FLINT IN THE BONES

EVA ST. JOHN

First published 2025 by Mudlark's Press

Cover art by Patrick Knowles
Map by Theodor Jurma
City Logo by Eva St. John.

First paperback edition 2025

ISBN 9781913628185

www.mudlarkspress.com

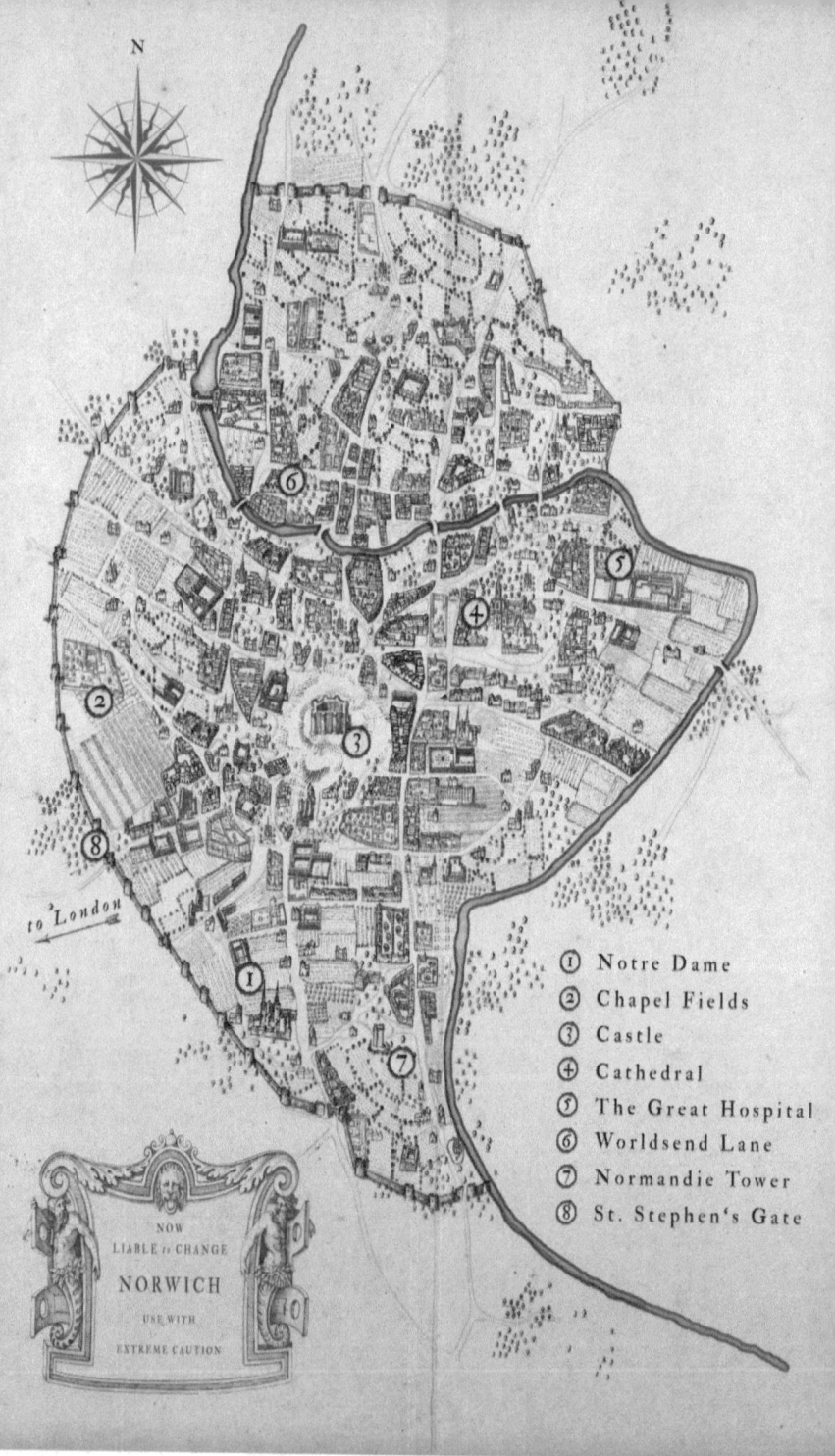

N

① Notre Dame
② Chapel Fields
③ Castle
④ Cathedral
⑤ The Great Hospital
⑥ Worldsend Lane
⑦ Normandie Tower
⑧ St. Stephen's Gate

to London

NOW
LIABLE to CHANGE
NORWICH
USE WITH
EXTREME CAUTION

This one's for Sunny.
You may remember him as Marigold.

Dear Reader,

A dreadful thing happened twenty years before our story begins. If you wish to know more, head to the back of the book under Author's Note, and download the free novella, **The Fatal Night.**

It contains no spoilers and can be read before this book or after.

Chapter One

 No matter how hard you try to escape your roots, the truth is you are always heading home. No matter how far you go, no matter how fast you run, at some point, your path brings you back to the beginning. Maybe it's magnetism, some intangible force pulling you back, or maybe it's simply magic. God knows I've had enough of that. I may not understand magic, but I sure as hell can't deny it.

Maybe my path home began the very day I jumped into the river and swam away, or maybe my journey home began here, crouched beside a wall in the pouring rain. My gun slapped to my side, sirens wailing overhead.

But I'm getting ahead of myself. I need to rewind a few hours and go back to base. London City Police HQ. There were lots of smaller stations around the city but my station, Westminster, was based at HQ. At eighty floors, it towered over Big Ben and St Paul's, but was in turn dwarfed by the other city skyscrapers. Progress never stops. Even when it should take a proper deep breath and pause.

HQ was dedicated to security, forensics, judicial. The top five floors, P1 to P5, were purely for practitioners. They even had a penthouse that had PP on the lift button. It's probably an indication of my maturity level that that delighted me far more than it should have. If they went by the common lingo of magician, they'd have MM, which at least sounds pleasurable. My personal term for the woo-woo squad would read WWS, which is close to wuss but not funny or accurate. They are scary individuals and don't find the term 'Woo-Woo' amusing.

Here on the thirtieth floor, we detectives run the business of keeping London safe. Hijacks, murders, kidnapping, smuggling, all the typical vices of a capital city in the twenty-first century. And as I was trying to catch up on some filing, it was my absolute pleasure to catch the attention of Captain John Wallace, head of the new recruits.

'Barnaby. This is Cadet Ollerenshaw.'

I looked up, smiling politely. Wallace was standing too close, as usual. I pushed my chair back and stood up. No one wants to have a conversation that close to someone else's groin. As I stood, I noted he had tightened another notch on his belt. His diet was clearly working wonders, as he mentioned tirelessly. He was currently making few friends, but he outranked me and I didn't want to antagonise any senior officer with my upcoming assessment looming. Though I'd be blowed if I would volunteer any compliments; he had a habit of reading too much into them.

Standing beside him was a young cadet in red. She was slim, tall, blonde and somehow made the uniform look tailor-made. I wondered how often Wallace had mentioned how much weight he could press. She was standing to attention and looked very serious. So far, I approved of her demeanour. Her hair was scraped back in regulatory fashion into a low bun and I noticed she had clocked my long hair hanging loose and then simply blanked it out. At least she was good at keeping her own counsel.

'Good afternoon, sir. Can I help?'

The cadet was holding a large bundle of case notes and I had a sinking feeling I knew what they were.

'Cadet Ollerenshaw needs to brush up on her processing of various cases. Thought you could help.'

'I am pretty busy at the moment.'

I really wanted all my backlog cleared before I attended my interview. If I could show a capacity for time management and paperwork, these would be points in my favour.

'The cadet is having trouble shifting out which files we process and which we send up to the practitioners, and you are particularly capable in this department?'

He trailed off and I sensed a bit of wriggle room.

'I'd love to sir, but the Doyle case really needs to be prepared for court tomorrow.'

'I just thought with your upcoming assessment… But if you're reluctant to help a struggling cadet…'

It wasn't wriggle room, it was a noose and I graciously complied.

'It would be my pleasure.'

'Right, well, I'll leave you ladies to it. Ollerenshaw, Detective Barnaby is one of our very finest officers. You'll learn lots from her. I'm just nipping down to the canteen. Can I get either of you a protein shake? No? Very well.'

And off he marched, shoulders back, head high. I tried not to roll my eyes and gestured to the cadet to sit down as I cleared space on my desk. As the police, we dealt with all breaches of law and order except those involving magic. Those cases were handled by the practitioners themselves. I had reservations about two tiers of judicial oversight, but that was well above my paygrade. Right now, my job was to help this cadet sort the wheat from the chaff.

'Right. Let's go through these one by one and you tell me if you think we should handle the case or if it should go upstairs.'

She took a deep breath, looked at me nervously, and then opened the first folder.

'Agatha Smith. Accused of making a man have sex with her after a night of clubbing by the use of magical enticement.'

I rolled my shoulders. This one was child's play, but it would be interesting to hear her reasoning.

'What's your opinion? Ours or theirs?'

She took another deep breath and then sat up straight, preparing herself.

'Relax. It's just you and me. I won't be writing an assessment on your performance.'

She visibly relaxed and shot me a quick smile.

'Okay. Here's how I see it. This case is ours. Some bloke is after a bit of revenge after getting wasted on a night out.'

'Anything else?'

'Well, given that the man is making false accusations of non-approved magic use, I'd charge him with wasting police time.'

I kept the grin off my face and nodded.

'Perhaps, but if this is the first offence, we can let him off with a warning and dismiss the case against her.'

She scribbled a note on the attached action sheet and then opened the next case file.

'Mr and Mrs Webster won–'

'Ours,' I cut her off. 'We get roughly fifty to a hundred reports of magical manipulation every time someone wins a jackpot prize. You'd be amazed at just how many friends and family aren't actually cheering on your every stroke of good fortune. Besides, all winners of prizes over a certain value are automatically checked by the practitioners. What was the amount?'

'A hundred grand.'

I whistled. 'Nice for them. Anyway, they will have been pre-checked. The practitioners get really crabby if you send reports up like this. It's a waste of their time and by the end of the day, they will make you bitterly regret it.'

She looked at me, her eyes wide in alarm, and I noticed she had perfect teeth as her jaw dropped.

'Do they curse you?'

'By the time you emerge from all the counter paperwork they send to reverse your decision, you'll wish they had. The only cursing will come from you.'

We ran through a few more examples and then paused at a more unusual case.

'Does it say he blew up a traffic light just by looking at it?'

She checked the notes again.

'Yes. Timothy Crow. Age forty-seven. After the lights blew up, he was reported to have shouted. "I did it. See. I did it!" When questioned how he did it, he said he had worked out the right words by himself.'

'What's his job?'

'Bus driver. According to the notes, he has made several complaints to Highways Division for inefficient signalling relays.'

I had my sympathies. Getting around London in rush hour was a nightmare, but we were still in the realm of coincidence and delusion. I pulled the case notes and had a quick read through before returning them to her.

'What are your thoughts?'

'Ours,' she said with confidence. 'Fantasist. You don't suddenly become a practitioner in your middle age.'

I stayed quiet and she looked at me nervously. 'Theirs? What have I missed?'

'A few things stand out. Look at his education. What did he major in?'

'Magic.' She groaned, but then tapped her fingers on the desk. 'But that's not enough, is it? Lots of people read magic. Doesn't mean they want to be practitioners. I did it as a minor.'

I was always curious about people who chose the sacred arts. If the option was to study magic or be dragged backwards through a vat of rancid milk without a nose plug, I'd be lying down in that pool of fermented curds and whey before they could offer me goggles. But that's just me. I have a troubled relationship with magic. My surprise must have been clear, because she nodded proudly.

'I did my degree as a science minor. Chemistry, Biology, Magic, Physics and Geology.'

She didn't strike me as a scientist. But then lots of people come into the police force from various walks of life.

'Daddy was furious. He said if you wanted to get ahead in life, you needed to major. Focus, focus, focus. But Mummy said that committing too early was foolish.'

'So your mother won out?'

I liked hearing people call their parents Mummy and Daddy. It reminded me of home, where that terminology was more usual. It was nice to have at least one or two decent memories of home. But of course here it simply meant her parents were probably loaded.

She laughed, now delighted at my statement.

'They both won. For my second degree, I majored in History.'

'And now you've joined the police?'

I imagined her parents were furious. Don't get me wrong, it's a noble profession and all that, but not what her parents had in mind.

'Why the police?'

I wondered what on earth this clearly very bright, privileged woman was going to say. Was she looking to make commissioner, a fast track to the top? Diplomatic Services. Practitioner Liaison?

'I want people to be safe. And happy.'

I tried not to laugh. Her earnestness was astonishing, but also, I'm not embarrassed to admit, a bit endearing.

'I looked at all the ways I could help and I felt the police force really gets to the heart of any situation.'

She was going to find out that the vast majority of criminals were not hard-done-by victims looking for a way out. They were hardened scrotes, happy to have a go.

'I meant the victims, of course. The perpetrators can go hang for all I care.'

I raised an eyebrow. 'Personality muting is harsh enough. No need to hang them as well.'

'Well, daddy says that we still have to feed them and that's an expense we could do without.'

'The vast majority make it back to a fulfilling life.'

I knew I was trotting out the party line, but in my mind, neutering the mind of a murderer or rapist just felt like they'd got away with it. Still, I reminded myself this way was best for everyone, except maybe the victims.

'When did you know you wanted to be a police officer?'

'As soon as I finished my minors.'

'So why take a second degree?'

'To ensure I passed selection. I needed to make sure they wouldn't overlook me.'

My God, this girl was driven.

'You weren't interested in becoming a practitioner?'

The prestige involved in being a practitioner was tremendous, as was having one in your family. The premature death wasn't a guarantee, but the death rate amongst practitioners was way above acceptable tolerances. But when your work provided free energy, it was amazing how acceptable tolerances could change. Of course, practitioners could work in any field, but the risk of disaster had become so great and so commonplace that the use of magic was now tightly regulated.

After the final debacle in the cartography department in Oxford, practitioners were regulated and only allowed to practise in a few fields. You'd think such restrictions would create a subdued and mindful individual. But that would show that you'd never met a practitioner at the height of their power. Rich, arrogant, complacent.

'Don't you like them?' asked Ollerenshaw. 'Daddy says they are worth their weight in gold. Without them we'd be reliant on energy from renewables, oil or nuclear. Can you imagine!' She laughed at the folly. 'Magic is limitless, free, clean, and so powerful.' She paused to grin at me sheepishly. 'That said, magic gives me the willies. It's either really boring or utterly terrifying.' She laughed again and looked at me expectantly.

I couldn't help but agree with her assessment. Ever since practitioners had managed to store wild magic and harness it into an engineered form, it had become the principal supply of energy. There was nothing glamorous about it, it just worked day in day out. That was the mundane side. Then there was the wiping of people's minds, splitting the earth, bringing the dead back to life side of it. Or, as Ollerenshaw put it, the utterly terrifying stuff. Those aspects of magic, though, were highly regulated and certainly not understood by those not trained as practitioners. We just said thank you for making the computers work and keeping the kettles boiling.

'I don't care about them one way or the other. They do a dangerous job and get well rewarded. Every person has to follow their own path.'

Historically, anyone could have a go at practicing magic, but over the centuries the practice had become refined and improved and with that improvement, more dangerous until at last it was finally regulated and only authorised personnel could practise. In fairness, trying to engineer wild magic was bloody dangerous and deserved to be closely monitored, and yet I felt the practitioners daily overreached.

I returned to our previous subject of Ollerenshaw's overachievement. I didn't want to dwell on magic.

'You know, you didn't have to study so much for the police force. You could have just applied through the open entrance exams.'

These were open to all, and no evidence of education was required. It was designed to make the force as inclusive as possible. If you passed the entrance exam and the interview, you were in. No one asked where you came from, what grades you got, who your folks were. So long as you didn't have a criminal record, you became one of His Majesty's finest.

'Oh my God. Who on earth comes in that way? Daddy says that's just a PR exercise. Can you imagine the sort that tries to join the police force that way?'

'Me,' I said tightly. 'I applied that way. I have no qualifications and, at the time, had no fixed abode. It's not a PR exercise, it's a lifeline.' I picked up the case file. 'Let's look at Timothy Crow again.'

Chapter Two

 I avoided looking at her, but I imagined she was desperately trying to walk back her words to a senior officer. I tapped on the case file.

'Why isn't he ours?'

'Um, because he studied magic, and er…' She fiddled with her pen. 'Look. I'm really sorry, I didn't mean–'

'Focus. Let's look at Timothy. When did he apply to become a practitioner?'

She looked at the case file and read through it quickly.

'There's nothing on here to say that he did.'

'Look it up.'

I pushed the keyboard towards her, but after a few keystrokes, she got locked out.

'I don't have clearance.'

Pulling the keyboard back, I placed my hand on the palm reader beside the keypad and once my security was cleared, I accessed the practitioner files. Obviously, I only had basic clearance. If I got my promotion next month, I'd be able to access slightly higher levels, but it wouldn't be much. The practitioners kept their information on a tight rein.

'Timothy Crow, rejected 1998, aged twenty-one.'

The screen went black and kicked me out. If I wanted further information, I would need to log in again.

'How did you know?' she asked, her forehead furrowed.

'I didn't, but it's always good to check. Now look at his records, see if he's ever changed his name.'

She typed on the keyboard and gave a small huff of surprise. 'Timothy Crow, born 1977 as Timothy Hamilton. Changed surname by deed poll in 1995.'

'When he enrolled into university. It all fits. Young man, desperate to be a practitioner. Changes his name to something he perceives as interesting. Studies at university, applies and is then rejected.'

I pictured his life, growing up embittered and rejected. His lofty dreams punctured by the realities of roadworks, mouthy passengers and faulty traffic lights.

'But why wait so long? That was a quarter of a century ago.'

'Because magic takes a very long time to learn, especially if you are doing it by yourself. Place his file in the practitioners' tray.'

Magic isn't some special skill that you are born with. You don't need to be a seventh son, or born under a special moon or whatever other nonsense the novelists like to invent. Admittedly, some people take to it better than others, but like all the other sciences, it's a hard slog, learning how to tap into the elements and manipulate them. And like some of the other sciences, it is highly unstable and dangerous for the individual studying it. But unlike the earlier scientists working with radiation, practitioners are able to harness magic into safe and clean power sources.

I yawned, ran my hands through my hair and then felt my body deflate as Ollerenshaw caught sight of the side of my face. My scars were on full display. Letting my hair fall forward again, I ignored her unspoken questions and spent the rest of the afternoon ploughing through the paperwork. As the day wore on, she got quicker at properly sorting through the cases and I was impressed by the rigour which she was developing as she went through the task.

'Ah, now this one goes straight to the practitioners,' she said with a trace of misplaced confidence. 'It concerns Norwich.'

Even the word made me shudder. I took a deep breath and then exhaled slowly.

'Not necessarily. What's the issue?'

'A trader has been falsifying her earnings, one Jenny Musgrove.'

Not a novel crime and didn't immediately warrant the attention of the practitioners just because it involved Norwich.

'Does she have a permit to trade with Norwich?'

Ollerenshaw riffled through the stack of papers in the folder. Trading licences were bitterly fought over. Despite the risks of entering Norwich, the rewards were vast.

'Yes, here it is.' She tapped on the keyboard and then nodded her head. 'All above board.'

'So why do you think this is for the practitioners? Unless there's evidence of her bringing in contraband?'

Trade with Norwich was highly regulated. For obvious reasons, items containing engineered magic were the most tightly monitored and well within the woo-woo squad's remit. Engineered magic in Norwich was like throwing matches into powder kegs.

'No. Just these financial issues.'

I shook my head. 'Mark it for the tax office. She has a licence, she wasn't smuggling. It's a normal crime.'

'But Norwich?'

'What of it?'

'Well, it's under the remit of the practitioners, isn't it?'

'Absolutely not. Norwich is self-autonomous and works directly with the British government and the UN.'

'But the wild magic?'

'That the practitioners were responsible for?'

'Daddy says–' I groaned but she carried on. 'He says it's their mess and they are responsible for it.'

'Says that out loud, does he?'

She blanched as she realised that she may have been indiscreet.

I waved my hand, everyone had an opinion about Norwich, but they did well not to mention them around the high and mighty practitioners.

Chastened, Ollerenshaw placed the file in the processed tray and we trudged on through the paperwork.

'There you are!' Wallace's voice roared across the room and I swear we both jumped. His demeanour had completely changed. Now he looked harried. 'Don't you have your handsets on?'

'No sir, I wanted Ollerenshaw to focus on the task at hand. The handsets can be too distracting.'

It wasn't the working updates and instructions that bothered me, it was all the other nonsense: *Swing by and pick up some sarnies! Who's for bowling tonight? If Jordan suggests a weekend of DIY one more time, I'll scream.* Obviously, the police handsets were for operational matters only, but police officers are only human and sometimes the domestic would spill into the professional. It was inefficient and non-procedural, but no matter how many times I raised a complaint, the situation would soon slide back to gossip. This was my official objection. My personal objection was the headache it provoked. Like most equipment, the radios were powered by engineered magic, and engineered magic gave me a headache. The more people chattered, the more my head hurt. So if I was concentrating, I generally switched mine off. If it was important enough, someone would soon find me in person. Looking at Wallace, I figured something important had happened. Now I had a black mark against me for not being operationally ready for whatever had just occurred.

'Well, whilst you've been playing at paperwork, other officers have been working.'

I tried not to react to the unfairness of that statement and waited for him to continue. Whilst he wasn't my boss, he was my superior, so I had to bite my tongue.

'There's been a prison break. We need all hands on deck.'

I was desperate to point out my shift had ended, but knew that would wind him up. I was relying on Turton to have ducked out on my behalf. Turton was my partner for operational matters and was a stickler for doing the absolute minimum.

Normally, I would be running down to provisions and grabbing a street uniform, but I'd had a bad night's sleep, the double-glazed unit was broken and the wind kept whistling in through the small crack, which was also how I thought the mouse was getting in. The mouse was actually okay. At least I had someone to talk to, other than my landlord to complain about the window. But my new mattress that I'd ordered had been delivered to an address in Scotland and the springs on my old one continued to dig into my spine. I was tired and grumpy and had just spent the past three hours training a new cadet and listening to the opinions of her daddy.

Turton would save me.

'Officer Turton is waiting for you down in the car. Seems he needs the overtime. Grab your gear and take Ollerenshaw with you.'

That was a step too far. Bad enough that I'd been manipulated into babysitting her for the afternoon, but now I had to take her out on active duty. The paperwork was going to be horrendous.

'But sir—'

'No arguments. If you'd been listening to your radio, you'd already be getting prepped. And this is good experience for Ollerenshaw. You can write a training report tomorrow.'

I inhaled, ready with a hundred counter arguments.

'Besides, it will look good on your application.'

I exhaled.

Ollerenshaw piped up. 'Will I be issued with a gun?'

Now Wallace looked at her properly.

'What are the regulations concerning cadets and E.M. guns?'

'No cadet may use any engineered magical device capable of inflicting harm until signed off by a senior officer following ten hours of live target practice. Section One. Paragraph three. Subsection one.'

'And how many hours have you banked so far?'

'Three.'

'And would you consider an E.M. gun capable of inflicting harm?'

'At full capacity, an em-gun can kill instantly.'

'So that's a yes?'

18

'Yes, sir.'

She looked embarrassed, but he clapped her on the shoulder.

'I admire your enthusiasm. But stick with Barnaby, she'll be carrying her gun and should be able to incapacitate him. Now, head down to provisions, and tune in to your radio for your orders.'

As he left, Ollerenshaw shuffled up her notes into a neat pile.

'Don't you like guns?' she asked, looking sideways at me. 'I saw your expression.'

One of the reasons I had chosen the detective branch rather than the patrol branch was there was less direct contact with engineered magic. Sure, in an office it was all around, from the kettles to the computers and lighting. But at least it wasn't on my hip or in my earpiece.

Like background radiation, magic is everywhere, but wild magic doesn't affect me. It's like in a thunderstorm. I'm aware of the ionised air and the electrical discharges, it's just part of nature. But getting electrocuted would bloody hurt. Same with engineered magic.

'It's just part of the job,' I said as much to her as to myself and was grateful she hadn't asked about my scars. Sighing, I grabbed my kit from the depot and having ensured that Ollerenshaw was properly equipped, we headed out. I was smarting over Wallace's comment that I *should* be able to incapacitate the prisoner. I was an excellent shot. Was he insulting me or was there something I didn't know about the escaped convict?

Chapter Three

'Has anyone got eyes on Cade?'

The prisoner was being referred to as William Cade. An unusual name for a practitioner and I suspected one they were using to deliberately hide his identity. I didn't care what he was called, I was hoping I didn't get anywhere near him.

My earpiece crackled as various squad members replied in the negative. This was a much larger operation than I had anticipated. It turned out that what I didn't know was that our escaped convict was a rogue practitioner and my gun skills in the face of his woo-woo skills would prove irrelevant. Many divisions were out on the street and the instructions were coming in thick and fast. The main one being not to engage. As soon as we located him, we were to call it in and let the practitioners subdue him.

'Okay, close the perimeter,' said Jones, our team leader and my direct boss. A good man, took care of his team and took care of the public in that order.

I stood up carefully and signalled to Turton across the street that we should move forwards. Howard Turton was my partner, not a bad person, not even a bad copper, but he preferred to be the last one at any shout. Paperwork was his special skill set and so far, we worked well together. In so far as we both did our job, and never communicated outside of work. This suited me down to the ground and, as he had a whole slew of friends both on and off the force, I doubt my failure to play besties bothered him at all.

I continued along my side of the terraced street, Ollerenshaw shadowing behind me. It being the evening, most people were home indoors with the curtains drawn, which was just how we police liked it. The general public loved to get involved. Without do-gooders, our job would be a lot easier. A helicopter passed overhead, its spotlight panning up and down the streets, sweeping the rooftops and generally drawing attention to the fact that a police action was ongoing. True to form, one of the front doors swung open ahead of me and a shaft of light spilled onto the wet pavement. A man stepped out and looked upwards. I cleared my throat, trying not to alarm him, given I was in full uniform with a baton on one hip, a gun on the other, and a riot helmet covering my face.

'Hi.'

He screamed. I removed my helmet to reassure him. *Just a woman, nothing to be scared of.* The fact that I could break his leg with the baton or send him flying with my gun was something I hoped he wouldn't focus on.

'Good evening, sir. Can I ask you to step back inside?'

He looked around, trying to regain the upper hand.

'Why? What's going on?'

Always with the questions.

'Nothing to worry about sir, but for your own safety, please step back inside.'

'Who is it?' shouted a woman's voice and presently his wife came to join him. She was wearing a dressing gown and carrying a glass of wine. She looked at her husband and then at me, frowning.

'Why were you screaming?'

I shook my head. 'That wasn't me, ma'am. Can I ask you both to return inside?'

'Why? Is there a woman out there? I heard a scream. Can we help?'

'There was no woman screaming, ma'am.' Saying ma'am to another woman always felt weird in my ears. Like I was in some American cop show. But I really didn't have time to establish her name and have a little chat about policing by consent and what a great job/terrible job we were doing.

'It's that manhunt, isn't it? You're after the criminal.'

'What's that?' said her husband, clearly not one to follow the local news.

'Someone's escaped from Norwich. It was on the news.'

Now he looked as alarmed as she did. I counted to ten. Very quickly.

'No one's escaped from Norwich. But we are following an escaped convict.'

'That's what I said.' Now that her initial alarm had passed, she began to get argumentative.

23

'Norwich is not a prison, as such. The prisoner we are trying to apprehend escaped from Belmarsh.'

'Is he in there because he came from Norwich? Because I heard that if you leave Norwich without a licence, they arrest you?'

A licence to leave Norwich. That was a new one.

'Norwich is embargoed. No one in, no one out. Now please get back inside. He may be armed.'

Honestly, we had no evidence to suggest that, but I had a job to do and it wasn't chatting to gossipy idiots. I certainly didn't want to say we were after a rogue practitioner. I put my helmet back on and immediately heard Turton shouting in my ear. Like a fool, when I'd removed the helmet, I'd failed to switch my radio loop over to my earpiece.

'Bish, I can hear something in the alleyway ahead.'

I looked across the road and could see he was inching towards a small one-way street leading to a mews. If Cade, our escaped convict, had gone to ground down there, we needed to proceed with caution. The occupants of mews houses in London were notoriously fussy about police actions outside their front door and were inclined to call up the commissioner faster than you could say, 'Sorry to bother you, ma'am, just trying to make the streets a safer place.' If it was possible, they were even worse than their neighbours on this street.

'Stand still,' I said into my mic, my voice muffled by an em-shield, ensuring the two gawping wallies in front of me heard nothing. 'I'll see if I can get a better angle.'

I turned back to the couple. Her wine glass was now empty and they were both standing on the pavement itself, presumably trying to see if they could see anyone and helpfully point them out. Presumably, my helmet with an infrared option, was no match for their self-belief in their abilities.

'Step inside now. The suspect is nearby. Any interference will result in additional arrests.'

They glanced back at me casually as they pointed over to the alley leading to the mews. No doubt having seen where Turton had pointed. The woman tightened her dressing gown and gave him a wave.

'Bish, get rid of them.'

I ground my teeth. What did he think I was doing? But I was trying to be nice. It was one of my daily goals. Be nice to people. Which, frankly, was quite often a complete waste of time. I lifted my visor and stared at them.

'There may be magic involved.'

That did the trick. They practically levitated, the speed with which they returned to the safety of their hallway and slammed their door shut.

'Could they have made any more noise?' snapped Turton. His voice echoing inside my head piece.

I hated working with these helmets. The engineered magic radiation buzzed and whined making my head throb.

I inched forward, staying in the shadows of the dirty brick walls. No amount of money or magic could keep London clean. She was a dirty old lady, and no amount of gentrification ever stuck for too long.

As I inched along the wall, I drew level with the opening to the mews. I could see the glowing red heat signature of a figure some thirty yards down the small lane. He was crouched down behind a large recycling bin and looking away from me. This end was closed to traffic and maybe he hadn't noticed that it wasn't a dead end. I inched closer until I could see him clearly.

'Full Broadcast. All units. I have eyes on the suspect.' I didn't need to whisper, the muffle field would ensure I wasn't heard by anyone standing more than an inch away. 'Navy chinos, white shirt, red trainers. Definitely our man. He's currently tucked behind some bins on Fawcett Mews.'

I heard the groans across various headsets.

'Okay,' said Jones, across the airways. 'That's perfect. Rogers and Frank, you're closest, get to the far end of the mews. Hammerstein and Lowe, go join them. Barnaby, Turton, block his exit. The practitioners are on their way. Cadet Ollerenshaw, stay back. Do not engage.'

Turton looked across the street and gave me the thumbs up whilst I waited for the go ahead. I checked my gun was primed. Single stun was loaded. All was good to go. I placed my hand on the gun and winced. Again, no issue with shooting someone, I just hated the feedback buzz. If I had fillings, I swear they would have vibrated out by now. As it was, my scars itched instead and I smoothed the skin on my neck and jaw in an attempt to relieve the irritation.

'Bish, proceed.'

I gestured to Ollerenshaw. Her face was tense with anticipation and I could see she was desperate to join me. Reminding her of her orders to stay back, I continued to creep along the wall until I had passed the entrance to the mews. Once out of line of sight, I ran across the road. Now Turton and I both moved towards the entrance of the mews, flanking each side. The idea of being this close to a rogue practitioner was making me skittish.

In the distance I could hear sirens approaching and wondered what twat had come in all action blaring. I could only pray that our suspect discounted the noise as just part of the London soundscape.

As I turned into the mews, Cade had had enough and was already on his feet, running straight for me. So far, he hadn't seen me.

'Stop! Police.'

I drew my gun and watched as he skidded to a halt, slipping on the wet cobbles and falling on his arse. He was a big man, more powerful than I had expected. I was grateful for the element of surprise, but it was short-lived as he sprang to his feet.

He lunged towards me and I fired my gun. Unlike ballistic guns, em-guns didn't miss as a bolt of weaponised magic zeroed straight in to the central nervous system of the intended victim. I expected him to fall, but he flicked his wrist and whilst he stumbled backwards, the shot had failed to inflict the damage required.

In my headpiece, I could hear Jones screaming directions at me. As he did, the convict waved his hand again. I could smell burning clutches and then a vicious stabbing pain pierced my ears causing me to rip the helmet off my head, throwing it to the floor. Immediately the pain evaporated. The convict was looking over his shoulder, eyeing up the possibility of escape back down the mews. When he looked back at me, he did a double take and laughed. I pulled my hair forwards and scowled. The last thing I need was a practitioner mocking me. Instead he smiled broadly and shook his head.

'Sorry about that, but I don't want them monitoring me.'

I set my gun to a higher setting.

'You can't escape. Hands up. Keep them still and apart.'

'I don't need to use my hand to deploy magic, you know,' he said with a smile, causing me to pause. I knew next to nothing about practitioners, but I certainly wasn't about to get beguiled, no matter how charming his voice.

'I don't care. Hands up.' My gun was still aimed at his chest and I wished to God I had my helmet on. I needed to know just how soon help would be arriving. No doubt that was the other reason why he had sabotaged it.

'You know, you could just let me go?' He tipped his head sideways and then ran his fingers through his short hair in frustration. The tracks of his fingers creating paths in the dark wet hair. 'What do you say?'

'I say put your hands in the air.'

Instead of complying, he took a step back. He was just about to run when his lazy smile turned to alarm. His eyes opened wide and he sprinted towards me. All of a sudden, I could smell diesel and burnt clutches. I could taste blood in my mouth and knew that a serious discharge of engineered magic was building up and it wasn't coming from him.

Chapter Four

I've always been able to sense magic. It's something slightly out of place. Wild magic tasted of oranges or honey, it smelled like lavender in winter. Sometimes the air in front of me would shimmer or I could hear the trickle of water through a distant cave system. It was never the same, but I always knew there was magic in the air. Engineered magic was sharp and itchy. It smelt foul and scratched the back of my throat. It whined through my ears and always gave me headaches.

A car tore up the mews and screeched to a halt in front of us. Two women and two men dressed in practitioner robes and carrying staffs leapt out of the car and ran towards us.

Cade lifted his hand and I yelled out a warning to the newcomers. I fired my gun, only to feel a sharp pain in my hand as it shattered.

From behind I was aware of shouts and footsteps running towards me and then a blast of heat swept past as Cade barrelled into me, lifting me completely off the floor. I was cocooned in a pocket of air as flames rippled around us. He shouted loudly over the sound of the fire.

'You're okay, Bish. When I put you down, get the hell out of here. If they ask you, tell them nothing.'

I wanted to demand how he knew my nickname, but seconds later he shoved me away from him. Stumbling, I fell to the side of the street, hitting some dustbins as I came to a halt.

Jumping to my feet, I spun around. Four practitioners now circled him. I was without my gun or my helmet. I should have made a tactical retreat. But I continued to watch and record the event on my body cam. I was the only police officer on the scene and someone had to record the evidence. I crept forwards. Cade was now standing still. He glared at me.

A tall, skinny woman in her sixties muttered a few words, then grunted. Cade flicked his wrist, his temper barely concealed.

'Sorry, Amber. Is that the best you can do?'

The woman began muttering in earnest when the other woman cut her off.

'Come on, Cade. You can't stop all four of us. Amber is simply trying to help you.'

From the look on Amber's face she didn't appear to be interested in dispensing help. Unless it was of the permanent and fatal variety.

I wondered why they didn't fireball him again and realised that the fireball hadn't been for him. It had been for me. One way to remove witnesses was, I supposed, to cremate them. I stopped creeping forwards and Cade smiled briefly. He had told me to get away and here I was advancing. Now, as I stopped moving, he nodded his head. Was I taking instructions from an escaped convict, against four of his colleagues. Admittedly, they had tried to kill me.

As he stood still, the four of them advanced until they were standing on each side of him. In a blink, he leapt forward, grabbing Amber by the neck. Pulling a knife from his belt, he swung around, slicing through her carotid artery. As blood sprayed out, Cade was still turning and thrust the blade of the knife into the chest of one of the men. Even as the practitioner was collapsing, Cade grabbed the remaining woman, yanking her off her feet and shoving her against the fourth practitioner. I flinched against the fountain of blood, but I'd seen worse. It was the suddenness of it, and coming from a practitioner, that caught me off-guard. He had saved my life but then taken theirs.

The two remaining practitioners scrambled to their feet as Cade sprinted towards the houses and did something unexpected. He turned and ran straight into the wall and disappeared.

I had witnessed many stabbings, but it had been ten years since I had seen anyone run into a wall. We used to call people that could do that 'map runners', but I didn't know they existed in London. The situation was now completely out of hand and I inched away. Grabbing my radio, I shouted for immediate back-up, emphasising that Cade had killed two practitioners.

The younger woman was back on her feet and had run to the spot where he had disappeared and was performing lots of hand and verbal incantations. This appeared to have no effect. She paced back and forth, then stopped. Grabbing her staff, she swung it at the bricks. I saw the rage on her face just before the rod connected with the wall. The entire side of the house shuddered and then in an explosion of dust and mortar the wall collapsed around her, leaving the interior of the house exposed. I could just about hear someone screaming inside, above the noise of the falling masonry.

The last remaining practitioner stepped over his dead colleagues and strode towards me.

'Officer. You are under arrest for obstructing practitioner manoeuvres.'

I cocked my head.

'Am I bollocks? You just tried to kill me. I have it recorded.'

He waved his fingers, then smirked at me. I felt a prickle of ozone and knew my body cam had just been wiped.

'Have you, though? I think you'll find your file is blank.'

When we go out and about, we always have either our body cam or helmet recording. It's a digital file and has been known to fall foul of magical interference. Which is why I always livestream. It costs me private credits, but it gives me peace of mind. Too often I messed up my own recordings, and this was a good way to ensure I had proper evidence. I smiled up at him and waited until the female practitioner joined us.

She was about my age, which meant that she was both very talented and bloody good at her job, as she was clearly in charge of operations. That, and she'd just torn a house apart. She was sweating heavily and the dust from the mortar smeared across her face.

'Did he say anything to you before we arrived?'

I stared at her, trying to decide on the best course of action. I really needed Captain Jones to get here as soon as possible. If I was about to be locked up, I'd rather it was in a police cell rather than a prac one. He'd be furious, but he'd be on my side.

'No ma'am.' Cade had told me to say nothing. He had saved my life, but he had also just killed two practitioners. I felt silence was probably my best recourse for now.

She smiled at me but I noticed her eyes didn't join in.

'I understand my colleague has placed you under arrest. It's highly regrettable, but I suggest you remain silent until you are back at the practitioner holding suite.' She continued with her dead shark smile. 'For your own safety, you understand.'

I nodded and raised my hand.

'What are you doing?'

I pointed to my raised hand.

'Permission to speak.'

She frowned and looked at her colleague before turning back to me.

'What?'

'I don't want to countermand a direct order from a practitioner, but I have information that you might find helpful.'

'Have you remembered what he said?'

'Not quite. It was more to do with your colleague here. He seems to be under the illusion that my recording of the events, including you fire-balling me, has been erased.'

Both pracs stared at me. He continued to sneer, but her face had become guarded.

'The thing is, I livestream everything. Obviously, this conversation is not, as your colleague just warped my camera with his little finger twiddle, but up until he did that, everything was on a live back-up.'

Now it was my turn to smile. My smile didn't reach my eyes either.

The man took a step towards me and the woman kissed her teeth. Just once, but he stepped back so sharply I laughed.

'Well then, officer,' said the woman thoughtfully, 'I deeply regret any harm that you think may have befallen you. We were simply trying to incapacitate the prisoner before he hurt you.'

Now her smile was a challenge.

'And that's what you're going to write in your report?' I asked.

'I don't think I'm going to tell you what I shall be placing on our report.'

I shrugged. I could hear lots of sirens now and a helicopter was hovering overhead, illuminating us. I needed their version on record before they tracked down my livestream and deleted it. I have been advised that practitioners can't do that and it would be a massive breach of prac oversight. But you know what? I don't believe them. By and large, practitioners are fine. They keep the lights on, literally, and in almost every walk of life, they are upstanding citizens, all pulling together for the common good. But the ones in the judicial and security systems? Them I trust as far as I could spit, having just eaten an entire pack of crackers. And I had just witnessed one practitioner evade capture by killing two and then escaping from a woman who had the power to tear a house down. I was so far out of my depth I was drowning.

I could hear footsteps running up behind me, but I didn't want to turn my back on either of the pracs.

'Detective Barnaby. Report.'

I almost sagged in relief as Captain Jones came and stood beside me. He'd bollocks me later on, but for now I'd probably receive his unwavering support in front of the woo-woo squad.

'Sir. The convict escaped. Two practitioners have been killed.'

'What!'

'That isn't what happened,' said the woman dismissively. 'Our colleagues simply collapsed as they exhausted their reserves. Your officer is confused. She fired her gun at Cade whilst he was casting a spell. He shot a fire bolt at her. We shielded her, but naturally it's hard for her to make sense of the events.'

'That's not how it happened,' I said quickly, trying to get my side of events out before they tracked down my recording. Firing a gun at a practitioner whilst they were casting a spell was a big no-no for all concerned. The engineered magic from the gun could combine with whatever the practitioner was casting and could cause a catastrophically bloody mess for all concerned. That or any nearby dog would start to quack. The results were chaotic and unpredictable and that's why there were strict laws about aiming guns at practitioners.

Jones glared at me. 'Barnaby, I know you have a solid record with identifying practitioner cases, but this is not one of those times.'

I noticed that the woman had narrowed her eyes and was watching me closely when Jones said that. I never told anyone I could sense magic. I just put it down to lucky hunches. The last thing I wanted was to draw the attention of a practitioner. They guarded their skills tightly and anyone showing a natural talent was made to register for the profession, unless, of course, you took holy orders. Failure to volunteer ended in a small procedure that rendered you incapable of performing magic. Or much else. It was the same procedure for murderers and the like, although not quite so severe. So it was a lobotomy or taking the cloth. The options to avoid becoming a registered practitioner were not great for anyone with some inherent sensitivities. I spoke quickly.

'Maybe I got confused.' I turned to the woman, who raised an eyebrow.

'And where is Cade now?' asked Jones.

I was about to reply when the woman cut me off.

'He ran past two of your officers. They didn't notice him.'

I drew in a quick breath, but she continued.

'Unlike this officer. Barnaby, is it? No doubt this makes her an outstanding officer. It's a fine line between reckless and brave. But she witnessed a dangerous event and was lucky not to have been killed.'

That felt like a warning. You could drive a truck through the holes in that story, but at least I was exonerated.

He looked between the two of us, then nodded his head.

'Okay, Madam Thaumaturge, I have that on file. I'll send it over to your department for confirmation, and then we'll send it over to jurisdiction for a ruling. If you agree?'

The woman nodded as I tried to melt into the shadows. She was a thaumaturge, top of her field, a real power broker, and I'd pissed her off.

'Barnaby,' snapped Jones. 'Get back to the station and write up your report. Take Turton and Ollerenshaw with you.' He turned to the thaumaturge.

'Medics will be here shortly and we need to evacuate those in the building where the wall appears to have fallen off.'

I noticed he wasn't asking how it happened.

'You can do what you like with the street and the house, but my own people will come and help our colleagues, and until they are seen to, no one else is authorised to come onto this street.'

Jones hesitated. A woman in her nightgown was now stumbling over the rubble. Her partner in pyjamas was helping her as they tried to make it to the street.

'Thaumaturge, we have wounded civilians—'

'And I have wounded practitioners. We'll let you know when we've finished. We need to track Cade's last movements before any of your clodhoppers come lumbering in here.'

I saw Jones ball his fists, then turn to me.

'Detective Barnaby.' I turned, wincing, waiting for the other shoe to drop. 'Once you have filed your report, consider yourself on suspension until we rule on the use of your gun.'

I nodded. Waving at Turton and Ollerenshaw to join me, I fled the scene as quickly as possible. All chances of my promotion seemed to be sliding down the drainpipe and into the gutter along with the rest of the London debris.

As we climbed into the car, my thoughts were racing. I had a thousand questions, but the main one was this.

How did this Cade know my nickname?

Chapter Five

As we headed back to the station, Turton drove. I figured if he was concentrating on the road, he'd be less likely to tell me off. I was wrong.

'Are you insane? Why did you challenge him?'

'You saw that?'

If I had some witnesses, that might help me when I came to write my report.

'We did, right up until the four practitioners arrived and told us to stay out of sight.'

'You were so lucky,' said Ollerenshaw breathlessly. 'Imagine what would have happened to you if they hadn't arrived.'

'Saved by the woo-woo squad. Lucky me.'

'Don't call them that,' said Turton. 'It's disrespectful.'

'Gosh, is it?'

Silence fell for all of two minutes. Ollerenshaw had been sitting in the back, her eyes darting left and right. Now she spoke up again.

'Do you think this will go for or against me? Daddy says I should never interfere in an ongoing practitioner investigation.'

'You'll be fine,' said Turton. 'You did everything by the book and followed every order. As did I.'

She smiled gratefully, and now Turton turned to me.

'Did you actually speak to the woman? Did you notice? No sash, I wonder why?'

As I said Turton was a good copper, but his skills didn't include observation.

'Thaumaturges and above don't wear sashes.'

A cyclist swore at us as our car swerved into their path and slewed back on track again as Turton recovered from the shock.

'If we could get back to the station in one piece. I'd hate to have to die with an unwritten report on my timesheet.'

He nodded furiously. Clearly, the same horror had occurred to him. I sighed and leant my head on the side window. I wasn't going to mention that I'd been suspended. Knowing Turton, he'd try to kick me out of the car lest my disgrace somehow affect him. Did I mention good copper? Just happens to be a shit partner.

'Did she speak to you? What did she say?'

'She said thank you. She said I was exemplary and invited me to join her for coffee whenever I'm next passing.'

'Wow. Bloody hell, Bish. That's amazing.'

Ability to detect sarcasm was also not part of his skill set.

Back at the station, we parked up and returned our equipment. Turton remained below for a quick fag break and Ollerenshaw and I headed up in the lift in silence. Wallace was waiting for us, giving us the benefit of his utter contempt, all previous jollity now evaporated. He whipped Ollerenshaw off for a debrief. As they walked away, she turned and mouthed a quick apology my way.

I refused to feel guilty. He had palmed her off on me, and now she had got dragged into a disciplinary offence. This wasn't my fault, although she was a cadet, the buck stopped with me and I knew that too would be added to my disciplinary report.

The main floor was busy. Officers sat at most desks, writing reports, tapping on computers, adding data, searching for connections. I was used to being ignored but today this felt very intentional as heads looked up and then their eyes quickly slid away.

I headed to my desk and pulled my laptop towards me. After a few keystrokes, I discovered that my most recent livestream files had somehow failed to be saved. Imagine my surprise.

I then switched to reports and wrote up the version of events that the female thaumaturge had suggested. It was at least some of the truth, if not the whole truth, and that would have to do.

I was startled out of my notes by a bellow of cheers and hooting. Turton had entered the room and was mobbed, as people wanted to know what had happened. A few people glanced my way, but not many, and I went back to my work. Friends were overrated. As was praise. I'm lying, obviously, but I don't have the knack of being likeable. At least not here.

It was enough that I did my job well, in my eyes at least. Popularity contests are for the pretty girls, the ones without scars on their faces, chips on their shoulders and more baggage than a sherpa can handle.

Turton sat down at the desk opposite me, but before he could start his notes, several colleagues flocked around him, eager for the inside story.

'So tell us, Turton, were you really there as the practitioners did their thing?' asked Jodie breathlessly, looking over at me. She was the sort of detective that made you wonder about the quality of the admission procedure.

I stared at her, then shook my head. I may have also sneered.

'No. Barnaby was closer,' said Turton. 'She saw what happened. I was instructed by a thaumaturge to hang back.'

There were some appreciative whistles when the others heard a thaumaturge was in attendance.

'Who was the practitioner that had escaped? Did you see him?' said Jodie again, all flashing eyelashes and gasps.

'I heard he was a practitioner from Norwich who had come to London,' said Max, a good-looking, well groomed, muscular heart throb in his late twenties. Clearly in love with his own image and no doubt planning to reach Chief Constable by the time he was forty. He'd probably make it as well. It was certainly my goal. I had risen quickly and then stalled. I was a good detective, but apparently my interpersonal skills were holding me back.

'To do what?'

'Start an uprising?'

I swear the IQ was falling with every utterance. These were His Majesty's finest and they were jabbering like children.

'He managed to escape from a secure practitioner's prison,' I said curtly. 'He wasn't from Norwich. Being from Norwich isn't a crime, nor is leaving it, and Norwich doesn't have any practitioners.'

'So how did he get away?' challenged Max.

'It's classified.'

'Yes, but you can tell us. We're all officers.'

'What part of "classified" don't you understand? Shall I call up to the fiftieth floor and ask them to explain it to you?'

Max glared at me as several of his colleagues sniggered at his expense.

'I bet that's why it's classified,' said Jodie. 'Who would be a greater threat than a practitioner from Norwich?'

The others stared at her in alarm.

'Jesus. Are you all stupid? I just said…' I tried counting to ten but stopped at three. I hit send on my keyboard and then pushed back from the desk. My shift was over. A crappy end to a crappy day. I'd picked a fight with a group of practitioners, they tried to kill me, the prisoner saved me before killing two others, he escaped by map running, everyone cheered for Turton, and my fellow colleagues were idiots. A crappy day in a long line of crappiness. Day in, day out. My life was shit, but it could be worse.

I had got as far as the lift when Turton shouted from his desk.

'Bish. See you later.'

'End of shift, partner. I'm heading home.'

'What about Jodie's party?'

I looked back across the office to Turton's smiling face. The others had returned to their desks, but I could see them wincing. Max was typing furiously. Gina was digging for stuff in her bag. Jodie had been walking across the office floor and stopped dead. She scowled across at Turton, his smile rapidly fading. I could practically see Jodie's eyes rolling from the other side of the room. Someone to my left laughed. My money was on Max.

'Oh yeah,' said Jodie, her head cocked to one side. 'Didn't you get the invite? Sure. Join us.'

I wondered if she could have sounded more pissed off.

'And why would I want to do that?' I asked.

The lift pinged behind me and I stepped into it and watched as the doors slid closed. That was right, crappy day and no friends. Life was great. Still, at least Basil the mouse was waiting for me. If he hadn't also buggered off.

When I had first arrived in London, I had found my approach was not conducive to making friends. I didn't have the knack of smiling at the right jokes. Hell, half the time I didn't understand the jokes. I rarely spoke lest my accent gave me away and spent every spare hour watching TV shows and muttering their sentences back to the screen. When I did talk, I said what was on my mind which, trust me, did not go down well. In the end, rather than actively try to engage and make friends, I went for passive neutrality and had reached the state where I was practically ignored on a daily basis. Not liked or disliked. Just not noticed. If it wasn't for my excellent work rate, I would fail to leave so much as a crumb of DNA.

It was time to grab some food, some sleep, and work out what tomorrow would look like.

Fired, friendless and fucked up.

Chapter Six

I took the tube back to Tooting Bec and walked the last half mile to Streatham. I lived in a unit for shift workers and one of the stipulations was no parties, no children and no broadcast noise. It worked perfectly for me.

'Hi honey, I'm home!'

The flat was silent. I walked over to my slippers and looked inside. Two tiny brown eyes shone back at me from the depths of the sheepskin.

'You can't stay in there forever, you know? What about your family? They'll be worried.'

I was lucky to have a ground-floor flat and opening the patio door, placed the slipper outside. Basil had turned up in my flat just before my shift. I saw him sprint across the floor and I nearly hit the ceiling. It was a long time since I had seen a mouse indoors and I was embarrassed by my reaction. Stepping off the sofa, I tried to capture him but he shot across the room and made a beeline for my slippers. I tried to shake him out, but he wasn't budging and there was no way in hell I was putting my hand in there. Mice bites are painful and bleed like buggery. If it hadn't been for the rain, I'd have left my slipper outside. Instead, as I was running late for my shift, courtesy of mouse antics. I left him where he was.

And now twelve hours later, he was still here. I closed the patio door, made a coffee and picked up a book.

The following morning, Basil was gone and I dressed for work. I pulled out a long sleeve blouse, with a high collar and a pair of trousers. It was going to be a hot day by the look of the steam rising off the patio, yesterday's rain gone in a heartbeat. July had been sweltering, and whilst the storms of the past few days had been welcome, they hadn't really broken the humidity. But at least it gave us something to talk about. Decades ago there had been talk about the practitioners altering the climate, but following the catastrophe in Oxford, all practitioner work was put on hold. And it was universally agreed that something that had the power to obliterate the entire human race was not to be tinkered with by practitioners, no matter how much they insisted they knew what they were doing. Interestingly, when pushed, none of them were prepared to say it was risk-free and that was the end of that. That's the problem with practitioners. In small-scale projects, everything is fine and dandy. It's when you try to do something new or revolutionary that the likelihood of the planet ending up as a pile of goo was quite high.

I walked and then caught the tube, aware that this might be my last time. If I couldn't be a detective, what could I do? I was good at my job, excellent, in fact.

Maybe I could go freelance? Helping to uncover infidelities and tax evasions. Or maybe a bounty hunter. That at least sounded more fun. Maybe I could rescue mice for a living. It would be nice to retrain and become an architect or a doctor, but they required people with exams and I had none. As a police officer, all I had to do was prove my worth, and I did. Every day.

Arriving at HQ, I said good morning to the receptionist who asked what floor I wanted. I reminded her that I had worked there and had done for the past nine years. I only convinced her when I showed her my warrant and then took the lift upstairs.

The first lift was full, so I waited and after three lifts filled up as I let people on ahead of me, I finally marched into the fourth lift and was glared at for my rudeness. Walking to my desk, Turton dashed across, looking worried.

'Chief Commissioner Hill has asked for you. Said you're to report immediately. I was very clear in my report that you did nothing untoward, except for firing on a practitioner.'

I tried not to laugh. Firing at a practitioner was punishable by a fine, imprisonment and dismissal from work. Hardly "nothing untoward".

I sighed. 'It's okay. You wrote what you thought you saw. Now if you'll excuse me.'

As I walked back to the lift, everyone turned and glanced over. I walked in silence and waited at the lift.

After a minute of the silent censure, I took the stairs. Hill's offices were only two floors up. It was mostly small offices rather than open plan stations and I headed along the carpet, another feature we were lacking in the detectives' pool, towards my boss' boss' boss. At least I was getting fired from on high. Because of course I was getting fired. Why else would I be dragged all the way up here?

Letting the secretary know who I was, I was ushered into a large office overlooking the city. The view was magnificent and the open windows were making the most of a faint breeze. I smiled. One thing I have always managed was to be able to enjoy the simple pleasures. But then I caught a whiff of a burning clutch pad and stalled.

'Good morning, Detective Barnaby.'

I stopped, smiled and nodded at the chief commissioner as he sat behind his desk. His lips were dry and I wondered if he'd been drinking again. He was a heavily overweight man, with grey hair that resembled a Brillo pad. It was said that in his prime he was a fearsome detective. I suspected he paid people to say that. It was more likely that he was a fearsome politician to have risen all the way up the greasy pole. The breeze wafted his pungent aftershave around the room, but there was no hint of alcohol. Maybe something else was making him nervous. I looked around and saw the female thaumaturge from last night, standing in a corner of the room behind me. A thaumaturge ranked very highly amongst the practitioners and weren't to be trifled with. Whilst their word wasn't actually law it may as well have been. What they wanted, they got. Yesterday, I had witnessed her rip the front of a house off. I needed to tread very carefully.

Today she was dressed in a smart trouser suit with her hair slicked back. She was wearing minimal make-up, which made her red lipstick stand out and as she smiled at me, I could see that her teeth were uniformly small and white. I was reminded of tiny little tombstones.

'Good morning, ma'am,' I said as neutrally as I could and tried to slow my pulse down. At the very worst, I had been expecting to be fired. With the presence of a practitioner, my punishment could be worse. My memory could be expunged.

Two chairs sat in front of the desk and Captain Jones sat in one of them. I was surprised not to see my Union rep, but no doubt they were on their way. No dismissals without due diligence.

'Please take a seat. We'd like you to help us with something.'

I stared at the captain, who pointed to the second chair. I sat down carefully. Hill's tone seemed too jovial, and I felt unsettled.

'Will my union rep be joining us?'

The chief commissioner looked at me and tilted his head.

'I don't quite follow?'

'I'm being dismissed, aren't I?' I got that out in a bit of a rush and stared at him. I'd faced worse men than him, but I really didn't want to lose my job.

The two men looked at each other and then the CC laughed.

'Did you let her think she was being fired, David?' he turned back to me. 'Typical David, hey, keeping everyone on their toes.' He chuckled, pressing the intercom, and asked his secretary to bring some drinks in. 'No, you aren't being fired. In fact, we want your help with something.'

He paused as the secretary brought the drinks in and I was alarmed by the presence of biscuits. I definitely wasn't getting fired, but I was beginning to think something worse was afoot. Jones nibbled his biscuit morosely. As the door softly clicked shut, Hill continued.

'We think we know where Cade is heading. He is a practitioner and a murderer and we need him captured as soon as possible.'

'Who has he murdered?' I asked.

The chief commissioner looked over my shoulder and the woman walked around to the front of the office.

'Two practitioners. You witnessed it last night.' Her gaze held a challenge and I looked over to Jones, who was staring ahead, his jaw clenched. I noticed that as he clasped his hands, his knuckles were white. I turned back slowly to look at the thaumaturge.

'You said yesterday they hadn't been injured.'

'That was for the official record. You and I both know the truth.'

'We followed his trail and found five more victims. Defenceless citizens, including a teenager and a child.'

Hill pushed a selection of photos across his desk. All the victims were in similar poses laying in the rain, stab wounds clear in the flash of a police camera. The kid was still holding her mother's hand. She was wearing a fluffy pink skirt and a tiara. It looked like they had been walking home from a party. In another photograph a teenager lay sprawled across a pavement, a skateboard lying on its side. In the final photos, a man was slumped against a rubbish bin, his phone still in his hand. The last picture showed an old woman. A bag of groceries spilled out on the surrounding road.

'Why did he kill them?'

'Maybe they got in his way,' suggested Hill.

The woman shook her head. 'Unlikely. He is, or was, a very talented practitioner. Now he has become unstable.' She paused and looked at the three of us as she spoke. 'This goes no further. If I hear any rumours about this, I will know where they started.' Clearing her voice, she spoke again. 'In the course of our training, we can sometimes fall foul of mental degradation. The ability to harness the magic can have a negative effect. This results in a benign state of apathy, similar to when we wipe the impulses from murderers and the like.

Sometimes it can cause death but occasionally the degradation can lead to worse things.'

I thought "worse than death" didn't sound great, but I held my tongue. It was fascinating to get an insight into the practitioners and I was curious.

'All practitioners, whatever department they work in, undergo monthly reviews, to assess degradation. We are very good at catching any issues and can help the individual towards a healthy exit from the field. But it seems that Cade was either capable of masking his issues, or the illness came on rapidly. We had just detained him but he escaped. He is now dangerously out of control. We think he killed these people in confusion. His mind is unravelling.'

I sat in silence. He hadn't seemed confused when he saw me.

'Can I ask? Can practitioners read minds?'

She looked at me and scoffed.

'No. That's for the television shows. Why do you ask?'

I didn't know why, but I didn't want to let her know he had said my name. Already I was doubting myself.

'I just wondered if he could hear what people were thinking and that's why he lashed out at them.'

She shrugged. 'No doubt he perceived them as a threat or he was simply enjoying himself. We don't know. But he certainly wasn't reading minds.'

I fell silent. Bish, wish, dish, fish. He could have been saying anything, but the way he looked at me? The confusion in his eyes and that moment he looked at me and laughed. For a second, I thought he knew me, but was this more evidence of his degradation?

'It's not contagious, is it?' asked Hill, giving me palpitations. The last thing I wanted was to be infected with some bizarre magical virus.

She snorted. 'No, he isn't contagious, but he is lethal. Which is why we have to apprehend him.'

'How much of a lead did he get?' I asked. 'Surely, we can alert the cities. Birmingham, Manchester? Did he go west? Bristol.' Christ, I wasn't thinking. 'He's gone to Dover, hasn't he? He's making a break for the continent.'

The CC shook his head and stared at me intently and reality hit me like a car crash. I may have even recoiled. Turns out I really hadn't been thinking.

'His last known point of contact was on the A11,' said the thaumaturge. 'I was able to catch a trace of his location before he muffled me again. He was a mile north of Wymondham.'

I looked back and forth between the three of them as the blood drained out of my face.

'He's going to Norwich.'

Chapter Seven

There was a buzzing in my ears and I thought I was going to vomit or faint. Jones passed me a glass of water but my hands were shaking so much that he removed it and made me put my head between my knees. After a few deep breaths, I began to feel normal again. I was appalled to see a fine sweat had broken out on my arms and when I looked up, the CC was staring at me with poorly disguised revulsion. The woman just stared impassively. I looked across at Jones.

'I'm not going back. You can't make me.'

I swear he looked sad. 'You have to. You're the only person we can send. There isn't another detective who was born in Norwich.'

'Then send a bounty hunter, an officer. There has to be someone.'

'There isn't,' said Hill. All sense of avuncular goodwill had now disappeared. 'There's only you. Consider this your way of paying us back the favour we did of employing you in the first place.'

'How did you know? My health records are confidential.'

No one knew I was from Norwich. I had worked so hard at concealing my past, but I couldn't fool the medical examiner when I first arrived. However, it turned out that her aunt lived in Norwich and had died in the cataclysm. She decided not to report me.

'Of course we knew. It was classified, but it's on your permanent record.'

It still didn't make sense. I knew it wasn't on my service record, only my medical one, and that was confidential.

'Did you look at my file?' I said to the woman. 'Who are you anyway? You don't have the right to open my medical files.'

I turned to my captain. 'Did you know as well?' He had always treated me with respect. I had never sensed a moment of fear or ridicule from him. He accepted I wasn't a great team player, kept myself to myself, but he always appeared fine with that.

'I only found out this morning when the chief commissioner called me in and explained what was about to happen.' I must have tensed, waiting for his disgust, but he simply shook his head. 'And I don't care. People talk a lot of shit. And most of the shit I've ever heard is about Norwich. Far as I'm concerned, you are one of my best detectives. Which is why I really hope that you take this job. William Cade is scum and he's taken refuge in your birthplace. Those citizens are vulnerable and he's our mess. Only you can get him out.'

I turned back to the practitioner who had watched my rising panic with barely concealed contempt.

'Send a practitioner. He's their mess.'

CC Hill spoke quickly.

'Thaumaturge Millicent Aethelflaed Persephone has already explained how destabilising a practitioner in Norwich would be.'

I memorised her name. I would investigate her later. Practitioners were given their first and second names but got to choose subsequent ones. I wondered why she had chosen Persephone but that was for later and I needed to focus on the task at hand.

'By her accounts, there's one already.'

'Yes,' she drawled, her voice low and amused. 'And a second one would be exponentially worse. Try to see it from our point of view. We're trying to save your home, even if you aren't.'

My laugh was ugly and loud, and I saw Hill recoil. Persephone simply smirked.

'You're trying to save my home,' I spat, 'after your wanton and arrogant behaviour nearly destroyed it.'

'Barnaby,' snapped both men at the same time, but I would not be stopped.

'Sorry sirs, but you have no idea what it was like.' I paused, swallowing hard. 'Millions died, the daily smell of burning corpses, the sky black with oil fires, collapsing buildings, broken sewers.' I shuddered as old memories swamped my thoughts. 'The very ground beneath your feet convulsing through the centuries as it tried to stabilise. The screaming madness as we tried to comprehend the swirling timelines.'

I stuttered to a halt.

'And if you don't get Cade, it will all start up again.'

'It never stopped!' I shouted.

'Of course it did,' said Persephone dismissively. 'Norwich is practically stable these days. I understand it's been months between quakes.'

'After twenty-five years, you call that stable? Not knowing if your house will still be standing in the morning. Not knowing if a new influx of old timers will be bringing the plague with them again. And all because of your bloody meddling.'

'Officer Barnaby!' Hill shot to his feet, but Persephone waved him back down.

'Let her have her say. The fact remains, she needs to get Cade. A practitioner can't because they'll make the situation worse and a non-resident can't because they don't have the innate resistance to the magic in Norwich.'

I panicked, trying to get out of this.

'We could leave him to it. He won't survive long.'

We all looked at each other. Were we prepared to inflict the sort of torture that Norwich inflicted onto a fellow human? Then I remembered the photos I had seen and the two murders I had witnessed and thought it couldn't happen to a more deserving person.

Jones read my expression and shook his head.

'I agree, but how much damage can he do before he's driven completely insane? He's already murdered seven people. Added to that, his very presence may cause quakes. According to Thaumaturge Persephone, you can't be affected by the magic in Norwich. That's correct, isn't it?'

I swallowed and tried to calm my nerves.

'The magic can affect anyone, but people who were living in Norwich at the time of the cataclysm seem to be shielded from the worst of it. Some residents succumb, but generally locals are safe. But I've been gone a long time. I don't know if I'm still protected.'

Hill steepled his fingers again.

'You have some natural protection. If you find yourself succumbing to the madness, just leave.'

He made it sound so easy. The problem with going mad was that you generally didn't know. Now it was my turn to lean back in my chair and get my shit together. Funnily, now the decision had been made, I felt a weight lift from my chest. And I certainly would not embarrass myself again in front of these people who had never spent a single day living with the horrors that I had, growing up. And I'd be damned to hell if the practitioner saw any more of my fear.

'Right, then. When am I going? What's been arranged?'

Jones gave me a nod and I was perversely pleased by his approval. Now Hill took the lead.

'You will liaise with the Norwich police force, or whatever they have.'

'Do they know I'm coming, sir?'

'We dispatched a messenger last night when we saw where Cade was heading.'

'Have they replied?'

Hill shrugged. 'Not yet. But it's only been twenty-four hours. Who knows what they're doing? It is Norwich after all. It's not like they can pick up the phone or send an e-mail.'

'Very well,' I paused, thinking through the logistics. 'I will be fully armed, won't I?'

'According to the treaty, no items with any engineered magic may enter the city walls. That includes your gun and baton.'

'What about a phone?' asked Jones.

'No phones. Besides, Norwich doesn't have a network.'

'Are things still really that shit?' I asked and then waved my hand dismissively. Of course they were. Dumb question. 'Well, they've got their reasons,' I said, oddly needing to protect my old neighbours. 'You don't know what it's like. But look, I think I should have some form of defence. Cade is a practitioner.'

'I think by the time you find him, he'll be a gibbering wreck.'

'Nonetheless.'

'No. No weapons containing engineered magic,' said Persephone, folding her arms. 'But we do concede you'll need something.'

I closed my eyes. If she suggested a sword, I may be forced to run her through with it.

'We're sending you with a revolver and a dog.'

'Are you mad?'

Her jaw dropped. She had probably never been spoken to like this by a junior officer, or anyone for that matter. 'I beg your pardon?'

'Dogs are banned. Any idiot knows that.' I appreciated I wasn't doing myself any favours. But dogs had become unmanageable, hunting in packs, prone to random attacks and sometimes rabid.

'I have investigated and dogs were banned when you lived there, but shortly after you left, they experienced an influx of wolves and now dogs are once more man's best friend. I understand there are issues involved but no doubt they will be explained to you when you arrive.'

I stared at her in silence, trying not to wipe my palms on my trousers. As a child, I had been attacked twice by a dog and was now scared of them. Just another joy of living in Norwich.

'What about rabies?'

'All under control now, I believe.'

I really didn't want a dog. I didn't want anyone to see my fear.

Jones cleared his throat. 'You don't need to take a dog, but the exclusion zone is currently overrun with wolves and bears. A dog might save you.'

I suspected I was less scared of the wolves and bears.

'I'll have a gun. Surely?'

'You will. With authorisation to shoot Cade on sight. But a revolver won't be enough if you get attacked by wolves between the walls. You are taking the dog. We can't risk you failing to get to Norwich because you're more scared of a dog than a wolf.'

The derision in her voice made my skin flush and I wanted to smack the stupid smile off her face. Instead, I simply nodded my head. It was just a dog and trained police dogs probably didn't go around attacking their handlers.

Persephone continued speaking.

'Regarding Cade's arrest. Shoot him on sight. Try not to kill him, but don't allow him to speak. However you incapacitate him, gag him immediately. Bind or break his fingers. It is vital that you render him impotent as fast as possible. But as I said. Please don't kill him. We want to rehabilitate him.'

I rolled my eyes. This mission was damn near impossible. I'd need the most amazing amount of good fortune to catch him unawares, then shoot him without killing him before he could raise a spell against me.

'I don't stand a chance. He's a practitioner. Besides which, last night I saw him map run.'

Immediately, she flicked her hand and I smelled burning rubber again. Around us I was aware of a muted noise, as if I was underwater listening to voices above. Beyond the bubble, Hill and Jones had turned to look at us and were speaking urgently, although I couldn't make out their words.

'Listen carefully, Eliza Barnaby,' said Persephone, her voice crystal clear. 'Map runners don't exist.'

'I saw him run into a brick wall.'

'You didn't. And even if you did, you will not mention it to anyone.'

'I thought map running only worked in Norwich.'

Map running was a neat trick if you could do it. You simply shifted your focus and saw where an old road or footpath used to be and then you took it. Rather like those hidden eye pictures that had an image hidden within. In Norwich, those hidden paths were literally embedded all across the city following the practitioners' cock-up.

She paused and stared at me, her lips tightening.

'Do you know any map runners?'

'No,' I lied. The way she had asked concerned me.

'So why do you think you saw him map running?'

'Because I've seen it in the past.'

'Where? Who?'

'Norwich. And I never caught their names. Several people would do it. They stopped after all the accusations of witchcraft and burnings, though. I didn't know you could run the maps in London.'

'You can't. It doesn't exist. Remember that.'

With a flick, the background noise returned to normal and Hill cleared his throat.

'Is everything alright?'

'Yes,' snapped Persephone. 'I was simply passing on some information. Please don't enquire further or I shall be forced to charge you with interference in practitioner business.'

Hill blanched and quickly assured her he had no intention of asking me any questions. Jones returned to miserable silence.

'Now,' said Persephone, all smiles. 'You need to go to the medical department for your jabs, collect your dog, pack a bag, and head off. A car will take you to your apartment, then drive you to the border. You should be there in three hours. And then you have a ten-mile walk. If you're quick, you'll be at the walls before nightfall.'

My jaw was properly gaping open. That was a ridiculous timetable. The jabs alone would make me sick as a dog. The dog would need to get used to me. I had to pack. And then a ten-mile hike.

'Cade has already had a day's head start. God knows what havoc he is wreaking.'

She handed me an envelope, which I took reluctantly.

'Those are your entry papers, your licence to carry a weapon and a map of the city.'

I dropped the envelope and leapt out of my chair away from it, staring at both men and glancing over to the door. The envelope lay between me and my exit, but I could swerve around it. No way was I stepping over it.

'Relax, Barnaby. It's treated.'

She scoffed and walked forwards, picking up the envelope and pulling it out to show me. I felt sweat soaking the back of my blouse.

'Look. It's just the outer perimeter, the walls themselves, the main check points and gates.' She pointed to a few familiar features within the walls. 'I believe these are the churches, all fifty-two of them, and I think that's the castle or the cathedral?'

'It's the castle, ma'am. That's the cathedral,' I said, trying to keep my finger steady as I pointed. 'Could you put the map away please?'

'For God's sake, detective. I assure you, the map is treated and has been tested. There is no latent magic in it. It is inert!'

'And yet I can already feel it pulling at me.'

'Well that's on you, isn't it?' she snapped.

'That's the whole bloody point!' I swore. 'In all these years of research, have you still not grasped that the magic in maps goes two ways? It is not an inert item in the hands of someone who recognises what it represents.'

'I have already said—'

I snatched the map from her hands and tore it quickly into pieces, not looking at the images as they fell.

'We don't take maps into Norwich.'

Chapter Eight

 'Both sleeves, please, Detective Barnaby. I'm afraid you're getting lots of jabs, aren't you? I'd say be brave, but you already are brave aren't you, heading into Norwich.'

Doctor Williamson was the jovial sort. He was embedded directly within the police force and often patched us up before the other medics arrived. I didn't know him well, but at least he was a familiar face. Now he moved between the sterile cabinets, pulling out various ampules with safety warnings on them and lining them up. I was going to look like a pincushion by the end of this.

'Right then,' he said as he approached me, syringe in hand. 'This one has some pretty nasty side effects but it can't be helped.'

I leant away from him.

'What's it for?'

'Bubonic Plague. Not something I recommend.'

He laughed and flicked the end of the syringe.

'I don't need it.'

'Doctor's orders.'

'Check my records.'

'Have you had a shot before?'

I shook my head and grabbed his wrist.

'I said, check my records.'

'You can't travel to Norwich without it. And you certainly can't return. The only exemption is if you have already had it. You know the rules, detective.'

He wasn't laughing now. I had a hold of his wrist but the patronising tone was still present. I stared at him until he moved away and I released his wrist. Heading over to the laptop, he typed in a few more commands and shook his head. 'Nothing here.'

'Go further back.'

'Eliza. I have worked with you for years. I think I know the medical history of all my colleagues.'

He paused and sighed, then tapped the keyboard again and then looked up in surprise. 'You have classified files. Why do you have classified files?'

'Before you lined up all these jabs, are you telling me you didn't check my childhood history?'

He looked flustered as he tapped the keyboard. 'There was no need. These jabs are standard for any visit to Norwich. Although it's exceedingly rare for anyone to visit. I can't even remember the last time. And you're not from Norwich.' His voice trailed off as his faith in that last statement wavered.

'Shall I grant you access?' I asked sweetly, cutting off his bluster. It wasn't my fault he hadn't done his job properly. I typed on the keyboard, placed my palm on the pad and allowed my eye to be scanned. Classified medical records could only be accessed with the patient's permission. Which again begged the question, how did CC Hill find out?

As the files loaded up, I went and sat back down again. I had no need to see the contents. Most of the details were writ large across my skin, the psychological traumas hidden under a veil of bravado. I watched as his faced paled and I smiled.

'Why didn't you say you were from Norwich?' He had sat down now and was staring at me.

'I assumed you knew.'

'But you had the bubonic plague!'

'Yes.'

'But that's dreadful.'

'I am aware.'

He looked at the screen again.

'You caught it in the summer of frogs?' I nodded. For a while, our calendar was a bit out of whack and we got used to marking the years with major events. The summer of frogs was pretty major. Nothing compared to the amount of people that also died from the black death, but the summer of frogs was an easier name to live with than the Year Everyone You Knew Died.

'But the death count for that outbreak was catastrophic. You were very lucky.'

I pulled back my hair, revealing the scars from my buboes.

'I guess.'

He choked on a laugh, trying to lighten the mood.

'At least all you have to show for it are a few scars.'

A few scars. I wanted to grab the metal tray with all the ampules on it and smash it into his face. I imagined punching and kicking him, his soft body crumpling to the ground as I tore the room apart. The noise of falling lockers and breaking glass filling my ears. I took a deep breath and steadied myself. I spoke in a low monotone, proud to keep the quaver out of my voice.

'I was eight. My mother and my ten-year-old brother died, Dom didn't even last the second night, Mum clung on for a week. The following year, my father died from the sweats. When I was twelve, I got smallpox. I don't need that jab either.'

By the time I got to the dog kennels, I had all but composed myself. The doctor's response had shaken me and I knew I was an emotional wreck. Too many memories were being dragged to the surface. I had spent a decade repressing them and now they were spilling out of me. And now I was going to the kennels. I wondered if I was going to get to the city wall by the end of the day, or just simply collapse in a heap of tears in a corner somewhere.

When I was seven, I had been running errands for my mother. I was late because I'd been messing about with friends down by the river. John's mother made the best fishcakes and he'd promised to bring some the following day if we helped him catching trout. The time flies when you're lying on a riverbank, your belly on the grass and your arm in the water carefully tickling fish. I promised myself to only catch one, but the sun was warm and Pete had caught two, so I had to beat him. Anyway, I was late and ran back across the meadow and startled a wild dog. I was lucky that I was so close to the shops. A butcher came running out with a machete and dispatched the animal. The dog had bitten my thigh and shoulder, shaken me like a rag. His saliva and my blood splashed my face as I screamed, terrified that he would clamp his powerful jaws around my head next.

Remarkably, my shoulder healed faster than my leg and I walked with a limp for a while, but my father insisted on daily physio until I was walking without a cane. He also insisted I walked our pet dog, Mr Wagsalot, daily. He didn't want me to develop a phobia. Even after my father died, I exercised every morning and evening until my muscles completely recovered themselves and the scars faded out to white tracery. My second negative encounter with dogs was with Mr Wagsalot himself, but I tried not to dwell on that.

The dog warden turned out to be surlier than her dogs as I pushed through the double doors and into the kennels area of the station. My arrival seemed to set off the animals, who all started barking from their cages. It was a cacophony of noise as the various barks echoed off the breeze block walls and metal pens. It was too much and I ran outside, slamming the door behind me. As I doubled over, trying to catch my breath, I heard the door open and looked up to see the warden smirking at me.

The officer in charge had a face like a slapped arse and I could feel her contempt for me rolling off in waves.

'They get boisterous at breakfast. We don't normally allow visitors, as it upsets them.'

I was concerned that the tracks of my previous tears were evident or that my fear was. Either way her attitude was unnerving. I remained silent. She was in charge and happy to prove it. I didn't need any more aggro today, so I stood patiently. Which appeared to annoy her.

'So you're taking one of my dogs to Norwich?'

'Not my choice.'

'Not mine either. Waste of a damn fine dog, if you ask me. Come on.'

We headed back inside and I shook my fingers as I tried to calm myself. Adrenaline stabbed my skin and I tried to steady my heart rate. She strode off down the kennels past the Alsatians and rottweilers as they jumped up against the metal cages, barking loudly.

'Noisy bunch,' she said fondly. 'They'll rip your throat out on command, you know.'

I moved to the other side of the corridor and ignored her laugh. Turning right, we carried along the concrete passageway past quieter dogs, face down in their bowls. Tails whipping from side to side.

'There's your dog. Useless sod really, which is why I was prepared to release him on this suicide mission.'

'It's not a suicide mission.'

'Bears and wolves, I heard.' She snorted. 'And that's even before you get to Norwich. God knows what freaks you have lurking in the city.'

I ignored her and looked into the cages, but couldn't see which dog she was pointing to.

'Which one is it?'

She pointed to a kennel to one side where a small dog was eagerly looking out of the grills, his tail wagging hopefully.

'We haven't fed him. Waste of food and will keep him keen.'

'That's cruel,' I said involuntarily. I didn't like dogs, but I wasn't a sadist.

'So's taking him to Norwich.'

I stared at the dog.

'That's a spaniel,' I said, proving I knew something about dogs and the something that I knew was that spaniels weren't known for their ferocity.

'Oh dearie me, were you hoping for something aggressive? Those dogs have been trained for years. Our officers rely on them to save their lives.'

'And what about this dog?'

'Bloody useless.' She began counting off on her fingers. 'Trained as a sniffer dog. Kept overreacting. Won't attack humans. Frankly, he should have been turned over as a pet, but no one wanted him.'

'So what is he good for?'

'Calms the other dogs down. And kids love him. Maybe he'll be good with bears. You'll have to let me know.'

Giving an ugly laugh, she grabbed a lead from the wall and approached the cell. The dog leapt around in circles.

'Sit!' roared the handler and the little dog quivered on the spot. She walked into the cage and clipped the lead onto the collar. 'There's a tracker in his collar which should tell us the location of the bears, I guess.' Her laugh was even nastier this time, and I snatched the lead from her hand.

'What's its name?'

'HRE57.'

'Bloody hell, that's not a name.'

I looked at the white-faced springer, who was looking up at me expectantly, his tail wagging furiously.

'Right then, Harry,' I said, trying not to shudder. 'You're with me.'

Chapter Nine

 An hour later, Harry and I were sitting in the back of a car driving north towards the checkpoints. No matter how hard I had tried, the dog kept moving towards my side, making me flinch every time. I'd packed quickly and shoved in a few essentials. Slippers being one. Minus mouse. Then stowed the rucksack in the car. I'd told the driver to step on it and we arrived at Wymondham just after one. There was no way that I was going to be out after dark.

Traffic started to really thin out until we were the only car on the road. It wasn't long after that that I could see the huge metal wall ahead. Five metres tall, it created a barrier between that part of Norfolk and the rest of the country. The barrier ran from King's Lynn to Wymondham and over to the broads. It didn't enclose all of Norfolk as the affected parts on this side of the wall had been stabilised. But honestly, very few people lived there. The initial cataclysm had been enough.

The barrier stopped at the broads. You couldn't stop the rivers from flowing, but you could sure as hell stop the people on them. Or you could try. Besides, magic and water were an uncanny mix. The Norfolk Broads provided their own unique barrier.

The Wymondham checkpoint was the only checkpoint for traffic. The wall was electrified and under constant surveillance. For obvious reasons, there were no magic barriers. The practitioners had argued but had been overruled by the United Nations and that was the end of that.

I hadn't paid any attention to the officer who had driven us here but having parked at the barriers she got out and hauled my backpack out of the boot and handed it to me as I climbed out of the car. We waited for the dog to join me. He was excitedly sniffing all the unfamiliar smells and looked like a dog with two tails.

The officer was about my age and she bent down and fondled the dog's ears.

'He sure is a funny-looking springer, but if I had to choose a dog to walk beside me, I'd choose a springer as well.'

I immediately warmed to her. At least she didn't seem to think I'd chosen this dog as bear food.

'I'm sorry I've been distracted. I'm Eliza Barnaby.'

She nodded her head.

'Yes, Bish. I know who you are. You apprehended the Quaglia Sisters. I think this is braver. I don't know anyone else who would do this. Go and get that scum.'

I shuddered remembering Sam and Lel. For years they had fooled everyone with their smiles and charm. Infiltrating the private school system they had created a blackmail network spreading across the country and out into the commonwealth and the world beyond.

Behind their public pretence of lovely young women, they had run a team of violent extortioners, thugs that carried out their bidding, inflicting terror across the globe. Despite my successful arrest, they had escaped a jail sentence on a technicality and I still ground my teeth about their evasion.

Now I was on the trail of an even scarier prey. And yet it was the destination that terrified me. It made me laugh that this police officer thought I was brave. So brave I couldn't even tell her where I was born.

'I'll be okay. I have the dog.'

She laughed. 'Indeed you do.' As she had been talking, she kept glancing over to the checkpoint and slowly edging back to the car.

'Thank you for driving me. I'll take it from here.'

With a quick wave, she hastened back into her car and sped away. I slung my backpack onto my shoulder and headed towards the low-level buildings. Outside, a large lorry was waiting. A driver firmly ensconced in his cab, pointing back towards London, patiently waiting for the next consignment of imports. Silks from the seventeenth century, spices from the eighteenth, minerals from the twelfth century. All of history's treasure and precious goods all filtering through the mess that was Norwich. Despite the general fear and revulsion surrounding my beleaguered home, people were still eager enough to buy its wares. One thing Norwich wasn't short of was commerce.

I sighed and headed into the building. Inside, it looked like any normal office. Chairs, filing cabinets, and a bell on the desk. I walked forward and rang it. A woman dashed through a door from an inner office and smiled at me. She was in her mid-thirties and dressed informally in jeans and a red and blue striped t-shirt. Around her neck was a whistle and a stopwatch.

'Detective Barnaby?'

I nodded.

'Right, well, we're expecting you. In fact, you might be able to help. Follow me.' She opened a flap on the counter and I walked through as she gave me a quick once over.

'Rucksack is a good call. Last idiot came with a wheeled suitcase.'

'I wanted to keep my hands free, plus I wasn't sure about the state of the road.'

'Mostly good,' she said over her shoulder as we walked along a carpeted hallway. 'I understand the bridge is out over the Yare, so you'll have to wade that bit. Good job it's summer, hey? You know what it's like in winter.'

As she chatted, I realised she had to be from Norwich.

'Are you local?' It was as polite and non-intrusive as I could get.

'Yep. Born on Ber Street, 1605. Arrived fifteen years ago in one of the little quakes. I work here and commute fortnightly. My name's Marjory.'

She stopped and stuck her hand out.

'I'm Bish,' I said, smiling as I shook her hand.

'Bishy Barnaby! I love it.'

I grinned back at her. 'When I had measles, Mum said I looked like a ladybird and with the surname...' I didn't need to explain any further.

'It's perfect. Now, if you'll just come through here, you'll see our problem.'

We walked into a large waiting room full of comfy armchairs and side tables. To the side were signs of baths and showers and further on, dormitories. Sitting on one of the chairs was a police officer who glared at Marjory and then cowered back into his chair as he saw me.

'I'll let him explain himself. In the meantime, can I take care of your dog? He looks like he might like some food and water and I'll sort his tags out.' She looked cross at the policeman and shook her head. 'When you've worked out what to do with him, I'll see you at the decontamination bay.'

Taking Harry's lead, she walked away. Harry paused, looking at me, and I was absurdly moved by his nascent loyalty. Although as soon as Marjory rattled the treats tin, he was gone.

I turned back to the officer, who now rose to his feet. He stank of sweat and his clothes were rumpled. Looking at the insignia on his shoulder, I saw it belonged to my own police station and I had a sinking feeling I knew who this was.

'Are you the envoy who was supposed to warn Norwich that a violent practitioner was heading their way and that a detective was following, to apprehend him?'

He waved the envelope at me again.

'I'm not going to Norwich. I don't get paid enough.'

'Yes, you do. Plus, you'd have received a danger payment.'

'What good is that to me if I'm dead?'

'For Christ's sake, man. You've allowed a dangerous criminal to increase his lead. I'll be reporting you for this.'

'You'll have to come back first. No one survives Norwich. It's full of demons and sudden death, ghosts walk the streets and suck the life out of you–'

'For fuck's sake. Stop that drivel right now. There are no demons, no ghosts.'

'What do you know?'

'Because I grew up there, didn't I?'

He stepped back and, throwing the envelope at me, ran towards the main entrance.

I watched the coward run and then stuffed the envelope into the top pocket of my jacket. Picking up my rucksack again, I followed the signs to the Decontamination Suite. Following the instructions, I stripped off and place my clothes and rucksack in their own chamber. After some pretty rigorous scrubbing I redressed, feeling uncomfortably tingly. Following the arrows, I entered another room and was just in time to see Marjory snap a pierced red tag onto Harry's white ear. Harry flinched and then returned to his food.

'Don't worry, I gave him a painkiller first.'

'But why tag him? His collar is chipped?'

She screwed up her face apologetically.

'The chip set the alarms off, must have some em-tech in it. Sorry.' She handed me a plain leather collar, with an old-fashioned silver disc on it. 'I've already put both your names on it.' I turned the disc over in my hands. Bish on one side, Harry on the other. It felt weird seeing our names together like that and I watched in concern as he continued to wolf through his food, seemingly oblivious to the red ear tag.

'So what's that for?'

'Part of the Norwich licencing act. All dogs must be instantly identifiable as safe. Any dog without a tag is shot on sight. We had a dreadful rabies outbreak about five years back. If it's not one thing–'

'-it's the end of days,' I quipped back.

For people living in Norwich, "the end is nigh" was yesterday. And today. And tomorrow. I laughed, what else was there to do?

'My colleague was supposed to inform Norwich of a murderer heading their way. He was last tracked on the A11 one mile north of here. Beyond the wall.'

She looked at me sharply.

'When was this?'

'Yesterday.'

She held my gaze and shook her head slowly, her jaw clenched.

'Not possible.'

I agreed with her but I wanted to hear her explanation and gestured for her to continue.

'This wall is double gated. You've seen for yourself anyone trying to get in or out has to breach both gates. And they can't scale the wall without setting off a whole range of alarms.'

'Could there be a breach further along the wall?'

'We check it every shift change. I've been here a week, so that's when we last rode the wall and checked for issues. There was nothing.'

'So something might have happened in the meantime?'

She frowned and then screwed her face up.

'If that bloody idiot had told me when he arrived, I could have gone and inspected the walls whilst he was here. Damn.'

I wanted to stay and help her but I had to get across before the sun went down. The mystery of how Cade got in would have to wait, for now speed was critical. I had to get to Norwich and warn them. As I stroked Harry's ear something about what she had just said struck me as odd.

'You said people can't break in. Who the hell wants to break into Norfolk?'

'Bloody Wizards. Who else?'

I looked at her in shock.

'Are you serious? What the hell are they thinking?'

'Power, hint ut?' Her accent was getting broader as she became agitated. 'That's all they ever want. All that bloody wild magic unleashed out there, they reckon as what they can harness it.'

'Are they mad?'

She raised an eyebrow.

'Sorry, stupid question. Of course they're mad. Do any ever succeed getting through?'

'Once or twice, not recently mind.' She looked cross that they had managed to evade her security, but they were practitioners, God knows they had the skill set for subterfuge.

'What happened to them?'

She smiled and I shivered.

'I saw one, went up like a firework. He screamed for hours. I taped that and sent it up to London. We haven't had another attempt since then.'

I shook my head. I couldn't comprehend the folly of trying to harness the wild magic in Norfolk. I didn't know much about how it worked but even I knew that you didn't try to hug a hornet's nest whilst covered in honey.

'Okay. As soon as someone else comes to the gate, I'll inspect the wall and send a message to the sheriff. I imagine you'll be stationed at the Watch House.' I nodded. I had no idea where I'd be stationed or how the Norwich police system operated these days but I was certain that Marjory would send a bird. 'Now, I have an apology. We're out of horses.'

I stopped examining the ear tag and looked at her in surprise.

'Horses?'

'I know. How twenty-first century are we?'

I laughed and leant back on the table. I hadn't expected a horse, so the lack of one wasn't an issue, but it would have been nice.

'How's that working out?'

'Surprisingly well. Around the river, the horses get as mad as March hares. But they are great at outrunning the wolves.'

'But you don't have any for me?'

Marjory winced and started rummaging in a large metal trunk.

'There's a large trading party gone across, and as no one else was scheduled, we let the spare horse go as well. Here–'

She stood up and handed me a dagger and a gun. The gun looked suitably antiquated, but the blade on the dagger was nice and sharp.

'I have my own gun. A revolver.'

I showed it to her and loaded the bullets.

She watched as I tried to get back in the fluid action of opening and loading the old revolver. 'You'll be expected to hand both weapons over when you get to St Stephen's Gate. Peter's on guard duty. Proper jobsworth and a bit handy if you get my drift. You'll have to go through decontamination again when you get over there. Make sure you keep the curtains pulled all the way across.'

I wasn't bothered by lecherous creeps. Them I could eat for breakfast but a second decontamination didn't appeal. I was still tingling from the one I'd just endured.

'Two decontaminations?'

'Norfolk is still a source of potential risk. We don't know what you encounter as you cross. So it's a belt and braces approach. No one wants the plague.' She looked at my face, 'Again.'

I nodded. 'Fair enough.' It was funny, for years I had been in constant turmoil about my scars. Marjory treated them as nothing more or less than what they were. They didn't signify I was ugly, or that I was the citizen of a terrifying city, infecting all in my wake. In her eyes, I was just someone that once got ill and survived.

'So what exactly does decontamination look like over there? When I left there was a groundswell for leeches being the cure to all ills. And trust me, I am not applying blood sucking slugs to any part of my anatomy.'

'Oh my God,' she laughed. 'I remember that. My mum swore blind by leaches until she had her first ibuprofen and then she was born again. Whipped us all down for every vaccination and pain killer going. No more chewing on willow bark for us.'

I nodded along, laughing.

'There was a lad on my street whose mum didn't hold with the new-fangled nonsense until she was visited by the devil. Two pain killers later and it was a miracle.'

We were laughing now and swapping shared experiences until I remembered that time was ticking.

'So, my decontamination?'

'Soap, shower and a change of clothes.' She shrugged. 'You're fully vaccinated and you've been scrubbed on this side. The only real risk is fleas, lice and ticks in the grass. Avoid any wildlife. Use your bullets only if a wolf attacks. Don't use it to scare them off. Try to avoid sitting down in long grass. Never ever step off the road. Only enter the water if you have to.'

'You said the bridge was out.'

She paused and shrugged.

'A fair point. Well, then you'll have to. But otherwise just avoid the environment as much as you can.'

She handed me a belt for my dagger, an apple, a flask of water, some sandwiches, and Harry's lead.

'Come on, then.'

We walked to the end of the room and she pressed a button on the wall. A large glass door slid open and she gestured at us to enter the room. As the door slid closed behind us, I turned and waved and was happy to see her waving back and giving me the thumbs up. The other door slid open and Harry and I walked into Old Norfolk.

Chapter Ten

 I stepped out into the sunshine and laughed at myself. I had been psyching myself up, expecting a land infested with plague-ridden fleas and slavering wolves circling behind stunted trees. Instead, the birds were singing, the sun was shining and the grass was swaying gently in the breeze. And all was quiet, just like the landscape behind me. I turned as I heard someone banging on a window and stepped forward and looked up at the sentry tower. Marjory was waving and shooing me on with her hand. She also waved a pair of binoculars at me and grinned. Accepting her admonishment, I began to walk. It was nice to know she was watching me for as long as she could.

'Okay dog, no time to dawdle.'

The little dog wagged his tail, his white face turned up at me, and then we set off. Initially, I let him pull on the lead as he excitedly moved back and forth across the road, but I remembered my instructions and reluctantly called him to heel. The dog didn't even come up to my knee. God knows what use he would be if we met wolves. Maybe the warden had a point. Maybe I could use him as a sacrifice whilst I made my escape. Or maybe he would wag them into submission. God knows, the tail seemed to be in constant motion.

The path ahead was clear. It was the old A11, a tarmacked dual carriageway. On either side, there was the odd cluster of rusted cars pushed off the road, now overgrown with plants and bushes. As we passed a crashed helicopter, we startled a deer that leapt up and bounced across the road and off into the long grass. It was all I could do to hold Harry back on his lead as he strained to chase.

After a mile or so, I turned and could no longer see the watchtower, I was now on my own until I reached Norwich. I knew there were a few old stately homes beyond the wall, but I didn't really know where they were and I certainly couldn't run to them in time if I got into trouble. I came to a section where the tarmac had disappeared and I walked along old sett stones. It wasn't as comfortable as the tarmac, but I marched on. I didn't remember this section when I left, but that was all part of the deal. The landscape changes.

And that's the nub of all of Norwich and Norfolk's problems. Some twenty-odd years ago, there was an accident in a cartography department in Oxford. Everyone knows that maps, like books, have a latent wild magic in them. Normally, that magic is contained and only affects one person at a time. Well, following a magical experiment by those oh so safe and clever practitioners, a load of magic spilled into a cartography drawer holding the historical maps for the city of Norwich and the surrounding countryside of Norfolk.

The spell somehow activated the maps' inherent magic and then fused and blended the maps. Imagine a fire or a flood, but rather than destroying the maps, this event fused and melded the differing sheets together.

Initially, the incident was met with shrugs from the practitioners and glares from the cartographer. It didn't occur to anyone that the physical entity of Norwich might be suffering. If suffering was the right word to describe the horrors taking place in the city.

A city and its representation goes two ways. A fact not previously understood. Up until then it was felt that as a city changed, a new map had to be drawn up and the old map abandoned. But anyone that has ever studied an old map will tell you, those lines still have a pull. An attraction that turned out to be more than idle curiosity or nostalgia. So when a city changes, the map changes. And apparently the opposite is also true if enough practitioners fuck it up. The maps changed, and so did the city.

We learnt a lot about magic that week. First, we learnt just how magical maps were and then we discovered just how much latent wild magic resided in bricks and mortar.

There were two main consequences. Blending a modern-day city map with a Tudor map meant that some of the Tudor inhabitants were pulled forward in time if their buildings still existed. A Tudor family living on Elm Hill found themselves waking up in the same building, just four hundred years after they went to sleep. And of course, it didn't just stop at the one map. All the time frames were affected. So not only did that Tudor family wake up in their house in the wrong timeframe, so theoretically did every inhabitant for each generation of maps up to the present day. Not everyone was pulled through, but the reasoning for that is the subject matter of many subsequent papers and symposiums.

All I knew was we had gone to bed with four souls in the house: me, my brother, my mum and my dad. We woke to over a hundred terrified, angry, confused and arrivals. Our home was suddenly filled with Tudors, Georgians, Victorians etc and they all claimed the house as theirs.

The second issue was that buildings disappeared or reappeared. The buildings at least risk of change were the oldest, those that appeared on every map and those that were made of stone. Or those that were most loved. Human memories imbued the stones and bricks with a magic that, until that moment, had never been quantified. For example, the St Augustine's flyover didn't stand a chance and was gone in the first quake. The people driving along it mostly plunged to their deaths. Only one high-rise survived. Modern office blocks vanished, some factories reappeared.

Beyond the innate protection of the city wall, the villages and towns were annihilated. New suburbs and dormitory villages disappeared in the blink of an eye. Having only appeared on the most recent map, they had little to lock them to the land. All across the county, new houses and roads disappeared, leaving only ancient manor houses and the old settlements.

That first night the population of Norwich rose from around 140,000 to several million, and then plummeted to 36,000 over the months as people died from an exciting array of options. The first, most basic, was that a building collapsed on top of you. Conversely, the modern building you were currently occupying disappeared with you along with it. You could die of an exciting range of historic illnesses or if you were from the past, then some of the modern diseases would wipe you out. Cholera and polio were all on the table, as were the black death and the sweats. And of course, so much unleashed wild magic drove people insane. Hallucinations were terrifying and simply trying to get your head around what had happened fritzed a lot of people's hard-wiring.

That was when we also began to understand that a sense of place was a real thing. Those residents that had lived in Norwich all their life coped with the changes the best, even better if they came from a long line of locals. People who weren't born and bred suffered the most.

Water mains ruptured, streets were flooded with sewerage, electricity pylons came down. Anything powered by magic went doo-lally. It would be hard to imagine a worse event. The United Nations certainly couldn't and threw up a ten-mile exclusion zone around Norwich, banned magic, evacuated all those that wanted help then burnt the bodies. My God, the pyres were dreadful, but there were simply too many corpses to bury. The UN sent in medicine and money. And then they buggered off and left us to it.

Chapter Eleven

I figured I was well over halfway. At least I hoped I was, as the sun was beginning to sink. I hadn't heard any wolves but a barn owl flew past in the late afternoon sun and I knew it was time to be safely behind the Norwich city walls. I broke my sandwich in half and shared it with the dog, then made a mess of trying to pour water into my hands to share with him. I was fairly unsuccessful, partly because my hands kept flinching every time his mouth came close to me, but he kept wagging his tail so I didn't feel a total failure. In the end there was more water on the stones than in either of our mouths, but we'd soon be at our destination.

Then the stones abruptly ran out and I was looking at grass. I tried not to get concerned. The route was still obvious, but only just. I couldn't see Norwich yet and the thought of just wandering around in the dark filled me with panic. There were a few safeholds along the way, but without a map I didn't know where they were. I hadn't even got to the Yare yet and I most certainly didn't want to cross that in the dark.

In the distance, I saw something moving towards me. At first, I thought it was a mirage, shifting in the heat, but as I moved closer, I saw it was a caravan of traders riding their horses and pulling carts towards me.

Cars were a waste of time as most used an em-engine and those that didn't couldn't handle the road surface. I thought a tractor would work, but then remembered that Norwich had very limited fuel supplies. An oil depot had been wiped off the map leaving broken pipes that had burnt for weeks. A choking black cloud had drifted across the countryside forcing us to stay indoors as the fire burnt itself out. I remembered the lorry and the minibus waiting on the other side of the barrier. They were waiting for this caravan.

I kept walking until I came alongside the lead wagon, as they slowed the horses to a halt.

The wagon driver seemed a relaxed sort and tipped a straw hat to me.

'How do?'

His accent was broad Norfolk and I smiled to hear those soft rolling tones again.

'How do,' I replied. 'Have I far to go?'

The man was in his fifties and looked well fed and well heeled. He wore a gold signet ring on his pinkie and looked every inch the gentleman trader. His straw hat, however, came straight out of Tess of the D'Urbervilles and he took his pipe out of his mouth.

'Not far at all. And I reckon as we've made your journey a little easier?'

I tilted my head up.

'That sounds promising.'

He swung around on his bench and called to the back of the convoy.

'Boys. Come forward and tell our intrepid walker what you've done.'

Two lads in their early twenties swaggered forwards, rifles slung on their backs.

'We shot eleven wolves.'

'Twelve.'

The man on the wagon laughed. 'It'll be twenty by the time we get to Wymondham. Unless you saw any along the way?'

'No, just a deer that scared the Dickens out of me.'

The three men laughed.

'Reckon your mighty hound wanted to play with that one?'

One of the lads bent down to ruffle Harry's fur and he pulled out a bit of food from his haversack. 'May I?' I nodded, and Harry enthusiastically gulped it down.

'What about yourself? We've got mostly just fabrics and spices on this crossing, but there is some chocolate?'

I looked up and grinned.

'What sort?'

'Belgium, 1850s.'

I tried not to lick my lips as he laughed and threw me a bar. Modern-day chocolate is all well and good, but until you've tried some of the old foods, you have nothing to compare it to. I took a bite and sighed with pure joy. The richness of the cocoa and milk combined with unrefined sugar and lashing of vanilla and cardamon was a treat that I hadn't tasted in years. I certainly couldn't afford it in London. This stuff only went to the top tables and the fattest purses. I felt like I was ten again when such treats were becoming commonplace.

I studied their wagons and the horses, the air wasn't that warm.

'You look bone dry. I was told the bridge had gone.'

'The repairs were finished this lunch, which is when we set off.'

'Well, you've got to make hay whilst the sun shines,' I said.

Who knew when another little quake would screw things up? The problem with the fused map was that for a while, the practitioners tried to fix the problem. From this, you may understand that they made everything, if not worse because that wasn't possible, then a continuation of awfulness. With each attempt to separate the maps, they created another quake. The main problem was that the practitioners didn't understand what they had done or how the magic was working, so not only could they not explain it, but they also couldn't fix it. They had argued for years that they should be allowed to experiment, but it was felt that might involve the total annihilation of Norwich and, for once, the practitioners were overruled.

What Norwich was desperate for was stability. So the maps were sealed away. Over the years, parts of the map occasionally dried out magic and we'd get a quake, a bit of Georgian Norwich previously unaffected would suddenly become fused and hey presto, a new flux of periwinkle fops and guttersnipes.

'I'd offer you a horse but you're nearly there,' said the trader and I shook my head. He had further to go than I had.

A young woman on a sturdy looking pack horse trotted forward.

'She can have mine,' and she swung off the back, removing her paniers.

'Well now, Anne.'

'Well now, nothing. She's still got three miles to go and those dead wolves will attract other predators soon enough. I can sit up by you.'

He took off his hat and scratched his head, looking between the two of us and then shrugged his shoulders.

'Well, that's me told, hint ut? Boys, help her up.'

And within minutes I was up on the horse. Harry's lead had been extended with a piece of rope.

'I'd buy you a drink when you're next back, but my visit is fleeting.'

'Work or pleasure?'

And after we'd all finished laughing, I said I was here on police business.

'Sounds serious. Can't remember the last time we had outsiders calling.'

I was about to point out I was from Norwich then stopped. What did it matter?

'Afraid it is, but it will be sorted soon enough.'

'And it's not something that we can take care of by ourselves?' His tone was friendly, but I recognised a hint of belligerence.

'I'm sure it is, but as yet Norwich isn't aware of the situation. I have no doubt the Norwich police force are more than capable of the challenge.' I stared at the two lads. 'No doubt the force could do with good officers, if you've ever had a mind to change your career.'

'Enough of that, you baggage,' laughed the trader, waving his hat in my direction. 'My sons are the best form of defence my caravan has.'

I laughed back, baggage was not meant unkindly.

'You can't blame a girl for trying to poach the best for her own team.'

One of the horses snorted and the moment passed.

'Before you go, when did you come to Norwich?'

'Two days ago. Some of my team aren't Norwich born, so we keep it short.'

That fit the timeframe for William Cade's escape.

'Did you pick up any hitchhikers or see anyone along the way?'

'Not a soul.'

'Could someone have smuggled their way through the checkpoint as one of your party?'

He narrowed his eyes.

'We are a legitimate enterprise under God's law and the King's eye. If you are suggesting–'

I cut him off. I didn't have time for his outrage.

'I'm pursuing a dangerous criminal. He got past the barriers somehow.'

'Well, it weren't with us.' He put his fingers to his lips and whistled loudly. As he did, the horses got ready to walk on. I hadn't said he could go, but by the same token, I wouldn't get anything else out of him.

'I'd best let you get on. Safe travels and I hope you get a good price for your goods.'

'Flemish silks, stunning lapis lazuli and the finest malmsey. That should be enough to fund the boys' gap years.'

As he drove forward, I manoeuvred my horse and kicked my heels. I had ridden a horse the sum total of five times when I was training for the mounted police. Those five times suggested I might be a better detective than a rider. I knew my thighs would ache before I got to the walls, but for now this was a relief. I had only gone a few hundred metres when one of the men turned back and rode up alongside me. He was about my age, with slicked back hair and dressed by Ralph Lauren. On his finger, he wore a matching gold ring to that of his father's. Business was clearly profitable.

'You'll have to excuse him. He gets twitchy if people suggest he's playing fast and loose. He's a very fair man, but people always suspect the wealthy.'

'It's okay, I'm the law. I suspect everyone.' I smiled as I said it and he tipped his head in acknowledgement.

'I just wanted to let you know. I asked everyone and no one has seen or heard anything unusual, beyond the obvious, either coming here, in the city or on the way out.'

I appreciated it.

'What "obvious unusual" did you encounter?'

'Anne saw bits of Hethersett flick in and out as we arrived.'

I winced. I hadn't seen any flickerings and had hoped they'd passed.

'You were all safe, though?'

'Yes. Although we had to send Miles back to wait in the lorry. He was already suffering. Seeing ghosts everywhere, people walking through walls, hearing cock-fights. We'd only got three miles from the barrier and Father said enough.'

'Was it his first time?'

No one knew how quickly outsiders succumbed to the wild magic, some could endure it for days, even weeks, others collapsed almost immediately.

'No, that's the shame of it. He's been with us for the past six trips. Damn shame to lose him. He can smell a rotting dodo from five metres.'

'Do they rot easily?'

'Like milk in a heatwave and about as tasty. And if one carcass begins to rot, it spreads to the others within hours.'

I realised I was getting side-tracked.

'And no one saw any walkers or newcomers in the city?'

'No.' He slipped his hand into a pocket and pulled out a slim silver card case. Flicking it open, he pulled out a calling card and handed it over to me. On it was the name Daniel Thwaite and a phone number.

'When you get back, give me a call. We'll get some drinks.'

I looked at him, surprised. It wasn't unheard of for people to try to gain an inside edge with the police force, but he was barking up the wrong tree if he thought I was that sort.

He laughed at my expression.

'Just a drink, honest. Just one ex-Norviker to another.'

Reminiscences weren't my deal either but I took the card politely. Saying goodbye, I headed on. I turned back to see he had safely rejoined the caravan and saw with surprise that he was still watching me. No doubt checking I could actually ride the horse properly. Shrugging, I shook the reins and we headed on our way to Norwich. The breeze was blowing my hair back into my face and now that the caravan had passed, I tucked it behind my ears again and carried on.

'You okay down there, Harry?'

His tail wagged and I had to settle for that. I was happier now that the dog was away from me and I relaxed a bit more. I was on a horse and making better time. Even if we encountered wolves now, I would be able to escape.

Had William Cade made it this far? Given the amount of security coming through the barrier, I had discounted the Wymondham Crossing as his point of access and yet his last ping had been along this road. With any luck, he had been caught up in a wave of wild magic that still scoured the land beyond the city wall. Only a few people could withstand those waves. When one hit, people simply vanished. Never to be heard of again. The smell of honeysuckle was getting stronger and I decided we must be approaching the River Yare. The Yare, unlike the Wensum, didn't cut through Norwich but flowed a few miles south of the city. Wild magic rarely crossed water and as a wave of magic hit the river boundary it ricocheted back on itself and flowed back across the land. This was why horses were so jittery approaching rivers and why they were a waste of space over by the broads. It was also a dangerous place for humans. Being in the river was fine, a place of safety. Climbing out onto the banks could spell disaster.

As we approached the bridge, I saw I had somehow over emphasised the "bridge" aspect of it in my head. When I had last crossed it ten years ago, it had been a tarmacked road. Now it was a collection of planks. And at the end of the planks stood a wolf.

Chapter Twelve

The wolf's pelt was matted with blood and I prayed it was his.

I came to a halt. From below, Harry was growling and as I looked down, I could see his tail had finally stopped wagging. He was crouching and his hackles were raised.

The horse was twitching and stamping on the spot, and I could feel the awkwardness of the pack on my shoulder. One wounded wolf probably couldn't hurt me up here on the horse, but what about the dog? It seemed that as push came to shove, I was reluctant to sacrifice my hairy companion.

The wolf looked to be three times Harry's size and I made a mistake. I decided to save him. Grabbing the rope, I hauled Harry up as quickly as I could, choking him on his collar, with his legs swinging in the air until I could grab the scruff of his neck and pull him up onto the saddle with me.

I desperately tried to hush him as he stamped his feet and began to turn on the spot. Which is when Harry growled by the poor horse's ear, and the wolf took a step forward onto the bridge.

Picture a clown car, if you will, one where the doors flap open and closed and passengers are shot into the air. I imagine the next few seconds looked remarkably similar.

The wolf limped towards us and Harry went ballistic, barking and straining as I held onto his collar. I wrapped his lead around my arm as I gripped on to the reins, trying to urge the horse back off the bridge. When Harry started to bark, the horse lost it. As far as the horse was concerned, the wolf on his back was now more terrifying than the one on the ground and he started to buck, rearing up then slamming back down, making the wooden planks tremble as he kicked back. I held on for maybe one buck and then I was sailing through the air. I expected my impact to come quicker than it did and just as I figured it out, I hit the water below.

With the rucksack on my back, I sank like a stone. My arms and legs were flailing, trying to find purchase in the weed-filled current. All I wanted was air. So desperately. I couldn't rise to the surface and I twitched and jerked, trying to rid myself of my anchor. At the moment I decided I was going to die, my arm jerked and I felt the rope that was wrapped around it go taut. Hauling on the rope, I pulled myself towards the surface and felt mud beneath my hand as I struggled to rise.

I was kneeling on a small islet. Harry and his lead were entangled in a stunted willow tree and it was that tension that had saved me. Stumbling to my feet, I removed my backpack, freed Harry and then sat back down again, coughing out the river water.

Harry wagged his tail.

'Bloody hell, dog. That was close.'

Looking around, I could see the bridge some hundred yards to my right. I had fallen into the faster, deeper flowing section but now on the bend in the river there were just a few shallow islands. I hauled my way through the water, wading up to my thighs and clambered up the banks grabbing onto the plants to pull me up. The injured wolf was long gone.

'Okay,' I said, 'Let's figure this out. On the plus side, I'm alive and so are you, so yay. On the downside, I'm soaking wet, I've lost the horse, we're still a mile from Norwich, the sun is setting and I have no idea which side of the bridge I'm on.'

Harry went for a pee and then wandered around. I was too tired to care that he wasn't on a lead. I knew I had to get up and start walking, but what if I walked in the wrong direction? I didn't want to be out here in the dark. A howl echoed across the air and Harry ran back towards me and sat at my feet.

'It's okay, boy, I don't need you to protect me. Or did you want me to save you?' I laughed ruefully and slicked my wet hair back, pulling duckweed out of it. 'I think we need to work on our technique next time, but for now, let's hit the road.'

The howl had made my mind up. I would walk in the opposite direction. It wasn't much to go on, but it worked for me.

Moments later, I was rewarded by the sight of a battered metal sign lying in the grass, baring the historic phrase. 'Welcome to Norwich. A Fine City.' The sign was rusty and moss had grown on it, but at least it was still doing its job. I was nearly home.

As Harry and I continued, I couldn't help but feel a sense of unease. The howl was still ringing in my ears, and every step we took felt like a risk. Water from my backpack dripped down my legs and my trousers chafed. The sky was turning dark and the trees lining the path seemed to close in on us. I knew we had to keep moving, but every rustle in the bushes made me jump. Harry seemed to sense my fear and stayed close to my side, his nose twitching as he searched for any sign of danger. For once, I welcomed his presence.

Another owl hooted and a wolf howled in the distance again and then I heard the sweetest of all sounds, church bells. Over the sound of the bells, a second wolf howled over to my right.

'Come on, Harry. Time to kick it up a gear.'

Jackdaws squawked overhead as they settled into the tree roosts and the odd bat flitted past. It wasn't fully dark yet, but I was definitely running out of light. The sun had set and twilight was fading. The bells gave me hope, though.

'That's Little Mary, and that's St Crispin. I think. Oh and here comes the cathedral, rising above them all.' I listened to their joyful peal. It had to be nine pm, the only time all the churches rang together was on the quarters, three, six and nine. Everyone agreed that midnight was unnecessary. Otherwise, the fifty-two churches took turns to ring the hours. As I left the woods, I could finally see the wall ahead of me.

The city wall was seven metres high and made of flint. During the cataclysm it had reared up, the tumbled down city wall reverted to its former glory, having been marked on all maps and symbolising to the citizens their city's boundary. Its walls offered stability and protected the city from the waves of wild magic that swept across the Norfolk landscape. It wrapped around my entire childhood and was the most solid and terrifying thing in my life. Home sweet home.

Two howls rang out behind me. They were much closer and I pulled the knife out of its sheath, drew my gun from its holster, and ran. The wet rucksack bounced against me, and Harry ran alongside. He tried to turn and face them off, but I yanked on the lead and pulled him along, sprinting for the city gates, screaming at the top of my lungs.

I was ten metres from the wooden gates when a heavy weight slammed into my back and I was thrown forward.

As I hit the ground, my face scraped against the rough stones that lined the city's entrance and Harry's lead pulled free from my hand. Pain exploded in my head, and I struggled to regain my senses as the two howls grew louder. Harry barked fiercely and lunged towards the attackers.

I heard his yelp, and my heart filled with fury. Stumbling to my feet, I ignored the pain and charged at the wolves, shooting as I ran. Harry was lying still on the earth and I wondered numbly if I had brought him to his death. The wolves were fast, but I was ferocious. I had spent a day being chased out of London and sprinting towards Norwich, returning to a home that I hated, chasing a criminal who was the stuff of nightmares. I was footsore and fed up and now the only creature that had shown me any warmth in ten years was in pain and it was my fault.

My bullets missed the first wolf but clipped the second one. I didn't even have time to register the shots as the first one threw itself at me. I dodged its jaws and slashed with my knife. Blood spurted from its wounds as it howled in pain then lunged at me with its teeth bared. Sidestepping, I plunged my knife into its flank. It fell to the ground, whimpering and writhing in agony. Stabbing it again, it fell silent. It was huge and for a second, I just leant on it. Its fur was warm and soft as its ribcage heaved one last time.

The other wolf backed away, growling low in its throat. I knelt there, panting, covered in blood, and watched as it limped into the night.

Chapter Thirteen

 Harry came running back to me, wagging his tail and licking my face. I hugged him tightly, grateful for his loyalty and bravery. All sense of fear I had of him had dissipated as we fought to save each other's life. I didn't know how I felt about other dogs, but this one had somehow stolen my heart and I felt the wonder of a new friendship. Patting Harry all over, I couldn't find any cuts, although he flinched when I held his paw, so I made a note to bathe that later. I stood up, readjusting the backpack.

Two men were now running towards me, high-powered rifles raised as I stumbled in their direction.

'Are there any more?' shouted one of the men.

'Don't know,' I gasped, pointing at the dead wolf lying on the ground. 'Two of them. They came out of nowhere. A caravan I passed earlier said they had killed a pack of ten.'

One of the men spat on the ground.

'Reckon it's time for another hunt. That's the eighth attack in the past week.'

The other guard continued to look out into the dark, then shook his head.

'You're not wrong, but tonight we need to get this traveller and her fearsome hound into the city. We can send the militia out tomorrow.' He went to ruffle

Harry's head, then pulled his hand away and stepped back. 'Are you fully inoculated? Papers.'

'Yes. All in my pack, although they might be wet.'

The two men looked at me closely, then swore again.

'Don't tell me the bridge has gone already?'

I shook my head, the shivers beginning to set in as my teeth chattered.

'Fell off my horse. Landed in the river. Harry here saved me.'

I leant down and patted Harry on the back and was rewarded with a wag of the tail. I was also pleased to see he wasn't limping.

'Okay, well at least that solves one mystery. A riderless horse turned up a while back. Come on, then.'

I followed behind, making sure not to close the gap that they had insisted I keep. The old inhabitants of Norwich had passed on the sweat, the plague and the pox. We gave them influenza and herpes. Which turned out to be just as lethal. I walked through the small door set within the huge wooden doors of the sally port and looked up at the gigantic flint walls towering overhead. I surveyed the walls as I walked, noticing for the first time that on this section each block of stone was knapped, leaving a hard, shining surface. Knapped flint was as sharp as the devil. It could cut through silk and paper, would carve bone, skin a rat and from time to time slice a jugular. But that was the knap edge, the face of the flint was as smooth as satin and shone like the night sky.

I don't know how I didn't notice it before, on this section of the gates, but just placing my palm on the icy surface helped settle my nerves.

The light from the torches and the moonlight reflected off the walls with a brilliance that almost hurt my eyes. Most of the wall was rough, but here at the gates the flint was knapped in the same fashion as the Guildhall and I wondered if the same craftsmen had done it.

'Miss?' I turned around, lost in thought. 'Over here, please.'

A short man in a three-piece suit was standing with a clipboard. A fob watch was tucked into his waistcoat and a bowler hat sat firmly on his head. The two guards waved me away as they returned to the Watch ports and I walked across to the contamination rooms.

There then followed a lengthy perusal of my wet papers and I was given a change of clothes and pointed towards a changing room with a rather ineffectual curtain. I turned and glared at him.

'I have had a very long day. I am on the trail of a killer. I've been attacked by wolves. They nearly killed my dog and if I have to endure a Peeping Tom, I swear to you I won't hesitate to draw my blade again.'

The man took two rapid steps back and stared at me in confusion and then laughed nervously as he pulled at his shirt collar.

'My name is Carl. Carl Butcher.'

I stared, mortified.

'Did you think I was Peter?'

'Marjory said he was on the gate today. I'm so sorry. I really am. It's been a horrible day. I'm so sorry.'

He held his hands up and started waving at me to calm down.

'It's okay, Peter was working today, but he bit off more than he could chew. A caravan left this afternoon, with a particularly feisty woman riding shotgun. When she changed clothes, he took liberties and she took revenge.' He was smiling now. 'He had to go home early with a broken nose, two black eyes and a smashed tooth.'

I winced. I could imagine which girl it was and I smiled, remembering her offer of a horse.

'I think I met her. She gave me her horse.'

'You didn't hold on to it for very long, did you?'

'No I did not.'

'Go and change. The clothes are warm and dry. We'll get yours back to you after they've been frozen.'

Freezing, it turned out, worked just as well as any magical device for decontamination. It was just a little slower. I was warming to Carl Butcher. As an immigration officer, he was efficient and welcoming. I tugged on a pair of light trousers and a t-shirt, then feeling a mild chill in the air, I added the jumper. Finally, I slipped my gun belt back on and returned the gun to its holster.

I pulled back the curtain and Harry ran forward. I was surprised by his enthusiasm.

'I've only been gone five minutes.' I laughed in protest as he kept jumping up at me.

'Not had a dog before?'

'Not for a very long time,' I laughed. 'Is this normal?'

'Completely. Now, excuse an old man for being nosey, but it says here you were born on Elm Hill and your surname is Barnaby. Were your folks Paul and Carrie?'

I knew this was likely to happen. The thing about Norwich is that the inhabitants are sort of static. We don't have people move in and out from other areas, other time periods yes, other cities, no. Which meant that after a while you really get to know your neighbours. In one sense, Norwich is just like a very large village. I stared at the man in front of me. I didn't recognise him and I normally have a good eye for faces. I tried not to sound hostile, but they had died twenty years ago and it remained a sore point.

'They were my mum and dad, yes.'

'I knew them. We hung out. Your dad more. I wasn't used to hanging out with girls. Wasn't done when I came from.'

I raised an eyebrow.

'Hampton Place, 1883. My wife didn't make it. I woke up in my bedroom, with ten other people.'

'It must have been terrifying?'

'It was. But that morning I found your father. He was in the middle of a fight with three men. I felt the odds were ungentlemanly, so I joined the fray. After that we found a kindred spirit in each other. It didn't take long to realise he was as scared as I was.'

He cleared his throat.

'He was a good man. And your mother was an angel. I was so sorry when they died. I offered to take you in. Lots of us did, but you chose the orphanage.'

I blinked. I remember being told of all the offers I had for re-homing, but I was done with caring for people who died on me. The orphanage seemed a safer bet.

'Thank you. I—'

He waved his hand.

'Forget it. Norwich is a hard city.'

He pulled out the paperwork that I had handed him. How different would my life have been if I had accepted the comfort of strangers? He could have gifted me a secure childhood and kept the memories of my parents alive. I drew a deep shuddering breath, wishing I hadn't come back.

'Now,' he said, clearing his throat. 'I see you have a licence to carry that gun, but that doesn't count for Norwich. You'll have to convince the sheriff.'

I made a judgement call. I knew I should tell the sheriff first about Cade, but I really wanted to keep my gun by my side. Especially following the wolf attack.

'This is between you and me for now, but I am on the path of a rogue practitioner. He has to be shot on sight, or else he might attempt a spell in the city.'

Carl crossed himself.

'An actual spell? Here? Where there's so much wild magic washing around. Is he insane?'

'Apparently, yes.' Although he had seemed quite reasonable when I met him. But then he had killed two people in front of me and then a further five, so I was no judge of character.

'You can keep your gun. If the sheriff kicks up, well, I guess we'll have some discussion about it. But I'm the gatekeeper and I say you can have your gun until he says you can't.'

I smiled gratefully and surprised myself by yawning, then laughing sheepishly. The day was catching up with me.

'Now then, I looked at your papers. Two envelopes were labelled *Confidential*. I didn't open them, but I can't let you proceed into the city without knowing their contents or their recipient.'

An immigration official that stopped at the word Confidential? I was impressed.

'Those papers basically say what I've just told you. So I'll need to head straight to the sheriff anyways. Or whoever's in charge of security, basically.'

I could have phrased that better, but he got the drift. He opened the window and, leaning out of it, called to someone named Michael. Then he turned back to me and shrugged.

'I know, I could have used the intercom but I like to save the electricity for essential items.'

'Is it still bad?'

'When did you leave?'

'Ten years ago.'

He chuckled. 'Heavens, it was bad back then, wasn't it? We have a canny system now, but it's wise to be frugal, especially in summer when the river runs slow and low.'

'Water turbine then?'

'Yes, and coal.'

I was curious. The Wensum was volatile at the best of times. Dropping a turbine into that seemed high risk.

'How stable is the river?'

'Solid as the walls. But slippery. If you stay long enough, you should go and explore.'

'How about the docks?'

Growing up, the docks had been highly restricted. They were a point in the city where the boundaries were dangerously fluid. The Wensum provided one of the city's boundaries. As such, it protected us, but historically it was a lot wider and deeper. It was an area where the timelines fluctuated rapidly.

'They're safer these days. Besides, you're an officer of the law. You can go anywhere. Speaking of which...'

The door opened and the guard who had earlier helped me fight the wolf walked in. Presumably

Michael. This time, he wasn't carrying a rifle or a gun. On a denim shirt he wore a gold badge with the cathedral spire and castle engraved on it. He wore black jeans and heavy boots with a utility belt on his hip, a baton slotted down the side. I took him for some sort of officer of the law, but wasn't sure what the system was here.

'Thank you, Mike.' I liked how Carl said Mike. As though it killed him to abbreviate Michael, but was doing his best to humour someone he respected. 'Detective Barnaby needs to see Sheriff Hitchman immediately. Is he at work or at home?'

'Work. He's on a late one after that incident.'

Clearly, Mike wasn't prepared to elaborate on the incident in front of me and I let it go. I was the outsider, after all.

'Very well,' said Carl. 'Could you accompany the detective and take her there?'

The last thing I wanted was an escort.

'It's okay, just give me the address. I'll know the way.'

The two men looked at me. Mike snorted but Carl was at least more tactful.

'I have no doubt you do. But ten years is a long time in Norwich. Besides, Michael, Mike could do with the exercise.'

Mike grinned and slapped his flat stomach.

'As if. Anyway,' he said, turning to me with a curled lip, 'outsiders don't get to roam around Norwich on their first night.'

'How old are you?' He looked several years younger than me. 'I bet I've lived in Norwich just as long as you have.'

He scratched his chin.

'Maybe, but I've lived here more recently and I never left.'

'No one's stopping you.'

'Why would I want to? This is a fine city.'

We glared at each other for a bit until Carl rapped his knuckles on the table.

'Mike, stop being antagonistic.' He turned to me, raising his eyebrows. 'Do forgive him. Mike is born and bred, lives over by the docks and plays for the Canaries. He can be prone to jingoism. Now, do you know where you'll be staying? No. Very well, I'll have your items sent forward when we find out. Now, off you go.'

And with that he shooed us out of his office and I stared down the winding length of St Stephen's Street.

Chapter Fourteen

 I followed Mike, choosing to ignore him as I looked around. So far, most buildings were the same, but now there was a sense of prosperity to the city. I gave a huff of surprise. Norwich appeared to be doing very well for itself.

Lights shone from windows, people were milling about. The vibe was relaxed although I was attracting a few stares. Or Harry was. There was a row of large canvas tents running alongside the wall in either direction, but St Stephen's Street still ran downhill towards the castle. I couldn't see it in the dark, but assumed the lights on the hill were coming from its windows. Little lanes ran right and left, and I tried to remember where the police station was.

'Are we going the right way? I thought the station was by the Guildhall.'

'It is.'

'Then wouldn't it be quicker to cut through the back lanes?' I said, gesturing to the little alleys on our left.

He stopped and walked back to me, standing in the yellow light of a streetlamp and scratched his chin again.

'Not worth the aggro, what with the curfew.'

'Still?'

That surprised me. In the past we often had curfews, but this didn't look like a city under need of martial control.

'Not Norwich, just the Threads. Those lanes have become very popular with the Puritans, and they've been getting twitchy about—' he broke off. 'Look, when were you born?'

'1996.'

He exhaled deeply. 'Excellent. Then you know what I mean. These oldies can get peculiar notions about what's acceptable. The Puritans have taken it into their heads that nighttime is for sinners. Plus, they also have a real thing about women in trousers.'

'And we allow that sort of nonsense? Self-imposed curfews and the like?'

'No, but it's Norwich. These things take time. Trust me. With the problems we are having with the Strangers we don't want to stir up any further divisions.'

I stared at him.

'The Strangers? They're the nicest people in the city.'

The idea of the Strangers starting a grudge match was ridiculous.

'You have been gone a long time, haven't you? Look, the Strangers are now a faction to reckon with and if keeping them and the Puritans apart keeps Norwich on an even keel, then we turn a blind eye.'

Community policing at its finest. Well, it wasn't my problem and we took the longer way to the police station, although in honesty there wasn't much to it. I was just trying to prove to Mike that I knew my way around. Which was dumb of me as I didn't know the current situation. I walked on and luxuriated in my lightweight trousers on a warm summer evening. If the weavers wanted to wear woollen petticoats, that was their own affair.

Nightingales were singing over the noise of the patrons of the local pubs. On one side of the wide road a man was sitting outside playing the pipes, a merry little tune that rose into the air and mingled with the pipe smoke of the old boys sitting outside the Crown and Anchor on the other side of the road. On the pavement, old men were playing board games and tutting to themselves about the youth of today.

At another table, a young woman was busy crocheting something that looked like it might be a blanket or a cardigan. However, when I looked closely it appeared to have at least four sleeves. As she beckoned the waiter for another cocktail I wondered if that was playing a factor.

Mike saw me raise an eyebrow and quickly explained.

'Daisy Rowley. Purveyor of the finest sheep wool jumpers.'

I frowned. 'But they have four sleeves? Unless, we can now add mutations to the list of Norwich's charms.' Honestly, I wouldn't be surprised. When it came to Norwich anything went.

He looked at me and scoffed. 'Of course they have four sleeves. One for each leg.'

I stared back at the girl merrily crocheting in the light spilling out from the pub and tried to understand what he meant when the penny dropped. 'Sheep wool jumpers! She's making jumpers for sheep!'

'Indeed she is.'

'But sheep-' How to point out the bleeding obvious. I tried again. 'Sheep already have. I mean-' I faltered again and Mike grinned as he gave Daisy a wave, then spoke softly to me, careful that the girl wouldn't hear.

'First time Daisy saw the sheep getting sheared she was so concerned for them getting cold that she went straight out, bought some wool and made them a jumper. Norwich has a way of changing the way some of us handle the world and I think Daisy is handling the world just fine.'

I watched as she finished her cocktail and bundled up her needles for the evening and thought he might have a point.

Above the evening sounds were the scents of a summer evening: pipes, wood smoke, hops, and honeysuckle. It took me back faster than I expected and I had memories of playing with friends in the chapel fields, picking blackberries and earning pocket money by rounding up the geese that invariably broke loose. It was a good gig until Mrs Hope caught us freeing the geese through her binoculars. God, we'd got bollocksed for that little wheeze and had to do community service for a month, but it had been worth it.

I had been seven when the cataclysm had struck, so I only remembered Norwich as it is now, a blurred mix of timelines. Before, it had just been like any other city. Manchester, London, Birmingham, Glasgow.

A shriek of laughter spilled onto the street as a hen party piled out of The Bull. All the girls were in cheap veils and one girl was wearing a bright red L on her chest.

Some things never change.

Seeing Mike, she shouted enthusiastically and ran towards him, an admirable feat in those stilettos. Her friends ran to catch up. Mike groaned and turned my way.

'Give me a minute.'

I think he was planning to quietly take her to one side, but she sprinted forward and jumped up, wrapping her legs around his waist, and planted a huge kiss on the side of his face. With her arrival, we were plunged into a cloud of perfumes, notably Chanel No5, Opium and most obnoxiously of all, this season's new fragrance from Givenchy. As he gently placed her back on the ground, she turned, laughing to one of the girls.

'Sal, look it's Mike. It's your brother!'

Sal swayed forward and peered at Mike, then punched him playfully on the arm.

'Lo Mike.'

'Hello, Sal. You all having fun?'

'We are,' shouted the soon to be bride and then finally noticing me, she peered at me closely and tried to act sober. 'Hello. I'm getting married tomorrow. Do you want to come? Mike's coming, aren't you Mike?'

'Yes, Lucy. Where would Andy be without his best man?'

'Is she your date?' Before he could answer, she turned to the group of giggling girls. 'Look! Marvellous Mike has a girlfriend. Told you he wasn't gay!'

'Lucy, for the umpteenth time, I am gay. This is Detective Barnaby, from London. She's here on work.'

They all stared at me now, the giggles faded away.

'She's new,' wailed a girl with heavy red lipstick and a plunging neckline. 'Lucy, a newbie on your wedding eve. This is such a bad omen.'

The other girls took up her cry and now the laughing girls were all weeping. Lucy stared between us and her friends in mounting panic. Mike sighed deeply and shook his head.

'Come on, Lucy. You don't believe in old wives' tales.'

'But remember that time a new one arrived and then the plague began, or when Mrs Harrison failed to curtsy at the moon and all the beer soured?'

'The beer soured because Mr Harrison failed to tend to the hops properly on account of punching Mrs Harrison, who ended up unconscious and unable to curtsy to anyone or anything.'

'But the plague?' sobbed Lucy, her mascara running down her cheeks.

'We can't stop a plague just because of a wedding, Lucy.'

I felt Mike wasn't helping things, as the girls all started wailing again. The old boys across the way were enjoying the spectacle, and a few more had spilled out to watch the drama. There was nothing half as enjoyable as street theatre, especially when the players were so pretty. The piper had even started to play a lament. We were moving into full Greek tragedy. I stepped forwards.

'Hello, Lucy. My name is Eliza Barnaby. I was born in Norwich in 1996. I went to school at Bignolds for a bit. I'm local. I probably even went to school with some of you,' I said, addressing the other girls, although in fairness, they all seemed at least five years younger than me. 'Well, that's when I turned up.'

Mike raised an eyebrow, but I wasn't about to explain that school was more of an option for me. Back then, we were just trying to stay alive and rebuild. School was something of a parental aspiration. If you had parents.

'Bignolds. Really?' hiccoughed the young bride, wiping her tears off her face.

'Sure did. Mr Spynke was there. Worst human being in the entire universe. Stank to high heaven and if he thought he could grab a quick grope, he would.'

'He still does. Or at least he did until one of the fathers chopped his hand off.'

'No way!'

'Way!'

Justice is harsh in Norwich, and serious criminal activity, rape, murder, etc are dealt with by banishment. They are sent down the river and beyond the walls. The magic is worst there and usually screws people's minds. Death follows soon after and if it doesn't, the wolves will.

The girls were all huddling around me now, telling me what all the teachers were doing these days.

'And Mrs Bilney—'

I cut off the young woman. 'That witch is still a teacher?'

'Yep.'

'Bloody hell. Norwich. The gift that keeps on giving.'

The girls laughed with me and just like that, the mood changed.

'So, I'm not a newcomer and tomorrow you are going to have a fabulous wedding and if I'm free, I should love to join you.'

The girls were roaring with enthusiasm, and the piper started a jig. Others spilled onto the street and little dances broke out up and down St Stephens Street.

Mike had been watching the group with his expression wavering between pride and despair. As we stepped away, he cleared his throat and looked at me awkwardly. His earlier bellicose manner evaporated.

'Sorry about that. Lucy and I have been friends since childhood. She's just a bit…'

'It's her hen party. Nice to see people being happy.'

In fairness, I had been surprised by the scene. In my mind's eye I had remembered Norwich as a place of fear and terror. I'd forgotten the laughter. Life on the edge does that to a community. The highs are epic, the lows are lethal.

Leaving the impromptu street party behind, we headed towards the heart of Norwich's civic centre. As we walked past St Stephen's Church, my breath caught in my throat and stuttered to a halt.

'Everything alright,' asked Mike, looking back at me.

'I'm fine.' How could I explain the urge to light a candle for the fallen? Once a week, I used to visit each church within the walls and light a candle for the lost.

I walked again, but found myself muttering words I thought I would never say again.

'Mum, Dad, Dom, Barnaby, Mrs P, Anya, Billy.'

The list ran on as I mumbled through the names I had remembered every week until I fled to London.

'You sure you're okay?' He was looking at me dubiously, and I stopped mumbling.

'Honestly. I'm not losing it already. When I was a kid, I used to light a candle for everyone I'd lost.'

'That would have been a lot of candles,' he said in a matter-of-fact tone, but not unkindly.

'We only did one candle for everyone. Fen used to say if we lit a candle for each person we'd lost, we'd have burnt the entire city down.'

'Who's Fen?' he asked as we carried on walking.

I shrugged. 'A friend.' My best friend, my partner in crime. She'd cried when I left and called me a traitor. I wondered if I needed to add her to my candle list as well.

'We can stop, if you want to go in,' said Mike, looking back at the church. 'Lots of people still light candles. I do.'

I almost said yes. I looked at him again. My first impressions of him had been clouded by his hostile attitude and my own response to being back in Norwich. Seeing him with his sister and listening to him talk about the candles made me pause. If I was going to work with the local police force, I would need to rid myself of my preconceptions. I had left Norwich barely more than a kid. I was returning as an adult and I had a job to do. I needed to focus.

'I can do it later. Let's go.'

With a quick nod, he turned and I followed him into the heart of the city. The marketplace sat in the centre, a large open space filled with temporary pitches. Surrounding the square were shops and other building.

I've seen sketches of the old city hall. A great big modernist structure overlooking the market, a huge clock tower soaring above the city. Now all that remained were the lions, great bronze statues that children would ride and pretend to fight each other on. Administration is run out of the Guildhall, a large, beautiful flint knapped building standing as majestic as any church, if not more so. Commerce is run from the Livery Halls and policing is based in the Watch House with the jail over on Bridewell.

We climbed the steps up to the front door of the police station. The Watch House, as Mike called it, was one of those buildings that had been pulled forward and were effectively new structures. The old Tesco that had once stood on its foundations didn't stand a chance. These imported buildings hadn't endured the centuries of time. No twisted floorboards, no creaking steps or leaky roofs. Cutting edge technology for the eighteenth century. However, that was where their mod cons ended.

Unlike the Guildhall across the street. The Guildhall had stood on that spot on every map and was in place when the maps merged and so there was nothing stronger to wipe it away. And there it stood, with old, twisted floorboards, creaking steps but also flushing toilets, running water and electricity. Buildings that had always existed endured. With the added benefit of plumbing. When it worked.

'Don't forget to wash your hands,' said Mike as we entered the main reception. I pulled out my tube of sanitiser and he shook his head, pointing towards a sink and taps.

'What the hell? Running water?'

Mike gave a goofy grin.

'Damn right. There was a big cholera outbreak about seven years ago. After that, the city underwent a massive engineering project. It's a bit Heath Robinson, but it's withstood every quake since then.'

I scrubbed my hands with the soap and patted them off on a paper towel.

'That must have cost a lot?'

'We're a very wealthy city. Don't forget the trade routes.'

Wealth in London is so obvious, so blatant, that for a moment I had looked at the old buildings, the trees and pastures and took Norwich for a dangerous sleepy backwater. I'd momentarily forgotten the vast wealth and what said wealth could do to stabilise a city.

'Follow me.'

I walked along the wooden corridor, running my finger along the polished surface. This was a rather unlikely police station. No smell of wet concrete, no open plan office and overhead fluorescent lights.

'Where in the blue blazes are the reports?' A man's voice shouted from a room off the hallway. Which goes to show that the more things change, the more they stay the same.

'Okay, now,' said Mike. 'Sheriff Hitchman's a great guy. You'll really like him. Just ignore the temper.'

Chapter Fifteen

 We walked into a large room filled with smoke, the smell of tobacco leaves mingling with the roses in a flower vase. There were lots of desks and filing cabinets, and the floor was lined with large rugs. The far wall comprised a row of heavy curtains and no doubt looked out over the market square.

'And who the hell are you?' A tall man in a three-piece suit and side whiskers pointed his cigar at me. He was well muscled and had bruised knuckles. If I had to bet, I'd guess he was a part-time boxer. He also seemed in charge.

'Detective Barnaby, sir. I'm here from the London police force. We have reason to believe a dangerous murderer has entered your city. He is also a practitioner. I'm here to arrest him and bring him back.'

He looked me up and down and then laughed.

'Just little old you? You'll be mad within forty-eight hours and dead within a week.'

'Only if I have to listen to your nonsense the whole time.' I also looked him up and down, then held his gaze as he glared at me. 'I'm Norwich born and bred.'

'Blow me sideways, so you're a quitter?'

It was my turn to blink. The last time I had been called a quitter, I was eighteen and crying. I wasn't that girl any longer.

'No sir, just wanted a change of scene from the pestilence and piss-poor urban planning. Elm Hill, 1996.'

He paused and then dismissed me with a sneer. It was the height of rudeness not to exchange placements, but the sheriff didn't strike me as someone big on manners. I bet HR had a hoot with him.

'So London lost a wizard and needs our help.'

He turned and addressed the rest of the room. Including Mike, there were two other people present. One was a woman in her fifties. She had been writing in a ledger, but now poured a glass of red wine from the bottle on her desk and sat back to watch the scene unfold. She was wearing regular clothes, trainers, jeans and a white t-shirt from Head in the Clouds. I only mention this because the other man in the room was dressed in yellow silk knee-length trousers, with white stockings and black patent shoes with gold buckles on their uppers. His jacket matched his yellow silk trews, and all he was missing was a wig and a large, feathered cap. Instead, he wore his hair in long blond curls and gave me a lazy smile, his brown eyes twinkling.

'And has London lost the art of communication?' snapped the sheriff. 'Why has no one sent word?'

I held the paper from the courier out. He took it and opened it, then frowned.

'This was written yesterday. Says a detective would be following.'

I tipped my head and the chap in the pantaloons laughed whilst the woman with the wine glass raised a toast to me.

'So why do you have your own letter of introduction?'

I grimaced. My colleague's fear made our force look incompetent in front of the Norwich crew.

'They were out of horses at the border and the courier was too scared to walk.'

The sheriff shook his head and then held out his hand for my other envelope, which I duly passed over. I watched as he read my credentials and then read the details of Cade's recent crimes.

'So we have a bloody wizard, who's gone doo-lally-tap and you need our help to get him out of here?'

'Yes, sir.'

'Yes, sir,' he mimicked me. 'Have you nothing else to say?'

'I do, sir. You have to distribute his likeness throughout the city. Tell the citizens not to approach him under any circumstances. He is dangerous and unstable.'

'Oh I do, do I, missy?' he growled, 'anything else that I should do?'

This was clearly a man about to explode, but I ignored the threat and ploughed on.

'Yes, all officers on the streets should carry guns, and shoot at first sight.'

'Would you like us to kill him or merely incapacitate him?'

His anger was very close to the surface now as he chewed and puffed on his cigar.

'Incapacitate is fine. The practitioners want him back alive. I understand it is very difficult to engineer magic whilst you are in pain.'

I had said what needed to be said and now I would wait for the volcano to erupt.

'Well then, missy. Here is what we are going to do. I don't give a rat's arse about the commands of a bunch of magicians. We will not be putting his image everywhere causing a full-scale panic. We will not be arming the City Watch, and you, missy, will not be wandering around the streets of Norwich with an unlicensed gun.'

'It's not unlicensed.'

'It is unlicensed in my bloody city if I say so,' he roared.

I recoiled slightly as Harry growled by my side, his warm body pressed against my calves.

'I am here in this city to recapture William Cade. If you do not permit me a weapon to halt Cade and defend myself, then my death will be on your head. I imagine that will cause a lot of bureaucracy, most of it involving practitioners entering the city to clean the mess up.'

I stared at him and watched a red flush creep up his neck. He glared at me and then poked his cigar in my direction.

'We could put him in the river for you. Save you having to drag him back. Saves a bullet.'

'Thank you, sir, but the practitioners want him alive if possible.'

He took a drag of his cigar and stared at me before blowing a fume of smoke in my direction.

'I couldn't give a rat's arse what the wizards want, or what their lackeys need. Is that clear?'

I coughed and waved the smoke from my face.

'Perfectly clear.'

I bit my tongue, desperate not to lose my rag in front of a senior officer, no matter how provoking. Now, as he flicked through my paperwork, he scowled.

'Where's the details of Cade's initial police report?'

I frowned, then realised I had overlooked a basic aspect of Cade's files. There were no details of his original incarceration. Plenty of details regarding his recent murder spree, but nothing prior to that.

'Maybe they were concerned the confidential documents would get lost in the crossing,' I said stiffly.

'They don't trust a little lady like yourself to not die or lose the papers?'

'Maybe they assumed you wouldn't understand the reports. Decided to keep it down to simple things, like pictures.'

'Woo! That's fighting talk, mistress,' joked my laughing cavalier. 'Joseph, I think she's got the measure of you. Desist with your rudeness.'

I turned and looked at him. I didn't need some dressed up dandy to come to my aide, but a bit of civility wouldn't go astray.

'Thank you…?'

'Detective Willoughby, if it pleases you,' he said sweeping his arm in a low bow. I bit my lip. For God's sake, is this what passed for a police force in Norwich? Thanking him stiffly, I returned to the sheriff.

'I don't know why they haven't sent the full details.'

'Give me bloody strength. Right then, Alys, take notes. You,' he snapped, jabbing his finger my way. 'Give me a description of this Cade.'

The sheriff was holding Cade's photograph in his hand and I wondered what more he wanted from me. I pushed my shoulders back and began a formal report.

'Cade is a large Caucasian male, approximately six foot two. Muscular in appearance, broad shoulders, long legs, could have been a sportsman. Dark wavy hair, swept off his face, blue eyes.' I paused, uncertain how much more to say.

'Do you think we're stupid?'

I had clearly failed a test and continued to stare straight ahead, not catching anyone's eye.

'No, sir.'

'So why are you telling me what he looks like when I'm holding a picture of him in my hand? I want a description. You're my only eyewitness. Tell me what you felt.'

I tried again.

'I approached the suspect—'

'Pig's teats, woman. I don't want a police report. I want your observations. Your instincts. Do London coppers not have them?'

'Okay.' I ran through the scene in my head and tried to marshal my thoughts. This was not how we gave our reports but this was Norwich, they did things differently. 'I was nervous when I arrived. Arresting practitioners is pretty unheard of and this was a huge operation. The situation was serious, but when I saw Cade, he seemed unconcerned. He was almost playful.'

I paused and looked over at the sheriff to see if he was going to shout at me again. I felt uncomfortable being so subjective. Catching his eye, he waved me on and I continued.

'I shot my gun at him, but he cast a spell and the shot failed. He suggested I should let him go.'

'Were you tempted?'

'No. He didn't appear to be using any magic to coerce me.'

'How could you tell?'

I wasn't about to tell him I could sense engineered magic. I knew what sort of trouble that would land me in, in London. I had no idea what the Norwich reaction would be. I had to step lightly here.

'Well, I didn't let him go, so there's that.'

He raised an eyebrow as he continued to puff on his cigar.

'And how did you feel?'

I hadn't considered that before and paused.

'I felt safe.'

The sheriff snorted.

'Was that before or after he murdered two practitioners?'

'Before.'

'And why do you think that was?'

'Because the practitioners that arrived to apprehend him tried to incinerate me and he shielded me from them.'

There was a silence as the sheriff looked at Alys and Willoughby and then back at me.

'Is that normal?'

'Being incinerated by practitioners or being saved by them?'

'Either.'

I pursed my lips thinking back to how close my life had been snuffed out.

'All fatalities involving practitioners are investigated by themselves. I'm led to believe they are few and far between and always accidental and within acceptable tolerances. Because of this I can't state how normal this is. I have insufficient data.'

He raised an eyebrow.

'And how many of these perfectly acceptable accidental deaths occur a year?'

'No idea, sir. The reports are confidential. Only the designated next of kin has access.'

The sheriff paused and looked at me keenly.

'What does "designated" mean?'

'It means the person that the victim designated to be able to read the report. This designation has to be updated weekly or else it lapses.'

Willoughby looked at me keenly and cleared his throat.

'So any victim needs to know in advance to nominate a next of kin, otherwise the incident report is never viewed.'

'Correct.'

'Who is your next of kin?'

'Police officers are exempt.'

'Your reports are open?'

'No. Our reports are never witnessed. We work in tandem with the practitioners and the official line is that we would never be the subject of deliberate hostile action.'

Willoughby laughed and stared at the other two incredulously.

'And what do you think of that?'

I closed my eyes. What did I think of that? Of their brutality. Their arrogance. Their complete disregard for the law and human life.

'I think it stinks. But when I say one of them saved me, that's what I mean when I say I felt safe. I have never heard of any practitioner going out of their way to help anyone.'

'Indeed. And what about afterwards?'

I knew he was mocking me, but if I thought about it, I had still felt safe. I mean not safe so much as in absolute fear for my life, but my fear was coming from the other practitioners. I shrugged.

'So basically, your practitioners are above the law?'

'More or less. If magic was involved, then they are judge and jury. In all other matters they are subject to the same laws as the rest of us.'

'So if a magician stabbed you with a knife?'

'He'd be arrested and go to jail.'

'And if he used magic to incinerate you?'

'He would continue with his life. I wouldn't even be a statistic.'

The more I talked, the flatter my voice became as I tried to keep my emotions in check. The sheriff looked at me, took another puff and then exhaled, blowing the smoke away from my face.

'Moving on. How did he escape? That isn't in the report either. Why didn't the other two practitioners stun him or whatever it is they do?'

'My impression was that either he was stronger than them or they didn't want to risk harming him.'

'So what? They just let him run away? Having killed two of their colleagues?'

His voice raised in disbelief.

'Not exactly, sir. As he attacked them, he took advantage of the confusion and ran into one of the houses.'

Hitchman narrowed his eyes and I knew he was one step ahead of the story.

'When you say he ran into the house?'

'He was a map runner.'

Alys hissed and poured herself another glass of wine. The sheriff swore and Willoughby watched me closely as I then replayed the thaumaturge's reaction as she tore off the front of the house in fury.

'With all her power, she couldn't follow him?' said Willoughby thoughtfully. I turned to him, grateful for his mellow tones after the sheriff's jabs and retorts. 'Tell me, are map runners common in London?'

I shook my head. 'I've never seen one, she looked appalled when she saw what he had done. I think it took her unawares. She also forbade me from mentioning it in the official report and talking to anyone about it.'

'And yet here you are,' said Hitchman, stabbing the air with his cigar, 'talking to us about it.'

I was getting used to his insults now and was getting the measure of him.

'I felt it was pertinent knowledge, sir. Do people still run the maps here?'

He looked over at Willoughby, who shook his head and then across to Alys, who shrugged.

'I've heard some people still do it. I mean, it's not illegal. Just frowned on.'

I relaxed a fraction and was going to speak again when a shrieking pain sliced across my brain. I felt a wave of cold water flush against my skin and I thought I was going to throw up. I had forgotten just how much this hurt and I gripped my head in my hands, trying to stem the pain. Harry was barking as the cavalier rushed forward and helped me into a chair.

'What's wrong?' said Willoughby. 'How may I assist you? Pain killers, perhaps?'

I tried to nod my head, but the pain was excruciating.

Which was precisely when the bells began to ring.

Chapter Sixteen

The noise of all the city's church bells ringing at the same time is dreadful. This wasn't the joyous peal of a set of bells chiming across the sky. This was every church ringing a single bell in continuous warning. There was no melody and the only person dancing to this tune was Death himself.

I was still shaking as I tried to run outside, but Harry's desperate barking stopped my flight. I knew what this was. He didn't. I made my way back from the entrance and ignored the look of contempt from the sheriff and surprise from the others. I had acted like a coward and knelt down to reassure Harry and hide my face from the others.

'Pig's teats,' swore the sheriff, pushing me out of his way as he grabbed a radio from the table. I moved out of his way and away from the door. Harry was whining and I tried to reassure him that the disturbance would soon pass.

'Where is it?' roared Hitchman into the mic. 'I don't expect the bells to be the first to tell me.'

He took his finger off the button and we all waited for a response. The woman had moved her wine off her desk and Willoughby had grabbed two radio sets and threw one at me. Before I could respond, Hitchman's radio started transmitting.

'Sorry, sheriff. St Augustine's, no signs.' Another voice crackled over the radio. 'Elm Hill, no signs.' Followed by another, 'Colegate, no signs.' As the various call signs came in, we waited in silence.

'Where in damnations is the source?' muttered Willoughby.

'Sheriff.' Another voice called in over the airways. 'Dorothy here. I'm at Finklegate at the moment. I think the first bell came from St Etheldreda's. I've been trying to raise Officer Lightfoot. Have they checked in with you?'

Back in London, we'd already have a map of the area up on a screen triangulating the position of our officers and trying to establish the focal point of ground zero. Here, maps were a non-starter, which meant that everyone already knew the street layouts and where the churches were in relation to each other. My memory was hazy and I muttered to the cavalier-come-police officer.

'St. Etheldreda's, is that near the junction of Rouen Road and Kings Street?'

He nodded and looked tense, as well he might. Rouen Road was long overdue a quake.

'Is the tower block still there?'

'Yes. Or at least it was this morning.'

'Damn.'

Modern-day concrete structures fared the worst in the maps meld. Normandie Tower Block had long been a source of local amazement. Even in my time, people shook their head at its resilience. Ten years on and I was willing to bet people thought they were safe if they moved back in.

'How many residents?'

'Not too many. Few trust it. In a bad winter, the tent folk sometimes move in, but not for long.' He then shushed me as the sheriff had started talking again. I hadn't been shushed since I was a child and I struggled to bite my lip. That was the problem with good-looking men the world over, they thought they were God's gift.

'Willoughby, get on over to the tower. Take her with you.' He said, throwing a utility belt at me. It was a beautifully tooled leather belt with a variety of pockets hanging from it, some larger than others. 'Let's see what London's finest has to offer.'

I removed my current belt and placed my gun in the newly designated holster.

'No gun.'

'I am licenced to carry a weapon.'

'Not in bloody Norwich, you're not. You're a Londoner. You're used to those baby guns the wizards made for you.'

I bridled at his tone.

'I can use a revolver. If Cade is around, he needs to be shot on sight. He can't be allowed to attempt a spell.'

'If you see him, tell Willoughby to shoot. You can shout bang if it makes you feel better.'

'Sir, I need the gun. Cade's my responsibility.'

I needed to be where the action was. Chances were that Cade had set this off and might still be in the vicinity.

'Lord, help us from magicians and their lackeys. Very well, take your bloody gun, but if you shoot any of my citizens, I'll send you down the river myself.'

He turned his back on me as he pulled some ledgers onto the table and started making notes, then looked over at me.

'You still here? You seemed to remember how to run out of a building just now. Let's see how you perform as a grown-up.'

The rebuke stung. I'd faced riots, fires, bomb threats and terrorist actions. I'd never once been accused of cowardice.

I slapped Willoughby on his arm and hoped he wouldn't tell my hands were still shaking.

'Right, let's go.'

'What about your dog?'

'He can stay with me if you like,' said Alys, looking up from the ledger. She was standing by the sheriff as they began scribbling notes and taking in instructions from the radio calls. 'I'm Alys Attwell by the way, Upper Goat Lane, 1350.'

I did a quick double take, which made her laugh.

'What can I say? I love me some nail varnish.'

It was true some of the oldies assimilated at an astonishing speed, others lost their minds, but Alys had clearly embraced the twenty-first century. Manicures and all.

'Your accent is very impressive.'

I knew she'd have had to have worked hard to shift her speech patterns. That far back and they were speaking Middle English. Chaucer scholars had been delighted until they realised people didn't care much for being treated like a walking almanac.

'Thanks. Cheers. Whatevs,' she grinned at me. 'I tend to go with whatever sounds good on the day.'

'Hell's pizzle, woman. Focus,' shouted the sheriff. Alys quickly apologised and she gestured to Harry to join her.

'He'll be fine with me,' I said. 'He's a trained sniffer dog.'

'Okay mistress,' snapped Willoughby, his impatience showing. 'Let's go.'

I glared over to Alys expecting some moment of sisterhood, but she smiled blankly and continued scribbling notes, her attention back to the unfolding disaster. Instead, grabbing Harry's lead, I headed out of the room and out onto the street. My first encounter with my work colleagues had been a disaster and I hoped that I would be able to acquit myself properly on our way to the quake zone. I knew I didn't need to prove myself to anyone, but at the moment I was feeling wrong-footed and stupid. Why hadn't I asked about Cade's initial conviction? Magician's lackey, that really stung.

Outside, the market was milling with people standing around in packs. A boy saw us approach and ran up.

'What's up?'

Willoughby crouched down, looking the boy in the eye.

'There has been a quake over King Street way. Nothing to alarm us here. Spread the word, but let us stay focused and trust in the Lord. Agreed?'

The young lad nodded and ran back to a small crowd. I watched the news spread through the crowd as Willoughby walked in the opposite direction.

'Why aren't we running?'

'Are you in such a hurry to die? What help will we be, then?'

'I–' I broke off. The truth was I didn't know the rules for a quake. 'I left when I was eighteen. The procedure for civilians was to just vacate the area until it was deemed stable.'

'Well, you're not a civilian or a child anymore, Miss.'

'It's not Miss or Mistress, it's Eliza. Detective Eliza Barnaby, 1996.' The honorifics for women were complicated depending on who you talked to, but Miss was usually respectful but suggested youth and or a lack of power. Mistress was for women with agency, it bore no resemblance to a marital status. That was what Mrs was for. No honorific suggested intimacy or poverty. However, I was an officer of the law and didn't wish to be addressed by my gender.

He stopped and gave a courtly bow.

'Nathaniel Willoughby. Third Baronet of Hiverton Manor, fourth son of Earl Hiverton and doubtless expendable. In my time, 1748, I was a gentleman philosopher, today I am Detective Willoughby. It is my delight and honour to meet you, even if the occasion is inauspicious.'

I blinked a few times and then nodded my head.

'Thank you. I–'

'Now don't dawdle, my dear. We have work to do.'

Wrong-footed again, I strode to catch up. We weren't running, but we were certainly setting a quick pace. His silver-tipped cane hit a little staccato beat as he walked along the pavement.

'Let us first acquaint you with the contents of your belt. You have a notepad and pencil, a torch, a whistle, a holster for your gun, a baton and a wristwatch. Guard that with your life, Hitchman is very particular about his watches.'

He pulled out a fob watch tucked into a small pocket in his waistcoat. 'Personally, I prefer the fob watch but the Sheriff feels the wristwatch to be a more modern piece of equipment.' I put it on as Willoughby talked and hoped that I might manage to curry some favour with the sheriff. Plus, without my phone I was struggling to know what the time was.

Willoughby nodded in approval and carried on talking. 'And if we're lucky, Alys will have packed the large pocket with some sustenance. The sheriff also felt you would need a stipend whilst you were here.' He passed me a purse heavy with coins and I stuffed it into one of my belt pockets. I had a quick look at my other equipment and saw that the baton was like the ones I was familiar with but carried no stunning capabilities beyond that which a sharp flick of the wrist could administer.

'I understand your batons can deliver a charge that stimulates the nervous system of the assailant? A useful tool.'

'It is. But I generally use my gun. It delivers the same "stimulations".' I said it in a light tone and Willoughby smiled back at me.

'But that stimulation carries various charges? Yes. All the way to the grave?'

'Yes, our guns can incapacitate or kill.'

'Do you always carry it?'

'As little as possible.'

'I find that we are in agreement. A gentleman should be able to respond to a situation without resorting to violence when he can help it.'

Well, I was no gentleman and I tried not to carry an engineered gun because it gave me a headache. But I was glad I had a gun on my hip if I was going to confront Cade again.

'You're wearing a gun at the moment,' I pointed out. It looked incongruous against the yellow silk britches.

'It's a quake. Who knows what we will encounter? I am guided by the philosopher Baden-Powell in situations like this. I like to be prepared.'

I grinned to myself as we walked on through the city. The large bag swung on the side of the belt. On the other side, my gun was secure but heavy. It would take a while to get used to the new configurations, and I tried not to swagger as I walked.

'From what we have ascertained, it appears that Normandie Tower has gone, and any potential inhabitants. More alarming, we may have lost Officer Lightfoot. A greater tragedy.'

We walked in silence as I waited for him to say more.

'You don't ask why it's the greater tragedy?' he said, looking over his shoulder at me. 'I wonder if that shows a lack of curiosity on your part, or if you already understand the situation. Which, given your recent arrival, suggests you don't.'

Wrong-footed and now chastened. Annoyed, I spoke quickly.

'The tower block was always an ugly piece of modern architecture. The fact that it survived so long has been a mystery. Anyone living in it when there are alternatives was foolish. Losing an officer is a serious concern and I hope that we simply discover the quake has fritzed her radio.'

'Quite. Although Officer Clive Lightfoot is a most splendid gentleman, not a lady.'

'My apologies.'

'There is no point in apologising for that which you did not know. Come on, my dear.'

I gritted my teeth.

'When did you arrive?'

'Ten years ago. Just after you left, by the sounds of it. I was visiting the fine city of Norwich on behalf of my father overseeing a thorny legal issue relating to wool shipment. Naturally, I had made my repose at the family townhouse, the ancestral house too far for a day's ride and back. Imagine my surprise when a small quake hurled me forwards in time. There was I, and several others, standing in my dining room, all of us at sevens and eights. The room was filled with peculiar furniture, unfamiliar to all. Our oak dining table once commented on by the High Lieutenant himself had been replaced by what appeared to be a single sheet of glass in the most outrageous proportions, fully six feet long. One elderly gentleman was standing in nothing other than his night shirt and holding his commode. Turns out he was my great nephew.'

I cut him off, ignoring his story which bore all the hallmarks of a long ramble. People's first night stories tended to.

'So you've been here ten years? Which should be enough time to know that we don't call women "my dear".'

He looked sideways at me and laughed.

'I call everyone "dear". I do not single you out for particular attention.'

I was ready to hit him but chose to pat Harry instead. It was funny the speed with which I was finding him to be a comfortable presence rather than a menacing harbinger of doom.

'That is to say your beauty has not cast its spell upon me. I assure you I shall not bother you like some unwelcome dog howling at the moon. You are an officer of the law, equal to myself and I will treat you as I would myself, or any other fair creature. Is that acceptable, my dear?'

I was still reeling from his comment about my beauty, so I walked on in silence. Harry wisely kept his opinions to himself. I wasn't yet able to tell if his tail was wagging sarcastically or in approval. One thing I knew to be true was that I wasn't beautiful. I had a run of smallpox scars running down the side of my face joining some plague scars on my jaw. Back in London, I told people it was a chip pan fire. They accepted it readily enough and agreed that my hair down was a good choice. I hurried to catch up with him again and noticed he was frowning.

'We'll head down King Street, it's more stable.'

The street lighting pooled along the pavements as people were hurrying towards us.

'Up ahead,' I muttered, careful not to further alarm the passing civilians.

'I can see it,' he said, referring to the absence of streetlamps.

'Here,' he passed me a wind-up torch. I looked at it and shook my head in surprise. When had I last relied on one of these? I might loath magic, but damn, it had its uses.

'Willoughby! Where do we go?' A young mother and two children had stopped in front of us. She was in her twenties and in a dressing gown. The children were both in pyjamas. All had slippers on and looked terrified.

'This evening's hospitality is in the Octagon Chapel, if it pleases you. They'll have beds and food ready. More details at the top of the road. Tell me, is your house still standing?'

Of course it was, I thought. Look at them, they were in bed or ready to turn in. If their house had gone, then they would be too. I was about to point that out when she confirmed it was, and he carried on.

'Well, then. Nothing to worry about. You know how these quakes work, they don't spread.' He turned to the little boy. 'Where do you live?'

'The Music House,' he said boldly.

'Well, bless my soul,' he chuckled and patted the girl's doll on the head. 'That house was standing when I was a boy, the same age as you. I would wager that you live in one of the safest buildings in all of Norwich. Now why don't you take your mother and sister over to hospitality?'

'Will we be safe?' asked the mother, her voice shaking.

'You have my word on it. But best leave the area for now until we secure it. Yes?' He gave her a deep bow, and I watched in surprise as she and her daughter dropped short curtsies and the little boy bowed. I'd forgotten about the bows and curtseys. They then hastened along the street with the others.

'It's always best to focus on questions where people can give positive answers. Cuts down the panic. Don't you agree?'

He walked away, leaving me and Harry staring at his back. He seemed permanently one step ahead of my thoughts and it was doing my head in. I wanted to prove that London officers were just as good as Norwich ones, if not better, but so far, I just seemed to be pointing out the obvious. I strode forward, determined to catch up without actually running, and soon we were alone and heading towards the dark. Underfoot the tarmac stopped and turned to grass.

Willoughby spoke into his radio.

'Just passed Music House Lane, heading north. Tarmac and streetlights have gone.'

Alys' voice came back across the static.

'Noted. The Watch will start creating an exclusion zone. Any sign of arrivals yet?'

'None so far. I shall keep you apprised.'

We walked along the grass. The air was fragrant and I saw a hedge of sweet cecily swaying in the moonlight.

Harry was sniffing the grass excitedly, running this way and that until I bent down and called him to heel. We were in dangerous territory. We hadn't stepped back in time. Time had stepped forward to us.

Chapter Seventeen

 'I presume both your jabs are up to date?'

He had paused and opened one of the larger pockets on the belt.

'There's insect repellent in here, spray your feet and legs, no point in getting bitten. The dog's as well.'

I quickly obliged and envied him his long white socks.

'Okay, you also have sedatives. Do not use them unless a person is dangerously out of control. They collapse immediately and are difficult to move to a place of safety. You have sweets which will help with the children and the baton is for the men. The women are usually the best to deal with.'

'Why? Because they're more compliant?' I asked tartly.

'No, because they don't ask so many vexatious questions.' He fixed me with a solid look, then closed his bag. 'Ready? And remember, they are terrified and you are terrifying.'

'I think the dark may be our friend?'

'How so?'

'Well, they'll be feeling odd, and no doubt the air smells differently, but they can't see much.'

He turned and nodded.

'Agreed. Now let us proceed. And let me talk first. They are used to male voices of authority.'

I rolled my eyes, but he was right. I could hear birds over by the river crying out in the night, and an owl flew overhead. I wondered if it was the same one from earlier and was surprised by how long ago that seemed. My stomach rumbled and I helped myself to one of the chocolate bars, much to Willoughby's disapproval.

'Nothing for your noble companion?'

'What? I was told chocolate is bad for dogs. Besides, I shared a ham sandwich with him at lunch. He's had food at St Stephen's Gate and food in the Watch House, which is more than I've had. So if it's okay with you, I shall have some food now before I deal with our new refugees.'

I was sharp with him because I was sharp with myself. Harry had been happily trotting alongside me all day and was probably just as keen as I was to go to sleep.

I rummaged in the pocket again and found some jerky and tore off a little strip for him. Kneeling down, I could pick out features in the landscape.

'Willoughby,' I whispered, 'there's a track over here.'

We made towards it and stepped onto the packed earth. It was the width of a cart and clear of weeds. Ahead, I could just about see a row of houses in the moonlight, but nothing else. It had been a long time since I had been here, but I was certain that the tower block stood in this area. To my right, I could see lights up on the ridge above us.

'This looks like a small quake radius.'

He pulled out his radio again.

'Approaching the site of Normandie Tower. There are lights above us on the hillside. I would suggest that Ber Street is unaffected.'

'Agreed,' replied Alys. 'The Watch are evacuating the area now. We're sending them to the convent. Secure any civilians. We're closing the surrounding perimeter, but it looks like the wall and the river will take care of those boundaries.'

'Small blessings. I shall keep you informed.'

Securing his radio to his jacket, he turned and whispered to me. 'Are you prepared?'

I nodded and he pulled out a bell from his rucksack and started to swing it as we walked forwards.

'Oh yea, oh yea. All good souls, gather here.'

He rang again and I heard a door open and someone walked forward holding a candle aloft.

'Who goes there?' It was an older man dressed in a brown tunic with bare legs and bare feet. 'Away with you.'

As he approached us, he took in Willoughby's finery and bowed quickly.

'I dun't mean no disrespect, fine sir.'

It was as broad a Norfolk accent as I had heard in a long time, but I could understand him, which meant he was at least Tudor and above. He also viewed Willoughby's dress as familiar, so that ruled out the nineteen hundreds.

'None taken, good sir. But I need you to raise your family and your neighbours.'

'Well, I dun't see as how I can do that, my lord. We've a busy day tomorrow and we needs our sleep.'

Willoughby rang his bell again, calling out into the darkness.

'Sir, please. You'll wake everyone up,' implored the older man.

Now a second figure joined him, holding a candlestick ahead of her. I could smell the tallow of sheep wax and was taken back to a time when I slept in the eaves of the house in the same bed as my brother, my mother telling us fairy stories.

The figure came alongside the man. She was a similar age to him in a pale linen shift, her long grey hair plaited to one side.

'John. What be the matter?'

'This fine gentleman wants us up. I don't know why.'

'He's drunk, is why. Go home sir and leave us Christian folk to our beds.'

'Dearest madam—'

I cut him off.

'Good evening. My name is Eliza. What's yours?'

The woman held her candle towards me and then took a step back.

'Why are you dressed as a man?'

I smiled to myself.

'Good. A woman that asks questions. Your name?'

'None of your business, my lady. Or is it my lord?'

'A woman that asks questions and has some wit. Perfect.' I liked her already. 'The river is rising and we need to evacuate you and your neighbours.'

'There's been no rain.'

I took a deep breath. Maybe I should have left this to Willoughby.

'Look, Norwich has been hit by a disaster of a biblical nature. I can't give you details, but you have to trust me. If we don't get you to a place of safety now, you shall be left to wander purgatory for the rest of your days.'

She stared at me. Something in my voice if not my words themselves convinced her.

'Very well, John. Wake everyone up. Go on. Get, get.'

She turned back to me.

'And where are we to go?'

I looked to Willoughby for guidance but he had drifted into the dark, no doubt looking for other arrivals.

'Willoughby,' I shouted into the dark. 'Do they still go to the Great Hospital?' The hospital had been standing since 1250 and was deemed a suitable spot for new arrivals. Very few would be unfamiliar with it.

A distant voice shouted back yes, and I turned to the woman who was watching me carefully.

'I know the hospital. We'll make our way there. Is the river really rising? Only I need to move the livestock if it is.'

A certain amount of honesty was required.

'No, the river isn't rising. But it is imperative that you leave now.'

'You talk funny, you seem odd and you dress like a boy. Why should I trust you?'

'I was born on Elm Hill. Norwich is my home and I would protect its citizens with my dying breath.'

'Even us? Who are we to you?'

'If you live within the walls, it's my duty to protect you. There is danger all around and I need to protect you and the other city residents.'

Willoughby had returned and he cleared his throat. I jumped but I notice the matriarch didn't. Her nighttime vision and hearing was no doubt far superior to mine.

'Mistress. Fetch a cloak. We have escorts coming to help you on your way.'

'To the Hospital? I know the way, lord. There's no need to disturb any others.'

'Even so, you will need a cloak.'

Grumbling, she returned to her house, a small cottage standing in a row of three surrounded by a well-tended enclosure.

More people had come out and the woman sent them all back in again, telling them they were walking to the hospital and get a cloak and, for those that had them, some shoes. There was a lot of muttering and grumbling, but she seemed to rule her neighbours with an iron fist and they did her bidding. A couple of the children came forward to pet Harry and were soon laughing as he licked their faces.

'How do we get them to the hospital without freaking them out?' I asked.

'It's all in hand. Look.'

Walking towards us were six monks. There was something familiar in the stride of one of them, and as they joined us, I saw Mike wink at me before he resumed a devout countenance.

'Good people,' called out Willoughby. 'These monks will guide you.'

'We don't need no guidance, begging your pardon, lord,' said a younger man. He was wearing boots and trousers, a cloak wrapped around his shoulders as he held a woman's hand. Three children stood in front of them and the woman held a baby in the crook of her arm.

'I am sure of that, but the monks are here for your protection against the dangers beyond.'

I noticed Willoughby didn't say where beyond was or what the dangers might be. Reluctantly, the group followed the monks with three monks leading and three monks behind.

'What happens now?'

'The lamps of the street have been extinguished, and the citizenry beseeched to douse their lights. We shall escort them by the most ancient of pathways to shield their eyes from the anachronisms of our time. Upon arrival at the infirmary, they shall be met with vaccinations, a place of rest, hearty sustenance come morning, and thereafter, a revelation most startling. Fear not, for we have honed our expertise in such matters.'

He was right. I was impressed by how well we had evacuated them.

'And what of us?'

'Now we shall sleep.'

'What, here on the ground? There are beds in there.'

'Please,' he scoffed as he lowered himself to the ground. 'The earth is cleaner. At first light, we'll round up the animals, inoculate them and then wait for the fumigation team.'

'And what of Officer Lightfoot?'

I knew Willoughby must be worried about him.

'In truth, he would have come forward when I rang the bell, if he had heard me. Now I pray he was simply knocked out by the quake wave and we shall find him in the morning nursing the mother of all headaches.'

I had a fine woollen cloak in my bag and I placed it on the ground, bemused at how my first day in Norwich had panned out.

Harry snuggled up alongside me and I tried to find a soft piece of ground.

'Willoughby. What if any wolves came through?'

'Within the city walls?'

'Oh yes. Sorry.' I felt stupid. The ground was hard and I wished with all my might that I wasn't back in my stupid home city. 'Good night.'

'Detective Barnaby,' his voice drifted through the darkness. 'You were very impressive with the arrivals. You displayed no fear and you and Harry calmed their nerves. Not bad for your first day back in Norwich.'

He fell silent and I stared up at the moon, thinking of London.

'Thank you. And please, my friends call me Bish.'

Silence fell again and I thought he must have fallen asleep when I heard him again.

'Goodnight then, Bish. Goodnight, noble Harry,'

Chapter Eighteen

I woke up covered in dew with the birds breaking the dawn light. I had probably slept for all of five minutes and now the birds were going hammer and tongs. I sat up and stretched. Willoughby was still asleep. His gold satin outfit seemed strangely at home amongst the grass and I left him alone as I found a bush and then started to explore.

I was standing in a large field. Ahead of me was a row of three wattle and daub buildings, I would say mid-seventeenth century, given their haphazard construction. Down towards the river I could see various wharf buildings and some boats at dock. Above me I could see the ridge of buildings where Ber Street ran. So far, the meld had only affected a small section. I walked ahead past the houses and after a few hundred metres found tarmac. I made my way back to the houses and walked around the back. All three gardens were one large plot, fenced in and housing two pigs and a brood of hens. I scowled at the rooster and was about to make my way back to Willoughby when a man stumbled out of the river mist.

'Hello! Where am I?'

His speech patterns were modern, and I spotted a radio attached to his belt.

'Officer Lightfoot?'

'Yeah.' He looked confused. 'At least I think so. Man, my head is killing me. Have you got any water or painkillers?'

Physically he looked fine, although his eyes were heavily bloodshot. One half of one of his whites had turned completely red. Telling him to follow me, I headed back to my backpack. Willoughby, remarkably, was still asleep, and I gave him a quick shake as I rummaged in my belt. Harry ran forward to say hello to the newcomer and I handed him some chocolate. He ignored Harry and snatched the bar from my hand as he fell to the ground and shook Willoughby.

'Willoughby! What did we drink last night, and did you pull this totty or did I?' he gestured his bar of chocolate in my direction and continued to gobble the bar.

'Hey, Willoughby,' I said, 'looks like your mate Officer Fuckwit isn't dead after all. Blessing, hey?'

I walked away from them, sat down and pulled out some dried meat to share with Harry.

Willoughby stretched and quickly sat up, holding Lightfoot's face and staring into his eyes.

'Clive, this is our colleague, Detective Barnaby. She's here from London and I won't stand to hear you talk about her like some doxy. Is that understood?'

Lightfoot swayed and blinked a bit.

'Shit man, how drunk did we get?'

He wasn't really paying attention to his surroundings or Willoughby, and was speaking on a small loop. I'd seen this behaviour before. Being in the direct vicinity of a quake can cause a deep mental trauma as your brain tries to keep up with the wash of wild magic swirling around you. Drunks and children fare better. Sleepers also handle it just fine, so long as their building is still there in the morning. If it's not, sometimes you wake up on a street, sometimes you wake up in an "old" old house or more often you just disappear to who knows where.

For now Lightfoot was on repeats and Willoughby looked over at me and nodded.

'What now?' I asked.

Willoughby stood up, patting his colleague on the shoulder and walked over to join me, brushing down his clothes as he did so, before sitting down again.

'Good morning, Bish. I trust you slept well?'

I laughed.

'Morning to you, too. I slept like a log.'

He raised an eyebrow.

'A log that was freezing cold and being kicked all night long.'

Now he laughed and I offered him some meat.

'So?'

'So, I need to get him to the doctor. He might shake this off, he might not. He doesn't seem aware he was in a quake. I expect that the Watch team will be here presently.' As he spoke, I could hear distant handbells slowly getting closer. 'Hark, the cavalry.'

I rolled my shoulders in relief. 'Can we leave the site when they get here?'

'What is this? You're abandoning our fine lodgings? What possible delights does the fine city yonder have to offer, that this field full of stones does not?'

I made a play of looking around and then shrugged.

'I don't see a bathtub?'

Now Willoughby looked around, puzzled.

'Can you not see the river?'

His face was a picture and I laughed in delight, throwing some grass at him.

He stood up and offered me his hand.

'Come on, my dear. Let's find you a bath.'

The bells were ringing closer now and Willoughby shouted out in response as a few teams of people converged on our position. Laughing, they all reunited and lots of people came and hugged Lightfoot. I tried to feel pleased for their happiness, but instead I just felt a little out of place as the team fell into well-practiced roles. Calling Harry over to me, I slipped him back on his lead and walked back along the track. Willoughby was occupied and I figured I would see him back at the Watch House. Harry tugged at the lead and started to pull towards the long grass.

'What have you found, boy?'

The poor thing was probably starving. Did spaniels eat rabbit, or was he flushing out a pheasant? A large bird exploded out of the grass in front of us, causing Harry to bark in alarm. Its massive wingspan startled me and I laughed in embarrassment. Hopefully, none of the team had heard me shriek. I turned around and saw Willoughby laughing as he headed my way.

Great. Professional London detective startled by a bloody bustard. They were enormous birds, and I watched as it loped off slow and low down over the river and onto the fields beyond. Harry continued to pull on his lead as I waved to Willoughby, then turned my attention back to him, mortified that he might have disturbed a nest. He was straining on the leash in a patch of grass that was a good three feet high. Tall wild fennel sweetly scenting the air as he pushed through their stems and then he dropped to the floor. My heart sank. Police dogs only did that when its quarry has been found.

Reaching him, I saw a bare female leg sticking out of the longer grass and realised that Willoughby must have had to sedate one of the arrivals after all when he wandered off into the dark last night.

I pushed the grass aside to check she was alright and saw she would never be right again.

Chapter Nineteen

 Leaving Harry in his guard position, I walked quickly towards Willoughby.

'Bish, did that little bird scare you?' He paused. 'What's wrong? Where's Harry?'

'We've got a dead IC1 female over in the grass.'

'A dead what?'

I recalibrated. He might call himself a detective, but this wasn't a police force that worked in the same way as the rest of the country.

'A dead woman, she's been murdered.' I thought of Cade. He had stabbed seven people on his way to Norwich, two in front of my eyes. He was an unstable practitioner. Now, here I was standing by a dead body, killed by a knife in the vicinity of a recent quake. And we knew quakes could be triggered by spells or engineered magic. Was this the work of Cade or a coincidence?

'Are you certain?' asked Willoughby.

He strode past me and then headed towards Harry. As he reached him, he patted him on the head and then leant over the body. The woman was naked and had been stabbed in the throat. A cross sliced open her torso, from her breasts to her pelvis, then a lateral cross through her belly button.

He crouched down, his dumb yellow satin trews strained at his knees, as he stretched his hand out to move her hair off her face.

'Stop!' I stepped forward in alarm. 'What are you doing? We need to wait for SOCO?'

'What do our socks have to do with this?'

Christ. This was a mess, we had a crime scene and a murder victim and we were tripping over acronyms.

'SOCO. Scene of Crime Officers. The ones that gather forensics.'

He nodded his head and then returned to the murder victim and removed the hair from her face. Pulling out a notepad from inside his jacket pocket, he began sketching. He didn't take his eyes off her face but spoke softly.

'That's us, Bish. We don't have a SOCO team. Our detectives are expected to gather the evidence. We're the first people on the scene. We have five senses and sharp brains. It's down to us.'

He beckoned me over and showed me the sketch.

'Do you agree that's a fair likeness?'

It was. It was beautiful, she looked like she was simply sleeping. It was so much kinder than the harsh flash of the morgue photographs.

'We have cameras, don't we?' I despaired at how backwards Norwich was. How did they get anything done?

'We do. But they're back at the station. We need to show her likeness to people in the area immediately.

And when we find her people, this will be an image that won't destroy them.'

I took a deep breath. I kept underestimating the citizens of Norwich. Time to recalibrate. Again.

'Come here,' he gestured for me to step forward into the crime scene. 'Let's study the scene together. Call Harry away, he might be on evidence.'

'Unlikely, he's a trained sniffer dog.' Nonetheless, he was going to get in the way and I called him to one side. He moved willingly, content that his job was done.

'Okay. Let's look.'

I crouched down over the body. It was rare to be so close without SOCO having bagged and tagged everything first.

'I take it you don't recognise her?'

Willoughby shook his head and gently rolled her to one side. Her cheeks were dark black.

'She's been resting here for several hours, although her bones move freely. I would say rigor mortis has passed.'

I agreed and then watched in astonishment as he leant forward and sniffed her body.

'What the hell are you doing!'

'I have five senses, Detective Barnaby. I will employ all of them to ascertain any evidence I can.'

Chastened once more, I chose my next words carefully.

'Have you divined anything?'

He sighed and then sniffed her hands.

'Nothing beyond soap and sweet cicely.'

I could have told him that, but I bit my tongue.

'Have you seen a killing like this before?' I asked.

He rolled her back and then removed his jacket and placed it over her torso. It was a sweet gesture and I was touched by his kindness and smiled.

'I suppose a London detective mocks my prudishness?'

There was a small challenge in his voice.

'No. I was thinking you were preserving the crime scene, as well as her modesty.'

He cleared his throat and stood up.

'Indeed, I apologise for underestimating you.' He looked back at the victim. 'And no. We don't get many murder victims here. Actually, that's not correct. We do, but it's pretty obvious who did it. Partner, colleague, the jealous lover, the cheated monger. All those are pretty clear to fathom. But a woman left carved up, naked in a field. That is,' he paused and walked around the body, 'unusual.' He bent over to pick something up.

'Wait.' I knew it would annoy him, but if there was evidence, we might get some fingerprints.

He stood up and glared at me. 'Did you think I was going to pick up the knife? We might not have SOCOS or many murders, but we still know how to preserve evidence and not leave our prints on murder weapons.'

I winced and walked over to where he was standing. Lying in the grass was a long blade, smeared with blood.

'Is that a butcher's knife?'

'Or a tanner's.'

I thought about it. Both removed skin from flesh, flesh from bones. Either worked. 'Now what?'

'Now we find out who killed her. I'm afraid your bath will have to wait a little bit longer.'

I glanced over at the river.

'Looks more tempting now, doesn't it?' he asked, a grin stretched across his face.

I laughed, which might seem brutal given our current situation, but all it shows is that you haven't been to many scenes of violence and brutality. And be thankful that you haven't. But for those of us that have, we use humour to get past it.

Willoughby picked up his radio and pressed the button.

'Sheriff? We have a dead body.' He paused as the sheriff's voice boomed out across the airwaves.

'Right you are. Masonry collapse or brain fritz?'

'Neither. This is a murder. Looks like a weird one. Victim is naked and has an upside down cross carved into her body.'

'Hellfire!'

'I shall have some of the Watch stand guard. Can you send some doctors down to retrieve the body? We've also got a knife.'

'I can do that. Do you recognise her?'

'No.'

'Okay. Get back here when the Watch takes over. Freshen up, then come into the office as soon as you can. Is the quitter still with you?'

I raised an eyebrow.

'If you mean Detective Barnaby, then yes, I'm still here.'

He didn't even pause and certainly didn't apologise.

'Fine. We've set you up accommodation in the Great Hospital. Go change your clothes or whatever it is you women do, then take a picture of the victim and show her to the arrivals. See if they recognise her.'

Willoughby shook his head.

'Sir, those arrivals are brand new. They are going to be highly discombobulated. The detective asking about a murder victim will only make things worse for them.'

I raised my other eyebrow and spoke to both of them.

'I am perfectly capable of conducting an interview with vulnerable and compromised suspects, in line with the current codes and conduct of the London Police.'

There was laughter on the radio.

'There now, our high and mighty quitter has it all under control. Report back to the Watch House as soon as possible.'

The radio went dead.

'Why does he call me a quitter?'

'Because you left?'

'No, I mean he says it like it's a thing? Like it's personal but not like it's a proper term. Lots of people left Norwich.'

Willoughby ran his hands through his hair.

'In the beginning. And then they couldn't. I guess he just loves the city so much he can't understand anyone abandoning it. And God knows, sometimes it's all hands on deck around here.'

I would not be made to feel guilty for trying to find myself a better life.

'What about you? Do you never feel constrained by the walls?'

'Occasionally, I wonder about the world beyond, but then I wonder what happens to us. Do we return to our own timeline? Do we die? Do we arrive somewhere older? I love where I am and how good my life is already so I don't see the need to travel. Everything I want is right here.'

In the early days, it was quickly observed that those who had been pulled forwards in time were unable to leave the safety of the walls without a high level of risk. A few made it across Norfolk and adapted to their new lives, but most simply disappeared as they walked away from the walls. The safest way to leave was via the boats, protected by the river, but curiously few of the old timers found a life at sea held any appeal.

Willoughby pressed the radio again.

'Mike, I need you and Giles over here immediately.'

He turned and handed me the sketch he had made earlier and started on another one.

'Do you need anything else?'

I stared at the young woman for a bit longer and then leant down and sniffed her. I didn't pick anything up, but I didn't know how good their autopsy facilities were and I needed every clue I could gather.

I had been sent to Norwich to catch a killer and he had already struck again.

Chapter Twenty

Harry and I walked away from the scene. I wished I could be like him, full of excitement at what the new day held. I had an escaped murderer, a new victim, a sheriff that thought I was scum and a partner that wore pantaloons.

William Cade was a monster and his exposure to Norwich had made him worse. God knows what was going through his mind as he had carved a cross into that woman's body, but one thing was certain, this pattern would speed up. I prayed that he died before he killed again, but that wasn't something I could rely on. I needed to find him as soon as possible. My mind was churning and I swore again that I hadn't had time to read his profile properly. I was working blind and was going to have to start from scratch to catch this killer. The question was, how quickly could I do it?

The streets of Norwich hadn't changed as much as I expected. It was more volatile when I was a child, but if I thought about it, by the time I was a teen, all the major quakes had happened. It was amazing that Normandie Tower had lasted as long as it had. Heading onto Bank Plain, it was much as I remembered, although there were more horses and carts moving people and goods about. Marigold was directing traffic and he waved at me as I passed. I doubted he remembered me. He just waved because it made him happy, his yellow washing-up gloves shining against his black skin. I waved back, delighted to see he was still thriving. The cart drivers were careful to avoid him and tipped their hats as they passed him, standing in the middle of the road. Happily, no one actually followed his capricious directions.

People were sitting outside cafés enjoying their morning cappuccinos, reading their papers or books, or catching up on the night before in small groups. No doubt last night's quake was the principal topic of conversation, but there was a remarkably relaxed air.

I was also attracting a lot of attention, or rather Harry was. I'd already seen a lot of cats, but not a single dog yet. People clearly weren't scared of dogs, though, judging by the amount of people that kept asking to stroke him.

As I reached the cathedral, I found myself walking inside. Yesterday, I hadn't lit the candles. Today I would. Inside, the cathedral was exactly as I remembered it. Dark against the bright sunlight and smelling of incense and stone dust. Light flickered down through the massive stained-glass windows and people milled around in silent prayer or talking quietly as they walked the stations of the cross, their voices muted in the echoing space. The choir was rehearsing and the voices of the choristers soared up, filling the tall, vaulted ceilings. I felt my stomach churn and walked over to the wall of candles.

Like all the churches, the cathedral had a bank of candles that could be lit in remembrance of the dead. I picked up a fresh candle and tipped its wick to the flame of another candle. My hand shook as I tried to catch the flame and remembered all the times I had done this before with Fen. I took a deep breath, trying to rid myself of her memory, and held the candle out again.

'May I help you?'

I turned and saw an old woman in a richly embroidered purple cassock. Her long hair was silver, almost white, and it was held back in a long plait. The wrinkles around her eyes creased further as she smiled kindly at me.

'Has it been a while?'

I choked back a bitter laugh.

'About ten years, give or take.'

'Then you are our guest from London?'

I nodded, wishing she would go away. I wanted to light my candle in peace. Clearly, strangers with dogs were quickly identified.

'Why did you stop lighting candles when you were in London? They have churches there.'

How to explain to this busybody that every time I lit them in London, I felt like a traitor. Fen's accusations ringing in my ears. The new life I was struggling to forge was being swamped by my guilt and loneliness. In the end I stopped, the only way forwards was to completely break with the past.

I shrugged.

'I was busy.'

She nodded her head.

'I imagine it was easier that way.'

I looked at her sharply and leant forward, my annoyance keeping my hand still, as the candle took flame and I set it upright. Picking up another candle, I lit that one as well.

'Is that for this morning's victim?'

I turned and looked at her closely.

'Who are you? That information is confidential.'

'My apologies, I'm Isidora, the Bishop of Norwich.'

I was wrong-footed and stared at her.

'Do you still go by Bish, or did you leave that behind when you left for London?'

I pulled Harry towards me and took a step back, watching as she put her hand to her mouth in dismay.

'I'm a fool and a rude one at that. My apologies, sometimes I put the cart before the elephant. One day I'll remember to think first.'

Whilst I tried to untangle her metaphors, she carried on.

'As bishop, it's my job to keep an eye on my flock. I pray for them all daily, but I pay particular attention to those that are far from home. No matter how long they've been gone. And when one pops back, I am, of course, immediately nosey.'

A female bishop, in Norwich of all places. I wondered how well that had gone down in some quarters. The Cromwellians were probably still griping about the karaoke bars, but I imagined they were fine with female emancipation. It was the Freemasons who were probably freaking.

'Have you broken your fast yet? I haven't and I would love company. Even better, I have a ridiculously large, walled garden where your dog can run off the lead to his heart's content.'

I had been prepared to say no right up until the point she had mentioned Harry and by the look of her impish grin, she knew it.

'I have work to do.'

'The sheriff will understand. Now, come with me.' She smiled again and I felt torn. Harry was standing by my side looking between the two of us expectantly as I decided what to do. The clergy were nearly as dangerous as practitioners for all their talk of peace and love. The fact that they were permitted to practise magic or, in their words, miracles, meant they were the one group of people that the practitioners viewed with caution. I simply avoided them. They meant well, no doubt, but I couldn't be doing with them.

'Good girl. I admire someone that accepts defeat so graciously, it is a lost skill.'

I followed her as she walked through the cathedral. People bobbed and bowed as she passed. Occasionally she made the sign of the cross and I found myself champing at the bit. I really did have work to do, but I wasn't prepared to get on the wrong side of the most important member of the clergy in Norwich. After a few more benedictions, we passed through a wooden door and headed along a small stone corridor. At the end, the bishop opened another wooden door and we walked into daylight.

Chapter Twenty-One

 Blinking, I took in a large garden overflowing with flowers spilling out from the borders and onto the lawns.

'There, that's better. I aways wonder who the people are bowing to. It makes me nervous.' She pulled off her cassock to reveal a simple linen gown underneath. 'Heloise, Abelard!'

No sooner had she shouted, than two enormous wolfhounds came bounding over from the far side of the garden.

'Meet our new guests, Eliza and Harry.'

I hadn't told her our names, but she already knew about the murder victim, so I knew she was well-informed.

The two dogs all but ignored me and zeroed in on Harry. I let him off his lead after some encouragement from Bishop Isidora. The dogs were so big and bouncy that I was worried for Harry but after a minute I could see she was right. He was having the time of his life as the three of them zoomed around the lawn.

'Now, you must be famished. A ten-mile walk, a dunk in the river, attacked by wolves, then straight out to a quake event and sleeping on the ground. When did you last have a proper meal?'

I wondered who her source was.

'Yesterday morning. Although I had a sandwich for lunch and some sweets for supper.'

'And I imagine you shared all of that feast with Harry.'

I grinned self-consciously. How could I eat if Harry went hungry?

'The pair of you need a proper meal right away. Break your fast like a king, sleep like an angel. That's what they say.' She paused and looked at me. 'That is what they say, isn't it?'

I winced slightly.

'Oh, squirrels. I'm always getting my idioms wrong. I'm trying to sound twenty-first century and I keep messing up. What is the saying?'

She looked at me expectantly as she waved at me to sit down.

'Breakfast like a king, lunch like a lord, dine like a pauper. The other one is sleep like a baby.'

I wondered when she came from. I didn't want to ask as she hadn't volunteered, although she already appeared to know my inside leg measurement. I came in sideways to see if I could get any more information out of her. After all, I was the detective. Her name could have come from any era but her accent was heavy. I was sure she was an old timer, but I would have loved to know how she became bishop. As far as I was aware, female clergy were a twenty-first century thing.

'When I left Norwich, I was sure we had a male bishop?'

'Tony Wyatt. An absolutely lovely man, isn't he? He retired a few years back in order to play more tennis. I still turn to him for advice. His top tip has always been to make sure the tombola runs smoothly during the summer fete. I thought he was joking until two people both won the star hamper. Goodness there were ructions. Of course, Tony came back like King Solomon himself to sort things out.

Anyway, I arrived about ten years ago. Came in the same quake as your new friend Nathaniel. At least I hope he's your friend. Lovely man. Learn to ignore the arrogance and the flirting, that's all for effect. And his outfits!' She giggled, making me relax further. 'That man is such a butterfly.'

I looked around the garden. Isidora had directed us to a pavilion with a pergola running the length. Honeysuckle and climbing roses hung down from the canopy, providing shade and a sweetly scented air. The house itself was a large flint and red brick building, but as far as I knew, this wasn't the bishop's formal residence.

'I thought the palace was on the other side of the cathedral?'

'It is, but what on earth do I need such a grand place for? I didn't want to be Bishop but Tony insisted, as did others and I found myself in the hot light. This is more than I need. It seems enormous to me, plus this one has the bigger garden. I find I have a hankering for the sky.'

A young novice in a full-length white tunic came out. Her eyes were downcast and she bobbed, as she got to the table. Her long brown hair fell to her waist and she wore a heavy brown cross on a long-beaded necklace.

'Mertle. I have a guest for breakfast. She could do with something hearty. And an extra bowl for her dog, please.'

The young woman left with another small curtsy, causing Isidora to tut.

'Honestly, I cannot stop the curtsy. The Victorians seem to have it hard-wired into their DNA. Sister Mertle is not the worst but the dear thing is so clumsy that when she curtsies, she invariably spills the tea set. Now, let's ignore work for a minute. Nothing good can be achieved on an empty stomach. Tell me all about London.'

For the next few minutes, we chatted about the capital as she proved herself to be up to date on current affairs, both in the UK and worldwide.

'We listen to the long-wave radio you know, and get papers occasionally, but nothing beats a first-hand account. I always chat to the traders to keep abreast of things.'

'Why?' I winced at my abruptness and hurried on. 'I don't mean to be rude. I just wondered what concerns Norwich has with the outside world.'

She tipped her head and stared at me.

'We have to work together. We need a future where we can safely co-exist. It isn't my intention that we should become a pariah state.' She chuckled. 'Well, more of a pariah state than we already are.'

Mertle returned with the food, and I was dismayed by how many sausages were on the tray in front of us. As she went to plate up the breakfast, Mertle managed to knock the tongs into the milk jug and as she jumped forwards to steady the jug, she knocked four of the sausages onto the floor.

I expected a flurry of apologies but she stood in silence her head bowed until she tilted her head and peeked a glance at the Bishop who was laughing softly.

'What a happy accident that you brought out so much food. Now I suppose the dogs had better eat them?'

With a quick bob and nod, the young novice grabbed the sausages from the floor and hurried across the lawn to treat the dogs.

'She may be clumsy but she's also canny. That girl is always looking for ways to spoil Heloise and Abelard. And today Harry will benefit as well. Everyone is happy.'

Grinning at the young woman's resourcefulness I tucked into my sausages as the Bishop went on to explain how Norwich was growing its future. They had funded an institute of medicine and biomechanical engineering that had no practitioner input whatsoever, based in Cambridge. Trade routes throughout the centuries were clearly exploited and she advised me to make friends with the Harbourmaster and the head of the merchants' guilds.

'Marjorie is brilliant, clearly off her rocking horse, but great fun and Charles is incredible at handling all the different guilds and getting the best price out of London.'

I dabbed my mouth with my napkin.

'I'm only here to apprehend a suspect, but I imagine I will visit the docks. If only to see if he was foolhardy enough to try and escape by river.'

She sipped her own glass of water and pushed her yogurt bowl aside.

'Back to work, then.' She sighed and I almost apologised, but she waved a hand, forestalling me. 'Tell me more about your mission.'

I tried to work out how much I could tell her. The clergy were literally a law to themselves.

'The practitioners have told me I have to keep this confidential.'

'Well, we wouldn't want to upset the most august practitioners, would we?' She said it lightly and I hoped that would be the end. 'However, this is my city and I would like to know what is going on, especially if they have lost one of their flock.'

'I don't think they call them their flock.'

'No, I don't suppose they do.'

I took a deep breath. 'It's just I don't know much about the relationship between the practitioners and the clergy and I would rather not annoy either of you. I know they permit you to practice miracles—'

She cut me off, placing her cup loudly on the table.

'They permit us nothing.' She picked up her napkin and dabbed at the spilt tea. 'My apologies, but honestly, I find the claims of the practitioners tiresome. Thank the Lord in his most benevolent wisdom, we have none in the city.'

This led me to a question which I wouldn't have normally dared to ask, but as the conversation had already been broached, I chanced my luck.

'Tell me, do none of the clergy practice miracles in the city?'

'How can we? Whether they are miracles or magic, they come from the same source and have the same consequences. They wreak havoc upon the city. I know beyond Norfolk, the clergy practice their miracles—'

'Not much. I think they try not to annoy the practitioners after the practitioners allowed them to be exempt from their sign-ups.'

'Allowed them?' She laughed loudly and I stared at her, confused. 'They allowed us nothing. We were once all the same. Wasn't our Lord, Jesus Christ, a practitioner himself?' She waved a hand dismissively. 'I suppose they wanted to go their own way but believe me, if they tried to move against us, they would regret it.'

'But the clergy don't practice much, I mean beyond Norwich. Back home, the clergy don't perform miracles much. What if the practitioners one day decide they are more powerful and ban you? Or at least ban you from performing miracles.'

'Ah, but they won't do that.'

'Why?' I was genuinely curious. I had never had a conversation like this before.

'Because they are not more powerful. They may have their magic, but we have the hearts of the people. They care more for us than practitioners.'

Sipping her tea, she placed the cup more gently and sighed. 'Well, I have had a lovely time with you. The song of the bees, the warmth of the sun, the scent of the roses and a lively conversation with a new friend. Even with such darkness in the world, I am grateful that God gives me these blessings.'

Calling the dogs to us, she stood up and Harry came bouncing across the lawn, tumbling and diving with the other two as they all ran towards us.

'Now, you haven't answered my question about your investigation. Maybe instead you could help me with a tiny investigation of my own. I know it's a liberty, but whilst you are here, do you think you could do me a favour? It's a tiny thing and I don't want it to interfere with your mission. Especially now that we have a new murder case.'

Clearly, this woman already knew everything the police knew.

'If I have time, I shall of course, help. What do you need?'

'It's such a small issue that I feel loathe to bother the sheriff but our socks are going missing. I don't wish to enquire directly. Bishop Investigates seems like using a cannonball to kill a fly. Maybe you could enquire down at the laundries and see if you can see if it's accidental.'

'The Laundries?' I asked, trying to moderate my voice. I was a detective, not some sort of school monitor.

'Yes, all our linen gets sent out. But not all of it returns. Silly, I know but…'

'Odd socks. I get it. God knows I swear my tumble dryer eats them. Leave it with me and if I get a chance, I'll pop in and ask around. I can play the role of ignorant incomer cop.'

She laughed at me and waggled her finger. 'No one will ever mistake you for ignorant.'

Sending me back through the garden gate, I had gained a bunch of roses and a bone for Harry. As posies went, they were an unusual pairing. I popped the bone in my backpack and headed on my way, feeling uncomfortable. I hadn't come out well from that conversation.

Bishop Isidora was a remarkably well-informed woman who clearly had the city's best interests at heart, and I hoped I would be able to solve her dilemma, as ridiculous as it was. In fact, it was so minor, I wondered if she was deliberately wasting my time for not telling her about the case and annoying her about the practitioners. Clearly, she knew it already, but I may have just made an enemy or at least annoyed someone powerful, no matter how sweet and old she looked. She was the bishop and not to be underestimated. Or maybe she was simply testing me?

The walk from the cathedral to the Great Hospital was a short one and I passed few people. This section of Norwich was mostly composed of church land. There was the cathedral itself, the school, the hospital and various related buildings. There was also a cracking pub and a gate onto the river. I had lived in this part of the city as a kid and had always loved it. It had always been the most stable area, given the age of the buildings. Every map had these streets and buildings in the exact same place for centuries. We were only affected by the first quake when the people came through.

The Great Hospital had been established in the twelfth century and had provided hospitality for pilgrims, crusaders, patients, the poor of the parish, and now the new arrivals, ever since.

I rang on the bell. Unlike the other churches, St Helen's had a locked door policy. No one wanted an arrival to stumble outside, unprepared. Beyond the church was a cloister, not as grand as the cathedral's, but in its smallness, it had an extra charm. It also made for a fantastic racetrack until the nuns would come and tell us off. I don't know why, but nuns always seem permanently surprised and disappointed by the reality of children. Personally, I think they spent too long fantasising about what a perfect child the baby Jesus must have been. But turning water into wine, that's the mark of a prankster if ever I heard of one.

Beyond the cloister was a collection of homes. Some individual houses, some long terraces built around a central square and all safely wrapped up inside their own red brick walls, waiting to welcome and embrace the weary traveller.

The door to the church swung open and a man stared out in exasperation.

'No deliveries. No dogs. No doxies.' He sneered at me in contempt. 'Away with you.'

Chapter Twenty-Two

 He was going to close the door again, but I pushed past and turned around to face him.

'I believe you have a room ready for me. If Harry is a problem, please bring me my bag and I'll find somewhere else.'

He scowled and looked me up and down. His long hair was unwashed and he wore a brown linen smock that stopped just above a pair of hairy knees and was tied at the waist by a knotted rope from which hung a pocket bag. On his feet, he wore a pair of wooden clogs that must have been a joy to anyone trying to sleep.

'Reckon as you've got the wrong lodgings. What are you? Off the boats? Your draunt ain't local, roight enough.'

'I aren't off the boats.' I said, finding myself quickly falling into his style of speech and wincing at how quickly the old phrases flooded back.

'Pilgrim then, hint ut? We don't take no pilgrims. You need to get back on the boat and leave Narwich. No place for you here. Specially not in them trousers. That's the devil's work, that is.'

I looked about, but the church was empty. Our exchange echoed across the cool whitewashed walls, but there was no help coming.

'Detective Eliza Barnaby. Elm Hill, 1996. Here from London. Now show me my room or bring me my bags.'

If his scowl could have deepened any further, he'd be spouting rain along with the other gargoyles on the church roof.

'Shoulda known yew were London. Now, yew lissun hare. Keep yon dog on lead and follow me.'

Looking down at Harry, I was convinced he rolled his eyes. We followed our delightful host through the church, past the cloisters and out into the lawned quadrant. We turned right and headed towards a cottage standing within a small garden.

'Roight. This is you. Ollust keep the dog on a lead and wear skirts. Small key is this door, big key is the church door. Curfew is seven pm. The refectory serves at six am and again at six pm. You ain't to bring owt else onto the grounds. Got it?'

I took the keys off him.

'Who are you, exactly? I mean, what is your job title?'

'Warden is what I am. Warden Josiah Sallop.'

'Well, Warden Sallop,' I said, keeping my voice as clipped as I could, 'I shall come and go as suits me. I am a detective on a murder investigation and will be working irregular hours. If I am around, it will be my pleasure to dine with the other residents. I have no intention of bringing anyone here. I know no one except for the bishop with whom I have just had breakfast. If I wish to invite her for dinner, I shall explain that she isn't welcome and we'll dine elsewhere. The dog is called Harry and he will always be on a lead in public areas, and I will never ever be told what to wear by yourself or anyone else.' I stared at him. 'Got it?'

Harry wagged his tail whilst we both watched the warden try to balance all that information. Clearly, the bishop won the day and he walked away muttering about dogs and skirts, but as he hadn't disagreed with me, I figured I had a new home for the next few days.

Unlocking the front door with a simple yale key, I was pleasantly surprised with the interior. Country modern, soft furnishing, deep carpet, bookshelves and board games. Looking around with a quick nod, I headed to the kitchen and tried the tap. I had running water. Although this was a modern kitchen, some modifications had been made to accommodate the limited supply of electricity. There was no fridge or freezer, but I found a door leading down to a small chilly cellar. A bottle of fresh milk sat on a marble work surface and there was some cheese under a cloche.

Heading back upstairs, I studied the small range. It appeared to be dual fuel running on electricity and a wood burner that no doubt provided my hot water. I ran up the carpeted staircase with Harry running after me as we explored the three rooms. Two bedrooms, one made up and a bathroom with a deep, freestanding bathtub. On a stand beside the bath was a collection of bottles and tubes and I figured I was sorted for soap, shampoo and toothpaste.

In the main bedroom, my rucksack was propped against the bed and as I moved it onto the bed, I looked out of the window and saw with a jolt that I had my own small, fenced garden.

Harry and I ran downstairs again, headed to the back of the cottage and opened a door into the small but perfectly formed garden. The lawn was lined by flowering shrubs, including a hedge of lavender, and in one corner sat a patio table and chairs and, by the back door, a bench with a bowl of water on the floor.

As Harry quickly helped himself, I thanked my benefactor. I headed back indoors and checked out the state of the food cupboards and found it was well stocked with dried goods, a loaf of bread and dog food. At least that's what I presumed the bone and scraps of meat were. I added the bone the bishop had given me for Harry and found a vase for the roses. Exploring the cellar a bit more, I found some butter and some cured bacon. Tonight I would dine on bacon butties or tagliatelle carbonara. Right now, I was desperate for a bath and a quick nap, but I needed to find someone in charge and ask if I could show the arrivals the image that Willoughby had sketched.

There was no way that I was going to ask the warden for help, so after a quick wash, I popped Harry back on his lead and headed off towards the quadrant.

It didn't take long before a woman in a long dress came out of one of the buildings and made a beeline for me.

'Detective Barnaby? I'm Marion Webb, arrivals officer.'

The woman was in her twenties, with straight brown hair and an engaging smile.

'The sheriff said you'd be on your way.' She motioned for me to follow her, and I headed toward the building on the far side of the quadrant. 'They've had their breakfast and are currently reading in the library. We find books with lots of pictures in them are a great way for them to understand the new world they've found themselves in. It helps to soften the shocks. So far this morning we've faced the excitement of running water and elasticated knickers. As usual, they were more impressed with the knickers.'

She opened a large wooden door and we walked into a small hallway. The door was glazed and I could see into a large double width room with windows out the back to more gardens. Inside, the room was lined with bookcases and sofas. The children were all sitting in a corner with their backs to the room. The adults were either praying or glancing at the books and then closing them again quickly. No one was sitting on the sofas. They either stood, or sat cross-legged on the plush carpet.

'What year have they come from?' I muttered.

Marion sighed. 'Want to guess?'

There wasn't much to go on. They were still in their shifts from the night before.

'Have they been offered clothes?'

'Of course. We have huge dressing rooms and arrivals can select anything that appeals, their time period or not.'

I looked at them again.

'Deeply suspicious. Refusal of gifts. Eschewing the comfy sofas. Praying. Are they Puritans?'

Marion smiled. 'That's why you're the detective. Puritans, 1640.'

'Oh joy.'

Some arrivals were trickier than others. 'Have the cavaliers and Roundheads buried the hatchet yet?'

'More or less. We've even had a few marriages. If things flare up, it's usually around the football matches. But each new set of arrivals jigs up the juices again. But that's our problem. Not yours. You go show them your picture, then you can get on with your job. The bishop will be on her way soon to formally welcome them to their new city. Then I can continue with the task of helping them adjust.'

She swung the door open and all the adults came to their feet. One of the men stepped forward. 'I demand to speak to your commander.' He was a big man with a barrel chest, thick calves and hairy toes. Over by the sofa rested a pair of boots and I wondered if maybe the sinful pleasures of a deep pile carpet had possibly seduced him. I kept my smile to myself.

Marion was about to reply when the woman standing next to him stared at me and cut him off with a flick of her wrist. It was the woman I had spoken to last night, and she appeared to be still very much in control. I noticed her shoes were still on her feet. When we walked in, she had been praying. Now she crossed herself.

'Are you a devil?'

I wondered how to proceed and then remembered how self-controlled she was last night. This was a strong woman who was simply freaked out. Direct measures for this one.

'Are you stupid?'

She recoiled slightly, and some of the children in the corner giggled. She glared in their direction and they quickly turned their backs again.

'I told you last night, my name is Eliza. I was born on Elm Hill. Nothing has changed since we last met. You are about to go through a lot of things and it won't help if you act stupid.'

'Are you in charge? A woman?'

'No. I'm a detective.'

She looked at me blankly.

'I keep the peace on behalf of...' I was about to say His Majesty, and caught myself in time. 'The state.'

'You're part of the New Model Army?'

'No. But I am responsible for civil disobedience.'

'Is that why you wear men's clothes?'

'No, I wear them because they're comfortable. Now. I need your help. We found a woman yesterday near your cottages. Do you recognise her?' I pulled the image out of my satchel. 'All of you gather round. Children too please.'

The children stayed still and I stared at the matriarch.

'I appreciate you are scared and confused. But I don't appreciate you acting stupid. I need everyone to look at the image.'

She jerked her head at the children, who all sprang up and dashed over to join the others. Twenty faces all stared at the sketch of our murder victim, their expressions ranging from blank to curious, but none showed a spark of recognition. It was a small blessing, but at least it meant they had one less shock to deal with. Whoever this woman was, she wasn't part of their community.

'Very well. And did anyone see or hear anything unusual last night?'

'Besides our being roused from our very beds and force marched across the city?' This was from the large man that I had decided was the matriarch's husband.

'Yes, besides that.'

Everyone shook their head.

'I heard a scream.' A little voice piped up and was immediately shushed by a bigger child. 'Be quiet, Beth.'

'But I did.'

'You did not!'

'I did by the grace of—'

'Beth Wilkinson,' said another woman. She was standing beside the two children and from her long-suffering look, I had her pegged as their mother. The man standing next to them cuffed the little girl across her ears. 'Were you about to take our blessed Lord's name in vain?'

'No, mother. But I did hear a scream.'

'You heard a fox,' said her brother scornfully.

'It weren't no fox.'

I decided to interrupt. I remembered my brother and I could argue for hours if no one stopped us.

'When did you hear the noise?'

She came forwards and stroked Harry, then smiled back gleefully at her brother before turning back to me.

'The moon had just risen.'

I turned to the others.

'Did anyone else hear this noise? Maybe you heard foxes and dismissed it?' More shakes of the head. 'Are you sure?'

'Do you take us for fools?' asked the matriarch. 'If we had heard foxes we'd have been up with our cudgels.'

It was my turn to acknowledge the stupid question. If they'd heard a fox, they would have worried for their hens.

'Well, thank you for your time. If anyone remembers anything odd about last night, before we met that is, please get in touch. Marion will be able to call me.'

'And when can we go home? Last night you said we'd be able to go home straight away.'

'I said as soon as it was safe.'

'And why isn't it safe?' she demanded, her hands on her hips.

'That will be explained to you shortly. The bishop is on her way and she'll explain everything.'

'What popery is this! Has Rome invaded? And since when has a woman ever been a bishop?'

Chapter Twenty-Three

 I cringed an apology to Marion and fled the scene, pulling Harry away from all the tummy rubs he was getting from the children.

Tucking the picture back into my jacket, we started to walk back past the cathedral. Rather than walk up Elm Hill, I headed through Tombland and along London Street. I wasn't ready for that trip down memory lane.

We passed Jarrold's and had a look in the windows. Being summer, they had a display of swimming costumes. I wondered what Mother Puritan would make of that red racer back? If knicker elastic was making the Puritans' hair curl, lycra was going to blow their homespun socks off.

The marketplace was buzzing with morning shoppers and I went to the first stall and asked where the closest bakery was and was thrilled to discover that Oelrichs was still going strong. Ten minutes later, I was heading into the Watch House with a box of goodies.

'Good morning. Who wants a cake?'

'I love new girl rules,' said Alys. This morning she was drinking coffee rather than wine and offered me a cup. 'Hi, I'm Alys, in case you forgot. We didn't get much chance to introduce ourselves properly last night, did we?'

'No, but tell me, you looked surprised yesterday, when I said where I was born. Is that not done anymore?'

'Not so much. Lady Julian said it was better to treat everyone as equals. She said–'

'Wait! Lady Julian arrived?' Lady Julian was world famous. She was a famous hermit from the 1200s and lived in a hermit's cell attached to St Julian's Church. If you've ever heard the phrase *All Shall Be Well*, well, that's one of hers. If Norwich had an honest to goodness goddess, it was Lady Julian. She had been my bedrock growing up. I think a lot of us clung to her mantra. A few words might seem like a platitude, but when you've got nothing else, they were a balm for a pitiful existence.

'Is she still in the cell? Does she communicate with people?'

How like her teachings to be telling us to put aside our differences.

'In her cell? No girl, Isidora has expanded her accommodation.'

'Isidora?' I grabbed a chair and sat down heavily. Horror consumed me. 'Is Lady Julian the bishop? Why is she called Isidora?'

'She is, and she's wonderful. Have you met her yet? She should be on her way to the Great Hospital. Isidora is her given name, apparently the name Julian came from the church, and honestly, she finds her new fame somewhat overwhelming.'

I was struggling to speak. Lady Julian was practically a saint. I prayed to her throughout my teenage years to make life better. Most of us did. I used to walk past the site of her cell hoping she would come back and somehow save us all. Even then, I knew that was a stupid idea. I replayed my conversation with her and wanted to die. God, no wonder she liked the sky above her. She must have been without it for so many years.

'Cat got your tongue?'

She smiled sympathetically and was about to speak again when an office door slammed upstairs and footsteps headed down.

'Back, then? Who's the victim?'

The sheriff wasn't in a good mood. I couldn't blame him, but it didn't help that he was so personally hostile. He walked over to the bakery box and helped himself to a croissant.

'Heavens, Alys. These are delicious. Did you go over to Oelrich's?'

Alys winked at me.

'No, Joseph. Eliza here brought them. New girl rules and all that.'

The sheriff swallowed uncomfortably and then put the other half of the croissant back in the box.

'Alright, let's stop mucking around. We have a dead girl on our hands and a killer on the loose. Where's Willoughby?'

He glared around the room.

'Did someone say my name?'

Willoughby walked in. He was still in a very elaborate jacket and half trousers, but this time apart from his white socks, his outfit was entirely black. Even his hair was pulled back and tied with a black ribbon.

The sheriff nodded.

'Right, let's begin.'

Willoughby crossed the room and made for one of the chairs over by a large leather-topped writing table. There was a bust of Descartes on the surface and a quill pen in an ink stand. I was certain that this was Willoughby's own desk. It also looked down over the market below and Guildhall across the way. I bet petty theft was kept low if you knew the detectives and city councillors were all watching.

As he passed the box, he looked in with an initial smile and then frowned as he chose a chocolate éclair.

'Which monster ate half a croissant and then put it back in the box? That's a flogging offence in my book.'

From where I was sitting, Sheriff Hitchman's face was a picture and I simply smiled back at him.

'If we can stop wasting our time? Willoughby, you're late. If the death of some young woman means nothing to you and you'd rather eat cake, then please let me know and I'll have you moved to the Watch for a few days.'

Willoughby whipped out a large white handkerchief, embroidered in lace, and dabbed his lips.

'I was delayed because I was collecting witness statements from King's Street. I have also been to the lab to see if they confirmed the knife matches the cuts on our victim.'

'And?' snapped Hitchman.

'They do.'

'Right. Next, we need to go and get witness statements from the arrivals. I don't suppose London has done that yet?'

He was still talking to Willoughby, but I replied. At least London was a better name than Quitter.

'I have.'

He drummed his fingers on his desk, an eyelid twitching as I saw him take a breath.

'And? Are you planning on making us wait for your report?'

'No, sir. No one recognises the woman.'

'Did you believe them?'

'Yes, because the children agreed. On the whole, most children make bad liars when in a group. I would say though that they are Puritans and very close-knit. The matriarch refused to give her name and they were all clearly scared, although putting on a brave face. Under these testing circumstances, they could be lying and I may have missed it.'

'Alright. Thank you for the arse covering essay. Right–'

'There is more to my report if you want to hear it.'

He stared at me.

'Now look here. I don't know how they run things in London. But here we don't allow some chit to talk to an officer in that tone of voice.'

I counted to five, there was no chance of getting to ten.

'And I don't know how you run things here, but in London we don't refer to women as chits, nor do we treat our detectives as idiots.'

I wanted to tell him that we also put food that had been in our mouths in the bin, but decided that was pushing my luck. There was silence in the room. The sheriff crossed his arms and raised an eyebrow, so I continued.

'One of the children, a young girl, said she heard a scream. Her brother dismissed it as a fox.'

'What do you think?' asked Willoughby and I was grateful for his intervention.

'I think a child raised on a smallholding used to the sounds of the countryside probably can tell the difference between the call of a male and female thrush, let alone that of a fox and a human.'

Alys riffled through the papers on her desk and pulled one out.

'It also tallies with a witness statement I have from a banker living on King's Street, closest to the incident site. Although he too said it could have been a fox. However, he was born in 1950. Norwich, for him, has always been built-up. He confessed he wasn't very good at nighttime noises, preferring the radio.'

Television was beyond Norwich with its reliance on em-technology. But transistor radios worked perfectly and it was one way that the people of Norwich kept abreast of world affairs, if they were so inclined. Generally, the musical stations were more popular, but most people tuned into City Sounds Radio.

'Was your girl able to give you a time frame?' asked Willoughby.

'Just after moonrise. She said it had cleared the beacon at Kett's Hill.'

Frustratingly, I didn't know what that time was. I'd meant to look it up, then remembered that I had no internet here.

'That tallies with Mr Johnston's statement,' said Alys again. 'About an hour after the bells chimed, the quake alert. He'd remembered coming out onto the street with his neighbours and then, rather than heading to the quarantine zone with everyone else, he headed back to bed. Said if this was his time to go, he'd do so in his own bed. After he heard the scream, he put his ear plugs in. Said, "bloody Norwich and its bloody noises" and finally fell asleep.'

'Right then,' said Hitchman. 'If our chicken girl and old timer are right, then the most likely source of the scream is our victim and she died in our time frame, which means that someone from here will know who she is.' He looked over to Alys, who had picked up a pair of knitting needles. 'Anyone filed a missing person's report?'

'Would have mentioned it if they had,' said Alys as she continued to knit.

Hitchman frowned and then let out a deep breath.

'Now, then. Onto our murderer. I'm not ruling anyone in or out, but the fact that London let slip one of their psychopaths makes me feel more inclined to him being our culprit. Detective Barnaby, perhaps you'd like to supply a little more information?'

'Yes, sir. What would you like to know?'

'How long had he been in jail and how did he escape?'

I squirmed.

'I'm afraid I don't know, sir. I was under the impression that everything would be in the briefing document I was asked to hand over to you.'

'This being the document in question?' He waved the sheet of paper in his hand. 'The picture of seven murder victims and a photograph of the practitioner.'

'Yes sir.'

'Well, as you can see, it's somewhat lacking in detail.' He pulled open a drawer of his desk and selected a cigar. Alys coughed loudly and opened a window. 'Well, if you didn't read the document, maybe you had the foresight to look this Cade up on one of your fancy computational devices?'

I winced as he began to puff, the smell of cherry tobacco filling the air.

'No, sir. There wasn't time.'

'Well, did you ask if he used a knife to inflict those wounds, or if he used magic?'

'No, sir, I didn't need to ask–'

'You didn't need to ask. What sort of a copper are you? Is this how London trains you lot? To not ask questions.'

'If you'll let me finish, I watched him stab the first two practitioners.'

Hitchman's eye's narrowed and he waved his cigar, telling me to continue. As I finished my statement, he stood up and walked around the room.

'So. Let me see if I've got this straight. A very powerful practitioner, on account of him killing two of his own and evading capture by the other two. Escaped, killed five people who got in his way and fled to Norwich. And the only thing your authorities did to solve the problem was to send some girl and her dog and a few photos to apprehend him. Have I got this right?'

The fury in his voice was making his words tight and clipped.

'I shall write to my bosses immediately and request the full files.'

He barked off a laugh and then roared at me.

'You will, will you? Thank you. That hadn't occurred to us dim-witted Norvikers.'

Harry growled and, in the silence, the sound of knitting needles slammed onto the table and Alys stood up.

'That's enough.' Everyone stared as Alys made her way to the box of goodies. We watched as she picked up the half-eaten croissant and threw it to Harry, who ignored it as he continued to stand in front of me, his shoulders low, his eyes fixed on the sheriff.

'Joseph, you went through this last night when she arrived. Making her go through it again now is uncalled for. She is not responsible for her dim-witted bosses. And it seems she has moved from one intolerable police force to another. Apologise to her now and calm her poor dog down.'

Everyone held their breath as he swore, before taking another drag of his cigar, ash falling to the floor.

'Right, maybe I shouldn't have raised my voice. I apologise.'

'Do you want me to write to London?'

He glared and I swear the tip of his nose went white as his face flushed red.

'No. I sent a message last night.'

'Very good sir.' I was proud my voice didn't waver. I hated being shouted at, but I was used to it. What had thrown me was Harry's reaction, and I was a trifle overwhelmed with how quickly we had bonded. 'What would you like me to do now? I think Harry and I should like to get out of the building.'

'Go with Willoughby. Head up Ber Street and see if we can identify our victim.'

'Right, sir.' I stood up in relief, but it was short-lived as he looked at the gun in my belt.

He pulled open his drawer again and I wondered if he was a chain smoker when he threw a gold disc at me.

'Only the law carries a gun. You'd best make it clear who you are. If I see you with that gun without your badge, I'll send you back to London.'

I pinned it to my collar and nodded once.

'Wear it with pride. Being a copper or a detective means something here.'

It meant something back home as well, but I wasn't going to get into an argument. Calling Harry to heel, I headed outside. In the fresh air, I let out a big sigh and then knelt down and hugged Harry as he tried to lick my face. A few minutes later, Willoughby joined us.

'Well done, Bish. You handled yourself admirably in there.'

I was still shaking and tried to keep the tremor out of my voice.

'Does he hate people that left Norwich that much?'

'I think he's usually just disparaging of them. But now he has to work alongside one and he has a killer on the loose and London are treating us like idiots. I'm afraid you unfairly became the focus for his worries and his frustrations.'

I saw he was wearing a gun on his belt.

'I thought Hitchman said you didn't wear guns, except under certain circumstance.'

'If my partner is wearing a gun, then so am I. If you feel you are heading into a difficult situation, then how can I protect you with just a whistle and a baton? This Cade needs to be incapacitated on sight.'

'I don't need protection.'

He stared at me and then gave me a courtly bow before handing me an apple slice and avoiding my statement.

'I thought you and Harry might share this. And I must thank you most kindly for the éclair. Oelrichs is a genius. Which is your favourite? I confess that the praline ring is above all others, the man's masterpiece.'

I took a deep breath and gave him a wobbly smile. I appreciated he was trying to lighten the tone.

'They were my favourite, but they didn't have any this morning.'

'Maybe tomorrow, hey?' He nodded and patted me on the head, which I found both alarming and funny. Old timers had really queer habits.

'Come on,' said Willoughby, smiling back at me as he took off. 'Let's go see the nuns.'

Chapter Twenty-Four

 We walked past the market and a few of the stall holders doffed their caps as we walked by. Given that I was in no distinguishing uniform, I assumed the deference was for Willoughby.

'Why are they doffing their caps?'

'Constable on the beat. That sort of thing,'

I noticed he tipped his head in acknowledgement.

'We police by consent here. But also through a relaxed attitude towards law and order. There are only twenty criminals serving time in Bridewell at the moment.'

'And how many have you sent down the river in the past year?'

'One.'

I paused.

'What's Norwich's current population?'

'Roughly 30,000.'

That was a very low set of figures and I said as much.

'It's different here.'

'For example?'

'We pull together in hard times, wrongdoers aren't tolerated. Most streets have their own stocks. Being drunk is fine, being drunk and disorderly is not. Stealing is wrong, but stealing to help others is tolerable.

Watering down of wine or cutting flour will see you in Brideswell.'

'The last person who was sent down the river. What did they do?'

'He ravished his daughter.'

'Fair enough.'

Ravishing was the more polite term for raping. The bastard deserved all he got. Going down the river wasn't an instant death. It was slow and lingering with madness occurring first.

'How do you deal with vigilantes if you are so laid back?'

'By not being laid back.' He laughed as we dodged in front of some carts. 'We are not nursemaids. The City Watch is as likely to administer a beating as a warning. And they really don't like vigilantes. If anyone is going to dole out a summary kicking, it will be them. And don't get me started on the Black Watch. Last riot we had to arrest as many of them as rioters.'

I wanted to object. The police were not hired street thugs, but this was Norwich. They did things differently here.

'Who are the Black Watch?'

'They are the gentlemen of the Watch with particularly short fuses. They do not have their own department. We all work together, but sometimes, when a certain physical skill set is required, the sheriff calls on the informal collective to come and knock heads together.'

It sounded like an in-built goon squad.

'And what about the militia?'

'They aren't part of the Watch. They mainly deal with issues beyond the wall but they do help us out with riots.'

'Riots?'

'From time to time, people like to blow off steam. It's quite normal for Norwich. Maybe once a year, the powder keg catches fire, but as I said, that's when the militia step in and of course the Black Watch go to town. Fine men and women. I admire their bravery. But in terms of general law and order, that's the domain of the City Watch and her detectives.' We turned down Surrey Street and Willoughby paused, adjusting his cuffs. 'Are you okay with flickers?'

'They've never bothered me.'

'Oh, I thought that might be why you left such a wonderful place,' he asked and I sensed a note of reproval.

'No, that would be the death, disease and quake aches.'

We walked towards Notre Dame in silence. There were a few detached dwellings from the nineteenth century and ahead were the walled gardens of the convent.

'We used to play in there as children,' I said, trying to build a bridge.

'What was the prize?'

'Getting some food out of the gardens without alerting the nuns.'

He laughed and I decided I liked the sound of it when it was with me, not at me.

'If flickerings did not cause you distress, I would suggest you wore them as camouflage?'

'Exactly. Of course, sometimes the nuns caught us and they'd be merry hell to pay.'

'What did your parents say?'

'Both dead, so I escaped the worst of it. Although the nuns kept suggesting to the authorities that I should be made a novice.'

'That would have been a waste.'

'That would have been a bloody nightmare. Still, it was fun.'

As we got closer, the building flickered and hordes of school children, dressed in bottle green and maroon colours, appeared on the streets, some running towards the school, others leaving in large packs, forcing anyone else off the street. We just sailed through their ghostly after images.

Flickerings were caused when a building just couldn't gather enough energy to be one thing or the other. Notre Dame School had generations of powerful memories, but Notre Dame Convent had faith and longevity. The convent mostly won out and over the years had become stronger as the school ceased to function when the meld occurred.

We walked up to the main gates and Willoughby rang the bell. All around us, girls in smart uniforms ran through the walls. Two girls were carrying hockey sticks and I could make out their laughter as they passed.

The door opened and a nun smiled politely at Willoughby.

'Detective Willoughby. What a surprise.'

Her tone suggested nothing of the sort, but she gave him a wink.

'Come on in, the kettle's on.' She turned to me. 'Detective Barnaby, I presume. I'm Sister Bernard. Please, step this way, and do excuse the girls.' She swatted at the image of a girl that ran her way. 'They are like midges at the moment. No doubt unsettled by the quake. Come along.'

Two little girls with wool blazers and felt bonnets ran past us as an unfelt wind blew against them and knocked one of their hats off. Absentmindedly, I bent down and handed the hat back to the girl, who thanked me with a puzzled frown and then ran to catch her friend, her hand firmly on top of her head keeping her hat in place.

Both Willoughby and the nun were staring at me in astonishment.

'Just how Norwich are you?' asked Willoughby. Interacting with flickers was not something that most people could do. For me it was second nature.

'I've got flint in the bones, me. Mum and Dad were both born here, and so were both of their parents. And apparently theirs as well. Although I had a great, great grandfather from Trowse.'

Trowse lying just beyond the river was practically abroad. I shrugged. The older your family was, the more attuned to Norwich you were. My brother used to laugh that we were Norviker thoroughbreds. Those of us that went way back had coped best with the quakes. Some of us could even sense them coming, as I had last night, and none of us were bothered by flickers. A few of us could even map run, but we kept that to ourselves. The early witch trials had taught us that lesson.

'Your headaches must have been appalling growing up?' said Willoughby with more insight than I'd given him credit for. Quakes were the product of engineered magic going horribly wrong and as such I could spot them a mile off. Wild magic, the sort that sloshed around the Norfolk landscape, caused me no trouble whatsoever.

'They were, but at least we were able to act as an early warning system. The flickerings were just a damned nuisance until we got used to them.'

'Speaking of which,' said Sister Bernard, 'please ignore this wall. Do you need my hand?'

She stepped forward through an apparently solid brick wall and I saw Willoughby flinch. I stuck my elbow out.

'Kind sir?'

He looked at me and grinned, looping his arm through mine.

'Lead on, fair guide.'

I followed Sister Bernard's footsteps through the ornamental rose garden whilst simultaneously walking through a maths lesson, an English lesson, and morning prayers. The girls, not the nuns. As we walked back out of the school block, Willoughby paused and touched one of the roses for reassurance, breathing deeply through his nose. Sister Bernard turned around and rejoined us.

'My dear Nathaniel. I am sorry the flickerings really are extreme at the moment. Sister Mary Margaret's rooms have always belonged to the Mother Superior. It's as solid as St Peter.'

'My thanks. It is such a bother to not be able to trust one's senses. I should learn to follow Harry's example.' We watched as Harry snuffled around the base of the roses. He then paused to pee, and Willoughby coughed. 'Or maybe following Mistress Eliza's example would be better.'

'Indeed, I am less likely to relieve myself in public,' I laughed, and now it was Sister Bernard's turn to cough and remind me of my manners. 'However,' I said quickly to Willoughby, 'I am very impressed that you can navigate these flickers. Sister Bernard is used to them. Harry doesn't seem to see them and I can tell the difference, so they don't bother me.'

This was one of the ways that people lost their wits. They couldn't trust their senses and eventually drove themselves mad.

We continued through the garden and into the convent. The main reception was double heighted and full of light and air and an absence of school children. There was a graceful double staircase swooping down either side of the foyer, and a nun was making her way down the stairs. Unlike Sister Bernard, she was wearing a full wimple, but there was no mistaking the fact that she was a redhead. The freckles on her alabaster skin gave her away, and I was reminded of similar features on a small green-eyed girl called Jennifer.

She stopped on the staircase, staring at me.

'Bloody hell. Bish!'

Shouting, she ran down the steps, her black robes billowing out behind her and I ran forward. I couldn't help myself. Jennifer had been my best friend. My partner in crime. My confidante and ultimately the reason I had left Norwich.

'Fenface!'

'Bish Bosh. I'm so sorry.' She was laughing and crying.

'No. it was my fault.'

'I shouldn't have said it.'

'You should have. I shouldn't have overreacted.'

We were swinging each other around, laughing. I couldn't stop the tears from rolling down my face and hugged her again as Harry bounced between the two of us, barking excitedly.

The last time I had seen her she had called me a traitor. I had called her a coward. Telling her she would die if she stayed. We had slung the most vicious insults at each other until she had run off into the dark and I slunk away into the river and beyond the walls.

A metal cane rapped the terracotta floor tiles, and we both whipped around to see a very stern Sister Mary Margaret glaring at us. She hadn't aged a day.

'Eliza Barnaby. I see you still haven't learnt any decorum. Sister Jennifer, did I hear you blaspheme?'

'That was me,' I blurted. I was still coming to terms with the fact that Fenface had actually made good on her threat to become a nun.

'Are you back?' she asked quickly before the Mother Superior could speak.

'Evidentially,' scolded the old nun. 'Get back to your duties. Detective Barnaby is here on duty. You two may catch up later.'

'I'll see you by the apple tree,' she shouted as she rushed off down the corridor with Sister Bernard shouting 'Walk!' after her.

Sister Mary Margaret looked at me sternly. 'Sister Jennifer is one of our most devout nuns. Please do not lead her from the path of righteousness.'

This was my second dressing down of the day and it wasn't even ten o'clock but I didn't care, it was so good to see Fenface again and incredibly she didn't hate me. I had been expecting hate. The sheriff's attitude towards quitters had simply reinforced my own negative opinion of myself.

'Sister Bernard,' said Sister Mary Margaret, 'could you please look in on Sister Jennifer and ensure she has calmed down? Now Detective Willoughby, if you and Detective Barnaby would care to join me for a cup of tea?'

She turned and walked into her office, and I trailed along behind my partner. I was positively dragging my feet.

When I mentioned that I didn't drink tea, she rolled her eyes and poured me a glass of milk instead.

'I seem to remember you preferred milk as a girl, yes?'

I mumbled an affirmative and I could swear that Willoughby was smirking.

'A delicious blend, Sister,' he said, having taken a sip. 'An Earl Grey from my own time, I think? They always balanced the bergamot better than the modern recipe.'

The Mother Superior smiled. 'This new generation is lacking in most things. Taste is just one of them.' I let Willoughby handle this interview. She and I had never seen eye to eye. She had walked out of the 1800s and found life in the twenty-first century had much to criticise. Although I wasn't the only one to notice that she had quickly vacated her small stone nunnery and made her way to the Convent of Lady Julian and promptly installed herself as the new Mother Superior, running water and sprung mattresses and all. The existing Superior had simply rolled over.

'Now, Nathaniel. I take it you are here to enquire after the dead woman?' She settled back into her armchair. 'I'm afraid I have heard of little that will help, although there have been reports of a stranger wandering along the walls at dusk.'

Willoughby pulled out the photo of William Cade.

'Is this him?'

She looked at the image and then crossed herself. Some of the old timers hated photographs.

'I haven't seen him myself, but I will have Sister Bernard show the likeness to the nuns who raised the concerns. Have you captured an image of the poor woman? Maybe I would recognise her at least.'

Pulling out the sketch from his satchel, she smiled at the paper as he unrolled it. Flattening the image, he held it up. The Mother Superior crossed herself and then kissed her rosary and muttered a prayer.

Neither of us spoke. Willoughby was about to shake his head at me, but saw I had no intention of interrupting her. We both waited in silence.

'I know this poor soul. Naomi Jenkins, she was quite deranged. She was one of those that lived in that tower of Babel. We would regularly visit and exhort those within to a place of safety. No child of God should ever live in such a monstrosity, but she was one of the very few who wouldn't move. Sometimes she would wander down to the river to swim in only the skin that our maker had clothed her in. I spoke to the dockworkers on many occasions, reminding them she was a child of God and not to be abused.'

'And did the dock hands heed your words?' asked Willoughby gently. It was quite possible that this was a domestic tragedy.

'They did, but sometimes Naomi would swear at me and tell me she enjoyed fornicating.'

My shoulder slumped. We had so many battered souls in Norwich.

'Do you think the men ever mishandled her?' I asked. 'Did you ever see signs of cuts or bruises?'

She looked at me and shook her head.

'No, I think both sides took what comfort they could find, but if a stranger encountered her...'

Chapter Twenty-Five

 The rest of the morning saw us going from door to door showing people the image of William Cade and enquiring after Naomi.

She had been born in the tower after the meld. She had taken to swimming naked in the river before the moon rose and sometimes sleeping with men for the fun of it. Naomi had enough food, and like all the city's lost souls, was taken care of in terms of health, money and safety. Right up until the moment she was murdered. Her carer said she was one of his less troublesome souls. He had fifty on his patch and she was one he could always rely on to be happy when they met. She was just addled.

We had less success with Cade. Several people had sighted a stranger wandering around the stone walls in the past two days. He had been heard talking to himself, often quite violently, but no one had been able to confirm that the man in the photo was the same person skulking in the shadows.

'So, now what?' I asked. I knew what I wanted to do, but I was the guest on this investigation.

'It's lunch. I say you reacquaint yourself with your friend. I'll go back to the Watch House and write up this morning's notes. Then I suggest we grab a bite to eat and head down to the docks. If Naomi was known down there, it's possible that one of her assignations went awry.'

A delicate way to describe having been murdered and carved up, but I agreed with his game plan and headed back towards the convent.

Jennifer was sitting on a bench just inside the convent walls. It was where we always climbed in and now I realised the nuns had placed it there to break our fall should we fall off the wall. A tiny kindness that I had never noticed before.

Looking at my friend, I paused to study her. Her hands placed neatly on her lap with her wimple framing her face. Her eyes were closed and I wondered if she was actually praying. I didn't want to startle her, so I called out as I approached.

'Ah ya got a loight?'

She flicked her eyes open, a huge grin on her face.

'Oi moight.'

I threw myself down on the bench beside her, grinning.

'I take it you don't actually smoke anymore?'

'Gave up the day I joined the convent. What about you?'

'Not long after I arrived in London. Turns out eighteen-year-olds smoking pipes and swearing like navvies wasn't "cool".'

'Since when did you care about cool?'

Since I was desperate to blend in and not draw attention to myself, I thought. Back then, very few people were allowed to leave Norwich. I had put my name in the draw and been unsuccessful, so I left one night via the river and walked to London. It had taken weeks and by the time I arrived, I looked like any old city beggar. I found a shelter that took me in. My youth was in my favour and I applied to the police force. The pay was decent, they had lodgings and best of all, an entrance exam. No qualifications needed. I faked my home address and started again. It was only during the medical that I had to properly disclose where I came from, but the doctor was kind to me and waved me through.

'Looking cool in London is also not cool,' I laughed. 'It's a tightrope, really. They all care desperately about not caring. Unless it's something that someone really popular cares about, and then that's the only thing that matters.'

'Sounds exhausting.' Fen pulled out two apples from her pockets and handed one to me. 'They don't taste as good if you haven't pinched them, but Sister Mary Margaret said she hoped you enjoy it, nonetheless.'

I took the apple and bit into it, its sweet juices filling my mouth.

'Tell her it tastes even sweeter knowing I'm not about to get caned.'

We munched our apples for a bit and then she looked me up and down.

'So you're a detective?'

'Yep. Look, I've got a badge and everything.' I pulled my hair out of the way and Fen laughed.

'That is proper fancy. Imagine you a copper. Talk about asking the fox to mind the hens.'

I gave her a playful punch.

'You know you should tie your hair back so everyone can see who you are.'

'And have everyone gawp at my scars?'

Fen blinked. 'Who the hell would do that? Is that why you grew your hair? To hide? Bloody hell, Bish. That doesn't sound like you.'

I bit my apple again and looked up at the sky.

'Not so much disfigurement in London.'

'Disfigurement? Hell Bish, you look like half the population and at least all your limbs work.' She shoved up her sleeve and pointed to the wasted left arm. That had been polio when she was fourteen. 'Is London really so shallow?'

I wasn't sure how to address the utter depths to which London's insecurities could sink a person, so I changed the subject.

'So, she's okay then, Sister Mary Margaret? And life as a nun is really okay?'

Fen gave my hand a squeeze and I was grateful that she was happy to drop the subject.

'It is, yes. I hated that we parted on such horrible terms, but I was sick of living in fear.'

'You! Afraid. Don't be mad.' But she'd said the same thing last time and I wouldn't hear it then either. I paused. 'Were you really scared?'

'Terrified. Every day. Running with you made me feel safe, but when you weren't around, everything loomed in on me. All I wanted was my own home. Knowing I'd be safe at night. Never wondering where my next meal would come from.'

'We could have got jobs. Found decent blokes. Had kids. That would have been safe?'

'I couldn't bring children into this world.'

'It's not that bad,' I protested, but God knows I had fled Norwich the minute Fen said she was becoming a nun.

'Your foster folk were good people.' Like me, Fen had lost her family in the plague.

'They were, but who knows when another outbreak of some vile disease hits us again? People are driven mad living here. When the bells rang the other night, I spent the rest of the night shaking in fear that more people I knew would have disappeared.'

'Is it really still so bad?'

She ate her apple for a moment and then threw the core over to one of the sheep in the pen.

'In truth, no. Things are a lot better. So much better, but I just can't shake the fear of being a child in Norwich. It seems to have got into my bones.' She paused again. 'Enough about me. I am very happy here in the convent. I made the right choice. What about you? Living in old London Town. What's it like? How many parties do you go to? Have you been in a car? What about a plane? How many friends do you have? What's your house like? Are you married?'

She got faster and faster as she sped through her questions and I remembered Fenface sitting on top of an oak barrel shouting out instructions to our little gang, laughing and bossing everyone around before the sun set and we all returned to our homes and shelters for the night.

'Still got the old verbal diarrhoea then?'

'Oh yes. I am daily reminded to keep my thoughts in an orderly manner.'

'Good luck with that!'

'I know. So tell me. London, all that you hoped?'

I ruffled Harry's nape to hide my face and then looked up, smiling.

'And then some. Wouldn't have left it for the world, but I'm really glad I had the chance to come back here and see you.'

'You'd have called on me? Even if we weren't involved in the investigation.'

'Absolutely,' I lied. I hoped that lying to a nun wasn't one of the many reasons that her God would smite me. I suspect it was. 'Look, let's catch up tomorrow. Are you allowed out?'

'It's not prison, Bish. We could go for lunch now if you'd like.'

I gripped her hand. I'd have loved that, but I was in the middle of a murder enquiry, plus trying to track down Cade. Catching up with old friends would have to wait.

'Would that I could, old bean! Would that I could. But one of us has to earn a living.' I kept my tone light, not wanting to remind her I was on a murder investigation. 'What about tomorrow?'

'Tomorrow it is, then.' She squeezed my hand back. 'I'll be praying for your success.'

I shrugged. I wasn't sure how much good that would do, but I didn't want to insult or mock her.

'Look, there is something you can do to help. Besides the praying,' I said quickly as she raised an eyebrow. 'The nuns over at the cathedral. Are they the same as your lot? The same order?'

'They're not. They're nice enough, but I don't think the two Mother Superiors get along.'

'Duelling nuns, hey?'

'Something like that. So what's up?'

'Do you get your clothes from the same place?'

Her face was priceless. 'Planning on a wardrobe upgrade? Had enough of your jeans? Maybe you fancy a wimple to hide your lovely long hair?'

'Wally. No, the bishop said some of her socks are going missing. I wondered if you had noticed the same thing.'

'Oh my God. You met her! Finally.' Fen clapped her hands in delight. 'I thought it was a dreadful irony that she arrived after you had left. How was it?'

'Honestly, I didn't know. She just said she was the bishop and to call her bloody Isidora. Lady Julian of Norwich and there was me talking to her like she was any old member of the clergy.' I groaned and put my face in my hands as Fen laughed kindly.

'Never thought I'd see you impressed by anyone.'

'Lady Julian!' I protested and Fen agreed my awe was justified.

'So she wants you to investigate missing socks?'

We were both laughing out loud now and the sheep had moved away.

'After all these years and when you meet her, she has a complaint about hosiery.'

'Darn it!'

And we fell about laughing some more. Eventually, we composed ourselves and I stood up reluctantly. I would have loved to stay longer, but at this rate I'd be late to meet Willoughby.

'Tell you what,' said Fen, 'I'll ask for laundry duties this afternoon. Then I can head over to the mill and see if they know anything about the case of the sinister socks.' I walked off laughing as she shouted out one final set of instructions. 'And tie your hair back. Be proud and let people know you are an acting officer of the Watch. That's a badge of honour.'

Chapter Twenty-Six

 I was still grinning as another nun came running over to chide her for shouting like a dock hand. I left her to it and Harry and I made our way towards the river. I wanted to revisit the crime scene on route. Lunch would have to wait.

It was strange heading down from Ber Street to Rouen Road. The tower block had been a constant feature on the landscape and now it was gone. The steps had also gone, so I gingerly made my way down the escarpment. The area was now wild pasture with a little row of houses. I wondered when they would be able to return. All that open meadowland was going to be tempting for livestock use. Of course it also made it vulnerable to new buildings via a quake, but that wasn't my problem. Later maps no doubt showed houses on this piece of pastureland. Another quake could restore them.

I slid the last few metres and walked into the pasture. I recognised a figure sitting on a chair outside one of the houses and I made towards him. He was whittling a piece of wood, the shavings piling up in the grass around his feet.

'Morning, Mike.'

He looked up at the sun.

'Afternoon's more like,' he said, and I checked my watch. I'd lost the knack of just knowing the time. 'Can I help?'

'Just getting a feel for the area in daylight. Meeting Willoughby down by the docks. What are you doing?'

'Watching.' His disgust was clear and I remembered that today he was supposed to be at his best friend's wedding.

'What for?'

'The usual. Make sure the pigs are fed, that the chickens don't get eaten. That no one steals any belongings. But mostly to watch out for stragglers.'

My puzzlement was obvious.

'A quake picks up waifs and strays. Roman soldiers out on patrol, goose girls walking their flock to market. Pilgrims asleep in the field. Depends how many maps were involved in the meld.'

'What about Cade?'

'Your practitioner?' He shook his head. 'Not a peep.'

'Will you make it to the wedding?'

He smiled at me, surprised that I'd remembered, and then nodded. 'Hitchman is sending a replacement presently. He's the best, you know.'

There was nothing to say to that, so I nodded politely, unable to vocalise an agreement, and headed over to the roped off crime scene. In the cold light of day, all there was to be seen was dark blood amongst the flattened grass. Two swallows swooped overhead and, in the distance, I could hear the sheep up at the convent. Life had a horrible way of going on. Death in the countryside always seemed so unsettling, its inevitability was more acceptable. There was nothing to see here, just life and death and ladybirds climbing up the grass stalks. Harry sniffing the ground, hunting out mice, his tail wagging furiously.

I turned away and, giving Mike a wave, headed over to the river. The Wensum provided Norwich with its eastern defences and, in many ways, it was even more powerful in keeping the coherency of the city structure intact. Magic and water don't mix. There is an innate power in water. It is always in the same place but always moving. You can never enter the same section of river twice. A lot of theoretic practitioners say water has its own power that eludes engineered magic. Whatever the cause, being on, or in the river, kept you safe, but the moment you stepped off into the landscape beyond, you faced the risk of wild magic. And if you stayed in the river too long, you were likely to be washed away to a different century as the river course changed over time. On the maps, the Wensum went all over the place.

Looking across the water, there were days when you could see football stadiums come and go, railways stations rise and fall. And as each quake raced across the maps, it crashed against the river and fell back on itself.

This was the southernmost section of the city and to my right I could see the wall running down to the final section where it joined the river. Traders sailed in this way from various centuries, unknowingly protected by the river. The dock buildings themselves were mostly wood and brick and if the arriving sailors thought things looked a little strange, their observations weren't welcome and no one sailed past the old bridge. Goods were unloaded, payment was made without question and off they sailed to their distant historic shores, none the wiser that they had sailed into the twenty-first century and back out again.

When they arrived back at Genoa, Antwerp, London or Seville, they had been paid handsomely for their cargo. Goods only went one way. The UN had decided it was fine for us to receive, but not to export. Which was a shame because I was certain the past would be grateful for elastic and ibuprofen.

I tried to imagine the direct path from the old high-rise down to the river. If Naomi was in the habit of a nighttime swim, I imagine she walked in a straight line. And then what? Would she have slid in off the jetty, or found a section of riverbank and walked in that way?

'Oi, petal. Fancy a tumble?'

I was shaken out of my reverie to observe a dockhand grabbing his testicles in what I presume was supposed to be a provocative manner. He was standing outside one of the wharfs smoking a white clay pipe and leering intently. I headed towards him, keeping

Harry on a tight lead and making sure my baton was ready to deploy. What I'd have given for an em-gun right now, but a length of steel would have to suffice.

'I'm sorry. Would you care to repeat that?'

'Oh very lah-di-dah. I said,' he licked his lips, 'do you fancy a tumble? I've got coins.'

'I imagine you also have crabs.'

He stopped, grabbing his crotch.

'And I daresay fleas as well. And when did you last wash your hands?'

'Why you smart mouthed little cunny.' He pulled a knife from his pocket and took a step towards me. I removed the baton from my belt.

'Oh, fancy a fight, is it? Maybe I'll take what I want anyway and give you a good kicking after, instead of a coin. Come on, then.'

I tried to decide the best way to handle this. I wasn't sure what to do with Harry. I imagined the dockhand would first try to incapacitate the dog before turning his attentions on me. It would be what I would do if I was planning on attacking someone. Eliminate additional threats. He was also expecting me to use the baton, seeing as how I had deployed it. I released Harry, passed the baton to my left hand and then stepped towards him.

'Changed your mind, have you?' He leered. 'Drop the stick and we can play nicely.'

I smiled, walked right up to him and punched him on the nose, driving my fist forwards. His head flew back in a spray of blood as he howled in pain. I stepped back and he ran at me. This time I ducked and swung the baton at his shins. As the steel hit bone with a satisfying crack, he fell to the floor. Harry was now barking and jumping back and forth at my attacker.

'You broke my leg?'

'Not yet I haven't. Shall I try again?'

'I'm going to call the Watch on you.'

I pulled out my whistle and started blowing. A few moments later, three men came running along the wooden wharfs. Now I had to hope to God they would side with me or I was going to have to throw myself in the river, assuming I could get to it before they got to me.

Two of the men were whipcord thin, their bare arms covered in tattoos and their teeth stained with tobacco. The third was broader and shorter. A bulldog between two hounds. The bulldog was the first to react.

'Get your dog on a lead, miss. Sam, you stay where you are.'

Sam, my would-be assailant, stayed on the ground but was now groaning loudly and claiming that I had assaulted him.

He looked between the two of us as I called Harry to heel. I didn't feel safe yet, but in calling Harry to me, I had taken a few steps closer to the water.

'Right then, miss. What are you doing down by the wharfs? This isn't a safe place, no matter how you're dressed.'

'I can walk where I like.'

'That you can. But some places are safer than others.'

'The magic doesn't bother me, it's the monsters I have issues with.' I tossed my head in the direction of Sam.

'Agreed.'

We all turned as a voice shouted from further along the wharf. Two people were running in our direction. It was Willoughby and a woman in suede trousers, a white blouse and a leather waistcoat. The man on the ground groaned. This time, he sounded like he meant it.

'Bish, are you okay?' Willoughby walked straight up to me. His eyes were narrowed and he was breathing heavily, his walking cane was raised high and I looked at the pommel in a new light. One swing from his cane and any attacker would be quickly felled. As he reached my side, he barked at the three men. 'What's happened?'

They looked nervously over to the woman, who was now standing with her arms on her hips and a mutinous expression on her face.

'Samuel. How many times have I warned you? Bill, Jake, Micah, were you involved in this?'

Bill, the bulldog of the three, spoke quickly. I noticed that Samuel had fallen silent and was now sweating heavily.

'No, ma'am. We heard a whistle blowing and we ran to see what was happening. The young lady was holding a whistle and a truncheon. Samuel was on the ground and her dog was barking at him. We didn't see what happened.'

'She attacked me. Set her dog on me. Then hit me with a metal bar.'

'In your face?'

'No, that's where she punched me. She hit me in the legs with the bar.'

He had raised himself to a seated position now and was rubbing his shins gingerly and pointed to the two large lumps that I had inflicted.

'Bish,' said Willoughby carefully. 'What happened?'

'This man asked me for sexual favours for which he would recompense me in coinage. I declined and then he approached me with a knife, saying he would no longer pay me and would take me as he wanted.'

The three men winced and hung their head. The woman folded her arms.

'Then what?' continued Willoughby calmly.

'I took evasive manoeuvres whilst ensuring Harry's safety and this man's incapacitation.'

Willoughby turned to the woman and nodded.

'Hortense, are you okay with the river?'

She nodded her head grimly. 'Absolutely. He's been on borrowed time for the past year. Not capable of learning a simple lesson, are you, Sam? This time you swim.'

He shot to his feet, but the three men blocked his exit.

'You can't do this. You need two officers of the law. You don't count, mistress.' He turned to Willoughby. 'The Harbourmaster don't count as an officer of the law.'

'No, but she does,' said Willoughby, pointing to me.

'She's the victim. I know my rights for the river. One employee, three contemporaries, one victim, two officers of the law.'

'You forgot the three strikes,' said the woman, 'and this is your fifth strike.'

'But you still need a second officer. Call Jacob.'

'We're not calling your uncle,' said Willoughby. 'You've shamed him enough. Besides, Bish here is not just the victim. Allow me to introduce Detective Eliza Barnaby.'

My hair had fallen forward again, covering my badge, and now I pulled it to one side, revealing the golden badge. That seemed enough for the three men as they closed in on their former workmate.

'No!' shouted Sam. 'After that quake, you know how unsteady the land is right now. I won't stand a chance.'

'Too late for that,' said Hortense. 'Boys, throw him in.'

'Wait.' I was all for summary justice, but this couldn't happen. 'Willoughby. This man could be our murderer. We know Naomi swam here, we know she was known to the men.' The tall man with an anchor tattooed on his forearm picked at his fingers. 'And we know he's happy to use a knife on a woman. He even told me he would carve me up.'

Willoughby frowned, but nodded in agreement.

'We have to interview him at the very least,' I went on.

'Yes, that's right,' shouted Samuel triumphantly. 'I could have killed her. You need to find out if I did or not.'

He was a sly bastard, I'll give him that. Presumably, he thought if he could buy time, he could somehow forestall his punishment. Although stepping up for murder was a risky move.

'Naomi were murdered night 'fore yestereve,' said the man with the tattoo. 'Samuel were in the stocks for twenty-four hours over at the Maddermarket for spitting at schoolgirls.'

Willoughby pulled out his radio.

'Alys. Can you confirm who was in the stocks at Maddermarket? Yesterday and the day before.'

We all stood silent as Alys consulted her ledgers.

'Samuel King. Address Polypin Yard. Works at the docks.'

Willoughby nodded, thanking Alys, and hung up.

'There you go, Sam. You're in the clear for the murder of Naomi Jenkins.'

Hortense stepped forward.

'Samuel King. I sentence you to the river.'

Chapter Twenty-Seven

 It all happened so quickly. One of the men removed the chains from the posts. Bill and the other man grabbed his arms and dragged him to the edge of the platform and with a practiced move, they shoved him hard off the edge of the wooden boards. He flailed desperately and then fell backwards into the water. I ran forwards. It was instinctive and Willoughby grabbed my arm.

'You can't save him.'

We watched as he tried to swim to the posts of the jetty, but the current was moving quickly and pulled him out to the centre of the river and then to the bank on the far side. Pulling himself out of the river, he stood and bent over. His hands on his knees as the water dripped off him and he tried to regain his breath.

'All gates,' said Willoughby into his radio. 'Samuel King has been lawfully dispatched to the river. Stay vigilant against his return.'

From the other side of the bank, Samuel stuck his middle finger up at us then climbed up the bank and ran against the flow of the river. Time splintered and I saw him walking in a crowd of football supporters all wearing yellow and green, cars and buses moved slowly, careful of the hordes as everyone moved towards the football stadium in the background and then just as suddenly the scene returned to green fields and not a single soul.

'Well, he's gone then,' said Bill. 'I thought I heard chanting?'

The others shook their heads. They hadn't seen or heard anything. I stayed quiet. I was shaken by the speed of justice. A man had just been obliterated from our timeline. He could be dead, he could be existing in a previous timeframe, we had no way of knowing. All we knew was that people dispatched to the river never returned. I shook my head. That was thinking like a victim. He died because of his own actions. I was simply an unwitting protagonist.

'Bish?' said Willoughby cautiously. I didn't need a partner treating me with kid gloves. I took a deep breath.

'Now what?'

He pursed his lips and, having looked across the river again, shook his head.

'Now we continue with our investigation. We already have all the workers' statements but Hortense suggested we might want to chat with Micah here.'

I nodded, but my brain was still spinning. Was throwing a man to his death, a change of existence, banishment, whatever, the right thing? And to do it so fast? And what had he actually done? Been unpleasant. Drawn a knife. Did his punishment fit the crime?

'Bish?' Willoughby was talking, and I turned away from the river. 'Are you well?'

I nodded again. Hortense and two of the men had returned to work, leaving the man with the anchor tattoo.

'The Harbourmaster thinks you may be able to tell us a bit more about Naomi?'

He picked at his fingers again, blood beginning to well at the base of his nail, filling the splits and callouses. Willoughby waited in silence. The best way to interview anyone was to leave them enough space to talk into. The compunction to fill it is an overwhelming trait in most of us. As officers, we quickly learn how to stay quiet and wait.

'She meant no harm. She just liked swimming.'

We remained silent.

'I never forced myself on her. She asked for it.'

When they say stuff like this, it becomes very hard not to speak. He must have seen my expression change and spoke quickly.

'Weren't like that. I meant as, she literally asked me. Said she was lonely. I said no for ages and she thought it was funny. She would swim upstream and then pull herself out on the ladder here. I'd watch her go in at the Waterfront Tavern and then I'd walk along the banks and wharfs ready to jump in if she got in trouble. But she were a natural. I'd watch her pale body, drifting through the dark water, and it felt like praying. Like she were an angel or summat. Her arm would break the surface to splash water at me. She'd laugh and then dive under the surface. I told her it was dangerous and she

253

said she didn't care.' He broke off and glared at us. His eyes were red with unshed tears. 'She were like that. Didn't care about rights and wrongs and shoulds and shouldn'ts.'

'So how long had you been intimate with her?' asked Willoughby, carefully. Harry had moved over to Micah's side and had sat down by his feet. The man's sadness was obvious, but that didn't mean he wasn't guilty.

'This past month. Asked her to marry me, didn't I. Like a bloody fool. She laughed and said we were married. She said she was married to me and the river and the fields and the sky. She used to say daft stuff like that all the time.'

'And how did that make you feel?'

'Sad and happy. Gave her a cloak, didn't I. I wanted her to be warm when she came out of the water.' He wiped his face with his hand. 'Is it wrong of me to ask if I can have it back? It's all I have to remind me of her.'

No cloak had been found and I looked at Willoughby. He shook his head.

'Micah, can you describe the cloak? If we find it, we will try to return it to you?'

'It was red. A long cloak in red wool with a cream linen lining. She said it made her feel like a fairy-tale princess.'

His voice broke for a second.

'Sir, I know you have already given your alibi, but would you mind telling me where you were the night before last?'

He rubbed his eyes with his fists and then wiped his cheeks dry.

'Over at Maddermarket with the lads. We'd been pelting Samuel with eggs. He used to bother Naomi and I went to town, egging him in the stocks. If I hadn't been so hellbent on punishing him, I'd have been with her, watching her swim. She'd have never died.'

He started crying again and Harry nudged his leg with his nose. This was what I hated about police work. Seeing humanity in all its misery laid bare.

'Thank you for your time, Micah,' said Willoughby. 'We'll be in touch when we find her cloak. And I promise you. We will find her killer.'

We walked away. Harry kept looking back at the man, but we gave him the privacy of his tears. I felt utterly deflated.

'Okay,' said Willoughby. 'We've ruled out the obvious suspects. It's time to consider Cade.'

We walked slowly along the wharf. Harry was nosing around all the barrels and piles of ropes, enthusiastically running back and forth on his lead.

'Last night when Hitchman had been asking you about Cade, I was under the impression that you might have more to say about the fugitive if the sheriff's interrogation style hadn't been quite so bombastic?'

I was getting used to Willoughby, but needed to be careful about what I said. He seemed very tolerant and hadn't been bothered by how sensitive I was to the flickerings at the convent, but I still hadn't gauged the public attitude to people who were sensitive to magic. That said, I could share what I knew about Cade.

'It's a theory, but I think Cade might be from Norwich.'

He hummed slowly as we continued to walk.

'Would you care to elaborate on your theory?'

'Well, he could map run, which we know is a Norwich thing and I have never seen or heard of it in London. And…' I took a deep breath. I hadn't told anyone this. 'He knew my name. He called me Bish.'

'You think he knows you? Did you recognise him? You said you felt safe. Could that be why?'

I pulled Harry close as he started to get excited by a pile of ropes and a second later, a rat shot across our paths and headed for the water. It gave me time to frame my words.

'That I don't know. I certainly didn't recognise him. Either from London or Norwich. But maybe, as you say, some part of me remembered him. I've been racking my brain since then and I've drawn a blank.'

'Very well. It's an interesting line of enquiry. We can look through the registers and see if a William Cade appears on any of them. If he's local, he might have somewhere to hide.'

'That won't work. I don't think William Cade is his real name. It doesn't follow the proper practitioner structure. I think they are deliberately obscuring his identity.'

'Well, maybe it's his birth name. It's worth investigating.'

I shrugged. Nothing in this case made sense.

'I guess. I don't know why Sheriff Hitchman hasn't issued his likeness throughout the city, though.'

'The sheriff is a good blade, he knows what he's doing. The last thing we want to do is cause a panic. Or worse, a lynching.' He smiled. 'This is good information, and I thank you for your openness. Now let us work together to see what else we can divine.'

'You think Cade's our murderer as well?'

'I have no solid evidence yet to support that hypothesis but I confess this is a likely lead.'

Chapter Twenty-Eight

 As we walked on, I fell back into silence. Willoughby seemed a decent sort, and I was grateful I was working with him. I was out of step in Norwich and was still finding my feet. Our first stop was the Harbourmaster's office, an imposing two-storey building. Thin red bricks below, timber beams with lime plaster panelling between above. The oak front door was double width, with iron studs. I was ready to follow Willoughby indoors when he turned back to me.

'You've been very quiet.'

'Lots to think about.'

'Did that villain take further liberties with your person than you mentioned?'

He seriously thought I was bothered by that.

'A man called me names and now he's dead. Justice in Norwich feels just a teeny bit utterly barbaric.'

Now it was Willoughby's turn to look disgusted.

'Mistress Barnaby. He has been in and out of Bridewell. He has regularly abused women. He took a knife to you. This wasn't his first offence by a very long shot. We don't have space in Norwich for long-term recidivists. You might call what we do barbaric. Even I would say it is brutal. But it has also prevented this city from succumbing to anarchy.'

He was pacing back and forth now.

'You know what this city was like? You grew up here. Tell me honestly.' He stopped and tilted his head. 'Hasn't the city improved?'

I wanted to say yes, because it had, but the price seemed hard to swallow.

'You are only seeing this from the final sharp end. But look at all the benefits. Of course, we still have petty crimes. But murders? We have a population of roughly 30,000. We are a city of really diverse cultures. In the past year, we have had one murder. That's it.

And rapes? Five. The women in this city are safe. They prosper. Our biggest issues come from sectarian violence, but we have that under control. Mostly, the people of Norwich are just trying to stay alive.'

He'd started pacing again. The dockworkers had given us a clear berth. Obviously, Willoughby losing his control was not a sight they were used to. Not that he was shouting, but he sure was exasperated.

'Okay.' I paused. 'Look, I don't know how I feel about it. I've only just arrived and yes, Norwich does seem improved. Vastly improved. And yes, those crime figures are incredible. But it's just…' I tensed. I knew I was being a hypocrite. I was glad he was gone. 'Seeing him just thrown in the river like that. It felt…'

It felt bloody perfect was how it felt, and that was what I was wrestling with. My job was policing, not punishment. Every rapist I sent to prison, every child molester that had their personality neutered. Every time I reminded myself that my job was to catch them.

It was not my place to dole out justice, to judge them. But when I thought about the victims, I wondered who we were serving? I knew every argument against capital punishment, and I agreed with just about all of them. I sighed. It was time to change the conversation.

'Let's talk to the Harbourmaster.'

'Very well.' He walked up the first step, then stopped and turned back. 'When Samuel climbed out of the bank, he ran for a few seconds, then disappeared. Bill thought he heard whistles, but you seemed to keep looking for a bit longer. Did you see anything?'

I shook my head. What was the point? Samuel was dead or as good as, what I'd seen was a scrap of aftershocks. A Norwich that was no more. Five thousand people died when Carrow Road and the railway station were wiped off the map. Despite all the love for the football stadium, it was made in metal and concrete. Being less than a hundred years old, it featured on very few maps and finally it was outside the city walls. I walked past Willoughby and entered the Port Authority building.

The ground floor was low-ceilinged with a few tables dotted around. Several people were busy at work, mostly men, and all appeared to be in rough homespun garments. One of the men looked up from his ledger as we walked in and he waved us upstairs.

To the weary sailor or trader, this scene wouldn't look out of place in any century up to the nineteenth. Admittedly, Norwich would look a little quaint in the eyes of any Victorian and positively medieval to an Edwardian, but it just about passed muster.

Harry had spent most of his time enthusiastically sniffing anything he could lay his nose on and as we climbed the oak stairs, his tail went into overdrive.

'Welcome,' said the woman I had seen earlier. 'I am Hortense Paine. Norwich Harbourmaster and one of the ruling heads of the city. I believe you are Detective Eliza Barnaby. Come to remove an unwanted individual. How may I be of help?'

She indicated two wooden seats with cushions and threw a bone in the corner for Harry.

'We have a lot of cats around here. Best to keep him occupied.'

Harry settled down to chew on the bone and I cleared my throat.

'Have you seen this man?' I pushed the photo of William Cade across the table to her, but she continued to look at me.

'No.'

The silence stretched out.

'Are you sure?'

'I assumed you were smart?'

I blinked and then caught up.

'The sheriff has already shown you the photo.'

'Yes, we had an emergency meeting last night. Which you would have known if you weren't busy getting your knickers in a twist with him about your status. Storming out of meetings shows a lack of professionalism.'

'My God, you people get really pissed at quitters, don't you? How about you focus on what matters?'

'Bish—' muttered Willoughby urgently.

'Nope. I have had it up to here with your bigotry. Yes, I left. Boohoo. Now I'm back. The outrage. If you could just answer my questions without insulting me, I won't be forced to write you up as uncooperative.'

The look on her face was priceless, and then she burst into laughter.

'Well, you have balls. No idea why you quit with a pair like that. Mind you, if I had a way to escape the plague, I might have taken it too.' She pulled open her blouse to show a series of buboes scars running from her breast to her armpit. I tucked my hair behind my ear to show that I hadn't escaped that particular ordeal. She rapped her knuckles on the desk in a way I often did myself and I found myself liking her.

'What do you want to know? Be quick, we have a galleon arriving. I need to make sure we're ready.'

'Thank you, Hortense,' said Willoughby quickly. 'If I can just—'

'No.' Hortense held her hand up. 'She lost him, she can ask the questions.' She looked at me with a raised eyebrow.

'He was last traced three days ago past Wymondham, heading for Norwich. We'd hoped that the wastelands might have taken care of him, but given the death of Naomi Jenkins, I now believe he successfully made it to the city. So we're visiting all points of entry.'

'You need to put an alert out on the radio,' she said sharply. 'Warn the citizens.'

'I agree.'

'Oh.' She muttered under her breath, then continued swearing. 'Joseph Hitchman, you stupid stubborn bastard.'

'Ah,' I said, catching up. 'The sheriff said it was my idea that the public wasn't to be alarmed, I take it? And you believed the sheriff would agree with some quitter about how to run his city. Now who's being stupid?'

'Bish!'

'Ah save it.' Hortense flapped her hand in Willoughby's direction. 'She's not wrong.'

She shook her head.

'What do you want to know?'

'What ships arrived in the last few days?'

'Several have been and gone. We have two in dock and they arrived today. They'll be gone by the morrow.'

That struck me as odd.

'Don't sailors want to stretch their legs when they reach port?'

'Not in Norwich, they don't. We tell them we're in quarantine. There's a bar, with rooms, showers, baths, hot food. No girls. There's only one exit and entry and no one can leave the port area without going through a security check.'

'What's the nature of the security check?'

'Jimbob and Dean.'

Willoughby nodded sagely.

'I'm sorry. Could you elaborate?'

'Jimbob knows everyone that works here. He sits on the gate. Dean barks at anyone that smells funny.'

'That's it?'

'Sounds simple, but you wouldn't believe how many times we've returned stowaways, deserters and sailors looking for a good time before they head back to their boats. Always feel bad about the stowaways because they'll probably get thrown overboard. But it's an uncertain future rather than a certain one. Descent into madness.'

'What about returning Norwich vessels? What do you do about them?'

'They're given a choice. We explain how things stand. We find out if their families were pulled forwards. If they want to join them, they are forever bound to the city. If they want to sail away and hope when they return, they do so to their own timeline, then that is also their choice.'

'What if they talk? Aren't you worried about them damaging the timeline?'

'Sailors spend half their time talking about mythical beasts and magic lands. What is one more tale?'

I wanted to know more, but I was drifting from the situation at hand.

'Okay. Moving on. Did you notice anyone in the past few days that was eager to visit the city? Anyone with a strange dress or an odd way of talking.'

I was mostly theorising out loud. Someone from London should have stood out like a sore thumb amongst a crew of Georgian sailors. Maybe he had arrived earlier, having been caught in a time loop? It seemed far-fetched, but I was grasping at straws. I couldn't think of a better way for him to arrive. She tilted her head.

'This murderer, that escaped from one of your prisons and made it all the way here, knowing what everyone knows about Norwich, thought he'd hitch a lift on a passing boat but did nothing to change his clothes or appearance?'

Her tone was as scathing as I deserved.

'Fair enough. Maybe an unusual accent?'

'In the past two weeks I've had two wherries from London. A barge from the Lowlands and blow me down if a bloody Phoenician boat didn't turn up.'

'Wow!'

'I know. And do you know what they all had in common? Unusual accents.'

I nodded. That's what comes of thinking out loud in front of smart people who don't care about playing nice.

'Can you think of anyway that someone could have got into Norwich via the port unobserved?'

To her credit, she thought about it.

'We don't stop. Even during a quake, hell, during a quake we're even more vigilant. At night, the sally gate is barred and padlocked. I have a key, as do the other city heads.'

'And who are they, please?'

She was not used to being interrupted and pursed her lips.

'The Harbourmaster, the Guildmaster, the Sheriff, the Bishop and the heads of the four leets.'

She raised an eye.

'If I may continue?'

I had been scribbling on my pad and paused. Norwich was split into four boroughs or leets in the local parlance.

'I know the names of the first four, but who run the leets?'

'Annabel Dalton on Timberhill represents Conesford. Thomas Valons on Surrey Street for Mancroft. Charles Brereton Pottergate for Wymer and Ipolite Martineau on Worldsend Lane for Over the Water. Do you require any additional information?'

I smiled as I finished scribbling.

'I shall speak to them all, in turn no doubt. Now please, what if Cade had got himself onto a boat?'

She scoffed at the foolishness of my question.

'If he came in on a boat, well, first he'd have to make his way throughout the Norfolk countryside unscathed and then happen upon a boat heading upstream that was prepared to let him onboard.' She shook her head. 'Honestly, the only way he made it is if he swam all the way upstream at night and then walked into the city further up the river. Course, he could have swum downstream, and tried to come in via the weir. Was he a good swimmer?'

I gritted my teeth. I had no idea, the files had been so flimsy. For the umpteenth time, I cursed the practitioners and their prejudice. The Norwich Watch were as good as any London police force, if maybe a little less by the book. A lot less, actually. The point was that London had inadvertently hampered this investigation and put the lives of Norwich citizens at risk. I was about to call time when I had an idle thought.

'What about smuggling?'

Hortense placed her palms on her desk and stared at me in silence. The fury on her face warned me not to pursue this line of questioning. Like any good copper, I ignored her.

'Didn't you hear me? I was asking about smuggling. Only I noticed a few things around the city that would suggest that modern-day goods are getting in.'

'That's acceptable under the embargo,' she snapped.

'Not this season's trainers or perfumes. Unless items younger than a year can now be traded. Shall I ask my bosses if the terms of the trade embargo have changed?'

She all but snarled as she rose to her feet.

'If there is smuggling, it's not coming through my port. Willoughby, maybe you would like to remind your partner that here in Norwich we stick to the investigation in hand.'

Willoughby had the sense to remain silent.

'I think you'll find Norwich policing is much the same as London's. If we smell a rat, we investigate.'

I rose to my feet and stared into her face.

'However, if you say there's no smuggling, then I'll take your word for it. For now.' I paused and smiled. 'Well, thanks for your time.' Harry had dropped his bone and padded across to me. I'd asked a bunch of questions, most of them were stupid and I gained no clues as to how the bloody hell Cade had got into the city. I had also wound up a powerful individual. 'Incidentally, what do you do about Vikings?'

She took a beat and then shrugged her shoulders.

'If they've come to trade, we let them. If not, we shoot them. Guns beat axes. I don't have time for troublemakers.' She had a cold grin as she said that and I left.

Back out in the sunshine, we headed through security. Jimbob gave me a funny look and Dean did indeed bark at me. Harry barked back, and Willoughby had to quickly introduce me before we headed back into the city.

'You need to tie your hair back. Especially with that gun on your hip.' He rummaged in a pocket, then handed me a black ribbon. I looked at it in bewilderment. I needed an elastic bobble, not a piece of satin to tie my hair back. What was I supposed to do with that?

'If you will permit me?'

He stepped forwards and took my hair in his hand whilst I stood there feeling deeply uncomfortable. It wasn't simply that my scars were all on display, it was that he was standing so close. I stood there as he pulled my hair behind my nape and then with a few quick twists of the wrist, my hair was neatly tied back.

'I've put a few pins in. It should hold for the rest of the day.'

I was uncomfortable as the breeze blew across my face and I was itching to pull my hair back.

'Detective. It's this or you lose the gun. If people can't see the badge, you will cause alarm.'

I muttered that my scars were likely to cause more alarm, but decided to grin and bear it. If Cade was in the city, and it seemed likely he was, I needed to be armed with something he couldn't incapacitate.

'Shall we proceed? What would you like to do first?'

'I want to find out how he got in. Now we interview each gate keeper, especially Heigham Gate.'

That was the gate closest to the weir and responsible for all upstream river travel. Hortense's comment about swimming into Norwich didn't seem so far-fetched if he swam with the flow.

'Agreed,' said Willoughby. 'Come on, then. One gate at a time.'

Chapter Twenty-Nine

We started at the bottom and headed north, but each time the answers were monotonously familiar. The gates were always closed. The ledgers were meticulous.

The gatekeeper at Brazen was very excited about a flock of lapwings, which were apparently early for the year. He had also heard several bitterns, a bird more familiar out on the wetlands to the east.

At St Stephen's Gate, I caught up with Carl Butcher, who petted Harry and showed me my own entry, the caravan's exit earlier that day and nothing else for the whole week prior. So far, no ledger had mentioned anything unusual prior to the quake, no one out walking, no ghost villages popping up and going again.

Walking along the inside of the wall, this section of Norwich was given over to park lands, orchards and allotments. A herd of cattle was wandering under the horse chestnuts, and I mulled over a theory that was taking shape about how Cade had gained entry.

As we headed toward St Giles Gate, the buildings had turned from individual cottages amongst the meadow, back to streets and town houses.

'Bish, would you mind? I need to call on someone?' He was fidgeting, but I couldn't see the issue. 'It's just that I'm at work, and this is a social call.'

'Are you kidding?' I asked in frustration. 'What will five minutes matter? It's not like we're actually making any headway.' Maybe a pause would give me time to process my thoughts. How the hell had Cade got into the city? My money was on the weir. For now, I was relaxed about the idea of a social call, plus I was interested to see who Willoughby was calling on. You can tell a lot about a person by the company they keep.

We turned into a courtyard. All the buildings were red brick and looked down onto a central fountain. A lot of the Norwich yards were higgledy messes of houses leaning on top of each other, roofs at various slants, often chickens running amok. But this one was a place of tranquillity, over the sound of the fountain in the centre, piano music drifted down from an open sash window.

Willoughby walked up the steps to one of the properties and rang on the doorbell. A head poked out from an upper window. She could have been Rapunzel, her hair was so long.

'Nathaniel!' She laughed and then disappeared from view. A few seconds later, the door was flung open by the same girl. She was an absolute vision. Early twenties, maybe. Her long blonde hair fell to a small waist. Her eyes, nose and mouth all seem to have arranged themselves across her face in a manner to elicit a smile. As she beamed at both of us, I couldn't help but smile back. She was dressed in a long regency gown of pale blue with pink ribbons tying off her shoulder-length puff sleeve. Another pink ribbon ran under her bodice and then the rest of the dress dropped as a simple tube to her feet. It was a gorgeous dress, the sort I dreamed of wearing except for the sheer impracticality of it. You couldn't ride a bike or a horse in it. Hell, you couldn't even run in it without hiking it up to your thighs. It was a dress for ladies to simply look lovely in. And this young lady did that very well indeed.

'Nathaniel. I wasn't expecting you so soon.' Her voice was as pretty as her demeanour.

He cleared his throat.

'Miss Lydia. I'm afraid I shall have to cancel our engagement this evening. If you would be so good as to pass on my apologies to your father.'

She scowled and a shadow passed over the sun.

'You're wearing black!'

She looked at him and then glared at me. I didn't take it personally. To her, I represented his work. Clearly, there was no other reason I was standing by his side.

'Lydia, I—'

'Yes, I know. You have a duty.'

He ran his fingers through his hair and then remembered it was tied back. He shook his fingers out of his locks, making a mess of it.

'A girl's life has been unnaturally cut short. Until the miscreant is found, I will not waste my time in idle pursuits.'

I winced.

'Waste your time?' her voice jumped an octave.

'That isn't what I meant.'

'And what if you never catch this killer? Am I to permanently be without my card partner?'

I snorted. I didn't mean to, but she was somehow equating our manhunt to her parlour games. This time her glare was laser focused and most definitely personal.

'Miss Lydia,' I spoke quickly. 'I apologise. It is also my sworn duty to capture this killer.'

She was about to reply when a voice boomed from further back along the corridor. Panic crossed her face, then a look of entreaty as she turned to look over her shoulder.

'What is the meaning of this, Lydia?' An older gentleman came to the doorway by her side. He was in modern dress, a buttoned-down pink shirt, and red chinos. 'Why are you standing in the open-air screeching like a fishwife?'

As she mumbled a quick apology, he shook Willoughby's hand.

'I see you have to cancel this evening. Thought you might.' Willoughby was about to speak when he held up his hand, placing his finger on his lips. 'Say no more, my boy, say no more. You have your job and we all sleep better because of it.'

He turned to me, raising an eyebrow, as Willoughby spoke quickly.

'Sir Nigel, please allow me to introduce Detective Eliza Barnaby. Mistress Eliza is on secondment from London.' He then turned to me, offering a deep bow. 'Eliza, this is Sir Nigel Hoxton, a good friend of mine. A demon at chess and lethal at cards. Certainly don't place a wager if he's in the room.'

Hoxton laughed. 'That's unfair.'

'Forewarned is forearmed,' I said, smiling. 'But I enjoy a game of cards and I certainly enjoy taking money from confident players.'

'Daddy—' Poor Lydia's voice trailed away.

Her father turned and tutted.

'Find your mother and explain your conduct to her.'

As she fled down the corridor, her slippered feet pattered on the floorboard. Even that was done prettily.

'I'm sorry for Lydia's outburst. She was very much looking forward to this evening.'

'As was I,' said Willoughby.

'Detective Barnaby,' said Hoxton. 'I hope to meet you again under better circumstances. Although it is my understanding that you will soon return to London?'

That felt more like a command than an enquiry.

'I'll leave when I've done my job.'

He nodded, then gave a very shallow bow.

'Glad to hear it. London is clearly well served by its officers. As are we.'

He smiled at Willoughby again.

'Now, Nathaniel. I must away and deal with my domestic issues. I shall see you anon.'

As he closed the door, Willoughby dipped his head, then took a deep breath.

'Oh, you are so in the doghouse,' I said, punching him gleefully on the arm. Something about being back in Norwich was bringing my old playfulness back to life. 'Come on, let's focus on work. The sooner we catch our killer, the sooner you can get back to the delightful Lydia Hoxton.'

He coughed as he re-tied his hair and smoothed it down on the nape of his neck.

'There is no understanding between Miss Lydia and myself. We simply spend some time together.'

'Well, I suspect Miss Lydia doesn't see things the same way. She seems a nice sort, though.'

He seemed ready to protest, then shook his head and I swear he blushed.

'The day is passing. If Cade did enter the city, I believe Heigham Gate would have been his best opportunity.'

I agreed. If Norwich had a weakness, it was at the point when the Wensum flowed into the city. The wall stopped on one bank and then continued on the other bank further upstream, where it carried on to create the northern perimeter of the city. This could be where Cade swam in.

My theory was soon quashed. It turned out this pair of gates were even more closely guarded than any other

275

gate and the weir. The turbine dam just beyond, which provided Norwich with its electricity, made life pretty tricky for swimmers if they didn't want to get paddled to death.

Crossing the bridge we entered the section known as Norwich Over the Water. It comprised a quarter of the city, was cut off from the south by the river and protected from the north by the wall. It was also the site of most of the factories. The air was not so sweet on this side of the river. Lots of coal smoke and woollen mills.

Two girls jogged towards us. They were in shorts and running tops, their ponytails swung from side to side. As they passed us, they waved at Willoughby, then carried on.

'Hang on.'

I turned and chased after them.

'Wait up.'

The two girls turned and smiled at me as I surreptitiously examined their footwear.

'I love your trainers!'

'OMG, I know, aren't they the bomb?'

I agreed that they were in fact the bomb, and then asked where they got them from. They mentioned a sportswear shop south of the river. As I thanked them, they bobbed a little curtsy and I returned with a similar little dip and then returned to Willoughby. Curtsying, I wondered which century they were from. They could have even been modern. The bow and curtsy had made something of a resurgence.

'What's the situation with modern goods coming into the city?'

'Tightly monitored.'

'Is this season's footwear on the list of acceptable items?'

'What with our own shoe factories? I don't think so.'

'In that case, Willoughby, I think you have a smuggling problem.'

For the first time since I had met him, Willoughby looked angry.

'That's the second time you've brought that up. Harbourmaster Paine has already educated you on that score and now it seems I must as well. There is no smuggling issue here. What there is, is a rogue practitioner on the loose. One that London failed to properly handle. You would do well to focus on your actual travails and not run after wild geese.'

As we walked on, I felt my playful spirit ebb away. Back at the Watch House, we wrote up our notes in silence and then I headed home. The trainers those girls were wearing had only just been released, I remembered Jodie back in the London office making a big deal about them. Norwich had a smuggling issue and for some reason, Willoughby was trying to hide it.

I had sat down for all of half an hour before my restlessness overwhelmed me. I headed back out the front door, Harry eager to head out into the evening scents.

Chapter Thirty

The evening was falling and the sky was tinged pink and red as the sun set behind the clouds. I could smell wood smoke from various chimneys mingling with the drowsy scent of evening jasmine. As I got close to the pub, the familiar smell of beer and hops filled my nostrils and I realised that what I needed was a beer and some intel.

The Adam and Eve was Norwich's oldest pub. It had always stood in the shadow of the cathedral spire and had once been a brewery run by the monks. Before I left, the brewery had been resurrected through the quakes and the monks were back in charge. Although they had taken a more secular approach to life.

Heading into the pub, most people turned and gave me the customary once over and then, seeing the now clearly displayed badge and gun, just continued to stare.

'A light ale please,' I said to the barman, chatting to a couple sitting at the bar. 'And do you have today's paper?'

A few minutes later, I was sitting in the corner of the pub, reading the news as everyone left me alone. Norviker News was a daily sheet and yesterday's quake was front page news. Naomi's murder was not and I wondered when the press went to roll.

I was unsurprised to find myself on the third page. Thankfully, they hadn't got a photo of me, just a lot of speculation about my appearance and whether I had triggered the quake. The paper suggested I hadn't, but it would keep readers informed should they find out news to the contrary. Following my story and the quake, there were plenty of exhortations to buy tomorrow's paper for further revelations. Details of when and where I was born had already leaked out and I wondered if I had the hen party or my colleagues to thank for that.

The rest of the paper had the normal sort of community reports, hatches, matches and dispatches. Successful operations, prize turnips. The middle section of the paper was full of business details and financial reports. Innovations and progress at the Cambridge facility. Value of imports and exports. I noticed an article on the Thwaite family, whom I had met on my ride across Norfolk. According to the newspaper's bio, Daniel Thwaite was single and rumours were he had caught the eye of a certain young lady on Ber Street. When I was a kid, that was where the brothels were, but now reading the paper I didn't know if they were having a dig, or sharing some genuine gossip.

The ads suggested that clothing retailers seemed to do a roaring business catering to all the centuries. Shoes and hats were also popular, as were hairdressers and make-up salons. Norwich really seemed to be past the worst of it. The back pages were dedicated to various team sports and it looked like football was as popular as hockey. I used to play hockey myself as a kid, running down the streets with a stick in my hand, knocking the hell out of a tin can as we raced past the beggars and jumped over the fallen masonry. Now they played on a pitch. I was getting old.

'May I join you?'

A light voice interrupted my thoughts and I looked up to see Marion Webb in a pair of tailored red shorts and a waistcoat. She looked a lot more modern than I had seen her this morning in homespun, but I was glad of a smiling face. Willoughby hadn't recovered his goodwill towards me and the end of our shift had been uncomfortable.

I smiled and gestured for her to sit down. She had a glass of cider and the condensation was running down the glass and onto the wooden tabletop.

'I know how it feels,' she said, wiping her brow and then pointing at her glass. 'I reckon we're heading for a heatwave.' She sat down and stared at me until I felt uncomfortable.

'I like your hair back like that,' she said finally. 'Surprised no one's asked to buy you a drink.'

I choked on my pint and laughed.

'I'm not.'

'Oh, the gun and the badge? Since when has that ever put a bloke off?' She had a gusty laugh and a few people looked our way. I scowled at them, and they quickly turned back.

'I meant my scars.'

'What about them? Jim over there has a prosthetic foot, so does Martha. Amputations, burns, scars — we have all sorts here and no one gives a sailor's spit. You do look tired, though. Have you eaten?'

I shook my head.

'Right. Let's fix that.'

Jumping up, she headed over to the bar and as I followed her back, I caught the eye of a man leaning against the bar, who raised a pint in my direction. I stared at him until he slowly lowered it back down, then quickly turned away.

Marion sat down again. 'Five minutes and food's on its way. When I get home, I'll pop some hair bobbles through your letterbox and some cream for the scars.'

'Does it make them vanish?' I muttered.

'Vanish!' She laughed loudly again and I tried to avoid scowling at anyone that looked our way. I failed. 'No, I'm not a magician, am I? But it will take some of that redness out and soften the skin somewhat. Just because you have to live with something doesn't mean you should suffer, does it? And stop with the glare. Now then, how's your day been? I've spent mine delousing Puritans. Yours has to be better than that, so cheer me up and spill.'

She finally paused and took a long swig of her cider and I was impressed she didn't choke. I thought about what I could discuss. I wasn't good at small talk or chitchat or even basic socialising.

'Are there still brothels on Ber Street?'

I was getting used to the laugh. I may even have smiled back.

'Are you looking for company?'

I blushed and pushed the paper towards her, pointing to the section about Daniel Thwaite.

'I was curious. He told me to look him up for a drink when I get back and I just wondered–' I trailed off, uncertain what I was asking.

'You wondered if he has a sweetheart there or if he rents his pleasures by the hour?'

I nodded mutely and had to endure her slapping me on the arm as she continued to chuckle.

'I wouldn't believe a word of it. There's always gossip about the traders. Go for that drink and ask him yourself. There's a few brothels on Ber Street, but not so many these days. They're more scattered around the city. Safe, healthy and well-regulated from what I hear, and the men and women are very much in charge. It's not like they have to do it, poverty not being a Norwich problem. But you know, some people enjoy it, and who am I to pass judgement?'

She raised an eyebrow, daring me to contradict her, so I did the smart thing and took a sip of my beer. How people made their living was not down to me. So long as they were safe and there of their own free will, that was enough for me.

'And how's your investigation going? Have you caught the magician yet? Or found out who the girl is?'

'I can't really talk about it. You know, ongoing investigation.'

'It'll be all over the paper tomorrow. I just, well, I was just a bit worried about the practitioner. I've never met one. They weren't so powerful back when I come from.'

Turns out Marion was an eighteenth-century girl when practitioners were just beginning to come into their ascendency, and as she'd only been here five years, she'd missed all the initial chaos.

'Should I be scared?' She spoke quickly and took another gulp of cider. Under all the bonhomie, this was what was bothering her. And maybe many others in the city as well.

'We're following several leads and hope to capture him as soon as possible.'

'But are we safe? What if he sets off another quake just by being here? Like he did with the tower.'

'We don't know that was him.' I tried to gather my thoughts and as I did, I noticed a few of the surrounding tables had fallen quiet.

'It's like this. Out in Norfolk, the countryside is awash with an excess of wild magic following the cataclysm and that magic causes pockets of instability.' I checked she was following along and noticed one or two heads from the neighbouring table nodding. 'Now, inside the city, those same levels of magic have been stabilised by the buildings, by the walls and the streets.

They have reabsorbed the wild magic and keep us safe from the fluctuations.'

'But what about the quakes? We still get those. Is having a practitioner in the city going to mess it all up?'

'No. At least I don't think so. First off, most of the quakes happened in the early days because of the maps back in Oxford warping and drying out. I believe that rarely happens now?' She nodded and I saw two people at another table having a muttered conversation before breaking off as I continued. 'Practitioners engineer magic with the spells and artifices. And that engineered magic is what causes the problems. Summoning wild magic to engineer when there is so much in the atmosphere is akin to standing on a powder keg and letting off sparks. It's going to end badly.'

'So this practitioner is really dangerous?'

I needed to choose my words carefully. I didn't want to terrify people and by now I clearly had the ears of half the pub.

'Not necessarily. If he doesn't cast a spell, he's harmless, and even if he does, it isn't a given that he'll set off a quake. You all live with the magic every day. Some of you may even lean on it a little. Doesn't mean you're practitioners or anything, but if the butter churns better than normal, or you remember the answers for your test, or any other small acts, you are using the magic and nothing happens.'

There was a sense of wariness as I said that, and I felt I had touched on a taboo subject.

'None of us are practitioners,' said Marion quickly.

'I just said that. I just meant that you've learnt to live with magic. We know it affects us. Some succumb to the madness, others get an A in their exams. There's nothing wrong with that. What we are hoping is that this practitioner succumbs to the madness before he does any damage.'

'Any *more* damage,' muttered a man on my neighbouring table and the pretence of quietly listening in had all but vanished as many faces now turned my way.

'We don't know Normandie Tower had anything to do with him. It could have been a straightforward map quake. I mean, who would have laid a bet on it standing this long?'

There was a lot of agreement in the room at that question.

'But what about the victim? I heard he murdered someone,' called out a woman's voice from further down the pub.

'Again, we have no evidence to suggest he was involved. We are not yet treating him as our prime suspect.' We were, or at least I was, but they didn't need to know that. 'We do ask that if you have any information, you let us know immediately and if you see anyone acting strangely – stranger than usual – that you report them immediately. Do not approach them.'

'What does he look like, then? Why haven't the police issued his image?'

Because the sheriff didn't want a mob chasing after a deranged practitioner who could then annihilate half the city. I chose different words.

'Sheriff Hitchman knows what he's doing.'

Invoking the sheriff's name seemed to cause several patrons to mutter and take a drink. The volume in the pub dropped and it seemed that the taste for gossip and speculation had been dampened by the mere mention of his name.

'Here you go ladies. Tatties and Links. And some for the dog as well.'

A young lad with an apron tied around his waist placed two bowls in front of us along with salt, vinegar and relishes. I leant forward and breathed in deeply as my mouth watered. In each bowl was a mound of small sausages and roast potatoes. The tatties' fluffy crispy edges were sprinkled with salt and thyme, the links were this side of burnt and perfect. I groaned with delight and tucked in.

As Marion chatted, I began to get an idea of how the city functioned these days. We didn't speak about magic again, but I saw from the reactions of the others that they were slowly embracing it, if not accepting it. The city was clearly thriving and desperate not to slide back into the anarchy I remembered. I hoped to God I found Cade before they did. Refusing a second pint, I headed home.

'I don't know, Harry. That didn't go as expected.'

I walked along the unlit streets, moonlight and memory guiding my way. Everything was out of step in my head, the reality of my experience was not aligning with my memories or assumptions. Harry was a dog. Dogs were terrifying. I was scared of dogs. Harry was wonderful. 'You are, aren't you? Look, I'm even talking out loud to you.'

We walked on in a companionable silence, Harry keeping his own council, me lost in my thoughts. After I had killed Mr Wagsalot, I had been wary of dogs, certainly, but had I been terrified? I didn't remember that. There were too many other things in Norwich to concentrate on. Everything in Norwich was scary.

It was only when I got to London and life became simpler that my fear of dogs bloomed like fungal spores seeping into my brain, hampering the pathways between rational thought and irrational panics. And that fungal bloom spread in my brain, I saw that now. Norwich itself became a canker in my mind, choking down the memories of the good times and only leaving the terror and despair.

London seemed so easy, so clean, and it was. Every time Norwich was mentioned, it was full of superstition and ridicule and I found I had cultivated a ground ripe for those seeds of revulsion to grow. I was desperate to forget the people I had let down and left behind, and in doing so I reshaped my reality.

Harry whined and I stopped, looking around me. For a moment, I didn't know where I was. It was darker here. I had wandered down a small alleyway, the moonlight ignoring this little stretch of tall, dilapidated buildings leaning over each other. The smell was also more astringent down here and I was careful where I trod. Night soil was a common occurrence and stank to high heaven. I swore to myself and ruffled Harry's neck.

'Nothing to worry about, Harry. I've walked into the maps, hang on.'

As he continued to whine, I turned around and walked back along the alleyway until I stepped back onto Pigs Lane and the twenty-first century.

'Sorry Harry, bad habit when deep in thought.'

That alleyway was once a shortcut to the Great Hospital, now long gone. I had often run it when no one was looking. It had been over a decade since I had last run the maps and I was a little surprised by how easily it had come back to me.

Now I'd have to go the long way round and concentrate. There was a killer on the loose and a terrified population. The two were a very dangerous combination and it was down to me to resolve it.

Chapter Thirty-One

I stretched out under the crisp linen sheets and groaned. The bells were chiming six and I had overslept. The skies were blue so I decided I'd wear a skirt today, the heat was already building and I could smell the lavender from the garden filling the air. It was going to be a hot one.

'Harry, I don't know how you manage in that fur coat.'

I pulled the skirt out of my rucksack but it was one of those dreadful suit skirts with a poly lining and I knew I'd be sweating by lunch, which only left my tailored shorts but I was on a murder investigation. If Willoughby was wearing black, shorts were probably out. Grumbling, I pulled my chinos on and made my way to the refectory.

Yesterday, Willoughby and I finished our investigations in virtual silence and then went our separate ways. He was clearly fed up with me and quite frankly I was fed up that the city's legal systems seemed to be wantonly turning a blind eye to localised smuggling.

He was right on one thing, it was not why I was here. I was here to apprehend Cade and the sooner I did that and got out of this hellhole the better. There were too many echoes stretching forward and slapping me off my balance. I had gone to bed full of resolve to get up early and try to crack the case.

I stretched and peeled myself out of bed, running over yesterday's events and my trip to the pub the previous night when a thought occurred to me and I sat back on the bed. I knew how Cade had entered the city and I was a bloody fool not to have seen it before. Slapping my hands on my thighs, I grinned at Harry.

'Now we're getting somewhere! Okay, breakfast.'

Popping Harry on his lead, we headed off across the quadrant. A few other people were also making their way there and they nodded at me as we made our way in. I wasn't in the mood to chat though and sat at the far end of a long trestle table. The room was already half empty and by the look of the plates stacking up over by the serving hatch, I was one of the later risers.

A young lad came over and offered me a bowl of porridge, which I eagerly accepted. He came back with a bone for Harry and a cup of coffee.

'Mistress Barnaby?'

It was the matriarch from the arrivals group. This morning she was dressed in a matching Puritan ensemble of plain black dress and white blouse embellished with a little hint of absolutely nothing. New arrivals were likely to lose their minds so had to be handled carefully, otherwise I'd have reminded her I was a detective.

'Good morning. Would you care to join me?'

She sniffed the air disdainfully and then sat down, her back ramrod straight as she frowned at my coffee.

'That drink is disgusting.'

'Would you prefer tea?'

She recoiled.

'Do you mean to tempt me with your riches? Do you think I will succumb so easily?'

I sighed.

'You still think this is hell, then. And we're all demons?' I drank my demonic beverage and smiled as the boy came over and refilled my cup. I noticed he kept well away from the woman's reach. She wasn't speaking, but she had clearly come over to say something. I tried again.

'What's your first name? You know mine and good manners would suggest we balance that, otherwise you are in my debt.'

'You speak like a devil.'

'What can I say?' I snapped. 'I am not a devil. There is no God, no Satan, no heaven or hell. You're in Norwich and it is the year of our Lord two thousand and twenty-five.'

I was only on my second cup of coffee. I was angry at Willoughby, angry at Norwich and angry at a world that had magic in it. That was my excuse for behaving so unprofessionally in front of a new arrival.

'An apostate!' She crossed herself.

'An apostate who has given you something and received nothing in return.'

I turned round and caught the eye of the young lad, who came across smiling.

'Please could I have a cup of tea? The one favoured by Lady Julian and a glass of water.'

Nodding he left with a smile. I turned my attention back to the woman and raised my eyebrow.

'Mary Turner.'

I inclined my head formally and then smiled. I'd have stuck my hand out, but I was worried she would view that as the prelude to an assault.

'It is my pleasure to meet you, Goodie Turner. I understand this is very difficult, but if I have any advice, it's to do as your children do. They adapt fastest and grow tall and strong. Those who resist their new circumstances become twisted and unsightly within their soul.'

'Blessed are the innocents.'

'Precisely.'

Our server returned and he placed the two drinks in front of me and then went to greet some women in Victorian dress. Goodie Turner was blinking at the sheer number of bows and frills on their gowns.

'Quite a sight, aren't they?'

'They are an abomination.'

'Are they really? I mean I'm more a one bow kind of girl but they're happy.'

'Life is not about being happy.'

I pushed the two drinks towards her. 'Lady Julian's favourite tea and a glass of water. I can't have my breakfast without sharing with you.'

Predictably, she drank the water.

'Now then. We have exchanged names, we have broken our fast together. What would you have of me?'

She looked torn. I really needed to get to work but there wasn't a person alive in this city that didn't know what it was like to wake up in a place you no longer recognised and the terror that came with it. I sipped my coffee and waited whilst the tea cooled.

'The night we met. I saw the girl.' She looked at me nervously, thinking I was going to be cross with her.

'That's very helpful. Thank you. Did you see anything else? I should love to hear.'

She relaxed a touch, by which I mean her shoulders softened slightly, though her back remained ramrod straight.

'I had woken up feeling strange. The air smelled peculiar and my head hurt. I opened the shutters and saw her walking towards the river. The moon had just risen so I could see her long hair and cloak as she walked through the field. I assumed it was Annie Lovell. She and young Tom have been meeting in secret. That were who I thought she were, in my tired state.

I got up and walked around the cottage. I could see no evidence of disturbance and the animals were also silent. When I went back to bed, I closed the shutters and saw her again but this time a man was following her.

I should have done summat but my head was pounding and I felt sick. I must have fallen asleep immediately, as I didn't hear any scream. Sometime after, there was a fearful banging on the door and that were when I met you.'

She finished her water in a single gulp. How must she be feeling, to realise that she could have prevented a murder? On top of everything else, she was experiencing. I decided to share something that I had never told anyone else.

'When I was twelve, I killed our pet dog. It had developed a madness that frothed at its mouth. He had been my companion since I was a child. He slept on my bed. After my parents and brother died, he was the only link I had to them. Then one day he attacked me. I ran out into the street as he pursued me, ripping at my clothes and tearing into my flesh. As I plunged my dagger into him, I felt myself stabbing my mother, my father. I was full of rage at their betrayal. Leaving me alone. Leaving me to fend for myself in a city of nightmares. I stabbed and stabbed until his blood and mine were indistinguishable. I spent the next week in a field hospital being jabbed and tested for rabies.'

Tears sprang up as I spoke. I sniffed, wiping them away, and I was grateful when she beckoned for a cup of coffee. As I drank it, she sipped her tea absentmindedly.

'Why do you tell me this?'

'Because we have all done things and will do things that we hate ourselves for. That we blame ourselves for. But we have to be kinder. This city will destroy you if you can't learn to forgive yourself.'

'But I could have saved her.'

'Who knows? Maybe you could. Maybe you couldn't. But if you hang on to your guilt, you'll destroy yourself.'

I took a deep breath.

'Do you know Lady Julian's mantra, "*All Shall be Well*"? Practice it. It's a tad fatalistic but at least it's a positive fatalism, which I can get behind.'

Talking about Mr Wagsalot had been good. I'd been carrying that for a few days as I got to know Harry. He was sitting by my feet right now, fully inoculated against rabies, as was I, and we would never have to go through that horror.

I sipped my coffee again and grinned weakly at her as she drank her tea.

'It's good, isn't it?'

She looked startled and then frowned at me as she placed the cup firmly back on the table.

'Were you able to see the man's face? If I show you a picture, would you be able to identify him?'

Removing the photo from my satchel, I placed it in front of her and I was gratified when she flinched. I had my answer. Cade was the murderer. She blinked and looked away from the image, her eyes darting back and then away again just as quickly. It took me a moment to realise that she was simply responding to the medium. A photograph was probably more devilry. I removed it quickly.

'I apologise. Our artists have new ways of portraying features. I didn't mean to startle you.'

She finished her cup and took a deep breath.

'It could have been him, but I only had the moon's light to aid my vision. However, the man I saw in the field was bald.'

I cursed. Cade had shaved his head. It was predictable. I wonder if he had done it to avoid recognition or if his descent into madness had already begun. The way he had carved poor Naomi's body suggested he had already succumbed to the wild magic.

'Oh, that smells lovely.'

A warm voice interrupted our conversation and Isidora came and sat down with us. Immediately, the server rushed to bring over three cups and a pot of tea along with some seeded bread.

'Good morning, Eliza. I see the early worm has caught the porridge.'

I giggled and looked up at her smiling, only to see her frown.

'Eliza, you've been crying?'

Honestly, the kindness in her voice nearly set me off again. I had serious awe issues around this woman.

'Goodie Turner has been sharing her wisdom with me, Mother.'

'Please, call me Isidora. These titles are very heavy for my small bones.' She poured three cups as I held up a hand.

'I have to go to work. Goodie Turner has just proved invaluable. We have a new lead on Naomi's killer.'

I stood up as Isidora made the sign of the cross, which my Puritanical matriarch copied. I curtsied because honestly, I had no idea what else to do. Goodie Turner was sipping her tea and I spoke quickly before she could cut me off.

'I think you are wrong about being happy. I think that's the most important thing we can strive for.'

'But not at the cost of someone else's happiness. Hmm?' asked Isidora.

'Well. No. But happiness is a good thing, right?'

'Happiness is indeed a good thing. Now go to work, my dear.' I was just about to leave when she spoke again. 'Incidentally, did you get anywhere with the issue of the–'

'Socks? I'm on it, on rather I have a nun on the case.'

She looked worried.

'Are you sure?'

'Don't worry. I'm on a mission from God!'

Laughing, Harry and I left the refectory, both of our tails wagging.

Chapter Thirty-Two

 For the first time since I had arrived, the office was empty. I thought the sheriff lived on the upper floors, but I certainly wasn't going to head upstairs and investigate. I headed over to a desk, avoiding Willoughby's, and pulling out a sheet of paper began to make notes.

We needed to circulate a picture of Cade with and without hair and we needed to alert the entire city. If everyone was looking out for him, he'd soon be found. I understood Hitchman's reluctance to alarm the people, but it turns out that ignorance is rarely the bliss that it purports to be. People just say that to justify keeping you in the dark and honestly, that's where the monsters lurked. Squinty bright lights and a raging gale blowing back the curtains. I'd rather be uncomfortable than cosseted.

'Have you closed their eyes?'

I jumped at the disembodied voice. No one had entered the office and the voice wasn't coming from the staircase.

'Hello?' I called out in the silence.

'You must close their eyes.'

The voice was coming from the vicinity of a large desk beside the staircase. I stood up and walked over.

'Whose eyes?'

'You know I can't say their names. They'd hear me. It's why I close their eyes, so they can't see me.'

I bobbed down and looked under the desktop. In the knee hole was a small man tucked into the far corner with a pile of index cards on his lap. I sat back and stared at him.

'Hello. Are you okay?'

'Of course.'

'What are you doing?'

He looked at me, puzzled, and waved a card.

'I'm filing.'

I sat on the floor and Harry crept under the desk and earnt himself a scratch behind his ears.

'My name's Eliza Barnaby.'

'Little bishy Barnaby, fly away home.'

I laughed ruefully. 'I don't know where my home is anymore. Where's yours?'

'Chapel Loke.'

I nodded and wondered how to proceed.

'Do you work here?'

'Of course.' He laughed and waved the index cards at me again. I heard the front door open and then footsteps along the corridor.

'Morning, Bill.' I recognised Alys Atwell's voice and rose to my feet. 'Oh heavens, Officer Barnaby you're in early.'

'Well, you know what they say. The early worm gets her porridge.'

'Why would a worm eat porridge?' She looked at me in confusion. 'Is this one of those modern sayings? Some days I wonder if I will ever learn them all. I tell you who is good at them, Bishop Julian. She is a marvel in God's truth. Now tell me, what are you doing on the floor?'

'Chatting to Bill.' I raised my eyebrows and knowingly nodded towards the desk.

'She hasn't closed their eyes,' said Bill from under the desk.

'Not to worry, Bill, I did it on my way in. How's the filing going?'

'She needs to know how to close their eyes.'

'I'll show her. You finish the filing, then I'll make us all a cup of tea. How does that sound?'

'They can't watch us if their eyes are closed.'

'I'm showing her now.'

Alys gestured at me to follow her and leaving Harry with Bill, we walked back out of the office and out to the front door and the carved wooded caryatids.

'Poor Bill thinks these statues are possessed by evil spirits.'

'Who is he?'

'An officer. He's worked for the City Watch for over ten years but recently he started acting oddly. You know how it goes. It's pretty normal for Norfolk. Gradually he refused to go on the beat as he thought all the statues were watching him. Now he comes to work with a blindfold on. The kids call him Blind Bill and will sometimes help him along if he's walking the wrong way.'

'Does he stay under the desk all day?'

'Usually. On a good day, he'll come out and join us but those days are getting fewer.'

Bloody hell, this city.

'At least he can still work.'

'It would be easier if he died.'

'Alys!'

'What? The Norwich madness goes on too long, if you ask me. Call it a day and throw yourself in the river. That's what I'll do if I ever go that way.'

'You don't mean that.'

'Why would I say it, if I didn't? What a strange person you are. Are all Londoners like you?'

'No I mean, it's just a bit brutal, isn't it? Wishing him dead?'

'It is what it is.'

She looked at me and then shook her head.

'You know what you need? Cake!'

I laughed in surprise.

'Yes, I suppose cake never hurt anyone.'

Heading off to Oelrich's I pondered Alys's words. Her generation were used to shorter, more brutal lives. Maybe she found our longevity a curse. It was very hard not to judge when people from other centuries looked at our own in despair or disgust. For all that Alys had wished Bill dead, I noticed that she had treated him with kindness and respect and maybe that was all we could ask for. Maybe with cakes, Willoughby and I may also have a better day working together. I didn't want a repeat of yesterday. If I saw any more evidence of smuggling, I would ignore it. It wasn't my issue.

'I don't know how they do things in London, but here in Norwich we come in to work at eight. Is that clear?'

I made my way through the desks, ignoring the sheriff as I placed a box of Oelrich's pastries by the kettle.

'And we don't waste our day eating cakes!'

Alys got up from her desk and gave me a quick peck on the cheek before helping herself to a choux bun.

'Bish was in at seven thirty. When you weren't here for the eight o'clock briefing, she nipped out for some cakes for us. Now that you are here, shall we begin?'

I went and sat down at my desk just as Willoughby bounced through the door.

'Sorry I'm late. Following up a lead. Oh, Oelrich's again? Bish, you'll be the death of me. Bill, will you be joining us?'

He picked up a small strawberry tart and smiled at Hitchman.

'What about yourself, sheriff? Will you be having the éclair?'

He winked at me and it was clear that he had put yesterday's outburst behind us. Inwardly, I relaxed.

'Not today, Willoughby,' said Bill's disembodied voice. 'But if there're any cakes left, I'd be happy to share with my new friend.'

I mouthed 'Harry' to Willoughby, who smiled.

'Sounds like a fine plan, Bill. Glad you're on top of it.'

Placing two cakes on a plate, he walked across the room and ducked down, handing it over as a thin white arm stretched up to receive it and then disappeared. Willoughby stood up again and spoke to the sheriff.

'I've just been speaking to Charles. He can get his runners to hand out a wanted poster with every news sheet.'

'I haven't authorised that.'

'Are you sure? I thought I heard you say it. And the Harbourmaster thinks it's an excellent idea.'

'She does?'

'Heard it with my very own ears. Now what have I missed?'

Sheriff Hitchman knew he'd been outplayed, but went with the flow. For such an angry man he was quick to change his mind when he could see the benefit.

'I think I know how Cade got into the city.'

The sheriff raised an eyebrow and Willoughby put his cake down.

'I apologise for not seeing the obvious sooner, but I think he simply walked in via the maps.'

'Go on,' grumbled Hitchman. 'How exactly would he have done that? How could he have got past the Wymondham barrier?'

'I think he just walked through it. He simply visualised a map in which the barrier didn't exist, and that is all of them after all, and just walked through. And then when he got to our city wall, he did the same thing. Walked through via one of the previous time layers and then walked into our timeframe.'

'Just like that?' said Willoughby thoughtfully.

'I think so. I've seen him do it before. I should have worked it out quicker.'

'You've been processing a lot of things in the space of a few short hours,' he said with a smile, and I felt marginally better. I wanted to share my suspicions that he was local, but Willoughby was still checking the registers and so far, had found no evidence for a William Cade.

The sheriff snorted. He clearly wasn't as forgiving as Willoughby.

'Interesting theory. Very well. Alys, draw up a flyer. Stress that he's not to be approached. Don't mention Naomi's murder. Or that he's a map runner. Don't want to scare the geese. Besides which, people will quickly put two and two together.'

He poured himself a coffee, ignoring the cakes, and then headed over to his desk gently tipping a cat off his chair and glaring at Harry as if to warn him.

Harry very sensibly ignored the cat. Although I noticed that his eyes followed it all the way out of the room and upstairs.

'Sorry sir, we need to change the image. I was speaking to Goodie Turner this morning.'

I let the team know what she said and about the shaved head.

'Did she positively ID the man as Cade though?' asked Willoughby.

'She was uncomfortable about the fact it was a photograph, but she said it could be him. He was tall, well built but bald.'

'But she saw him in moonlight having just endured a quake. It's not the best ID, is it?'

Hitchman slammed his hand on the table. 'Willoughby, why must you always question everything? London here has come on the trail of a deranged murderer. We have a deranged murderer and an eyewitness who places the man at the scene. What more do you want?'

'Don't you think sacrificing some woman in the night is a wholly different to stabbing someone whilst you flee from your jailors?'

In fairness, that change in MO had bothered me as well.

'It's in the air,' said Hitchman, his arms waving above his head. 'We know what Norwich can do to people. Imagine what it does to a practitioner. Damnation, I expect any minute now we'll find him dancing down the street bare buck naked and howling at the sky.'

Whilst an unpleasant image, it would make our job easier and to be honest I was hoping that he would have succumbed sooner, although few were driven immediately mad. Most could endure a few weeks whilst they gradually spiralled out of control.

The handset on Alys' desk squawked and she picked it up, pressing the broadcast button. The room filled with the tones of Mike's voice. If I didn't know better, I would swear he was holding his nose.

'Alys, tell the sheriff we have another body. Young woman, same carvings. I think she was killed before Naomi from the state of the body.'

The sheriff jumped from his desk, strode across the room and grabbed the radio.

'Location.'

'She's in the river where the Dalymond joins.'

'Secure the scene. Willoughby and London will be with you shortly.'

Putting the radio down, he glared at us.

'Why are you still here?'

We left. This time we headed north. Willoughby was walking quickly and ignoring all greetings.

'What's wrong?'

'Besides the death of another innocent?' He frowned at me. 'I was harbouring a theory that the killer came through in the quake. Disoriented by his new surroundings, he lashed out.'

'And now?'

'And now it seems that if the body is older, then Cade seems the more likely candidate and as you say he simply walked in through the barrier.'

'You're not convinced though, are you?'

'It's the change in kills. This would be so much easier if your bosses had seen fit to provide us with a full criminal report.'

He wasn't wrong. The change in MO was alarming and if I was back in London, I would have sworn blind this was two different killers but the chance of two psychotic murderers running around in Norwich seemed unlikely. Whatever I thought about the sheriff, professionally he ran a very tight ship.

He stopped and looked at me. 'About yesterday.'

I cut him off.

'Let's say no more. You were cross that I was focusing on the smuggling, but I'm not here to investigate that. In future I shall stick to the task in hand.'

He looked down at me, frowning as he ran his fingers through his hair and once again tangling up his ponytail.

'You need to stop doing that.'

'I agree. But I find myself surrounded by vexatious women.'

I looked around in surprise.

'I see no vexatious women.' I joined in his laughter and then apologised again.

'Genuinely, I don't mean to make your job harder.'

'It isn't that. It's just,' he paused as he re-tied his ponytail. My own hair was hanging in a plain strand along my spine. I felt uncomfortably exposed, but so far no one had pointed or screamed. 'I think you're holding something back.'

He jolted me out of my thoughts and I started to walk, trying to frame a reply.

'In what way?'

He was about to run his hands through his hair again and I tutted quickly.

'You need to get your tailor to put some pockets in your trews. Keep your hands in there instead.'

'You have a point. And I see you have sidestepped my concern. I feel you know more about this investigation than you are letting on and it concerns me. I can't capture a criminal or protect you if I don't have all the facts.'

I puffed out my cheeks.

'Okay. Now listen. I do not need protecting. I am an officer of the law. I have a gun on my hip and years of experience. I know what I'm doing.'

He stopped and bowed. 'I meant no offence. I did not wish to impugn upon your abilities as a detective or an officer. But I still feel you are withholding something.'

I noticed he hadn't mentioned that I didn't therefore need protecting. I imagine some things were simply hard-wired into eighteenth century gentlemen.

But it bothered me that he thought I was holding out on him. He knew I was attuned to the flickering, but having sensed the attitude towards magic I didn't want to reveal just how attuned I was. The last thing I wanted was for him to realise that I could also run the maps.

'I'm withholding a thousand things. You're just getting thrown off by the London vibe. Trust me, I'm not holding back anything relevant.'

'And that's all it is?'

'Cross my heart and hope to die. If I am keeping anything relevant back from you, I shall be sure to tell you.'

My abilities were not important and if it stopped him from looking at me like I was cursed, I'd be very relieved.

He shook his head and gave a quick ungentlemanly snort.

'Well, I feel utterly reassured now. Very well. Let us proceed. We have work to do.'

We were walking through a small residential area as we made our way to the Wensum. I could see a space being taped off on the other side of the bank. Goat Bridge would have been the most direct crossing, but I only crossed it at nighttime on account of it not actually being there in this timeframe. The fact that I could see it and use it was just one of my affinities to Norwich. Crossing in daylight would just draw attention to myself. Willoughby turned and walked downriver until we got to Whitefriars Bridge, which everyone could see and cross and then we headed back up to the crime scene. The air was foul with the smell of tanneries, coal and now something altogether more pungent. I could have done with a pot of Vicks and was about to impress Willoughby with news of this London marvel when he handed me a little purple glass vial.

'Dab it under your nose. It will help with the smell.'

The stench of rotting corpse was quickly masked with something astringent and peppery. My eyes watered and I wondered if the cure beat the condition.

The body was still in the water, trapped in the roots of a weeping willow. I clambered down the bank to get a better look at her. Again she was naked. Was this a pattern of his or of the girls? On her swollen wedding finger a large diamond ring bit into the flesh. This was no robbery.

Willoughby was standing on the banks above me. His velvet shoes were not suitable for scrambling down the bank.

'She was married or engaged,' I called up. 'Someone must surely have missed her and filed a report.'

'Agreed. Unless the husband is the killer. Can you hazard a guess how long she's been in the water?'

I looked at the swollen figure. The cuts had split the skin open and the flesh below had turned blue beneath the grey skin.

'A day or two at least. My guess is she went into the water almost as soon as she died. Her body probably got trapped somewhere along the riverbed. Do we have a pathologist?'

In my ignorance, I assumed they hadn't. And yet everything else I saw was evidence that Norwich was if not flourishing, then at least stable.

'Of course we have a pathologist. Who do you think processed the last body?'

Willoughby's tone was sharp and I snapped back at him.

'I've been here two days. I don't know everything.'

'May I suggest you assume we have everything that any modern city has and go from there?'

I wanted to point out all the things that they didn't have, but decided now wasn't the time for a fight. We had a second victim and no clues.

Grabbing the roots of the tree, I pulled myself up the bank just as two men in long blue gowns arrived. Behind them was a stainless-steel covered wagon pulled by two horses.

Not fast, but hygienic.

I moved out of their way as they assessed the scene.

Willoughby was off to one side, talking to the Watch. I had walked away from the crime scene, keen to avoid the smell, and had no desire to watch as she was pulled from the water. Out of the corner of my eye I caught a glimpse of red and then saw a cloak billow out into the lane. A man turned suddenly and ran away down a small passageway.

Micah had mentioned that he had given a red cloak to Naomi and so far, we hadn't found any trace of it. Plus, this man had run and police officers are like dogs. If they run, we follow.

I screamed to Willoughby and gave chase.

Chapter Thirty-Three

 The lanes around the factories were difficult at the best of times, but as my suspect fled, he was pulling over crates and animal pens and I found myself slipping on beer spills and dodging chickens and piglets. A goat loosed from its peg ran at me and I narrowly avoided it, only to slip on a patch of moss growing on the dank pebbles. As I turned into the next passageway, it was long enough for me to see a large bald-headed man in a red cloak turning a corner. I screamed for people to stop him, but they just cheered as I ran past.

I'd pulled my gun from my holster but I lost sight of him again. Instead, I sprinted along his trail of destruction. It was years since I had been here and I couldn't remember any of the shortcuts. I could see smart wide roads running left and right, but I had no idea where they would come out. For now, I had to pursue him along his own path. At the next turning, I saw a red cloak on the floor. Ignoring it, I sprinted on, jumping over some sacks of wool, ignoring the remonstrations of an irate merchant.

I realised we were heading back to the river when the chaos on the lanes stopped. A few people were looking out of their windows and then pulled them closed as I demanded if anyone had seen him. I ran to the end of the street and saw I was standing in a long terrace of tall Georgian townhouses, complete with elegant trees lining the pavement. The road was wide enough for two carriages to pass easily and as I looked up and down, I couldn't see a soul. I ran to the far end that led to the river and peered over the side, holding on to the ladder rails, but there was no sign of him.

Jogging back down the road, Willoughby sprinted out of the small side street.

'Where did he go?'

'No idea.' I bent over, my hands on my knees, as I regained my breath, my head splitting. I wasn't unfit, but he had a head start on me and was clearly fit himself. 'He was leaving a trail of destruction and then nothing. Did you see his cloak? We need to secure that. He has to be in one of the houses. This road or back along that lane.'

Willoughby looked up and down the road pensively, then pulled out his radio.

'I need the entire Watch on Worldsend Lane. Only those with the second body are to remain in post. Everyone else here now. This is an all-city call.'

A moment later, I could hear Hitchman on the radio as Willoughby brought him up to speed.

'It would be bloody Worldsend Lane, wouldn't it? I'm on my way.'

So far, not a single person had opened a door and it was killing me to know that our man was probably in one of these houses. Or worse yet, climbing over their garden fence and away off into the city.

'What's wrong with this street?'

'This is a Strangers' enclave. It's also the home of the Head of the North Quarter.'

'I thought the Strangers had settled around the merchant halls of Charing Cross.'

'They still do their business there, but recently they have moved to Over the Water in large numbers. It feels unwise.'

I thought about it. The Strangers were historically a group of refugees that fled religious persecution in the Low Countries. They had always been the most friendly group of people and, understanding the fear of persecution and the bewilderment of change, they were the most tolerant of Norwich's population but I remembered Mike mentioning that they had become difficult recently.

'Was the move forced upon them?'

'As in a ghetto?' Willoughby looked at me in disgust. 'Certainly not.'

'Then they are establishing a power base,' I mused. In a city as troubled as Norwich, social cohesion had to be carefully monitored.

'I like the phrase "power base". It speaks to the problem directly. And Worldsend Lane is the heart of their rookeries.'

'Hell.'

'Hell indeed. Because it's about to get nasty.'

Whilst Worldsend Lane was an elegant-looking street, it was surrounded by a host of lanes and yards, all populated with an effective standing army. Why had the city council allowed this to happen? Then I remembered this was the home of Ipolite Martineau. According to Hortense Paine, Martineau was one of the city heads and represented Over the Water. He was clearly a powerful man and carving out his own kingdom.

By now, the street was filling up with members of the Watch. By the time there were a hundred gathered around us, I could see lots of lace curtains twitching, but still no one was making themselves known.

Raising his voice, Willoughby shouted to the open windows.

'Two women have been vilely murdered in this city in the past week. One of them may be known to you. Her possible killer was chased to this location where he has taken refuge. My men will knock on every door for witness statements. If you know anything at all, please tell my officers.' He took a deep breath, then carried on. 'The man in question is tall, well built. He has no hair on his head and until just now was wearing a long red cape.'

Dropping his tone, he addressed the Watch.

'Two per house. This road and Pennyrunfast Lane. If any of you see him, grab him and restrain his hands, knock him out if possible. Otherwise, no physical confrontation with any house owner. Understood? Oh, and he dropped his cloak down Pennyrunfast. Start the door to doors there and someone get the cloak down to the pathologist at the crime scene. They'll have evidence bags.' He was about to speak when something occurred to him. 'Black Watch, stay by me. Now, the rest of you go and remember, nice and easy.'

A small team of about ten men and a couple of women stayed behind. One or two were grinning to each other. One guy was stretching and one of the women yawned before cricking her neck. Honestly, they looked like a student rugby team or a bunch of football fans on derby day.

As the rest of the Watch spread out, I wondered at Willoughby's concern. Before I could ask, I heard a horse approaching at speed. Riding towards us was the sheriff. He drew up and jumped off the horse, throwing the reins to me.

I had zero idea what to do with a horse, but I figured I could at least hold the reins. At least I wasn't trying to ride this one towards a wolf.

'Are you certain he went to ground here?' He was addressing Willoughby, but I replied.

'No, sir. My last visual of him was on Pennyrunfast Lane, before the Four Monkeys. He dropped his cloak by a brazier. After that, there were only a few more signs of his flight. So he could be in the tail end of Pennyrunfast.'

'Okay, well done with keeping up with him. And you're sure he's our man?'

'He ran.'

We couldn't be absolutely sure, but as a rule the police don't like it when someone runs. And we absolutely have a problem if they continue running after we've told them to stop.

'Did you see his face?'

'No, but his height and build fits the description of Cade. And like I said, he ran.'

'Not to mention, a red cape and bald head that fit Goodie Turner's account of the man by Naomi's body,' said Willoughby.

'Okay, that's good enough for me. Hopefully, this won't escalate.'

The tension between the two men and those of the Black Watch was palpable. If the Black Watch shared a trait, I would have to say it was broken noses and heavy ringed fingers.

'What is the issue with the Strangers? I thought they were peace loving and law abiding?'

'I wish,' snorted Hitchman. 'I've been saying for years now we were giving them too much leeway.'

Harry growled. In the distance I could hear an ugly noise building. We had both been in scenes like this before, whether on nighttime riots or Saturday afternoon football clashes. An angry mob was heading our way.

The Black Watch turned in the direction of the noise and Willoughby looked around, then grabbed my arm.

'Go down Pennyrunfast, now.'

I shook his hand off.

'Willoughby, I'm an officer of the law. I don't run.'

Which was a lie, but Hitchman had already called me a quitter and I didn't want to give him any more evidence.

Chapter Thirty-Four

Marching down the road towards us was a gang of men at least a hundred strong. They were uniformly dressed in dark blue twill trousers and a woollen waistcoat over white shirts with rolled-up sleeves. To me, they looked like they had simply walked out of the fabric mills and onto the street. They were shouting a song I didn't recognise, but reminded me of every anthem out there and simply boiled down to "Who are you?" and that other true and tested chant, "Come and have a go if you think you're hard enough."

Leading the pack was a tall man, similarly dressed although he also sported a jacket and a soft cap. The noise was reaching a crescendo, and I was berating myself as a fool for not running. We were outnumbered, but I noticed the rest of the Watch had stopped their interviews and had dashed back to stand with us. Harry continued to growl and I bared my teeth. I had my gun on my hip but was loath to use it against an unarmed mob.

The leader of the men held his hand up and the chanting petered away as he stepped towards the sheriff.

'A fine morning to you, Joseph. How's the wife?'

'What's the meaning of this crowd?' shouted the sheriff, ignoring the man's pleasantries. 'Do you want me to arrest you all for disturbing the peace?'

The man swung his arms out wide, playing to his audience.

'We heard our homes were being raided. Our women and children being harassed. We simply ran here as quick as we could in order to protect them.' He turned to the men. 'Ain't that right, boys?'

The "boys" roared their approval.

'Enough,' shouted the sheriff. He stepped away from the leader and addressed the crowd directly.

'A young lady has been found dead in the water. She was brutally murdered. A man we believe to be involved ran this way and then disappeared. Right now, a dangerous murderer could be holed up with your precious wife and child. His knife to their throats.' Now he started shouting, biting out each word. 'And. We. Are. Trying. To. Save. Them.'

One of the men in the crowd sprinted away from the group towards his front door. Flinging it open, he ran inside. A second later, the crowd exploded as the men ran to their various homes.

Hitchman turned to Martineau.

'And what of your lady wife, Ipolite? Not concerned by her safety?'

'It's Tuesday. She visits her sister on Tuesdays.'

'Very well. But I'm warning you. Try a stunt like this again, and I will see you before the magistrate. We have a killer on the loose and you are impeding our search.'

Willoughby cleared his throat.

'Excuse me, Master Martineau. Your sister-in-law is Mistress Rugge, I believe?'

Martineau paused. His smile becoming guarded.

'Yes, and what of it?'

'My apologies, sir, but I happened to know that Mistress Rugge is engaged with Miss Hoxton today. They are looking to purchase a new painting. I believe your wife stayed at home.'

Martineau looked nervously across the road at a fine double-fronted townhouse. It was the only property on the street with steps leading up to the front door and stood directly opposite Pennyrunfast Lane.

'Ipolite, let our men question everyone, or I will see you in jail.'

I don't know if he even heard him as he had turned and walked quickly towards his own house and ran as the door opened from within.

Hitchman breathed a sigh of relief.

'Really, Willoughby, I may mock your propensity for gossip, but never ever let me stop you.' He turned to the Watch. 'Why are you scratching your arses? Get back and interview everyone. I want answers.'

I was still feeling the shakes from a massive dump of adrenaline when Willoughby took one look at me and suggested sustenance.

'There's a great stand over at Whitefriars that specialises in particularly fine victuals, unless you would prefer not to eat in public.' I shook my head. Lots of people were funny about eating in public in Norwich. I think it was eating and walking that was the big sin, but I could never keep up with all the little rules. But that wasn't my issue, I simply didn't want to leave the scene. Naomi's murderer was in the vicinity and if it was Cade, I needed to be present.

'We'll come back if any of the interviews turn up anything interesting. Plus, Harry looks like he could do with a drink.'

I wanted to protest, but there was nothing I could do right now and I was desperate to sit down before my legs gave way underneath me.

I took one more look up and down the street, hoping to catch a glimpse, when something small caught my eye. In the gutter by the junction of Worldsend and Pennyrunfast lay a small white object. One thing you can say in Norwich's favour is that it's litter free, so that alone made the item noteworthy, but even from a distance I had a sinking feeling.

Walking over to the gutter, I picked up the little object. My headache was intensifying as music whined out of the cordless headphone. Springing back, my fist firmly clasped around the earbud, I sprinted down Pennyrunfast screaming at the top of my lungs.

'Don't touch the cloak!'

Chapter Thirty-Five

 Willoughby ran after me as Harry and I legged it down Pennyrunfast Lane. Front doors were open as members of the Watch were interviewing the inhabitants. Little children hugged their mothers' legs as the women shook their heads and shrugged their shoulders. This whole neighbourhood seemed to be determined not to have seen anything.

'What is it?' shouted Willoughby.

'Magic!'

All heads turned my way, and then doors slammed. A watchman was walking towards me with the red cloak under his arm. He gave a puzzled frown as Willoughby overtook me and told him to stop walking.

'Bish. Where's the magic?'

I took a step forward and my headache intensified. It wasn't a splitting headache, but having been in Norwich for a few days, my ever-present headache had gone. Now it was buzzing back into life and Harry was barking.

'It's in the cloak.'

Unsurprisingly, the watchman threw the cloak as far away from himself as he could, thereby hitting me in the face with it. A gentle thud settled down in the back of my cranium, making itself at home. The ache was familiar and I ignored it. Placing the cloak on the ground, I searched for pockets. The hem was crusty with blood and I winced at how I was tampering with evidence, but I needed to find the source of the music, and there it was. My hand grasped the hard rectangular outline, and I removed a phone from an inner pocket.

Switching it off, I showed it to Willoughby.

'What is that?'

'Trouble.'

I leant against a wall as Willoughby stepped away from me and pulled out his mike. I shook my head.

'Too close. Just go and tell the sheriff the situation. I'll wait here.'

Willoughby was going to argue with me, but I waved him off. Engineered magic was something I was more familiar with. I slid down the wall and watched him dash back down the lane. Harry shuffled towards me and licked my face as I hugged him and tried to think things through.

By my reasoning, this item had been in the city a few days. It may have triggered the last quake. It may trigger another one. I'd lived through quakes before, I could walk through timelines. I was probably the best person to hold the artefact before the disposal unit arrived.

A few minutes later, the lane filled with members of the Watch. Instead of interviewing the neighbours, they now evacuated them. On either side of me, the lane was rapidly being emptied. No one was screaming or crying, there was no panic as such, more a very determined effort to get as far away from me as was

326

humanly possible. Willoughby cut through the throng and came and sat down beside me.

'How are you doing?'

'I'm hungry and I have a headache. Other than that, I'm peachy. How about you?'

'I'm sitting on a muddy lane in black velvet trousers. My day is less than acceptable.'

I chuckled and then groaned.

'I really hate this fucking city.'

'This fine city?'

'This fine fucking city.'

He nodded.

'Normally, I would strenuously defend Norwich, but I think at this moment at least you may have a point.'

'How long until the retrieval unit shows up?'

'If you listen carefully, I think you can hear them.'

Indeed, there was a low rumble of tyres on cobbles as a vehicle made its way towards us. The electric engine declared by its very silence that here was yet another way that Norwich had embraced a modern-day solution to the lack of petrol and an inability to use engineered magic. A man in a boiler suit stepped off the quad bike and walked towards us. I noticed he kept his helmet on.

I got to my feet and Harry tucked himself around the back of my legs as he approached.

'What is it?'

'Phone. Sixth generation, about five years old.'

'Level of artefact?'

I shook my head. I had no idea what the scale was for items containing engineered magic.

'Is this a simple or complicated level of magic artifice?'

'Very complicated. This is an extremely powerful piece of engineered magic.'

'But it's so small,' said Willoughby.

'That's the nature of its power. This is a phone, a camera, a television, a satellite receiver. Our killer was using it to listen to music.'

I held out the white earbud.

'There should be another one of these lying around, unless he still has it.'

The guard stepped forward with a lead-lined box and told me to drop the earbud in.

'If you hand me the device, I'll try to switch it off.'

'Already done. I'm from London,' I said tiredly. 'I know how they work.'

I placed the phone in the box, removing my fingers quickly as he snapped down the lid. He then turned back to his quad bike and drove away at speed, a siren blaring.

'What will happen to it?'

Willoughby turned back to look at me as the sheriff strode down the lane towards us.

'It will be driven out of St Stephen's Gate and over to the Wymondham quarantine. I pray that brave man is not hit by a quake.'

Running around Norwich with a piece of engineered magic was a bit like standing on top of a hill waving a spear in the middle of a lightning storm, shouting that all gods are rubbish. Or so I've read.

'That's one hell of a job. When he gets back, we are buying him a drink.'

People think police officers are brave. We're not a patch on the militia.

The sheriff reached us, slightly out of breath. He had ridden in to stave off a riot and ended up having to organise a potential quake evacuation.

'Are you okay?'

I was surprised by the concern in his voice, and assumed he meant Willoughby.

'Has she lost her wits?' he said, looking at Willoughby in alarm. 'Has the device rendered her mute?'

'Sorry sir, I didn't realise you were addressing me. I'm fine.'

'You're sure?'

'Well, Willoughby promised me a hotdog, but so far I'm still hungry.'

Hitchman barked a short laugh and then looked relieved. Pulling out a cigar, he lit it up and then pointed it at me.

'Dog's pizzle, London. Go have your food. Both of you take the afternoon off. This is going to take hours to sort out. A murder victim, a near riot and a piece of banned technology. Balls, what a mess.'

'Any sign of Cade, sir?' asked Willoughby.

The sheriff spat on the ground. 'Would I be chatting to you about your bellies if there was?' Turning, he shouted at a fellow officer and stormed off.

'Come on,' I said, watching Willoughby's expression. 'God knows he's not my favourite person, but he's just frustrated. That wasn't personal.' I was going to say more, but my stomach rumbled.

Shaking his head at my unladylike behaviour, he grinned and offered me his arm.

Chapter Thirty-Six

 We sat down by a small fountain near the Jarrold's mill. From here I could see the comforting spire of the cathedral and I remembered that breakfast had been a long time ago. It was past lunch and I swore.

'What's the best way to get a quick message to someone in the city?'

Willoughby looked around and then pulled his whistle out and peeped three times. A minute later, a girl came running from around the corner, shortly followed by an older boy, mid-teens, coming from the other direction. They both sprinted towards Willoughby, but the girl got here first and then curtsied quickly.

'You have a message?'

Willoughby nodded and the boy stepped forwards quickly.

'I can run faster, Officer Willoughby.'

'I know. But she got here first. You know the rules. This isn't a priority message, Toby.'

The girl sneered at Toby and then blanked her face quickly when she saw me watching her.

'Actually, it is a priority,' I said. I had always hated that sort of smug smile. It belonged to sycophantic suck-ups, and I had had a gutful of them over the past ten years. She glared at me, but I ignored her. Mean girls thrived on attention. I turned to Toby.

'Can you run a message to Notre Dame?' He nodded earnestly and handed me a notepad and pencil. Whilst I scribbled out a quick note to Fen, the girl stared at the three of us, then turned on her heel and stormed off in a huff.

Sealing the note, the lad placed it in his pocket and asked if this was an official message.

'No, I just need to apologise to a friend for missing our lunch date.'

'Okay.' He handed me a chit of paper. 'Pay now, or on account?'

'Put it on my tab,' said Willoughby, and with that the lad nodded once, then turned and sprinted away.

'They seem young to be working?'

'One day a week spent working for the city. Four days of school, two days of rest.'

'They get paid?'

'Absolutely. They also get to choose what work they do. Message running, harvesting, piggeries, engineering. Speaking of which, let's eat.'

Mungo Jerrys did the best hotdogs this side of the river. I ordered mine with extra apple sauce and crackle sprinkles and rejoined Willoughby on a bench overlooking the river under a weeping willow. He passed me my coffee in exchange for his hotdog and we settled down. It had been a frantic morning and I was famished. I had also bought a second sausage for Harry and broke it up into pieces to let it cool down.

'Do you think that phone was capable of triggering a quake?' asked Willoughby, wiping his fingers and feeding a chunk of sausage to Harry.

I had just taken a bite of my delicious hotdog and wondered if it was a universal trait to wait until someone had a mouthful before asking a question. I glared at him and chewed quickly as he waved an apology. Gulping quickly, I now coughed and had to wait a full minute for the choking to stop.

'Better?'

I threw my eyes to heaven. 'Yes, much better, thank you.' I wiped the tears away and continued. 'I don't know much about how engineered magic triggers Norwich, but I wouldn't be surprised. What is certain is that listening to music via Bluetooth from a phone probably fritzed Cade's noggin.'

We ate in silence, considering the damage that engineered magic inflicted in Norwich.

'May I ask you something?'

'My mouth is empty. Carry on.'

'In London. Is a device that contains so much magic commonplace?'

I thought back to my own phone and how much I was missing it.

'Pretty much.'

'Even to the extent that your prisoners have such an incredible tool?'

'God no, they're expensive. Plus, who would let a prisoner have that sort of access to the outside world and that much entertainment? A phone is a privilege, not a right.'

Willoughby took a bite of hotdog and looked at me expectantly. I shrugged. I didn't know what he was waiting for me to say. Did he think phones were an abomination that no one should have? Did he think prisoners should have luxury items? The idea was ridiculous and then the penny dropped.

'Bugger. How did Cade get hold of a phone?'

'Could he have stolen one?'

I wiped my fingers with my napkin whilst I thought it through.

'It's possible, but phones are usually locked. They can only be used by the owner. He'd need to be able to hack it in order for it to work.'

'So what? Are you suggesting that he's a hacker now as well as a murderer?'

I threw the paper in the bin in disgust.

'I don't know. I didn't get a chance to read his files. Maybe the encryption broke when he entered Norwich? Maybe there's a spell practitioners can use?'

It was a rubbish suggestion and I knew it.

I jumped to my feet, startling some small birds that had gathered for scraps.

'Are you heading home?' said Willoughby, squinting up at me.

'What? No. Why would I do that?'

The sun was on my back and I stepped to the side, casting him into shade.

'Because we were told to go home for the rest of the day.'

I stared at him in amazement.

'There's a dead woman lying by the side of a river, another one lying on a mortuary slab and their killer is running loose. I am not taking the afternoon off.'

He was smiling up at me, and I glared back.

'What? If you want to go home, that's fine. But I'm not.'

He carried on smiling, then brushing crumbs off his lap, he stood up as the little birds swept back in.

'Good, because neither am I. Let's find out who she was and take it from there.'

An hour later, we were heading up Magdalene Street towards Barnes Yard. The home of a Sabrina Wise, a twenty-three-year-old woman employed by Fairfield and Sons, one of the local shoe factories. We were checking out her home first, then her place of work. Her parents had filed a missing person's report and the image they submitted was close enough to the bloated flesh that had been pulled out of the river. They also confirmed a recent engagement to a Percival Pottelbergh of Worldsend Lane. There wasn't a copper born that believed in coincidences and I knew we would soon be returning to have a friendly chat with the young fiancé.

Barnes Yard was in a completely different league of habitation. Old timber buildings leaning into each other, no gutters and a central communal water pump. Two children were playing hopscotch on a chalked-up grid, and Willoughby went and asked them to direct us to her lodgings. They pointed up an outdoor set of stairs. At the top was a single door.

'But she ain't there,' quipped the older of the two children, a boy with a smart expression. He shouted to his mother, then carried on playing.

'What?' shouted a voice from within a house across the courtyard.

'More from the Watch. Sheriff's men.' He winked at me and I decided this little boy was sprinting towards being an obnoxious teenager. A woman made her way across the courtyard. Her blonde hair was pulled back into a ponytail with two inches of roots showing along her hairline. She was wearing jeans and trainers and the air of a woman who couldn't wait for the school holidays to be over. On her hip was a laundry basket full of damp clothes and a bag of clothes pegs.

'Now what?'

She bent down, placing the basket on the floor under a washing line. Then stood up with a towel and two pegs in her hand.

'Good afternoon, mistress.'

'Don't start that bloody mistress guff with me.' She pinned Willoughby with a withering glare and then pegged out her clothes.

I stepped forward. 'May I?' After a quick nod from the woman, I helped her peg out the clothes as Willoughby moved over to talk to the children. He took Harry with him, and I was surprised by how glad I was that he looked back at me before padding over to play with the children.

'You're the one from London, yeah?'

I shrugged. It was obvious who I was.

'Reckon you're one of them quitters.' She pegged up some socks, I pegged up a tea towel. 'Quitters are losers that die or fail miserably.' She carried on putting out the laundry. Her words were more curious than challenging, and I let her speak. I needed information about Sabrina Wise, and I imagined this was her landlady. 'You seem to have done well for yourself, though.'

'Do you want help with the sheets?' I asked as I pegged the last garment. With a nod, we headed over to the other clothesline and I folded the pillowcases.

'How well did you know Sabrina?'

'She was my tenant, not my bestie. No, fold them the other way,' she said as I re-folded the pillowcase, because apparently that was important.

'So, what can you tell me?'

'What's to tell? It's like I said to the Watch. Young girl, first job. Her folks live over Friarsgate, but she wanted her own place, a bit of independence. They weren't happy with her lodgings, neither was her fiancé. Every one of them turned their nose up, but she said she was saving for her trousseau. She used to giggle when she told me that. She was a sweet girl.'

I nodded and moved on to the sheets, working with her as we folded them together.

'So why didn't you tell the Watch she was missing?'

She looked at the ground and stopped folding.

'Look, you see, the thing is… I hadn't noticed. And I feel dreadful about that, just dreadful.'

'So when did you notice?'

She snatched the sheets out of my hand and folded them in a messy tangle.

'When her rent was due. She hadn't paid, so I tried her rooms and saw they were empty. A coffee cup was growing mould. I figured she'd gone home for a bit, so I sent them a note. Which is when they turned up here full of panic, like it was my fault. Woollen merchants, you know how jumped up they are.'

She stared at the mess of sheets in her arms and shook it out, shoving half my way.

'I'm busy, you know. I have the boys, a job over at Jarrold's, and these few rooms I rent.'

'No one's blaming you, you know?' I tried to sound kind, but her guilt was muffling out any efforts of sympathy.

'If I had just noticed sooner—'

'She'd probably still be dead. What you can do now is help us find her killer.'

By the time she finished telling me what she knew, I was little wiser. Sabrina had been a quiet girl, friendly, polite, was nice to the children, paid her rent on time, occasionally a few girlfriends would call for her when they went out for drinks. Never ill, always left for work on time. Went to church regular as clockwork. A blameless life. And by all accounts, well off and about to marry for love.

At least I had her place of work. Fairfield Shoes, where she worked as an accountant. I folded the last piece of laundry and placed the pegs back in the bag.

'Is London really better than here?' she asked unexpectedly. 'You know Norwich isn't that bad, really.'

Ignoring her question, I handed her the peg bag, thanked her for her time, and headed over to Willoughby. Was London better? A thousand times better, but how could I say that to someone that was stuck here? Willoughby stood up as I approached, but the two children clung onto Harry as he tried to return to me.

'Please miss, can we walk him sometime?'

I'd said yes before I thought about it, then remembered that I'd be back in London, hopefully within the week. Cade was losing control. He wouldn't last much longer. I just needed to catch him before he killed anyone else. And then when I returned to London, Harry would head back to the kennels. The thought made me feel uncomfortable.

'Willoughby, we need to go.'

Back out on the street, I suggested we head over to her place of work and see if we could glean any clues. Willoughby had found out one interesting piece of information. The boys had seen a bald guy hanging around the entrance to the yard yesterday, although they didn't think it could be our killer, as they often saw him in church.

'He's someone they recognise?'

'Yes, which rules out Cade.'

I chewed it over.

'Could be a coincidence. There's more than one bald man in Norwich.'

Willoughby played with his ponytail and preened slightly. 'This is true, but I don't like coincidences.'

'You've said.'

We crossed over the river again and headed towards the shoe factory.

'Observe,' said Willoughby. 'Let us see if we find out anything at work. We will call on her fiancé when the situation at Worldsend Lane has calmed down. Then we are going to find her local church and see if the priest can tell us anything about his bald parishioners.'

'Assuming they attended the same church.'

Fifty-two churches were within the city walls. What were the chances that they both attended the same one?

Chapter Thirty-Seven

 Sabrina's boss was a fastidious little man who had little to say. She was a hard worker and he had been sorry to hear she was getting married. When I asked why, he looked at me confused and then Willoughby commented she would likely stop work. I rolled my eyes and thanked him for his time.

'Why should she have to give up work?' I snapped as soon as we left his offices.

'I'm sure she didn't have to. Young ladies may do as they wish these days.'

'Maybe they don't wish to be referred to as young ladies?' I snapped.

'You seem in a bad mood?'

I stopped and then apologised.

'I'm behaving like an arse. I get this way when I am first learning about a victim. It's just my frustration.'

'I feel the same.'

That was hard to believe from this man, who was the current model of restraint.

'I think I am the opposite of you. When I am on a case, I become sombre. When I am at rest, I am more effusive. Your emotions come to the fore when you work and are suppressed when you relax.'

It was a curious observation and I wasn't sure I agreed, but I was beginning to value Willoughby's insights and I turned away in annoyance.

'Let's go to church.'

He bowed with a flourish and walked along the road alongside me.

'I imagine you must be anxious to return to your own family?'

'I beg your pardon?'

Willoughby took a step back.

'My apologies. I was simply trying to talk of small matters and offer you the comfort of their memory.'

'Small talk and family chitchat. Is this the sort of chatter that you think entertains me?'

Even as I spoke, I winced. I really was acting like an arse.

'I have no family. I told you they died.'

'My apologies. I was referring to a husband or partner. Maybe children? Your friends and work colleagues?'

I stared at him in silence and then, tugging on Harry's lead, strode off towards Sabrina's parish church. Where we finally learnt something interesting.

The congregation, as suspected, had its fair share of bald-headed men and I had to smother a grin as once again Willoughby smoothed his own flowing locks.

'And what of Miss Sabrina herself?' asked Willoughby. 'Was she looking forward to her coming nuptials?'

'What young woman doesn't?' asked the priest.

'One that is being forced against her will,' suggested Willoughby. I liked his line of thought. Before we visited her would-be husband, it would be good to know if she was as enthusiastic as everyone said. Unfortunately, Father Walsey looked quite appalled at the suggestion.

'I have never met a sweeter couple.'

'So no trouble between the pair of them. No previous acquaintances who objected to the union.'

He twisted his hands together and shook his head vehemently.

'Absolutely not. Although–'

He broke off and Willoughby and I did all we could not to shake it out of him. 'Although' was always the precursor to something useful. He remained silent, and I guessed the nature of his concern.

'Did she say something whilst in confession?'

He looked relieved, and Willoughby sagged. He knew as well as I how hard it would be to get any information out of him. I tried.

'Tell me. Did she confess to something that you feel has a bearing on her murder?'

He thought about it. 'No. In fact, the matter arose later, following on from a conversation held in the confessional.'

'So what you think is relevant was not said under the act of confession but connected to it?'

He rubbed his hands again, and I knew I would get this out of him.

'Just tell us what she said outside of the confession. That's all we ask.'

The priest looked across at Willoughby, who nodded his head. Drawing a breath, he began to talk.

'She was concerned that her demeanour was attracting unwanted attention and asked if I had any suggestions?'

'Were her concerns warranted?'

'I can't say.'

Clearly, she had discussed this at length in the confessional.

'Did she seem worried?' asked Willoughby.

'She did, but I assured her, her behaviour was chaste and seemly and once she stopped work, her concerns would be ended.'

Great, it sounded like the poor girl had a stalker and being hidden away in the marital home was deemed a suitable solution.

'Was there anyone in particular whose attention was causing her concern?'

'I can't say.'

'Maybe a man with a bald head.'

He flinched, which told me everything I knew.

'Goddammit. If you just give me his name, I can talk to him. Maybe arrest him?'

'Officer Willoughby. Please tell your colleague to calm herself.'

'I will not. Two women have been brutally murdered. The blood of a third victim will be on your hands.'

The priest crossed himself twice and looked at Willoughby in horror.

'Sir, you know I cannot!' He was pleading now and I spun on my heels and stormed outside. We were getting nowhere. I needed to know who was bothering her so we could rule him out. Cade was most likely our killer, but we needed to know who this man was.

Willoughby rejoined me a moment later and took a deep breath.

'God's Blood, spare me from the confessional!'

'Did you learn anything else?'

'She had this conversation with our tongue-tied priest three days ago. Which keeps Cade in the frame, just. But I have concerns. Those two lads say the bald-headed man has been hanging around for weeks.'

'The same man?'

'They weren't certain.'

I groaned loudly and was concerned when Harry whimpered.

'I'm okay.' I ducked down and patted him on his flank and was happy to see him wag his tail.

'Detective Barnaby?' I looked up and saw that Willoughby was standing stiffly to one side. I had snapped at him entering the church, belittled his city and sworn at a priest, and yet he had still supported me against that priest. I owed my partner an apology and standing up, I stuck out my hand.

'I may have mentioned that I am behaving like an arse. I apologise.'

He eyed my hand and then shook it firmly.

'I find it wise not to argue with ladies. I agree you are an…' He said "arse" with a broad grin on his face and then laughed. 'I don't think I have ever called a lady an arse before. I prefer Bish.'

I grinned back at him.

'So do I. Now onto the fiancé and if I behave like an idiot again, please let me know.'

Returning to Worldsend Lane, we found it once more a place of quiet respectability and we walked past Martineau's house and knocked on number fourteen. A red painted door with brass fittings. The window curtains were drawn and on the doorstep was a small bunch of flowers. I bent down and read the attached card.

'In Deep Sorrow – Ipolite and Martha.'

As I stood up, the door swung open and a woman in her fifties opened the door. She was well dressed and I took this to be Mrs Pottelbergh, Percival's mother. She looked at the flowers and asked me to pass them to her. She scowled as she read the message, but when she saw me watching her, smiled politely.

'Forgive my poor manners, Officer Willoughby. We are a sad household today.'

'And I regret that I have to intrude on your grief, but I should like to speak to your son. Is he home?'

Waving us into the house, the light fell and I struggled to see in the dim hallway. The woman picked up a lit candle and we followed her into the front room. I was itching to throw open the curtains, but I didn't want to annoy Willoughby, so I sat in the gloom, grateful for the modicum of daylight that crept around the edges of the curtains.

A man cleared his throat and I turned as he entered the room. My first impression was that even in the gloom, he was ridiculously good-looking. Model worthy. He had also been clearly crying and as he spoke, we could hear the roughness in his throat.

'My mother says you have questions of me?'

His speech was formal and I wondered about the segregation of the Strangers. He should mix with others of his own age, from all ages, not aping the behaviour of his parents. Had he been born in this timeline or in another? It was idle speculation and I focused on the current situation. It was time I showed Willoughby that I could be tactful.

'Sir, we regret our intrusion and it is our intention that the murderer of Sabrina be swiftly brought to justice.'

He hiccoughed and then cleared his throat.

'You are the female detective from London. Sabrina would have loved to meet you. She always says that women are capable of anything.'

'She was most generous in thought,' said Mistress Pottelbergh, who came and sat down beside her son.

'We have some questions that you will find painful, but I assure you we only ask to find her killer.'

His mother straightened her back, but he waved away my words.

'Nothing could add to my pain. Ask away. No doubt you have suspicions of me?'

'No sir,' I lied. 'Not at all, but we would be remiss if we didn't ask about your relationship.'

'Really!'

'Mother. I want Sabrina's killer found. I don't want the detectives wasting time trying to decide if I am involved. Best they clear me now and get on with their investigation.'

I liked Percival. That's not to say I trusted him, but on the face of it he was saying the right things. He went on to bore us with the details of their engagement. He even volunteered his diary, which I expected Willoughby to dismiss on grounds of gentlemanly conduct or some such nonsense, but he took it without hesitation and flicked through it. After a few minutes, he looked at me and shook his head, before returning the diary.

I ploughed on.

'We have spoken to Father Walsey, who mentioned that Sabrina was concerned that she had attracted unwelcome attention from a man. Do you know who she was referring to?'

Mrs Pottelbergh hissed.

'Miss Wise was not the sort to be bothered by unwelcome suitors. She was devout and circumspect.'

'Indeed,' said Willoughby, 'but sometimes a fox will set his cap at an innocent quail. It is not something the quail invites.'

'I told her parents they should prevent her from working at that factory.'

'Mother. Sabrina knows.' He clenched his fists and coughing started again. 'Knew her own mind. She loved working there, and I was proud at the nimbleness of her mind. You yourself said she was very talented.'

'I did. But better that she manages her own household accounts from the safety of her own home where she is not subjected to the public gaze of strange men.'

They hadn't answered my question, so I asked it again and they both said no at the same time. Sabrina hadn't mentioned anyone bothering her.

'I spoke to some children that live in the same yard that Miss Sabrina was lodging in,' said Willoughby. His voice had taken on a curious, unthreatening tone. 'They mentioned that a man with a bald head had been hanging around. He also attended St Saviour's. Do either of you recognise this description?'

Again, their answer was short and sharp.

'Besides. How does this help? You know her killer. It's this madman from London. We've seen the posters. A murderer has entered Norwich and suddenly you have two dead women. Why are you bothering us with this nonsense?'

'Mother. They are doing their jobs.'

Mrs Pottelbergh stood up abruptly, forcing Willoughby to do the same. I had fewer manners, but rose nonetheless. Our time was done and we made our thanks and left, heading back out onto the light of the street. In an unspoken accord, we remained silent until we were clear of Worldsend Lane.

'Why would they lie?' I asked.

'Because they don't think it's relevant. They are convinced it's your man, Cade.'

'But why not tell us anyway? Percival said he would answer anything so as not to obstruct us. He even gave you his diary, for God's sake. So why not tell us who was bothering her? They both clearly knew.'

The quarter bells chimed for six o'clock and I was surprised by how quickly the day had gone.

'You know, she scowled when she saw the bunch of flowers from the Martineaus. Neighbourly rivalries, or something else?'

Willoughby walked slowly.

'That's interesting. Martineau has risen quickly. I imagine he's made enemies along the way. Dammit. It all comes back to Worldsend Lane, but I can't for the life of me see how.'

'I think Cade is hiding in this leet. And I think we need to flush him out before he kills again.'

We headed back to the Watch House, wrote up our reports, and then Harry and I walked home. I was surprised to find a bowl of spicy stew in a thermos on the front doorstep, with a note from Marion telling me to eat well.

Ruffling Harry's head, I made my way to the garden with a slice of cheese, my stew and a glass of red wine.

Pulling out my pencil, I began to make notes. The timings were all wrong. Cade had only arrived three days ago. He would have had to kill Sabrina immediately. Unless. Unless she discovered him swimming his way into the city. But I had already discounted that as the means of entry. Maybe she saw him acting suspiciously and tried to raise the alarm and he killed her. It was certainly possible, but if that was the case, he was more dangerous than even I had given him credit for.

A serial killer is usually rigorous. They plan their attacks. Cade was acting like a spree killer.

Chapter Thirty-Eight

 There was a note on my doormat when I came downstairs the following morning. Picking it up, I headed into the garden and let Harry stretch his legs whilst I read the letter.

So sorry, Mother Superior had us on lockdown yesterday following the murder but there is a new consignment of linen that needs to be paid for so I'm heading over there first thing. I'm going to ask some questions and hopefully you and I can solve the bishop's dilemma. Fingers crossed, if you are free for lunch, I will have the answer to the Serious Situation of the Missing Socks.

Lots of love

Fenface

P.S. The nuns are praying for you.

She added a sketch of a nun rolling on the floor laughing whilst the other nuns told her off. I agreed with Fen, nuns praying for me was too funny for words.

I grinned and folded the letter into my pocket. When we were kids, we were forever making up mysteries and then solving them. My favourite was Ten-ton Tony's Terrible Toupee. Fen's was something to do with Mistress Swanson, a barrel of ale and a dancing donkey. Now we were investigating missing socks. I hoped I would have time to have lunch with her, but it was unlikely. Cade needed my full attention. I was going to urge the sheriff to close down Over the Water, call in the militia and do a house-to-house search. It would be a massive effort, but I was sick of waiting to get lucky.

The weather was even hotter today and I looked at my very limited, nothing-suitable-for-a-heatwave wardrobe and surprised myself by choosing the linen shift that I had been handed at the entrance gates. It was baggy enough to be airy, light enough to be cool, and long enough to be respectful whilst in the middle of a murder investigation.

Half an hour later, I had to squeeze into the Watch House. The entire ground floor was chock-a-block with the Watch. The meeting hadn't started yet and I picked up Harry and shuffled my way over to Willoughby, who immediately stood up and insisted I had his seat as he sat on the desk. Harry tucked himself under it away from all the feet.

'What's going on?' I asked quietly.

'Full briefing. The sheriff wants everyone in on this. All leave has been suspended. All other investigations have been halted.'

A wave of silence stuttered across the room as the sheriff came down the stairs and made his way to his corner desk.

'Yesterday, we found the body of Miss Sabrina Wise. She was killed in the same manner as Miss Naomi

Jenkins, although the pathologist believes she was killed before Naomi. We have our chief suspect, and his image has been circulated throughout the city, both with and without hair. We have had an eyewitness report of Cade with hair from last week. We know our killer's head was bald when the quake happened. Detective Barnaby, temporarily joining us from London, saw him yesterday and gave chase but he went to ground in the Strangers' vicinity.'

'I have every reason to believe he will strike again if we don't stop him, so now, I want questions and observations. He is only one man. By the end of the day, I want him in custody. Questions?'

Willoughby stood up and everyone swung around to look at him.

'Are we certain that William Cade is our killer? The bald man was seen twice, but on neither occasion was his face seen.'

'Of course he's our killer. Nathaniel, we've discussed this and dismissed it. You yourself regularly quote that the most obvious solution is the answer.'

'But the London briefing notes are so vague. And the timing of these murders is so tight. He would have had to have started killing the minute he arrived.'

'Obviously, Norwich affected him immediately, driven him mad as he crossed Norfolk,' said Mike from across the room and several voices muttered their agreement.

'If that were the case, I would expect that he would have been incapable of functioning by now and yet yesterday Detective Barnaby chased him across Over and he was able to evade capture. Does that sound like a man driven mad?'

'We have a theory on that,' said Willoughby. 'We think Cade might be from Norwich.'

'And you didn't think this might be useful information?' roared Hitchman.

Willoughby paused, waiting for the muttering to calm down. I was glad I wasn't the focus of those baleful eyes.

'Detective Barnaby felt he may be from Norwich. I told her to keep her suspicions to herself whilst I checked the registers for evidence of his birth or arrival.'

'And,' said the sheriff, sarcasm dripping off his tongue. 'Would you be so kind as to share your findings with us now? We'd be delighted.'

I winced, but Willoughby shrugged it off.

'I found no William Cade that fit the age of this man. Of course he could have changed his name.'

'And why do you think he was from Norwich?'

I cleared my throat.

'Because he's a map runner, and he knew my name.'

'Could he have known you from London?' asked Alys.

'Possibly. But I didn't recognise him. I just thought putting that together with the map running, and the fact that he appears to be successfully evading us, he may be on his home turf.'

'And why do you think you weren't told this?'

I looked around the room as everyone waited for my response. The sheriff was observing me, but his temper seemed to have died down. The rest of the Watch ranged from hostile to curious, and I hated all these eyes looking over my face. I wanted to scratch my scars or pull my hair forwards. Instead, I counted on my fingers.

'Three reasons. One. They didn't tell me because, as with the other useful information, they withheld it.'

'Why would they withhold vital information like that?' asked Willoughby.

'Because the practitioners have been all over this case and they are the most secretive and powerful force in British society. However, there are other possibilities. Reason number two. He isn't actually from Norwich.' I was certain he was from here, but I had to keep an open mind. 'And three, and this is quite likely, they don't know he's from Norwich.'

'Why wouldn't they know that?' demanded Hitchman as he blew smoke into the air.

My face was on fire now and I wish I hadn't said anything. I took a deep breath and addressed the room.

'Because Norvikers are treated like scum, they can't get jobs, they can't get accommodation. Everyone is petrified of them. They think we carry death and disease in our pockets.'

'If I ever go to London,' said the sheriff. 'I will stand on the steps of their bloody Guildhall and I will proclaim as loudly as I can that I am a freeman of Norwich and bloody proud of it.'

There was a round of applause as people stomped their feet and slammed their hands on their desks. I ducked down to reassure Harry and to quickly wipe a tear away.

'I wonder,' said an elderly woman's voice, 'would you have done the same thing as an eighteen-year-old girl that had been walking for days? Homeless, hungry and desperate?'

As everyone turned to look at the main entrance, I stood up to see Isidora walk through the room to join the sheriff.

'Bishop Norwich.' He bowed formally and the rest of the room followed suit, in such cramped conditions it was tricky, but not a single person failed to show respect.

'I was just saying—'

She held her hand up and the sheriff trailed off.

'Your love of your city and your care of it are known to all, but some of our flock woke into horrific chaos, death and destruction. Many of them lost their entire families, their friends, their livelihood and their sanity. We should be more forgiving of those children that fled, hoping to find safety.'

I sat down quickly and ducked my head under the table, pretending to reassure Harry. To my side, a hand appeared with a white handkerchief and I dabbed my eyes quickly and then took a deep breath before sitting upright again. I avoided Willoughby's face in case he was looking kind or concerned. That would be worse than the hostile glances of five minutes ago.

Lady Julian turned to look at the rest of the room.

'I have come here this morning simply to offer support and comfort. We shall hold extra masses throughout the city today for anyone who is troubled by the recent events. I wanted you all to know that each and every one of you is in our prayers. The whole city is praying for you today. Now, please continue.'

The sheriff shuffled his papers and then straightened his tie as Isidora stood in the corner near some of the Watch officers, who all looked a little awed. A chair was passed over the heads of the crowd and a space was made for her to sit down. Before she sat, one of the guys, whom I guessed was part of the Black Watch, given his sheer size and sense of latent intimidation, took off his jerkin and wiped the seat down before allowing her to sit. By the time she was sitting, a teacup had appeared and she took a sip then sighed contentedly.

'Right,' said the sheriff, anxious to take control of the room again. 'Why is he targeting these women? Is there a connection?'

'Both women were found near the river,' called out a voice near the main door.

'Anything else?'

'They're a similar age and size and of course both women,' said Willoughby.

'What about work?'

'Jenkins did most of hers on her back,' said a man with a guttural laugh.

'If you have nothing useful to add, Jones, you can clean the streets for the next week,' said Hitchman, his gaze furious. The Watch officers standing by Lady Julian all looked suitably appalled as the sheriff continued. 'See if shovelling dung works better for you than spewing it.' The oaf who had made the joke now stood pale faced and confused. 'We know Naomi did on occasions have sex with men, but it was by all accounts, including her own testimony to neighbours, consensual and she never received payment.'

'So what did she do for money?' asked Mike.

'Small jobs, gardening, babysitting, ironing seemed to have been her main source of income.'

'Did the skyrise have enough electricity for ironing on a regular basis?' said Willoughby, surprised. 'I thought it was on limited supply given its precarious status.'

'It is,' said the sheriff. 'Who found out about the ironing?'

One of the Watch, a young man with a tattoo on his neck, raised his arm and then cleared his throat before reading from his notebook.

'According to neighbours on King Street, she would work several shifts over at Hartley's. She worked on the industrial presses, ironing the fresh linens.'

There was a small flurry of muttering from the other side of the room, and a young woman shot her hand up.

'Sheriff, we have a connection. Sabrina did the accounts for Hartley's.'

'No,' shouted another voice, 'she did the accounts for Fairfield Shoes.'

'Sorry Micky,' said the woman, her voice dripping with disdain. 'Did you interview her boss, or did I? That's right. I did. And he told me that Miss Case also earned some extra money doing the accounts for Hartley's.'

'Right, calm down,' shouted Hitchman. 'This is progress. We have a connection. Detective Barnaby, weren't you asking about the laundries the other day?'

My mind was spinning as a previous connection resurfaced.

'We have another point of connection,' I said. I had already started scribbling a note to Fen, telling her not to go to the laundry. I stood up and looked at Willoughby.

'At the first crime scene, you said Naomi smelled of soap.'

'It's a connection,' he said doubtfully, 'but it isn't the strongest one.'

'But don't you see? She had been swimming. You shouldn't have been able to smell any soap. The water would have washed it away. And for you to smell soap on her from another person, they must have a lot of soap on them, on their clothes as well as their skin.'

'Damnation! You're right. I should have spotted that.'

I didn't have time to mention that I had missed that clue as well.

'I need a messenger in here now. Can someone call one?'

Willoughby leant out of the window and blew his whistle. Within seconds, a small kid about eight with cute freckles climbed the drainpipe, leant in through the window, took my note and sped away.

'What was that about?' asked Willoughby, as all eyes watched us.

'I was asking about the laundry, but it had nothing to do with this case. I was helping Isidora–'

'The bishop.'

'Yes,' I stumbled over her name as panic was gripping me. If there was one thing that a nun, a hippie and an accountant had in common, it was that by all accounts, they were innocents. And Cade had a type. 'Bishop Julian asked for a bit of help with something, so me and a friend have been trying to get to the bottom of it. I just sent a note to the convent to stop her from getting involved.'

Lady Julian stood, handing her cup and saucer to one of the Watch. She smoothed her cassock down and tucked her hair behind her ears before clearing her throat.

'Sheriff, I may have made a mistake. A man came to me some days ago in the confessional. I can't disclose the nature of what he told me, but I was alarmed by the content.'

'What did he say?' said Hitchman, in a clipped voice.

The bishop shook her head.

'It was the confessional. I deeply regret I can't say.'

'Did he confess to murdering anyone?'

'Again, I can't say.'

'Bloody hell, woman, what did he look like?'

There was a hiss from around the room, but no one spoke.

'Joseph, it was the confessional.' I watched as the sheriff's shoulders slumped. For the second time on this investigation, we were being hampered by the clergy. 'I couldn't see his face. But I didn't have reason to believe his fantasies were dangerous. More than that, I can't say. I just thought he might have knowledge of the events.'

Hitchman exhaled deeply and ran his hands through his hair. 'Okay, and sorry for swearing at you. It's just—'

'Yes, I know,' she stammered. 'And I was very conflicted, which is why I tried to start an investigation without saying anything. The man smelled heavily of carbolic soda. I thought he worked over in the laundries somewhere. I thought if I could get the detective to start looking around the laundries, she might stumble on something.'

I stood up and shouted at the bishop across the room.

'I roped my friend in. She's a nun. We thought we were playing at a silly riddle over missing socks and stockings. She was going to go over there yesterday and start asking questions.'

Isidora clasped her hand over her face and then made the sign of the cross.

'I am so sorry. I didn't know how else to proceed. I didn't even know if he was involved in all this. I thought he was simply a troubled soul.'

'He may yet be,' said the sheriff, 'but we are going to need to work out who he is and eliminate him from our enquiries. Right. Today, I want everyone over at the laundries. Every single person from cleaner to owner is to be interviewed. Anyone with a bald head is to be brought here. Alys, who owns the laundries?'

Everyone watched in silence as Alys retrieved a large ledger and then started to flick through the page until she stopped and looked up at Hitchman, her eyes wide.

'Ipolite Martineau. Changed hands last month.'

The lines of enquiry kept heading back to this man.

'Well now, that's interesting. It's about time that Ipolite Martineau was properly questioned. Bishop Norwich, will you inform the other city heads? I want this to be as open and above board as possible. The last thing we need is the Strangers kicking off.'

'Hellfire.'

To my side Willoughby swore and it was so out of place I spun around to look at him. He in turn, was looking out of the window where I could see my messenger running back weaving through the crowds. He wasn't the only one, as three other messengers were sprinting in from the west of the city. All converging on the Watch House. No one ran at that speed with good news. Seconds later, they burst into the room.

'There's been another murder!'

'At the chapel fields.'

'A nun.'

Chapter Thirty-Nine

 I was already in motion as they piled into the room. When I heard the word "nun," I screamed at everyone to get out of my way and then I was outside, sprinting across the marketplace. There were too many buildings in my way. I would have to tuck down small alleys and narrow passageways. I began looking for older paths. Routes that were no longer available, except for a few. Once upon a time, these lanes were recorded on maps and because of the meld, still existed in a state of permanent limbo.

All it took for me to see them was a slight unfocussing of my eye, and there they were. Ancient thoroughfares, long-lost streets, open plains. I sprinted as fast as I could. Was I noticeable to the people occupying those historic realities? Maybe. Could our current citizens see me running into apparent brick walls? Almost certainly. That's why I only ever used to play run the maps in the dark. We used to lay bets about who could run the fastest from one point to another. A few of us could run the maps like me, others were just bloody fast. I didn't always win, but I'd arrive laughing, win or lose, and then Fen and me would collect our winnings and eat out for the evening. After a few adults were burnt as witches for doing the same thing, we quickly stopped any public display.

I sped up until I reached the edge of the chapel fields. Towards the city wall, a large group of gawkers were congregating around an apple arbour. I leapt over the lavender hedge and made straight for the crowd. Coming from the far end of the field, I saw Willoughby cantering towards the same point.

Shoving the ghouls out of my way, I could see the body of a nun lying in the clipped grass under the apple trees. She was fully clothed and a red stained cross marked the front of her white gown. Her wimple was missing, exposing her short ginger hair. Fen must have loved being a nun to cut off her pride and joy.

My wail alerted one of the people standing guard over the body, and he tried to restrain me as I pushed forward.

'Sorry miss, please stand back. Wait for the Watch.'

'I'm a detective.'

'Sorry miss, I know all the detectives and I've never seen you before.'

'I'm from London, you fucking moron. Let me through.'

The man picked me up and almost instantly collapsed as I punched him in the gonads and ran towards Fen. Disregarding every rule in securing a crime scene, I flung myself beside her and begged her to wake up. As I held her, I remembered all the times we played together, all our dreams and adventures. All now obliterated by my folly in involving her in a stupid side quest.

With my hand against her face I noted that her skin was clammy and blinked. I sat back with a jerk, checking her pulse. There it was, faint but irresistible, defying her final moments. My girl was fighting for her life and God knows she was not going to lose.

'She's alive!' I screamed into the crowd. 'Call the ambulance.'

Willoughby was kneeling by my side and checked her pulse as well and then shouted into his radio for help. There was so much blood, I didn't know if she would pull through.

'Who found her? Why didn't you call for an ambulance?'

I was shouting at the crowd, who had now fallen back in confusion.

'She looked dead to me. Some guy found her. I saw him with her. He'd been trying to save her. Had blood all over him.'

I looked around the crowd. Was it possible that this eyewitness had not been a good Samaritan but our murderer?

'Where is he?'

The man looked about and shook his head. 'Can't see him. He was that upset. I reckon he's gone home.'

'We'll need to speak to him. What's his name and address?'

'Don't know him but I think he lives over near the laundries near Stranger's Hall. Think I've seen him around those parts.'

Willoughby and I looked at each other. The coincidences were mounting.

'Describe him!' snapped Willoughby as I continued to press the palm of my hand into Fen's wound watching in despair as her blood welled up around my fingers.

'He's tall, a big bloke, easy to spot, what with his bald head.' The man looked around the crowd and then stopped. 'There he is.'

I jumped up, shouting at a bystander to apply pressure to Fen's chest. The fool was pointing to the far side of the field where I could see a tall man with a bald head walking away. Like other murderers before, Cade had hung around to see the aftereffects of his handiwork. Checking my gun was loaded, I loped slowly towards him. I didn't want to alert him and I didn't want to scare the public. Who knew what he might do? I had visions of him grabbing a bystander and thrusting his knife into their neck. Worse yet, he might start to build a spell. I was within a hundred yards of him when he turned for one last view of his handiwork when he saw me and legged it.

In the distance, I could hear a siren approaching. Norwich's only ambulance was racing towards Fen. There was nothing more I could do for her, but I could catch her would-be killer.

Blowing my whistle hard, I then let it go and chased after him. This time I could only run where he ran. Each time I lost sight of him, members of the public pointed in his direction and I sped on. At the end of a long lane, I saw him turn into a yard and I knew I had him cornered. I careered down the lane, grabbing the timber beam on the corner of the building to slow me down as I swung into the yard.

We were in a quieter part of the city and this yard looked abandoned. Was this where he had been hiding? The yard was empty and I blew my whistle again. He was in here and I meant to seal his exit until others arrived and we would do a door-to-door search. To the right of the yard, a door opened and a man walked towards me. He was around six foot, well built with a physique that suggested hard labour rather than working out in the gym, with a bald head showing the telltale shadow of regrowth. But now that I was staring at him face to face, I could see that this wasn't Cade.

'Are you a sinner, pretty lady?'

I drew my gun. I was desperate to look over my shoulder for reinforcements. I didn't even have Harry and I realised belatedly that I'd shot out of the Watch House without him. Now I was in an isolated yard with a madman.

'Lie on the floor and put your hands behind your head.'

He giggled. I hadn't expected him to comply, but the giggle from such a large man was unnerving.

'Why did you attack the nun?'

'She was asking questions about me.'

'No, she wasn't.'

'She was!' he roared and I took an involuntary step back as he giggled again. 'Sorry. I mustn't shout, it scares the pretty lady. She was asking about the socks. I do the socks. I make everything crisp. I clean.'

Where the hell was my back-up? This was my fault for sprinting off, but at least I had him cornered. Not that I felt great about that.

'I said lie down!'

He giggled again and pulled an em-gun out of his pocket. The smell of burnt clutch pad suffocated my nostrils and my head shrieked in pain. I fired my gun as he fired his.

As he fired at me, my body jolted and I screamed in pain. Pulses of electricity flowed through my muscles and then I fell over, crashing on to my side as my body thrashed uncontrollably. Helplessly, I watched as he staggered towards me. My shot had only clipped him and I swore at my mistake. He managed to tuck the gun away and slid a knife out of his pocket.

'Don't worry, pretty lady. I'll make you clean again.'

I couldn't even speak. Tears of rage filled my eyes as he leant over me and placed a plastic bag over my face and tied a cord around my neck. I gasped when he looked up, surprise washing across his face and then he was thrown backwards as someone leapt over me. It wasn't Willoughby as I had hoped, but I didn't care. I just watched in desperation as the two men fought. My rescuer was familiar and was clearly giving my assailant a run for his money. I wanted to warn him about the knife and the em-gun, but each breath was becoming more laboured. I struggled on the floor, trying to regain movement in my arms but the more I fought the more desperate my breathing. I could feel the plastic bag wet from my exhalations filling my mouth as I inhaled.

Black spots were forming in front of my eyes and I couldn't help but think what a shitty ending to my life this was going to be.

I had run away from Norwich so that I could die a peaceful old age somewhere nice and safe and boring. Yet here I was, back in a Norwich yard, my life rapidly dwindling. The black spots were joining and then just as I blacked out, a hand ripped at the plastic and with a desperate gulp, I sucked as much air as I could into my lungs, then started choking.

Strong arms levered me up into a seated position, cradling their arms around me as they removed the cord from my neck.

'Are you okay?' The man's voice was deep and concerned. I tried to nod, but it had been a powerful blast and I was still struggling to regain control of my body. 'Hold on.'

A minute later, I felt his arms under me as he lifted me up. My head slumped forward and I couldn't make head nor tail of who he was. After only a few steps, he placed me back on the floor, propped up in a corner of the yard. I managed to pull my head upright and could feel movement slowly returning to my limbs.

Crouched down on the floor in front of me was William Cade, complete with hair.

'Where?' It was as much as I could manage, but he understood me.

'He fled down Back Lane. I couldn't follow, I had to save you.'

'Shit.'

He laughed.

'Same old Bish. Always with the foul mouth. I couldn't believe it when I saw you back in London. I literally fell in surprise as I saw you coming at me, gun in hand.'

'Who?'

He pulled a face. 'You don't recognise me? I'm hurt. Still, I barely recognised you, where's my grubby little urchin? Never pegged you for a great beauty.'

I was pretty certain that at this moment, I was dribbling. My lips were slack and I could barely form a word. Great beauty indeed, but grubby little urchin sounded about right. I had so many questions but no ability to ask them.

'You – killer.'

He shook his head and helped move me upright as I slid to one side. Mortifyingly, he dabbed my chin with his sleeve.

'No.'

'Saw– You.'

He frowned and then chuckled as he sat down in front of me.

'I didn't kill them. Takes more than a few stabs to slay a warded practitioner. Mind you, they'll be lingering for weeks.'

'Others.'

It was killing me to only manage monosyllabic grunts, but he was quick to follow me.

'Did you see the bodies?'

I tried to shake my head, but it fell forwards. Once more I felt his hands on my face as he gently righted my head. This intimacy was intolerable whilst I was so vulnerable. His fingers were on my scars and I wished I could flinch. I closed my eyes until he removed his hands and when I opened them, he was sitting back on the floor again.

'Listen to me, Bish. I swear to you on flint and sky I didn't kill anyone.'

As he spoke the old words of my childhood, I stared at him.

'Who– You.'

This was killing me and I clenched my fist. He looked at my hand and looked back at me.

'Good, you're recovering. I'm going to have to leave you now, but it was nice to see you again. Now, I can't tell you much about your killer. I've been trying to track him as well, and I'm pretty sure he is living on Worldsend Lane. I'd have done more, but thanks to your investigation, my mugshot is up all over the city.' He stood up and I struggled to look up at him. He grinned nicely and tilted my head before stepping back again.

'There, can you see me better now?'

'Stay.'

'And have you arrest me and cart me back to London? Not likely. Got to say, when I heard London had sent a detective after me, I wasn't worried. Imagine my shock when I saw the same little Bish Barnaby on my trail. Blood ran cold then, I can tell you. Smartest kid on the streets.' He broke off as we heard a whistle out in the lanes. 'Time for me to leave, kiddo.' He leant forwards and for a second, I thought he was going to kiss me. I pulled away as much as I could and he laughed softly.

'Bish, I do not kiss girls who are paralysed.' Pulling my whistle to his lips, he blew loudly into it and then stepped back. 'One last thing. Do not tell anyone you can travel along the maps, or you'll end up drawing the attention of the practitioners. And God knows you don't want that! You could end up on the run, labelled a murderer.'

He looked at me carefully. 'Promise me, Bish. Not a word.' From where I was sitting, I saw Willoughby run into the yard and Cade stepped away from me. Then with a grin, he placed his finger on his lips and ran into one of the walls. For a brief moment, I could see fields from a time before these buildings existed and then Willoughby was by my side.

Chapter Forty

Norwich Hospital was located in the castle. Given that this was the most secure place within the city walls, it made sense. On every single map ever drawn of Norwich, the castle was always present. The castle was basically a huge stone cube sitting on a mound in the heart of the city and, along with the cathedral, marked the Norwich skyline. It became a conduit for a hell of a lot of people to come through, from lords and ladies to knights and serfs and of course plenty of prisoners as the castle had previously been a prison amongst other things over the centuries.

Now it was the hospital and home to most of the science labs. I was in a private room and frankly, I was impressed. Admittedly, my view outside was restricted by the stone arrow slit window, but everywhere else was polished stone and glass. My bed was fully orthopaedic and if I had actually needed to be in here, I'd be quite content, but the fact was, there was nothing wrong with me. The blast had worn off and except for a sore neck, I was fine.

Or at least I would be, if I could get out of this room. Currently, the door was being guarded by two of the Black Watch, who had been left strict instructions by Willoughby not to let me out of their sight and even more importantly not to let anyone in.

I could hear footsteps in the corridor outside, and I slid off the bed as the door opened. Willoughby and Hitchman entered the room and I stood up as straight as I could. As usual, Hitchman was smoking and I wondered how he had smuggled that past the nurses.

'Relax, London. Sit down.'

'How is Fen? I want to go and see her.'

'She's still in surgery, Bish.' I stared at Willoughby, trying to see if he was lying. 'I've asked her doctors to let us know the minute she's out.'

'She'll need guards.'

'Already arranged,' said Hitchman, and pulled over an armchair and sat down. Willoughby sat in the other armchair and I was left no option but to sit back on the bed or look silly standing to attention. And frankly, when I said I was fine, I was in fact still a wee bit wobbly.

'Tell us everything that happened.'

'Right. The first thing is the killer isn't William Cade and the second is that you have a serious smuggling situation going on.'

I had been tasered and that was weapons-grade engineered magic. There was no way in hell that should be allowed in the city.

The two men looked at each other, and the sheriff sighed.

'You were right. You warned me she'd work it out.'

'Wait, what? What did I work out? Hang on, did you already know Cade wasn't our killer?' I tried to jump up but sort of slid to my feet, and Willoughby leapt up to help steady me.

'No, not at all,' said Willoughby, settling back into his chair, as he convinced me to sit back down. 'We've known about the smuggling ring for a while. We'd been getting ready to break it when you showed up from London with news of an escaped killer.'

'London treating us like bloody fools,' snarled the sheriff. 'There you are, all full of London pomp and arrogance, spinning some tale about a deranged practitioner. Did they think we're such bumpkins that we'd fall for the pretty face and let you rummage through our networks?'

'I came here to catch a killer.' My voice was hoarse, but it didn't stop me from shouting.

The sheriff stood up and opened the door.

'A pot of tea and three cups in here pronto. Oh, and some honey. Hurry up.'

He closed the door and sat back down again, quickly stubbing out his cigar. He looked across at the arrow slit in dismay, realising his error, and tried to waft the smoke around. Glaring at me as I grinned in return. It was fun to see the sheriff on the back foot.

'I believe you. At least I do now. Although when you commented on those running shoes, I was alarmed.'

'Why? Are you involved? Are you running the smuggling ring? Did you think I was here to investigate you?'

'Use your brain. If we were running contraband, why would we be investigating it? We were narrowing down on our suspects, but if engineered magic is being brought into the city, then it becomes critical. I thought you were here because London had become aware of the issue and didn't trust us to resolve it properly.'

I choked back a laugh. 'Are you kidding? London doesn't give a rat's arse about Norwich. The rest of the world wishes we didn't exist. We represent the inconvenient truth of unbridled practitioners. To the general public, we're insane, plague-ridden inbreds. To the practitioners, we are a source of constant embarrassment. No one cares about us.'

I was panting now as the two men considered my words.

'I'm sorry,' I croaked. My words had been bitter.

'What for?' scoffed the sheriff. 'What do we care about their opinion? We're Norwich!' He winked at me as a tea service was wheeled in by a nurse in blue scrubs. She smiled at me and Willoughby and wrinkling her nose, scowled at Hitchman.

'I thought you'd like to know, Sister Jennifer survived her surgery. She's very weak and hasn't woken up yet.' She walked over to me. 'And the best medicine for you is a cup of tea and a spoon of honey. I'll leave you to it.'

'Can we talk to her?' said the sheriff.

'And what part of "she's asleep" did you not understand, sheriff?'

'I–' he spluttered to a halt as a blush crept around his shirt collar.

'You won't be talking to her today.'

'I'll talk to her–'

'You'll talk to her when we say so. Now, drink your tea and Detective Barnaby, you are free to leave when you wish.' She smiled warmly and hugged me. 'Well done, you saved your friend's life.' Turning, she glared at the sheriff. 'And need I remind you, smoking is not permitted on hospital property. For someone who apparently doesn't smoke, I would expect more from you. I am disappointed.'

We sat in silence as she left.

'That bloody woman,' muttered Hitchman.

'Your wife is a treasure and you know it,' said Willoughby, 'and she was right, Bish did save Sister Jennifer, and smoking is apparently bad for you.'

I dipped my head so that Hitchman couldn't see me openly laughing at him. Willoughby poured three cups of tea and offered me a spoon of honey. I think I heard Hitchman mutter something about choking on it, but I ignored him and focused on the issue at hand.

Fen had survived, and that was all that mattered. I tried to gather my thoughts but everything kept spinning out. Fen was alive. I should have known better than to involve her in even a simple investigation. Norwich remained a dangerous city.

'So, now what?' I asked, as Willoughby handed me a cup.

'Now you need to tell us everything that happened when you caught up with the killer. And why you are certain that Cade isn't involved?'

I was succinct in my report and relayed everything that had happened except for the bit where I thought he was going to kiss me because honestly, that was mortifying. And I kept silent about how I was a runner. Apparently, no one had reported me yet. When I'd legged it over to the chapel fields, I didn't care who saw me and I was certain there were witnesses, but so far, the jungle drums hadn't made it as far as the Watch House.

'Bloody hell,' growled the sheriff. 'Well, that confirms it. He's a Norviker. And a map runner as well. Damnations. What's your take on this, London?'

I'd been thinking of this the whole time I'd been waiting in my hospital room. I didn't know anything about practitioners being able to protect themselves, but it made sense. And as for him killing the other five people, I hadn't seen the bodies and the only evidence that Cade was the killer was the say-so of a thaumaturge. Beyond that, I was desperate to know who he was. Clearly, he knew me when I lived here, but to me, he was unknown. Had he changed so much that I no longer recognised him, or was he someone I didn't know well back then?

'I'm torn. My job is to arrest him, not determine his guilt. I mean it's not as if I even know why he was on the run from the practitioners in the first place. But he saved my life and for what it's worth, I believe him when he said he didn't kill anyone. However, that raises a different issue.'

'Why was he arrested in the first place?' said Willoughby. 'And why were you sent to recover him without being told he was a Norviker?'

'From what he said, I think it had something to do with him being a map runner or that he was originally from Norwich. I wasn't able to question him properly at the time.'

The sheriff scratched his head.

'Enough. He is not our main problem. We have a smuggling ring and a murderer and now we know the two are linked, and at the heart of it lies Worldsend Lane and the Strangers. How in hellfire do we do this without starting a riot?'

He clattered his cup down and stood up. 'Willoughby, put London up at yours for the night, would you? I don't want her unguarded. Bring her up to speed with the smuggling ring and see if you can think of some solutions. I'm going to speak to a few contacts.'

He threw the door open, told the guards to go do some proper work and then strode off down the corridor.

'I don't need guarding.'

'I know. But you could do with a good meal, a decent bath and some delightful company. Harry is already at mine. You may as well join us.'

Chapter Forty-One

 Nathaniel Willoughby lived in one of the Georgian town houses on Upper Saint Giles street. It was a red brick building with tall windows over three floors and stone steps leading up to a navy front door with a brass knocker.

We had left the hospital ten minutes ago and whilst it was no distance, I wasn't capable of walking briskly, so I pretended I was simply taking in the sights as we ambled through the arcade and bypassed the Guildhall. Opening the door, he didn't use a key. As a police officer, I was sorely tempted to advise him against such woeful security issues, but he was the law here and this was his home turf.

Inside, the main lobby was light and airy, with sunlight pouring down from a central rotunda. In front of me was a large, curved staircase and a corridor leading towards the back of the house and two doors to the left and right of the hall.

'Kevin!' Willoughby's voice echoed off the marble floor and he turned around to me. 'They are probably out in the garden. Can you manage that, or would you like to sit down?'

'I am perfectly capable of walking to the back of your house,' I said somewhat waspishly, and wondered who Kevin was. Willoughby smiled at me and led the way. This house was much bigger than I realised, but even so it wasn't an arduous distance and soon I was outside on a terraced patio with a wrought iron gazebo running the width of the house. Out on the lawn, Harry was playing fetch with a man a few years younger than myself. Seeing us, he dropped the ball and came running over, sweeping his hair back into place. He really was quite handsome. My guess would be Arabic or North Asian, blessed with dark hair, scissor sharp cheekbones and beautiful blue eyes.

'We were playing,' he said, laughing, and his smile was so infectious that I couldn't help but smile back.

Harry, having torn the ball to shreds, now looked around for some other amusement and saw me. He stood still for a second, then launched himself towards me. As he piled into me, I lost my footing and would have collapsed into a heap had it not been for Willoughby catching me. Today I had been embraced by a convict, a killer and a colleague, each making me more uncomfortable than the last. I was so unused to human contact, I had no way of interpreting them. I quickly pushed away and righted myself, then made a mad fuss of Harry.

'Your correspondence is on your desk,' said Kevin. 'There are a few letters from the houses.'

Willoughby frowned.

'Thank you, Kevin.' He turned to me. 'I'm terribly sorry, but I will need to read these in case I have to reply before sunset. Kevin here will see that you have everything you need.' He looked back at his assistant.

'I think Mistress Barnaby will be most grateful for a bath first.'

Kevin looked me up and down and winked at me. 'I'll say, you look a right state.' Before I could react, he ploughed on. 'There are evening clothes laid out for you and clothes for tomorrow. I shall have your current garments cleaned and repaired. Harry has been fed, had a run and now that you are home, I'm sure he'll settle down for a nice long sleep. Nothing for you to worry about. Now, come with me whilst his high and mighty attends to his lofty business. Chop chop.'

Willoughby rolled his eyes. 'It's best if you just do as he says. He can nag for half of Norwich.'

'And if I didn't nag, would anything get done?'

'Do you know I pay for this abuse?'

'Pay me more and I'll make my abuse sweeter.'

'How about I pay you less?'

'Naughty, the unions will be all over you. Fancy me going out on strike.'

The two men were chuckling through their banter and I got the sense of a warm friendship.

'Come on, Mistress,'

'Please call me Eliza.'

'Oh, this one I like. No airs and graces. She can stay.'

'Kevin!'

'Alright, alright. Eliza, follow me.'

Bemused, I followed him back into the house, with Harry trailing by my feet. Looking back, Willoughby had disappeared, so I decided to ask Kevin some questions.

'So, Kevin? Do you work here?'

'For my sins. I'm Lord Willoughby's manservant.'

That made me pause. I knew servitude was a thing when I left Norwich, but I was surprised to see it still in existence and said as much.

'Dearie me, I'm staff. Not a slave. And it's a good gig. Good salary, great living accommodation. I get to go to lots of fancy events and have the time of my life.'

I shrugged. It sounded reasonable.

'So what does a manservant do?'

'Well, now there's a question. What don't I do? Basically, I take care of his person and the house. He felt a larger staff wasn't necessary for his reduced circumstances, so I'm a bit of a secretary, cook, groom, tailor. I take care of his guests,' he bowed in my direction, 'and generally make sure that his day runs smoothly.'

'And you live here?'

'Indeed I do. And I have the entire top floor, my own kitchen, bathroom, games room, I love it.' As he was talking, we had headed upstairs and along a carpeted corridor. 'Now then, these are your rooms for the night. I've put a robe on the bed for after your bath, which is through there.' He pointed to a closed door. 'Come down when you feel like it, or have a nap. Either option is fine. The salon has lots of records and books and I can whip you up a nice cocktail if you fancy it.'

'How will I find you?'

He slapped his palm on his chest in mock offence.

'What sort of manservant would I be if you had to come and find me? I shall keep an ear out for you.'

'I might tiptoe?' I grinned.

'A challenge? I accept! Right, I shall carry on prepping for supper. Enjoy your bath. If you don't want to come downstairs, there's a bell pull by your bed. Ring that. Toodles.'

And he was gone. It was like being accosted by a human version of Harry. I looked at the robe on the bed. It was a banyan made in silk damask with a muslin lining. Beside it was a full-length white cotton nightgown and I wondered if Willoughby just happened to have a stash of women's clothing lying around for guests. Maybe they were his. I laughed to myself. Despite the cavalier bows and britches, he didn't strike me as a fan of ladies' garments. Maybe they were Kevin's?

I opened the door to the bathroom and Harry ran in ahead of me, skidding on the oak floorboards as the last of the sun's rays shone through the steam rising from the bath.

Chapter Forty-Two

Half an hour later, I was padding downstairs in my slippers, nightdress and dressing gown. I felt utterly ridiculous and completely out of place. I reached the staircase and whispered for Harry to come to heel and we made our way down the staircase. I wasn't sure whether to turn left or right when I heard Willoughby's voice behind me.

'It's left. And why are you tiptoeing?'

I turned and grinned. 'I was trying to outsmart Kevin and I succeeded.'

'Nope.'

I swung around to see Kevin standing with the door open to a large room beyond.

'You need to teach Harry to tiptoe if you want to get past me.'

'Okay, Kevin,' said Willoughby. 'Thank you for this evening. Why not take the evening off? Mistress Eliza and I will feed ourselves.'

'Oh, I don't think so.'

'I assure you, we will somehow survive. I'll sort out breakfast as well, so make a night of it!'

Kevin looked torn.

'You can ask Mistress Eliza all about London the next time she's here.'

'Oh my God, Nathaniel. You make me sound dreadful.'

'Ah yes, your cap, now wear it.'

'Monster!'

'I understand that to be a compliment in some dialects. I shall take it as such. Now, go before I change my mind. I'm sure Mark will be free.'

Kevin rolled his eyes and then, with a bow, turned and ran upstairs as Willoughby showed me through to the salon.

'You'll have to excuse Kevin. He often talks before engaging his brain, but I think highly of him.'

'I think it's reciprocated.'

'He reminds me of my brother. I think he would have been deeply happy in this era. It wasn't until I arrived here that I saw him in a new light.'

'Have you ever looked him up?'

'Never married. Died of old age. Title passed to a second cousin. It's not much to go on, is it? There are many days when I wished it was he and not I that had ridden to Norwich that day.'

For a moment, he was lost in thought and then grinned.

'But then I wouldn't have met a fierce London detective who runs down criminals and swears at bishops.'

I groaned. 'I didn't swear at her. Just sort of in her general direction.' It was lame and I had no idea how I would ever be able to apologise. Swearing at my childhood heroine and bishop to boot was just about the worst thing I could imagine. I was amazed that the sheriff was even speaking to me.

Willoughby offered me a glass of madeira and a plate of small treats that were to die for and explained why Kevin was worth his weight in gold.

Willoughby smacked his lips appreciatively.

'I'm only allowed these when I have guests.'

'I'd be inviting strangers over just so that I could eat these,' I said and helped myself to another one.

I was sitting in a deep armchair and Willoughby had put on an album. I was expecting something classical and was surprised by the eldritch sounds of Mysterons by Portishead.

'Is this okay?'

I nodded and sipped my madeira. If I wasn't careful, I would fall asleep and we had work to do.

'Shall we start with the smuggling or the problem with the Strangers?'

'Not the killer?' asked Willoughby.

'No, I think the use of the artefacts has created him. Constant exposure to engineered magic here in Norwich is lethal. And I think someone knows who he is and is covering for him. And the chances are that it's the same person who gave him the artefacts.'

'Do you think it was deliberate?'

I put my glass down. I needed to concentrate, and I could already feel sleep tugging at my bones.

'No. I honestly think this was a dreadful set of unintended consequences. But now we have a smuggling ring that is not only trying to cover their tracks, but they are also trying to shelter a psychotic murderer.'

Willoughby was reclining on his sofa and nodded sharply.

'I agree with your assessment. I think now that we have removed Cade from the equation, the situation becomes clearer.'

He wasn't wrong, but I was here to arrest Cade, not get involved in Norwich's other investigations. Now that the two investigations were no longer linked, I could focus solely on Cade. But someone had tried to kill Fen and I wouldn't be leaving this city until they were found.

'I'm not leaving until I have Cade and you have Fen's attacker.'

'What will you tell your bosses?'

I sighed. I didn't have a solution to that. What Cade had said compromised my relationship with my bosses and I needed a while to think it through.

'I'll sleep on it and see if anything springs to mind. So the smugglers. Tell me everything. Maybe fresh eyes can help.'

Willoughby leant back, marshalling his thoughts, and then began.

'Norwich has a tightly regulated mail system. Packages can come in. Goods arrive via barge and caravan from either the twenty-first century or before.'

'Do we get many historic caravans?'

'Almost none, these days. However the magic works, historic Norwich and Norfolk continue, their own timelines seem unaffected. Although there are still some clues that irregularities occur. Norwich being England's second city, then disappearing into obscurity. Then, once more, surging into prominence again. But I try not to lend my mind to it. I leave that for the scholars and historians.'

I agreed, trying to understand Norfolk's timelines was a nightmare. Far better to focus on the here and now.

'So it's only the Wensum that links us with the past and present on a permanent basis.'

'And the A11.'

I nodded, having travelled that way myself.

'And these smuggled goods are modern. They aren't coming through from quakes.'

'Precisely. Until this week, we were treating the venture with kid gloves. A pallet of running shoes, make-up, records. All of these things aren't harmful, but the traders have effectively "forgotten" to pay the city trade tariff on them. It's driving Hortense delirious with rage, but Joseph has persuaded her to remain quiet for now.'

'So you're confident that she isn't involved?'

Willoughby shook his head. Hortense struck me as pretty scary when I saw her. I wondered just how angry she could get.

'So what's her concern, loss of revenue?'

Given that the vast majority of trade came through the docks, it seemed the most likely option.

'No, professional pride. Whilst the smuggling goes on, it challenges her authority and tarnishes the reputation of her docks. She has more money than she knows what to do with. The same is true of all of Norwich and yet there are some that always want to be richer.'

'And what will they do with this wealth?'

'There's talk of lifting the travel embargo. It's a hot topic, as you can imagine, but we have a generation born into this new reality. They are growing up and want to travel. They want more than just to live and die in Norwich.'

This would be quite the step forward if the embargo was lifted. Free movement of people would be wonderful, but would it work?

'And those that are amassing money will splurge it on a new life in London.'

'Once again, you divine the issue at hand. Imagine you have a child who wants to make their way in the world. You could send them to university, set them up in London properties. This generation would burst onto the outer world like oligarchs, swimming in wealth.'

I couldn't decide if this was a good thing or a bad thing.

'Is it likely to happen?'

'In truth, I think we are a few years off. Talks are only in the early stages with the United Nations. And there's considerable opposition in Norwich as well. What if everyone leaves? What if they don't come back? Will their children born outside of Norwich be unable to return lest they are driven mad?'

He sipped his drink and waved his glass at me.

'Your arrival has set tongues wagging. You've been gone ten years and yet seem utterly unaffected by the city. Although, I think you have a closer affinity with the city than many.'

He raised an eyebrow and I shrugged. I wasn't prepared to say anything. The sheriff's reaction to Cade being a map runner had been unnerving.

'I mean, you were completely unfazed by the flickering at Notre Dame. I thought I was good with the flickers, but you breezed through it. You also interacted with one of the schoolchildren and I have never seen that happen before. Plus, you often seem to be looking at things that aren't there. When Samuel King climbed out of the river and disappeared, I'm certain you saw more than we did?'

The silence lengthened, and then I exhaled deeply. Willoughby was my partner and much of what I could do wasn't illegal or dangerous.

'Yes. I supposed I am a bit more in tune with Norwich than some. But it doesn't help us. Tell me why you suspect the Strangers.'

From his expression I knew he felt I was holding out on him, but from all the encounters I had had with the locals, I knew that their relationship with magic was still uncertain. I didn't want to witness their disgust or anger. Even more critically, I didn't want it getting back to the practitioners. Willoughby waited for me to say more, but as I remained silent, he ploughed on.

'I have a few reasons, some more valid than others.' He ticked off his fingers. 'The Strangers are the wealthiest district in Norwich and it's hard to see how. Especially as this wealth increased in the past five years since the Martineau family arrived.'

'His behaviour is out of character for the Strangers I remember from childhood.'

'Yes. Following his arrival, he quickly organised the workers in the area. Lots of neighbouring streets have clammed up. At first, I thought it was extortion, but I haven't been able to prove anything. Finally, and this is the least valid reason. I abhor the man. He is an empty vessel.'

In the distance, I could hear a faint chiming and Willoughby stood up.

'Shall we eat?'

We left via a different door and headed along a small corridor and walked into a modern kitchen.

'When I woke on the day of the meld,' said Willoughby, moving around the room, 'it was a strange new world, but I was eventually delighted to see that my home had remained a residence and that previous occupiers had superb taste.'

'Were they here when you arrived?'

'No, they'd been abroad touring Europe. For a while, the house was busy. All my staff came through, as did other owners and their entourages.'

'Presumably, you built this house?'

The law said that whoever had the earliest claim to the property had the executive right, but that subsequent owners and tenants also had rights. It was a horrible tangle, but it kept the lawyers happy.

'We did, or rather, my father did. Over the past ten years since we arrived, numbers dwindled as people died, went mad, or simply moved out. Some got married, others preferred to set up in their own dwelling.'

'And how did you feel about that?' I wondered if he felt lonely being the last man standing.

'Honestly, it was wonderful when the last one left. I still host dinner parties for the previous occupants. There are no hard feelings and I ensured everyone was as comfortable as possible. But the day the last person left was a blessed relief.'

'So, Kevin was one of your original staff?'

'Heavens, no. He came and knocked on the door one day. Handed me a letter of introduction from the bishop and informed me I had mud on the back of my hose. I thought I'd been managing nicely as a bachelor on my own after my housekeeper got remarried and moved out.'

I watched as Willoughby moved around the kitchen, whipping up an omelette.

'You will make Miss Lydia a fine wife one day,' I teased and was delighted by his blush. He even went so far as to fumble a mushroom and had to pick it up from the floor.

'Miss Lydia is simply the daughter of a dear friend.'

I nodded sagely and grinned over the top of my glass.

'As you say.'

'Indeed.'

'Indeed.' And then I giggled, and Willoughby flicked his napkin at me.

'Dinner is served.'

Chapter Forty-Three

Despite the fine linen and comfortable bed, my sleep had been troubled. I heard the churches chiming through the night and when the first blackbird started to sing at four, I was awake with him.

I didn't know what to make of Cade. The fact that he appeared to know me was still troubling. Was his attitude towards me colouring my view of him? He swore he was innocent and his words had the ring of conviction.

He certainly seemed to believe he was innocent, but I've known many criminals who, in a deluded state, were unaware of their crimes. Their conditions may have been tragic, but they were as nothing compared to the devastated families they left in the wake of their murderous rampages. Cade felt different. In his favour was the behaviour of London failing to send me with any decent intel. They almost certainly knew he was from Norwich. A critical piece of knowledge. But the fact was, I had to capture him and return him to London. That was why I was here. I would speak in his defence if needs be, but justice had to be served. If he was innocent, then he had to go through the proper channels.

I was also worried sick about Fen. I ran through a thousand scenarios where I hadn't mentioned Lady

Julian's request. Over and over, I replayed our conversation. Each time I found better conversations, a thousand if onlys. My guilt was drowning me and I had resolved to visit her in the morning and ask for her forgiveness. Having resolved my dilemma, I would roll over to try to fall asleep. I knew she'd give it, that she wouldn't blame me, but my stomach lurched when I pictured her shouting at me. Accusing me of cowardice, stupidity, recklessness. All the things she said to me when I left Norwich.

My final fear was purely selfish. Willoughby had skirted around my affinity to Norwich. He was only a step away from asking if I could map run. The sheriff had been angry when he heard that Cade could map run, but then the sheriff appeared to be angry at most things.

I threw the covers off and as I swung my feet out of bed I was reassured when my feet landed on something hairy. Harry stretched and then jumped up ready to go. I loved his enthusiasm and was increasingly wondering how on earth I was going to hand him back when I returned to London? Bobbing down I gave him a quick hug and then hurried to get ready.

It was six a.m. Willoughby had suggested we go to work early. A lot had happened yesterday and we needed to get ahead of it. Right now, the killer was ahead of us, but by the end of the day, I wanted him safely detained. Then I would focus on Cade. From the open window, I could smell coffee and decided to head downstairs in search of a morning brew and let Harry out for his morning necessities.

Kevin said there were clothes for me in the wardrobe and I went to grab a pair of jeans when I swung the door open and stared at a pretty pink regency dress. I mean, it was really pretty. Puffed sleeves with a pleated hem and lace trim. A ribbon bow under my bodice and lace and muslin around my neckline. I stared at it in horror before futilely checking all the drawers. This was the only item of clothing in the room. It was possibly the most ridiculous garment I had ever seen a police officer in and yet I could hardly go out in my nightdress.

I slipped it off the hanger and was grateful to see a zip in the back. Without help, I would never have managed to button myself in.

Sitting in front of my dressing mirror, I looked at the various hair pins that Kevin had laid out. I had attached my golden police badge onto the dress, anxious about making a hole in the fine fabric. Now I had to ensure people could see it. My reflection stared back at me and I gently ran my fingers over the scars, the red and white skin smooth under my touch. I had seen burn victims with far worse scarring, but there was no pretending my scars weren't also very visible. And yet, over the past few days, no one had fainted or turned their face in revulsion.

I looked at Harry in the mirror and I could swear his alarm mirrored my own expression.

'What's that you say, boy? I look like mutton dressed as lamb? I think you have a point.'

Sighing, I attempted to tie my hair back, and then with my hair looking suitable for something to nest in, I headed downstairs. At the bottom of the stairs I bumped into Kevin, who wolf whistled.

'You can knock that off,' I said sharply, but he shook his head.

'I will not. You look a picture, but let me just fix your hair.'

Gesturing for me to turn round, he quickly took hold of my hair and after a few quick moves stepped back and looked at me critically, before smiling. 'Perfect.'

I glowered at him as I patted my head, trying to see what he had done. From the feel of it, my hair was firmly swept up into some sort of bun on the back of my head. I gave my head a quick shake, terrified that it would come undone like someone's ridiculous idea of a librarian, but I was relieved and surprised to see it still firmly in place.

Thanking him, we walked together towards the breakfast room. 'You know, I'm sure this dress is lovely, but do you have any jeans?'

Kevin was carrying a tray of coffee, so I opened the door. Willoughby was reading the papers and stood up as I walked in. His face was a picture of dismay. My heart sank.

'I look ridiculous, don't I?'

'Not in the slightest. You look, if I may say, beautiful. It's simply that I asked Miss Lydia to select something modern for you. You're the same size and I thought she would send something suitable.'

'It has a zip? Maybe that was what she thought you meant by modern?'

He groaned and waved me to sit as Kevin poured us each a coffee.

'Kevin, why didn't you say what Miss Lydia had sent wasn't suitable?'

'Mistress Eliza looks fine to me,' he said, rebuking his boss. 'Besides, when you sent your note, you gave little guidance. "Female London detective injured. Staying night. Needs a change of clothes. Ask Miss Lydia for something modern." Where in that does it mention jeans?'

'Kevin, do you seriously think I can chase down criminals dressed as Jane Austen?'

He laughed and conceded my point.

'The mysteries of a lady's wardrobe are beyond me. Unfortunately, your own clothes have already been sent to the laundries so you'll have to remain as pretty as a picture for a tad longer. Now his Lordship likes kippers and eggs for breakfast. How about yourself and Harry?'

When I said we'd be happy with the same, Kevin left the room, calling Harry to follow him. The allure of kippers and a garden quickly persuaded Harry and he shot off after Kevin. Willoughby apologised again.

'We'll head off extra early. That way you can call into your lodgings and change.'

I sighed in relief.

'Thank you. I know we'll be very busy today, but do you think I'll be able to pop out for a while to see Fen?'

I buttered some toast and moaned in delight. The butter was amazing, it was so rich, there were flecks of salt in it and flavours I couldn't pin down.

'Does Kevin make his own butter?'

'No, it's fresh from the local dairy. But we have a fridge, so it lasts that bit longer.'

I'd noticed the fridge last night in the kitchen.

'Is there more electricity these days?'

'A bit, but we are all still restricted. I forwent lighting in order to have a fridge. Truly one of this age's splendid developments. We have an icehouse in the garden, but this really is an indulgence.'

Before I took another bite, I placed a napkin over my lap, tucked another into my bustline, and studiously ignored the jam. When I returned this gown, with a note of thanks, it would be without a single blemish on it. Having successfully navigated the kipper and eggs, Willoughby suggested we head out onto the veranda to finish our coffees and discuss the day ahead. However, we had no sooner stood up than the doorbell rang and shortly after, Kevin arrived with a message sealed in green wax, reserved for official correspondence.

Willoughby cracked the wax and then handed the note to me.

Meet me at Worldsend Lane at 7:30. Bring London, leave the dog. Going to interview Martineau.

'Right now?' I asked in dismay.

'Best time to catch him off-guard, after breakfast, before work.'

'And why not Harry?'

'Logic suggests we present him with no reasons for refusing our entry. He could legitimately decline the presence of a dog.' He turned to Kevin. 'Please keep Harry here until we return. We shouldn't be more than an hour. Do we have a shawl for Mistress Eliza?'

My heart sank. A shawl. In my entire life, I had never worn a shawl. As I slipped my feet into my trainers, I grinned at the contrast with the dress and begrudgingly took the shawl from Kevin and then allowed him to drape it properly after I tried to turn it into a straightjacket.

'Well, don't you look the picture?' he said again, grinning, as I hefted my belt onto my waist. 'Maybe if we–' He stepped forward and tried to rearrange the dress around the belt and then stepped back, shaking his head. 'Nope. I'm afraid I can't do anything to make that better.'

Willoughby stepped into the hallway and Kevin appealed to him.

'Are you really going to allow Eliza out in public looking like this?'

I was laughing at his distress.

'Honestly Kevin, it's fine, but look, I can remove the holster. I no longer need the gun. Cade is not an imminent threat anymore, so the gun is superfluous. Wouldn't you agree?' I said, turning to Willoughby.

'Indeed,' and he removed his own holster.

'Why not remove the belt entirely?' pleaded Kevin, 'the lines of the gown are being destroyed.'

He tried again to bag the fabric out above my waist and I swatted him off.

'Kevin, I'm a detective. I am going to work. I need the tools of my trade to hand. This dress doesn't even have pockets. Where on earth does Miss Lydia put stuff?'

'Well, in the first place, she doesn't carry batons. And as for smaller items, her maids and footmen carry them for her.'

I tried not to roll my eyes. She had done me a favour by lending me her clothes and I would not, absolutely, definitely not make a judgement call on her lifestyle choices.

Willoughby strode off ahead of me into the early morning sunshine and I tried to keep up, but the long sheath nature of my gown was not suitable for a long stride. I shuffled to catch up with him and then hoiked the skirt above my knees, only to see Willoughby openly laughing at me.

'Those trainers do not suit that outfit.'

'I'm calling it a Norwich mash-up. I plan to start a new range.'

He paused, swallowing whatever he was about to say.

'My apologies, I shall walk slower, you may drop your skirt.'

'Rubbish, let's not keep the sheriff waiting.' I walked away, my skirt bundled up in one arm, and soon enough Willoughby was walking alongside me.

'You know, I find myself in a position of discomfort. I have seen you in trousers, but seeing you like this, seems improper. Isn't that ridiculous?'

'It is, but it's down to the dress. The dress carries with it certain expectations and standards. Wearing it like this is improper. That said… When we interview Martineau, I shall wear it correctly. Does that help?'

He looked abashed.

'I am a fool to be swayed by such frippery.'

'It's understandable. This is Miss Lydia's dress and she would never behave in such a manner. You were brought up in a different era. I imagine the twenty-first century was one hell of a learning curve. God knows *we* found the learning curve to be difficult.'

'Would you elaborate?' He looked genuinely curious, so I tried to unpick it.

'When you all first arrived, we had to deal with an awful lot of things, but one of them was so subtle that at first we didn't notice it.'

'Plague, famine, fire. All these things have a powerful call on one's attention.'

'Indeed. But what we were initially most unable to deal with was the fact that we weren't actually right about how to live. There's a sense that, through time, we develop. That somehow, I am better than you, simply because I come from a later era. Which, living with all the arrivals, we slowly discovered was nonsense. And following that understanding meant that we had to learn to accept you as equals, even if your beliefs and attitude were often at odds with ours.'

'I concur. I think we all have much to learn from each other. I truly believe that Norwich will become a beacon in how to live a good life.'

That Norwich had something positive to say to the world floored me so much that I spent the rest of the walk in silence. We passed a few people who said good morning to Willoughby and desperately tried to avoid my eye. Although I noticed two ladies in Victorian crinolines nudge each other as they pointed to my trainers. I dropped my hem as we approached Worldsend Lane and patted down the dress, hoping I hadn't creased it too badly.

The sheriff was waiting for us at the top of the lane, standing in a cloud of cigar smoke and, for the very first time, looking at me warmly.

'Perfect outfit, London, but hand me your belt. It spoils the effect.' I was tempted to point out that he and Kevin were in agreement, but I didn't want to push my luck. He looked across at Willoughby and nodded. 'Now, I'm going to lead the interview. This will be very much softly-softly. Willoughby, you act the gentleman, I'll be the coarse copper. London, you keep your senses open for anything magical in the house. If you need us to withdraw, the codeword is Harry. If any of us use it, I will make our exit without alerting them.'

'Are you expecting trouble, sir?' asked Willoughby.

The sheriff stubbed out his cigar and placed it in a case.

'Always.'

Chapter Forty-Four

Hitchman knocked on the door.

'Do you think he'll be happy that we were seen calling on him?' I asked, looking over my shoulder. I could see at least three windows where the curtains were twitching.

'Probably not,' said Hitchman as we waited. 'Had it been just myself, he could pass it off as city business. With three of us, it suggests we're here on an investigation.'

The door swung open as a maid invited us inside. I had only seen the house from the outside, but now we were walking down the hallway toward the back of the house. Despite the bright sunshine outdoors, the corridor seemed gloomy and we were ushered into a parlour where Mr and Mrs Martineau were sitting waiting for us. It was a mark of discourtesy that we hadn't been received in the drawing room. Even I knew power games were at play.

I curtsied as I entered the room and accepted the offer of a cup of tea. Willoughby bowed deeply and Hitchman coughed loudly into a handkerchief. Mistress Martineau visibly winced. From the moment I had stepped inside, I was aware of a small headache beginning to settle, the smell of burning brakes filled my brain.

'What can I do for you, Joseph? Can't it wait for council?'

The sheriff burped, apologised and sat down heavily, making the spindly wooden chair creak.

'You asked to speak to myself and my wife. Is her presence necessary if you are going to behave in such an uncouth manner?'

Willoughby, who was already seated, bowed his head to our hostess.

'Mistress Martineau, thank you for permitting us to enter your gracious home at such an ungodly hour.'

'No hour is ungodly in the eyes of the lord.'

'And yet there are still hours that we reserve for our families and we are grateful that you entertain us during one of those.'

'It is the Strangers' way to always open our doors and our hearts to the outside.'

'You inspire all of us. Mistress Barnaby and I were discussing how much each century had to learn from each other.'

Throughout this exchange, her husband had been sat still watching the three of us. He was on edge but covering nicely. By allowing his wife to speak, he was able to conceal his anxiety. Now he spoke.

'Yes, why is the London detective here? No doubt she is connected to your outrageous search in our district yesterday?'

'You don't have a district,' said Hitchman quickly. 'No ghettos, no enclaves. Norwich is a free city and anyone may live where they choose.'

'And we choose to live together.'

'Sabrina Wise wasn't a Stranger and yet she lived and worked in these quarters. And now she's dead. Is there a connection?' Willoughby and I sat in silence as the sheriff jabbed away at his questions.

'Are you suggesting a Stranger killed her?'

'Are you aware of any bald-headed men acting out of sorts amongst your community?'

'Absolutely not!'

'And are you aware of anyone smuggling goods?'

'How dare you!'

'I dare because the man who attacked Detective Barnaby had a gun powered by engineered magic. He was also seen in this neighbourhood.'

'Let me get some fresh tea,' said Mistress Martineau, standing up abruptly.

'May I help you, mistress?' I asked.

'Why?'

'I wish to be helpful.'

'That is godly. Very well.'

I followed her out of the room and was surprised that she hadn't called for a maid. She was clearly agitated, but was it simply down to having officers of the law in her house?

'I am sorry that we have distressed you with our presence.'

She smiled nervously and nodded her head rapidly.

'We are God fearing. My husband is an honest man.'

'Of course he is. You have made a beautiful home here.'

We walked through a small room with a simple table and four chairs. On the walls were various oil paintings, all in heavy frames. Some were scenes of country life, others were portraits. I was struck by an impressionist painting but chose not to comment. As I walked closer to the kitchen, my headache increased and I tried to relax.

'This painter is very talented,' I said, pointing to a portrait of my host. 'This is a true likeness.'

She smiled. 'It is a sin of me to say so, but yes, I agree. I like it.'

I looked around the room and saw a family portrait. Husband, wife, daughter, son. The girl was pointing to a dove. The boy held a Bible, his long dark hair a halo of curls around his head. The son was looking boldly out of the canvas. His pale blue eyes proclaimed him as a young man with great conviction. The last time I had seen this face it was contorted, sweat pouring off his shaved head.

'Your children take their looks from you, I see.' And I was pleased to hear my voice wasn't shaking. 'Is your son a priest?'

'He is, yes. He is currently on retreat. Fasting in a hermit's cells.'

'And your daughter. Has she blessed you with grandchildren?'

The woman almost visibly relaxed as the topic moved from her son and onto her daughter and domestic matters. She moved through to the kitchen and then turned around quickly before I entered the room.

'Oh, I forgot. We are out of milk. Please let me escort you back.'

She was quick, but not quick enough that I didn't see an iPod sitting on the kitchen table.

'It's really no trouble,' I said, but the skin on the back of my neck was throbbing. As we returned to the salon, I expected someone to attack me from behind. The gloom was oppressive, and I imagined a killer lurking behind every door. I was relieved when we rejoined the men.

They had clearly been arguing, or at least Martineau and the sheriff had. Willoughby was trying to broker an accord.

'My apologies, gentlemen, we are out of milk.'

Her husband looked at her in astonishment and shook his head.

'Nonsense, woman. We have milk.'

'We don't. I gave the last to the cat. I forgot to tell you.'

'It doesn't matter,' said Hitchman. 'What does matter is working out a way to run a door-to-door inspection without causing any undue alarm.'

'And I've said, we are innocent.' Martineau was clearly riled up and looking forward to a fight.

'Then with God's blessing you have nothing to be concerned with' said Willoughby, his voice placating, but Mrs Martineau was having none of it.

'As my husband says, you will only cause panic amongst our community.'

'Look,' said the sheriff. 'You are up for election at the end of the month. You can either do it with my backing or without. If you are seen to prevent the law whilst they try to hunt down a vicious killer, I can't see that going well.'

Martineau growled and leant back in his chair. 'We need tea, wife. Send the maid for milk.'

I could see that he was settling into this discussion, but I couldn't stand here and waste time.

'I love the fact that you gave the last of your milk to the cat. Pets are such a blessing, aren't they? I've only had my dog Harry, a few days, but already I find myself very attached to him. '

'Your dog?' asked the sheriff, staring at me.

'Yes, Harry. I love him very much.'

He drummed his fingers on the arm of his chair and then stood up.

'Martineau, before the women get carried away talking about animals, can I suggest that you draw up some provisos for a house-to-house enquiry? I shall return this afternoon and we can work out a way to proceed.'

He bowed to his hostess.

'Thank you for your time.' He glared at Willoughby. 'Next time, stop interrupting me when I am trying to negotiate. Detective Barnaby, here in Norwich, we stick to the matter at hand not chitchat about pets. Is that understood?'

Without waiting for a reply, he turned and walked out of the room, leaving Willoughby and me to hurry out after him. He didn't look back at the house as he walked towards the end of the road. A messenger was sitting at the end of the road and I recognised young Toby. As we walked towards him, Hitchman started speaking quickly.

'Toby. No, don't look at me. Stay where you are. If anyone leaves the Martineau house, come and tell me immediately and do not acknowledge what I just said.'

We walked past the boy and I was impressed to see how after his first look at us he had returned to whittling a stick and did so until we had turned the corner and stood out of sight of Worldsend Lane.

Now Hitchman turned to me.

'Report.'

'The house is full of engineered magic. I could feel it as soon as I entered the building. I also saw an iPod on the kitchen table. That's why she changed her mind about letting me in the room.'

'Why would she let you join her if she knew that was on the table?'

'Because I don't think it was there earlier.'

The two men turned and looked at me.

'I think their son left it there. I was looking at a family portrait in the dining room and I was looking straight into the face of the man who attacked me. The man who killed Naomi and Sabrina. Their son is our murderer.'

Chapter Forty-Five

 Without missing a beat, the sheriff brought his radio to his mouth.

'Calling all Watch. We are about to raid the Martineau home. Suspect is Jan Martineau. He is believed to be within and is carrying magical devices.'

He rapidly sent directions, blocking off various streets in case Jan tried to escape across the gardens. A team were also deployed to the river.

Within ten minutes, we had a group of the Watch standing beside us wearing stab jackets. Mike's sister, Sal, looked me up and down in my pretty pink dress and I raised my hand.

'Don't bloody ask.'

I was about to take part in a raid dressed as Little Bo-Peep.

'Bloody hell girl, you look ridiculous. Here.' She thrust a stab vest at me.

There were about twenty of us huddled three streets away. We were attracting the attention of citizens heading to work or to school. We would need to be fast, before we lost any element of surprise.

'Okay, listen up. Jeremy and Paddy, you go in first. Break the door down. London, you come with me. Shout if you sense any magic. Willoughby, you're outside the house. I need you coordinating all the teams.'

'Sir, Bish is not properly equipped.'

'I'm in a dress, not a straitjacket. I'll be fine.'

Beside me, Sal slapped my back and murmured her approval.

'Right. Everyone in place. Now.'

Willoughby jogged over to me. He was still struggling with the way things had panned out, and he looked furious.

'You'll be alright.'

I nodded and smiled up at him.

'I know.'

He was about to say something else when the Watch around us surged forward and the sheriff hollered my name. With a jaunty salute, I hitched up my skirts and ran to the front of the crowd. I could hear Willoughby calling directions to the other teams as we jogged towards Worldsend Lane. Adrenaline was pumping through my blood and despite the inconvenience of my dress, I was ready for action. Hitchman held his hand up at the corner of the street and, looking back at us with a quick nod, he sprinted down the road.

I had enough time to catch young Toby's eye. He hadn't left his spot and I told him to hide. Then I was also sprinting. Paddy and Jeremy were in the lead. Despite their size, they were setting a fierce pace. They'd have made great second rows. They bounded up the door and then Paddy raised his boot and smashed through the eighteenth-century door lock and they poured in with the sheriff and me behind. I had suggested deployment of a battering ram but Paddy asked where the fun in that was.

Martineau had come out of a room into a corridor and was immediately grabbed by Jeremy and pulled out of the house. Mrs Martineau screamed and fled upstairs.

'London, can you sense any magical devices?'

None of us wanted to be tasered, myself in particular.

'No. Not on this level.'

'Okay.' He pointed to five of the Watch. 'Secure this floor, the rest with me.'

He raced upstairs, taking the steps two at a time. I tried to keep up, but this skirt was also not built for climbing at speed and I was overtaken by the rest of the team. Sal paused beside me, bobbed down and grabbed the hem at my ankles. She yanked at the seam and tore the dress up to my thigh with a satisfying rip.

'London!' roared Hitchman from above.

Thanking her, I sprinted up the last four steps and along a wide corridor. I paused. The blood was pounding between my ears. My breath was coming fast, but I had no headache.

'Clear. They must have removed everything.'

'Damnations. Paddy, break down this door and let's get Mrs Martineau out onto the street.'

Seconds later, the bathroom door splintered open and Paddy moved past me to restrain the wife. As he stepped forward to grab her, she shook a bottle in our direction. A clear liquid coursed through the air, splashing Paddy and spraying us all. He swore in pain just as the liquid hit my sleeve and jacket.

'Acid!' roared Paddy, and he shoved Mrs Martineau aside as he lunged for the taps. Hitchman covered his hands with his jacket, then ripped the sleeve off my dress, as I rapidly unzipped my stab vest, kicking it to one side.

'Paddy. How are you?' shouted Hitchman as I grabbed Mrs Martineau's wrist and wrenched it backwards, forcing her to cry out in pain as she dropped the bottle.

Paddy was muttering and hissing, but looked across at us in the small room. 'Blistered.'

'There'll be honey in the kitchen,' said the sheriff. 'Mrs Hitchman swears by it. Cover the blisters in it, then wrap your hands in tea-towels and get to the hospital.'

He shrugged his jacket off and threw it on the floor by my stab vest and looked at my shoulder.

'Did she get you?'

I shook my head. I had her face pressed against the wall and her arm pinned behind her back.

'I'm good, boss. Let's get her out of here.'

'Willoughby,' said the sheriff into the radio. 'Mrs Martineau is on her way out. I want both her and her husband in Bridewell as fast as possible.'

Two officers grabbed her from me and she began kicking and screaming as she went past us and lunged at Hitchman, who promptly slapped her hard across the face. This was not how arrests went down in London. It was, however, a damn sight faster.

Six of us were now panting, leaning on the banister, catching our breath as Paddy followed them downstairs and made his way to the back of the house.

'Right. Let's find our murderer. London, are you certain you can't sense a taser?'

'No, but he killed the women with a knife.'

'Good point. In pairs. Room by room. London, with me.'

We headed back along the corridor to a closed door at the top of the staircase. The sheriff quietly placed his hand on the brass doorknob and slowly twisted. In the silence, I heard a giggle and I froze. Craning my neck, I saw a trapdoor in the ceiling.

I tapped the sheriff on the shoulder and pointed above my head. We both looked up. 'He's in the attic.'

The next second, footsteps ran overhead.

'Jim! Get here, now!'

As one of the team ran towards the sheriff, no doubt to bunk him up to the ceiling, I sprinted downstairs, through the front door and down the steps onto the road. Willoughby had both Mr and Mrs Martineau gagged and in handcuffs. A group of ten officers of the Watch were standing guard, waiting for transportation.

'He's in the attic,' I panted. Unlike modern houses built with interior dividing walls, older attics were open spaces that ran the length of the terraced row. They weren't spaces used for storage, and their access points were small and narrow. Residents barely paid that space any attention. But they were a haven for adventurous children, clever thieves and desperate killers.

Willoughby blinked once, then grabbed his radio.

'Be aware, the suspect is in the attic space. He could exit via any house.'

He looked around and opened the radio again. 'Where's the wagon?'

'Ten minutes, a wheel's broken.'

'Hellfire! All units Black Watch to Worldsend Lane now. Alys, summon the militia.'

He closed the radio and looked at me.

'We're going to have to walk these two out of here. The longer they are out in the open like this, the greater the risk of a mob forming.'

I was about to agree when a whistle blew from further down the street. I snapped my head in the direction of the call and could see a watchman waving his arms and pointing. Beyond him, Jan had run out of the front door and was making a dash for it.

'River unit, he's heading your way,' shouted Willoughby. We sprinted down the street, quickly closing the pace on him. As he ran, he span about and waved his arms in the air. The first watchman caught up to him and tackled him. Moments later he collapsed in a spray of blood as a knife glinted in the sunlight.

'Killer is armed,' shouted Willoughby into his radio. 'Approach with care. Get a physician. Now!'

Eight of us had now caught up with Jan, who was laughing and spinning, his knife flashing back and forth.

'Okay. He's surrounded,' said Willoughby. He bent down to check on the fallen watchman and I saw with horror that Mike was clutching his chest, blood running out between his fingers. I ducked down beside him.

'It's not arterial, you'll be fine. Keep pressing on the wound and stay still or your sister will kill me. I'm already in her bad books for coming to work in a dress.'

He looked up at me and winced.

'Everyone's in her bad books. I'd better not die, or she'll kill me.'

I smiled briefly, squeezed his hand, then grabbing his gun, stood up. I could hear Mike try to speak, but his words were lost in a violent cough and I prayed to God that the doctors got to him in time.

I caught up with Willoughby as Jan was shouting in a mix of Flemish, English and pure gibberish.

'He's pretty far gone, isn't he?' I said to Willoughby, who nodded, never once taking his eyes off him.

'Alright, nice and easy, everyone. Let's herd him towards the river.'

We had just started to corral him when our radios buzzed.

'We've got trouble.'

At the far end of the street, a mob was forming. Willoughby swore and grabbed his radio.

'All units, Worldsend Lane Now. Run!'

Jan had been standing watching us approach, giggling and singing to himself. His hand was covered in blood from the knife and he absentmindedly ran his hand across his scalp, leaving streaks of blood on his face and head. His shirt was open and blood marked his bare torso where he had wiped his hand. One suspender held his trousers up, the other hung at his hip.

We were within ten metres of him when he gave us a lazy wave and then sprinted right, towards the houses on the other side of the road.

Now the thing about being a map runner is that most of the time, we don't see the older routes. That would be much too confusing. I can only see a road or passageway if I'm looking for it, which was why I hadn't seen it before and now I could see Jan heading straight towards it. Things fell into place. Jan could also run the maps, which explained how he had been able to avoid detection for so long. The Watch were faster than I was and had almost caught him. As far as they were concerned, he was running straight into a brick wall, but I was screaming behind them that he was going to escape, so they gave chase, nonetheless. And then he was gone. I watched as the men stumbled to a halt. Two even hit the wall, unable to stop themselves at the speed they were running. I had the standard double vision of watching them stare at a solid brick wall and simultaneously seeing Jan beginning to walk away down a dark lane towards a field. The men by the wall were crossing themselves. One had a rosary out and Willoughby was shouting into his radio.

I had no choice. This man had nearly killed Fen and had killed two other women. He was the source of the smuggling that had deranged his brain and would derange others and set off further quakes. He was destroying my city and I was going to stop him. I walked forwards, passing Willoughby and the others.

'Bish, wait, what are–'

And then I was on the lane. Willoughby's voice disappeared into the twenty-first century as I crept up on Jan.

Chapter Forty-Six

I didn't know when I was, but I thought pre-eighteenth century, although it could just as easily have been the thirteenth. The houses on either side of me were lime daubed and leaning towards each other, creating a gloom despite the high summer sunshine. I looked over my shoulder and Worldsend Lane had gone. This lane ran back a few properties and then ended in a dishevelled building.

In front of me, Jan was still skipping and giggling. Two women with laundry baskets on their hips walked past and he pulled at their skirts. They turned in alarm but seeing nothing, they screamed and dropping the baskets on the floor, ran past me. I hunkered down in the shadow of the building, but Jan continued on, paying no attention to their flight. I wondered if he had always been able to run the maps. Being able to interact with the people here meant he was strong. Had that ability developed with the exposure to the em-devices? Was he stronger than me?

Ghost-like, we walked through the lane until he stepped into sunlight and a grassy field. I moved quickly.

From the corner of the buildings, I could see the river to my right. A group of women were hauling sheets in and out of the water, laughing loudly amongst themselves. Jan had also noticed them but seemed to have had his sport and walked across the meadow. Over to my left, I could see the cathedral and castle clearly. A few churches also stood proud of the smaller houses and the wall wrapped around the city as far as I could see. This was a very early Norwich. If I concentrated, I could see later versions, but that made my headache, so I stopped. This far back, I was at a huge disadvantage. Jan seemed to be comfortable walking around, my head was beginning to throb. I had been too long from Norwich.

My problem was that the minute I made myself known, Jan could flee forward in time, running from map to map and I might lose him, depending on how well he could run. As a kid I knew of few better runners than me but I had been a long time in London. Jan had lived here all his life and had a brain fritzed by the engineered magic. He had nothing to lose.

If I kept him in sight, I should be fine. I stepped out into the sunlight and began to stalk him. Mike's gun was in my hand. My heart was thumping. I was standing in the middle of a meadow in a long pink gown bitterly regretting having removed my stab jacket.

'Halt. In the name of the law.'

I'd got halfway through my command when he jumped in surprise and spun around, staring at me in delight.

'Pretty lady! I can see your leg.'

I was standing in the classic marksman position, one leg forward, the bare skin showing through the split in the dress and my arms locked in a brace around my gun that was pointing directly at him.

'I will cleanse you of your sins.'

'Will you, bollocks!'

'I shall remove thine tongue, for thine profanity offends the angels.'

'Fuck off. Now. Put your hands in the air.'

That bloody giggle. He grinned and walked towards me. The closer he got, the more I could see how badly he was suffering. His left hand kept twitching and his eyes flicked left and right before focusing on me again.

'Stay where you are!'

He stopped ten feet away and I braced to shoot. I had let him get too close and was considering stepping back when he smacked the heel of his palm against his forehead and leant slightly to the right. His arm stretched out into the fresh air and as he pulled his hand towards him, it was holding a long cleaver. I squinted and could just about see we were also standing in a large kitchen. I blinked and cocked the trigger of my gun.

'Put the weapon down or I'll shoot.'

At this range, it was impossible for me to miss. Any sane person would know that and would place the weapon on the floor. He screamed loudly and leapt towards me, the cleaver high above his head.

I pulled the trigger.

There are moments in life when all one wants to do is swear very loudly and then contemplate the amount of alternative paths one could have taken to avoid a certain juncture. I could have been a shop girl selling make-up, I could have been a nurse, administering medicines, I could have been a kept housewife. Instead, I became a police officer. The sort who does her duty. The sort who swears to serve and protect.

The sort who forgets to check if there are any actual bloody bullets in her actual bloody gun.

The gun clicked and I stared at it in stupefaction. Mike had been trying to tell me. That was why he had stopped firing and had tackled Jan instead. He was out of bullets.

To my left, I heard a shout and saw William Cade sprinting from out of one of the cottages. Jan and I both turned, momentarily distracted by a voice that could clearly see both of us. That momentary distraction was all the time I needed. Pulling my arm back, I hurled the gun at Jan and was delighted when the hilt smacked him hard in the forehead. He stumbled two steps more and then collapsed on the ground in front of me.

'Hello, gunslinger!' said Cade as he jogged the last few steps towards me.

'Is that supposed to be funny?'

'A little bit.'

I was furious with myself and panting heavily. The last thing I needed was Cade showing up.

'You're under arrest as well.'

'What are you going to do? Chuck the gun at me too?'

I paused. This was ridiculous. I was here to arrest Cade, instead I had captured Jan.

'Looks like you have quite the dilemma. How to arrest an innocent man whilst dragging back an unconscious, guilty one? Let me help. Over to your right there's a dresser with a ball of kitchen string on it.'

I turned and squinted until I could see what he could see. My poor sight through the various time layers was really hampering me. Cade and Jan both had the advantage over me, but Jan was unconscious and Cade appeared to be helping. I picked up the twine.

'Excellent. Now start binding his feet and hands.'

'Doesn't it hurt your head looking through like that?'

'A bit. I find picking up stuff hurts more. My brain seems to scream that it's not actually there and then the headaches start.'

'Interesting.' I crouched down and pulled Jan's arms together. 'I'm the other way round.'

'Here,' he threw me a small knife. 'I'll be back in a minute.'

He jogged away across the meadow. I sat on my knees and watched as he ran off. For now, there was nothing I could do about him, so I took the knife, cut the string and bound Jan's ankles as well. At least I knew this man had actually killed people. As for Cade? This was the third time I had met him and each time he had saved my life. I was increasingly doubting the practitioners' allegations.

I stood up, grabbed Jan's boots, and began to drag him. There was no way I could carry him, but we hadn't moved too far from Worldsend Lane. I could pull him that far. Map running this far back was a tricky beast. Any maps from this time period were mostly fields and suggestions of roads rather than anything even barely approaching an accurate portrayal. I needed to get to a known point before I could rejoin the twenty-first century. Once back on Worldsend Lane, I could hand him over and await my fate. I knew I was going to be vilified for map running, but maybe they'd get over themselves in their rush to deal with Jan Martineau. I could then head back to my lodgings and work out what to do about Cade.

I slipped and fell backwards, landing heavily on some thistles. Swearing loudly, I jumped up and kicked the inert Jan.

'I think you'll find that that goes against the Police Officers' Handbooks on the care and provision of a detained suspect.'

Cade was standing next to a small pony with a rope around its neck.

'Quite the comedian, aren't you?'

'Yes. I find being hunted for a crime I didn't do hilarious. Now, move out of the way.'

'I'm perfectly capable of putting him on the horse myself.'

'Now who's the comedian?'

I didn't dignify his comment with a reply and moved out of his way.

'Well done. Nice to see you can change your mind. I'm going to need that.'

He bent down, heaved Jan into an upright position and then pulled him to his feet. Moving a deadweight the same size as yourself is not an easy job, but I managed to avoid lending a hand as I stood back and smirked.

He had got Jan upright, but getting him on the pony was another matter, as the dear thing kept wandering off. I stood and waited.

'Maybe,' he panted through gritted teeth, 'you could hold the horse steady?'

'If you're sure?' I asked sweetly.

'Bloody hell, woman, I liked you better when you were tasered.'

Grinning, I went after the pony, grabbed its rope and walked it back towards Cade. As I braced the animal from moving away, Cade threw Jan over the pony's back and stepped away. He wasn't panting as such, but his breathing was definitely laboured.

'Now, all you have to do is walk Dobbin here back to Worldsend Lane. Pull Jan off and drag him forward and let Dobbin wander back to her trough.'

It was a good plan but lacked one other person.

'Why don't you come with me and help drag Jan through?'

'So that you can call the Laughing Cavalier and have me arrested?'

I shrugged. I wasn't surprised that he hadn't fallen for that. As traps go, it was pretty pathetic.

'If you mean Willoughby, you might be surprised to know that he has had doubts about your guilt from day one.'

'He has? That's refreshing.'

'Well, I don't know about the crimes you were in jail for. But he didn't think you were the Norwich killer. Plus, he found the London dossier on you full of holes.'

'Clever little popinjay.'

'Do you find his sense of fashion threatening to your uber masculinity?'

If I didn't know better, I'd have suggested he sounded jealous. He looked at me in astonishment and burst out laughing.

'Okay, I suppose I deserve that.'

We had reached the edge of the meadow. The women were still washing their clothes and had their backs to us, which was just as well, because I really didn't need one of them coming over to reclaim Dobbin.

'Okay. I'm going to leave you here.' He handed my gun back to me and I tucked it awkwardly into my sports bra. He grinned at me. 'You really have quite the look going on there.'

I stared at him and raised an eyebrow.

'And you should wear your hair back more often.'

'What, to show off my pretty face?'

'Well, yes. But I meant that with your hair down, it looks like you're ashamed and hiding. That's not you.'

I was speechless. What did he know about me? He wasn't the one living in London with people gawking at my scars.

'I bet they don't even notice them,' he said, as if reading my thoughts. 'You're beautiful. People probably look at you because of that.'

'Yes. I've clearly been hallucinating when they called me Scar Face and Elephant Girl. Thank you for re-educating me.'

He had the grace to look embarrassed.

'Fair enough. Thought you were braver than that. The Bish I remember would have gone up to anyone who spoke like that to her and fed them their own tongue.'

I was incensed that he seemed to remember me and I had no recollection of him at all. 'Who the bloody hell are you?'

He shook his head.

'I'm heartbroken. Still, it'll be harder for you to track me if you don't know who I am. Now, as lovely as this has been, I have to go and you need to sort out this piece of filth.'

'But I–'

He held up his hand.

'No. There's no need to thank me.'

'What! That's not–'

He stepped forward and slapped Dobbin's rump, and she trotted down the street. I ran to grab the rope and when I turned around, Cade had gone. Swearing loudly, I walked alongside Dobbin. I would keep Jan on the back of the pony when we walked through. Willoughby and the sheriff might not be there anymore and I couldn't drag him more than a few yards. When Jan was in cuffs, I'd walk Dobbin back and send her home. That is, if she would walk through the map with me. Cade had suggested that she wouldn't, but then he had also said he struggled to bring items from one layer to another. Harry had no problems when he was on a lead. Maybe Dobbin would be fine as well.

I walked her and Jan through the wall and into the modern world. And immediately ducked as a flying pan whizzed overhead. It landed with a clatter on the cobblestones behind me. I had returned to a full-scale riot.

Chapter Forty-Seven

Unlike riots you see on television, riots in Norwich are often quieter than you'd expect. There are no overhead helicopters, no one with loudspeakers, no explosions and no Hollywood soundtrack. Instead, what you hear is the sound of men grunting in pain, shouting in fury, fists connecting with flesh. Missiles were being hurled and half the ground-floor windows on the street had been smashed, shards of glass hanging from their frames. One woman was swinging a length of broken wood with broken shards of glass attached. As she swung at a member of the Watch, another officer ran up behind and punched her down.

Chairs and kitchen equipment had been pulled out of the houses and were being used as weapons. Halfway down the road, it looked like the Watch had created a barrier out of men and riot shields. Had they got Martineau and his wife away, or were they also behind the cordon? The street itself seemed to be a fight between the Watch and the Strangers. I could also see groups of other men fighting the Strangers and at best guess other Norwich citizens had heard the fray and had lent their weight to the side of law and order. I spotted a few red uniforms and decided this must be the militia. That or they just fancied a scrap. There were very few women present. Women, in my experience, didn't go looking for a fight. The women here were Strangers and were defending their own patch.

'Oh dear, this doesn't look good, does it?'

I whipped round to see Cade standing on the other side of Dobbin.

'Got lost?'

'Thought I'd just check you were able to drag him over the map lip.'

'Me and Dobbin did just fine. But now we have a different problem.'

He looked around and stroked her ear as he contemplated the situation.

'Okay, follow me.'

Picking up the frying pan, he moved towards the crowd and pulling Dobbin, I caught him up. As we advanced, he shouted above the fray.

'Make way for the law!'

Walking towards a riot in which the law was very actively engaged, this seemed a ridiculous statement and yet as people turned, they stopped in their tracks.

Striding towards them was the man whose face had been plastered on posters all across town as a desperate criminal. In his hand was a frying pan that he was holding above my head as a shield. For my part, I was dressed in a long pink gown with a ripped sleeve and a torn hemline leading a pony with a man trussed across her back and holding a gun.

'Make way for the law!' shouted Cade again.

'I have the murderer!' I called in response.

In tandem, we walked through the riot and as we approached, the fighting around us would falter and stop. Looking over my shoulder, we were now in the middle of the crowd. Behind us, the combatants had now followed us, creating a wall of bodies. Ahead, the fighting continued. Cade was heading in the direction of the most intense fighting around Willoughby, Hitchman and the Martineaus.

Willoughby must have seen us approaching as he blew sharply on his whistle. The members of the Watch behind me also began to whistle and very quickly the noise of the fighting was drowned out by whistles. The rioters in front of us turned to look, and just like that, the fighting stopped and the air was silent.

We were now standing in front of the shield wall, and Willoughby smiled tiredly at me. There was blood running down his face from a cut in his forehead and his jacket was torn, but otherwise he seemed fine. Kevin was going to be furious when he saw the state of those buttons and I had to stifle a giggle. I'd always had a nervous laugh.

'Black Watch,' shouted the sheriff, 'guard Detective Barnaby.'

The crowd shuffled nervously as various members of the Watch moved forward to create a wall around my small party. Given the groans as they made their way through the crowd, they may have stepped on a few toes. With extreme force.

'Murderer!' A boot shot through the air and narrowly missed Cade's head, causing Dobbin to stamp her feet nervously. Jan Martineau slid off her back and crumpled into a heap beside me. The Watch had forced a space for us and now people could see his face. I could hear murmurs of worried recognition amongst some in the crowd. I pointed to Cade.

'This man is not the Norwich murderer.' My voice carried out across the mob. 'This man helped me capture him. This man has been hunting him like every member of the Watch. This man will be returning with me to London.'

I had been facing the crowd but turned now to look at the sheriff.

'Can we let him through so that he may return the horse and then we can detain him?'

The sheriff muttered to Willoughby and then shouted to the Watch to let him through. Taking Dobbin's rope from me, he bowed deeply and then winked. I glared back at him. I knew he was going to run and I hoped Willoughby realised this as well, but I needed him away from this mob. Crowds were capricious beasts and could turn in the blink of an eye.

'But he murdered Sabrina,' shouted an anonymous female voice.

I snapped my head back to the bulk of the rioters.

'No, he didn't. The man responsible for that murder is on the ground at my feet. Using smuggled goods, he allowed his brain to become addled by the engineered magic. That engineered magic also likely set off the quake at Normandie Tower Block. Poor sweet Naomi, an innocent soul, was murdered as she returned from her nighttime swim and he strangled her and then carved her up. But she was not the first!'

I was in my stride now and telling the crowd a story to stir and shame them. I needed them in the palm of my hand, and then I needed them to safely disperse before anyone else got hurt.

In London we would either kettle a crowd or use water cannons on them, but often that created more trouble down the line. Policing had to be by consent. Yes, riots had to be stopped and squashed with force but not so much that the police were seen as the enemy.

'His first victim,' I paused, 'that we know of, was poor young Sabrina Wise, daughter of the Coslany Wises. Many of you would have worked with her, wondered about her disappearance. Little did you know she had been cruelly murdered, then thrown in the river.' I made a sign of the cross and was pleased to see that others followed suit. 'And then just yesterday, his derangement growing even more violent, Jan Martineau attacked a nun.' I crossed myself again and this time everybody followed suit. 'But he failed to kill her. She was my childhood friend and now she lies in a hospital bed fighting for her life. And this,' I kicked Jan, who groaned, 'is the man responsible. He has their blood on his hands. And so do you!' What murmurs there had been now fell still. My next few words could spark the whole thing off again.

'This man at my feet is the son of Ipolite Martineau, your city representative. Many of you standing here had your doubts. You had your suspicions. You knew the lies you were being told didn't ring true and yet you said nothing. When we asked for information, you stayed silent. When we asked for help, you turned your backs. Two women are lying on the mortuary slab and another lies fighting for her life and you did nothing.'

'Fucking Strangers!' shouted an angry voice from the crowd. This was the moment when I could lose control.

'Careful,' muttered Hitchman by my side.

'But it wasn't just the Strangers, was it? It was you as well,' I called out to the back of the crowd. 'Each and every one of you. Anyone who bought a new pair of shoes for your boy. You knew they were probably smuggled, but you turned a blind eye because where's the harm in a pair of shoes? A record? A packet of fags, a bottle of whisky. With each and every blind eye, you allowed the smuggling ring to grow until they were importing items created by practitioners. Items which cause derangement here within the walls of Norwich. Items that trigger quakes. Each and every one of you has displayed signs of greed. Venality. You have shown a disregard for your fellow citizen.' I dropped my voice. 'You have behaved like Londoners.'

And now the crowd was united again in their common shame. They might not fight each other for a minute, but I was standing on bloody thin ice and I could tell from the way the Black Watch stiffened their spines that they felt the same.

'But in the depth of your failings, you ran in to help the Watch. You behaved like Norvikers. Willing to help protect the law. And maybe some of you answered that call a tad too enthusiastically,' a paused and allowed myself a chuckle and was relieved to see one or two bashful smiles appearing on some of the faces in the crowd.

'Maybe you swung your fists a little too gleefully and maybe we'll have a few words with you later about that, but when we needed each other, you stepped forward. And the Strangers, I know you had no notion of the depths of Jan's madness. You were defending your homes, defending your family because you felt that a great wrongness had been visited on you.'

I paused again as I looked around. I couldn't remember ever saying so much in public and felt desperately uncomfortable as everyone continued to watch me.

'You have been cajoled and manipulated by Martineau. Could you have stepped up to him, found a better representative? Yes, but hindsight is a wonderful thing. And there is not one of us standing in this crowd that hasn't looked the other way in their lifetime. Not one of us who hasn't taken the easier path.'

The crowd was relaxing now. I could feel the tension seeping out of the air. They were reverting back to individuals.

'Look at the person beside you. Tell them your name.'

The crowd looked at me in confusion.

'Now! Tell your neighbour your name.'

There was some low mumbling as people began to awkwardly tell the men they had just been kicking in the guts their name.

'Now tell them your favourite meal!'

There were a few laughs, but also some grumbling.

'This is stupid!'

'What. Don't you have a favourite meal? What are you, on a diet?'

'I am not!' shouted the anonymous voice in protest.

'You bloody should be,' called out another man's voice nearby, which caused a few more laughs.

'Go on. I mean it. Tell your neighbour your favourite meal.'

The noise from the crowd grew louder as people began to exchange information. I let them chat for a minute and then shouted for silence.

'Right.'

The crowd quietened and I could feel the sense of them as a single unit completely ebb away. I looked over my shoulder. Willoughby stood smiling down at me. I nodded and then turned to the sheriff.

'Sheriff Hitchman. Over to you.'

The sheriff dispersed the crowd and warned that arrests would be coming and sentences would be appropriate for the crimes carried out. As they returned to their homes, I imagined many bloody knuckles would be quickly washed in an attempt to hide their actions. Eventually, all that was left were the Watch, a few badly injured individuals and the Martineau family. Mrs Martineau was wailing loudly as her son was handcuffed and placed in the wagon. She and her husband were placed in another and as she climbed up into it, she turned and spat at me. Willoughby grabbed my shoulders and pulled me back.

'It's okay,' I said, 'her spit is probably less acidic.'

The cart trundled off and I looked around. Cade was nowhere to be seen.

'You let him escape, didn't you?'

Willoughby examined his fingernails.

Chapter Forty-Eight

'And he just let Cade escape?' asked Fen.

I poured her a glass of water and helped her adjust her pillows as she wriggled to get comfortable. It had been two days since the riot and I was making my goodbyes.

'Won't you get in trouble, returning empty-handed?'

'Probably.'

'You must be furious with Willoughby?'

I was about to agree, but I knew when I had sent Cade over to him that would happen, or at least I had a strong hunch. I had only met Cade a few times, but I was convinced that something was seriously wrong with his entire conviction. Besides which, he'd saved my life three times. He hadn't mentioned it, but I owed him a debt.

'A little, but I think Willoughby had the same instinct as me. Besides, now I know how he's been hiding, I can find him. But first I'm heading back to London to see if I really need to.'

'Will you come back?'

I fiddled with my watch and tried to formulate an answer. Had she asked me when I first arrived, my answer would have been swift, but now I simply didn't know.

'I like your hair like that.'

I stroked my ponytail self-consciously.

'It's a lot cooler.'

'I remember you with your hair hacked short.'

'And yours was down to your waist.'

'Doesn't really work under a wimple.' She ran her hand over her cropped locks. 'I do miss it though, especially looking at your hair. You look better with it up, though.'

'Do you think I should cut it off again? Go back to my urchin look?'

She laughed, then winced and I passed her some water that she waved away.

'I'll just want to pee and frankly, that's as sore as laughing. No, I like your hair up because it means you're not hiding. That's the Bish I remember.'

Her words echoed Cade and I wondered again who the hell he was. I was tempted to ask Fen who she thought he might be, but she was currently lying in a hospital bed because I had involved her in my investigations. Instead, I told her I would write and then hurried out of the castle. The last time we had parted had not been on good terms, but this didn't feel any better. All in all, a simple exit where I just left without saying goodbye would be better for me. However, now I also had to go to the Watch House. I was here on work and I had to sign off from the Watch House properly.

'Come on Harry, let's go face the scary man.'

Harry wagged his tail enthusiastically as we made our way through the Royal Arcade. I had popped in here earlier to one of the clothes shops and handed them Miss Lydia's dress. They promised to repair it as best they could and return it to her. I also asked them to choose a second similar dress to send back with it as an apology.

As I walked past, the lady at the counter gave me a little wave and I waved back. She was a nice sort, the friendly gushing kind for whom no issue was insurmountable. Plus, she kept giving Harry treats, so she was a winner in my eyes. Walking along Gentleman's Walk, Toby ran past me and gave me a quick salute. Today he was wearing his school uniform. It seemed he just enjoyed running everywhere. Miss Lydia was strolling along in the same direction with a group of friends, all giggling about something. She didn't even glance in my direction and when the other girls went to approach Harry, I noticed they all stopped at the same time and quickly returned to her side, giving me furtive side glances. I was certain that she would not miss me in the slightest.

I reluctantly climbed the steps to the Watch House. The room was almost deserted. Alys was chatting to Bill under the counter and Willoughby was at his desk writing into a ledger. Hopefully, explaining why he had allowed a known fugitive to escape. I let Harry off his lead, and he dashed over to his side. Today he was wearing pink satin knee-length britches and a cream frock coat with a lace trim over a pale pink shirt. If he wasn't so well built, he'd look ridiculous. As it was, I couldn't help but think how good he looked. He and Lydia made a fine couple.

'Bish! I was beginning to think you might have snuck away without saying goodbye.'

I snorted.

'You're late,' thundered the sheriff as he came down the steps. 'Don't think I don't have better things to do with my time than wait for you, London.'

He stomped towards me and handed me a thick white envelope sealed with green wax embossed with the official city seal.

'Hand this to your bosses. Although, I suspect they don't have the wits to follow my instructions properly. I still haven't decided if they are corrupt or incompetent. It may go some way to exonerating your failure to return with William Cade.'

I was surprised that he was prepared to help me, but kept my face blank. I took the envelope and placed it in my luggage. Standing back up, I went to take my watch off.

'Keep it. Maybe if you learn to look at it more regularly, you'll be better at keeping time.'

'I was visiting Fen.'

'Sister Jennifer. How is she?'

'Recovering nicely. The doctors say she'll be out in a few more days. Her wounds are healing well, and the sisters in the convent will be able to care for her.'

'Good. I'm looking forward to telling her that justice has been served.'

'Has it? Have I missed something?' As far as I knew, the three Martineaus were still being held in the Bridewell. I presumed the trial would be months off.

'We're holding sentencing this afternoon. We'll be reading your statement.'

'I can stay,' I said, surprising myself. I hadn't expected things to move this fast, but if it was today, I could prolong my visit.

'No. This is a Norwich matter and I know you are keen to get back to London.'

I tried not to feel snubbed and nodded in agreement.

'Will it be the river for all of them?'

'Can't tell yet, but not for Jan. Bastard died in the night. Massive bleed in the brain.'

I looked across at Willoughby, who nodded.

'Vengeance is mine, sayeth the Lord.'

The sheriff huffed and I suspected he had strong views on vengeance and who should be allowed to have it. Still, the man was dead and I knew Fen would be relieved.

'Right, I have work to do. Here.' He thrust a bag into my hand. 'Food. Oh and there's a bone for Harry.' He opened his mouth to speak again, then closed it, quickly patted Harry and stomped back upstairs. A door slammed and I turned to Willoughby.

'Well, I'll say goodbye, then.'

He stood up. 'Not here, you won't. I'm walking you to the gates.' Taking my bags, he waved at me to lead on. Alys startled me with a hug goodbye and having flustered my goodbyes to her, I crouched down to say goodbye to Bill and then Harry and I headed out into the sunshine.

As we headed through the city, we were stopped constantly by people waving and smiling at Willoughby. His change in outfit was a clear signal to the city that all was well. Several people also came up and shook our hands or bowed to us.

'Spam, egg and chips!' shouted one man from a carriage as he passed us and soon, we were being hailed with shouts of favourite meals.

'For what it's worth,' said Willoughby, grinning broadly, 'my favourite meal is turbot in a butter and caper sauce.' He looked at me expectantly and I thought about it. 'I haven't had it since I was little, but I love cockles and samfer, maybe with some bacon.'

'Can't go wrong with bacon,' laughed Willoughby. 'Next time you're here, if it's in season, I shall ask Kevin to prepare a dish.'

My mouth was already watering at the thought, when out of the corner of my eye I spotted a familiar figure and swore.

'Bloody hell, is that Half Cut Hannah?'

Willoughby looked across the way at and old woman sitting on the flight of steps up to St Peter Mancroft. She was dressed in layers of skirts and shawls and had a lace cap over her hair. By her feet was an empty begging bowl which she was ignoring as she read a magazine. Willoughby looked her way and nodded.

'You remember Mistress Busby then?'

'Hard to forget. Do you know one time her house was on fire and she had two little ones in there? Well, she ran into the building and shot back out a few minutes later with two bundles in her arms. Everyone cheered until she sat down, unbundled one of her precious cargo and began to drink gin straight from the ruddy bottle she'd saved! The crowd had to run in to rescue her children whilst she proceeded to get hammered.'

Willoughby laughed. 'I don't think I've heard that one. But I have heard so many others about her that I can well believe it.'

'I'm amazed she's still alive. I wonder if any of her children made it?'

'All seven did.'

'And I bet they are the terror of the town?'

'Not a bit of it. All upstanding citizens. A teacher, a nurse, a member of the watch, two are in the militia and so on. I think they all chose careers where they could keep an eye on their beloved mother and keep her on the straight and narrow. Or at least as close to it as they can. You know young Toby, he's her grandson.'

I shook my head in disbelief. Half Cut Hannah and her drinking buddy, Red Wine Jack, were infamous when I was a kid and their children were a tight-knit group who would steal to order. Norwich sure does funny things to people.

We walked in silence for a bit. We were now walking up St Stephen's Street, the wall reaching up into the sky, embracing the city and keeping it safe. I didn't know if I was ever coming back, but I was leaving with an odd feeling that I couldn't place. I had only been here five days, but I felt uncomfortable heading towards the gates.

'I reckon the sheriff would have something to say if I tried to return.'

'You jest?'

'Not a bit. The man loathes me.'

Willoughby stopped walking and looked at me.

'For an exceedingly fine detective, you can be a trifle blind. The sheriff clearly holds you in high esteem.'

I choked out a laugh.

'I'm not convinced.'

'In truth?' He began counting on his fingers. 'He has written a report in which he has been sure to exonerate your actions. He has allowed you to keep one of his precious watches. And finally,' he lifted the bag the sheriff had handed me. 'He has made you a packed lunch! And, I believe, included cakes from Oelrichs.'

I was about to protest when I saw a familiar figure waiting outside the gate and swore. Willoughby glanced ahead and frowned.

'Be nice,' he muttered. 'Remember who she is.'

'As if I could forget,' I hissed back.

Lady Julian, Isidora, the Bishop of Norwich, was standing by the closed gates in full ceremonial robes. Two priests, a monk and three nuns stood to one side watching us approach. I was confused by her presence. The last time I had seen her, I had sworn at her. Was she here to formally banish me? I felt sick to my stomach.

'Why is she here?'

'Dispensing alms, I should imagine. She regularly comes out into the city to talk to her flock and tend to their needs. I understand she's been out every hour over the past two days.'

As we approached, she walked towards us and waved her entourage back. Willoughby bowed deeply and then retreated, taking Harry with him, to leave us alone. I could see the tiredness etched on her face, and I thought she looked exhausted.

'Will you forgive me?' she asked, and I blinked in astonishment.

'What for? I'm the one who swore at you.'

'And rightly so. I'm a woman of faith, not a detective. I should have spoken clearly. My attempt at cleverness nearly cost the life of a woman. I am atoning for my sin of pride, but I hope that you may also find your way to forgive me.'

I continued to stare. This woman had been my guiding light throughout my childhood. She was probably the most important person in the city, and yet she was asking me for forgiveness. The idea was ridiculous.

'No matter. I ask too much.'

I realised she thought I was still angry at her. Seeing she was about to turn away, I stepped forward and surprising myself, embraced her in an enormous hug.

'You never ever need my forgiveness for anything,' I croaked, then quickly stepped back from her. I was annoyed at my sudden lack of control and stood stiffly, angrily wiping the tears off my face.

She raised a hand and wiped a tear off my cheek.

'You honour me. My burden will be lightened and I bless you for it.' Her smile was so warm, I nearly started crying again.

'Before you go, can I make a suggestion?'

I nodded.

'You admired me as a small girl because I was an anchorite, yes?'

'Yes. You were always taught to us as someone clever and wise and caring.'

'But did I also appeal to you because I was locked away, hidden in a cell, my back turned away from the outer life?'

I looked over my shoulder, making sure that Willoughby couldn't overhear this.

'A bit,' I mumbled.

'You know, I chose that life as a positive decision. I wanted to be closer to God.' She paused and spoke softly. 'I wasn't hiding.'

I gulped and nodded, not trusting myself to speak.

'You have been hiding too long. God didn't create you for you to hide. He wants you to shine.'

I felt awkward. I didn't believe in God, but I certainly would not say that to her. She looked at me sternly.

'*I* want you to shine.'

I straightened my shoulders and nodded again, biting the insides of my cheeks. At this rate, I might never speak again.

'Right then. Let's keep this boat on the road.' She raised her voice. 'Sir Nathaniel. I will continue on my rounds and leave you to your goodbyes.'

They bowed to each other and then, giving us both her blessing, she walked away. I watched as a group of small children came running up to her. One had an egg in her hand and all the party stopped to examine the wonder.

'Ready?'

'Yes. I really do hate goodbyes, though.' I was half hoping he would slap me on the back and be on his way, but he simply nodded as the gatekeeper came towards us leading a pony and trap.

'Good morning, Eliza. You'll be pleased to know the sheriff insisted we had transport for you on your return. He said it was too hot for the dog to walk ten miles.'

Willoughby mouthed, 'See?' and I shook my head in disbelief.

After a brief safety talk, the gates were opened. Leaving Norwich was an easier process than entering. At the Wymondham gates I would have to pass a health inspection, but as there were no current outbreaks of anything in the city and I was fully inoculated, I should sail through that.

'May I accompany you?' asked Willoughby.

I would have loved to say yes, but it would place him at an unnecessary risk. The wild magic didn't bother me much, but I knew it would be at least uncomfortable for him and potentially dangerous.

'I would like that, but another time maybe?'

'I understand.' He leant on his cane. 'You don't want to share your lunch?'

'Exactly.'

'Very well,' he said, smiling. 'It has been a pleasure getting to know you.' He lifted my hand and gently kissed the knuckles as he bowed.

I smiled softly and curtsied in return.

'The pleasure has been all mine.'

The gatekeeper placed my bags in the trap and helped Harry up. I felt awkward, but stepped away from Willoughby and turned to the gatekeeper.

'And you're sure the horse knows which way to go?'

'You'll be fine. Daisy here will head straight towards Wymondham and a bag of oats. She's as dependable as an ox, no falling in the river this time.'

'Well, time to go, then.' I climbed up onto the bench and shaking the reins, encouraged Daisy to walk forward. We trundled through the gate under the wall and out into the countryside. Knowing that the horse knew the way, I turned on my bench and looked back towards the city. The gates were already closing and my last sight was Willoughby holding his cane in a salute.

Chapter Forty-Nine

 A day later I was back in my flat and preparing to return to work. I was also due to return Harry to the pound, but I figured there'd be no harm if he stayed with me another day. I was sure that was best for him. Besides, it would be nice to see a friendly face when I returned from my bollocking at work.

I brushed my teeth, swallowed two ibuprofens and pulled my hair back into a high ponytail. I then teased a few strands out to partially cover my scars. Then, remembering Isidora's words, I pulled the hair back off my face. I also added some make-up, but no concealer and smiled back at myself. I thought I looked okay. I wasn't convinced that I projected confidence and happiness, but as the saying went, fake it 'til you make it.

Externally I looked good, internally I was a mess. I had slept poorly, my head was thumping from all the em-radiation and I felt miserable. Why, I wasn't sure, but I knew I wasn't looking forward to my debrief. I had been sent to Norwich with one mission and I had failed. Now it was time to face the music.

Leaving Harry looking morose at being left behind, I headed out. At least I would have a friendly face to come home to. Maybe I could pretend I had lost him but honestly, my flat was no place for a dog and I contemplated moving out. Could I get away with stealing a police dog?

The commute into work was the same as ever, distracted faces glued to their phones, tourists taking selfies then trying to find their wallets, commuters glaring at wheeled suitcases, beggars staring morosely at the pavement and all the while my headache had settled to a dull thud. Using my security card, I swiped into the building and nodded at the guard, who glanced up at me and then resumed his monitoring of the security screens.

I took the lift up to our floor. People were busy staring into their monitors. The air con was making the room unpleasantly cool. I could hear Brent complaining about the temperature and marvelled how nothing changed. In the past few days it felt like the world had turned upside down and yet here was everyone, plodding on as usual.

I made my way over to my desk, saw that in my absence my in-tray had grown alarmingly and switched on my computer.

'Hello partner!' I looked up at Turton, who had come over to join me. 'I heard you've been on a top-secret assignment. Anything exciting?'

'I doubt it,' scoffed Jodie, joining him.

I pushed back from my screen and smiled up at both of them. A proper wide smile, like I really meant it. They weren't my friends, but they were my colleagues and I had honestly never tried to engage properly with them before now. Jodie looked at me closely then raised an eyebrow.

'I like the new look, suits you. You know you can get foundation that covers those scars?'

I knew she was genuinely trying to be helpful, so I bit my tongue.

'Thanks, but I'm okay with them. Shows I survived.'

'I like that,' said Turton. 'I hadn't thought of scars like that. I always think of them as a mark of something that happened. Not an event that was overcome. That's pretty smart of you.'

I laughed. 'Not really, it's taken me about ten years to figure that out.'

'So what have you been up to?' asked Brent, coming over to catch up on the gossip.

I wondered how much I could say. I had been told expressly not to mention Cade, but the guys had obviously been told I was on a top-secret assignment so I figured I could tell some half-truths.

'I've been in Norwich. They had a murderer and I was helping.'

Their faces were priceless.

'You've been in Norwich?' Turton took a step back.

'It's okay, I'm perfectly fine. I was fully inoculated, plus there's no illness in the city.'

'But what about the madness?'

'Doesn't affect me. Norfolk dumpling born and raised.'

He took another step back.

'It's not contagious,' I laughed. 'You can't catch Norwich off me.'

'Is that how you got those scars?' said Jodie in a hushed voice. I nodded and tried to remain nonchalant.

'How old were you?' she said.

'I was eight when I got these ones and twelve when I got those.'

'That's dreadful. What did your parents do?'

'They died.' I shrugged.

'God, I'm so sorry. Is that when you came to London?'

'No, I was nine at the time. No one was allowed to leave Norwich.'

'That's so unfair. What did you do?' said Jodie.

'Foster care, slept on the streets. I was properly independent by fourteen and when I hit eighteen, I snuck out of the city and walked to London for a fresh start.'

'Bloody hell, Bish,' said Turton in astonishment. 'That's barbaric, forcing you to stay there.'

I was tempted to point out that it wasn't Norwich forcing me to stay, it was the outside world refusing to let me leave.

'Well, people have a really low view of Norwich.'

'That's just prejudice,' said Jodie firmly. 'I mean, clearly you are the right sort.'

At this rate, I wouldn't have any lip left as she carried on.

'I mean, look at you, you are probably the best detective on the force. Your clean-up rate is phenomenal, even with Howard here slowing you down.'

Turton laughed and nodded. 'She's not wrong.'

'Rubbish, you just like to do things more cautiously than me. Policing takes all sorts.'

'That's nice of you to say that. But they didn't pick me to go to Norwich, did they?'

'No, they picked me because I can withstand the magic. Besides, they didn't need me anyway, they pretty much solved the crime themselves.'

The ten o'clock bell chimed.

'Right, I have to go and be debriefed. Wish me luck.'

'Tell them you deserve a bonus.'

I laughed. 'Yeah. And after that I'll start hunting for a new job, shall I?'

'Fair point,' said Jodie. 'Oh by the way, we're all out bowling tonight. Want to join us?'

I tried not to blink too hard and nodded.

'Sounds like fun. If I survive the briefing, I'll let you know.'

I walked up the stairs, still marvelling at the change in attitude. I'd only been gone five days and everyone had changed. I skipped up the steps with my ponytail swishing on the nape of my neck. I was no doubt about to get chewed out, but didn't care. I wasn't pleased with them, either.

The chief commissioner's secretary looked suitably unimpressed by my lack of fear and trepidation. I wondered if she drank red wine and kept a cat in her bottom drawer. The odds were not favourable. A red light lit up on her desk. She stood, walked over to the door and swung it open for me.

I strode through and came to a halt as I saw the chief commissioner, the thaumaturge from my previous visit and a further man and woman I didn't recognise. They each wore the customary sash of a practitioner.

'Detective Barnaby. Please take a seat.'

His tone wasn't forbidding, but neither was it welcoming. I got the impression that he felt there were four people too many in his office right now.

I sat down and stared at the three faces.

'I'm Detective Barnaby. I know Chief Commissioner Hill and Thaumaturge Persephone, but I'm afraid I haven't had the pleasure of meeting either of you before.'

The woman looked across at Persephone, but the man cleared his throat and introduced himself as a simple bureaucrat, 'Here to make things run smoothly.' I tried not to roll my eyes. A practitioner politician. Here was a man that would do nothing to help me.

The chief commissioner picked up the letter that I had deposited yesterday afternoon and glanced at it before flicking it in my direction.

'Have you read this?'

'No, sir.'

'The language is particularly…' He tried to find the right words.

'Archaic? The Norwich vernacular can span the centuries. Would you like me to read it for you?'

I leant forwards, holding my hand out, which caused the bureaucrat to snigger and Hill to shoot back in his seat.

'The phrase I was going to use was Anglo-Saxon.'

'Ah, right? Well I have it on good authority that if you are referring to "fuck", then that isn't actually Anglo-Saxon.'

Persephone held up her hand.

'As fascinating as a discourse on the vulgar tongue is, shall we please keep to the matter in hand?'

'Right. Yes,' continued Hill. 'Whilst you were in Norwich, you captured a killer who had murdered two women whilst you were there.'

'But not Cade,' said Persephone.

'No, ma'am.'

'Are you sure?'

'Positive.'

'And you couldn't have just said it was?' she asked idly.

'And let the actual murderer walk free to commit more murders?'

She sighed and leant back in her chair.

'I suppose not, but it would have been convenient.'

'What would have been convenient was me having the actual case notes pertaining to Cade's history. That severely hampered my investigation. I'm afraid Norwich holds us in great contempt.'

'Oh dear, what a pity.'

'It's not on, you know. Treating a fellow crime force like that. It made us look incompetent or corrupt.'

'Are you sure you haven't read this letter?' said Hill.

'Quite, sir. But the sheriff made his opinions clear on a daily basis.'

I found myself smiling and could almost smell the cigar smoke.

'It says here that there were no reported sightings of Cade the entire time you were there. Is that correct?'

'Yes, sir. There were posters up all around the city but no one came forward and reported that they had seen him.'

Which wasn't a lie.

'Did you hear any rumours of people walking through walls?'

I looked at her and scoffed.

'I think that has all but died out. Just for the record, I also failed to spot anyone walking on water, flying through the air, seeing the future, or cavorting with the devil.'

I laughed and poured myself a glass of water, impressed that the water didn't tremble. Cade had warned me to keep my skills to myself and it looked as though the practitioners were actively interested in map running.

'So, what do you think happened to him?' asked the unnamed bureaucrat, tapping his pen on the table.

'I guess he never made it. Or if he did, the background magic drove him insane.'

'That wouldn't have bothered him,' said the female practitioner and then flinched as Persephone slapped her hand on the table.

I looked back and forth at the people sitting opposite me as though I had just learnt something new.

'Only Norvikers are safe in Norwich. Are you saying this Cade was from Norwich? Don't you think that was information I should have been made aware of?' I added an air of righteous indignation into my voice. 'And if we are going to discuss insufficient briefings, last night I tried to investigate him. I found no mention of him, his murders, details of the victims. Nothing. I remembered the names of the two victims and I looked them up. Nothing. I even looked up birth and school records. Nothing. It's as if they never actually existed.'

I glared at the chief commissioner.

'We clearly did a good job of covering it up,' said the bureaucrat, smiling.

'On what grounds?' I demanded. Last night had been the final piece of evidence to convince me that Cade or whatever his real name was, was innocent of the crimes he was being publicly accused of. In fact he was being deliberately framed. I didn't think I was going to get answers, but I was going to make it clear I didn't believe their lies. I stared at the practitioners until the man cleared his throat and spoke smoothly.

'Public calm. No one wants to think of a rogue practitioner.'

'I would suggest to you that the reason that I couldn't find a single whisper about these murders was not because you did a good job covering it up, but because they never happened. And if that's the case, what was Cade actually guilty of?'

The chief commissioner looked towards the thaumaturge, who shook her head.

'Very well. I think we'll count this as case closed.'

'But—'

'Detective Barnaby, we appreciate your efforts, but it is time to move on and discuss your future within the force.'

I sat still. I knew I was in for a rap on the knuckles, but this sounded like it was going to be permanent.

'Because I failed to apprehend an innocent man who had a head start and a serious advantage.'

'He is not innocent. Nor do I believe he's dead,' snapped Persephone.

'So, who is he?'

'That is not your business,' she shouted. 'Excuse me,' she said calmly, smoothing her skirt. 'I am disappointed that you failed in your assignment, but you have been given an opportunity to redeem yourself. Chief Commissioner?'

Now Hill spoke and he looked relieved that we were moving away from the domain of the practitioners.

'Yes. It seems Sheriff Hitchman has a smuggling problem and has suggested a permanent liaison officer be embedded in the Norwich force with an aim to stamping out the contraband ring and further, improving relations between Norwich and the outside world. He's suggested you.'

I stared at him blankly, trying to work out how I felt about that. Surprisingly my first reaction wasn't denial. Neither was my second or third.

'Well. I know you were reluctant to go, but we think this is a good idea. We would insist you were properly housed.'

'We would also expect weekly reports,' chuckled the bureaucrat. 'Consider yourself our first ambassador,'

'And we'd expect the briefing paper to be accurate,' drawled Persephone. 'Especially in matters concerning Cade, should you see him again.'

'Again?' I smiled innocently. Clearly, she didn't believe my story.

'As I said.'

We stared at each other and I felt my headache increasing as her frown deepened.

'Enough,' she snapped and my headache subsided. 'Will you accept this position?'

'I have conditions.'

'You do?' asked the chief commissioner.

I had already made my mind up when the job had been offered. The more I thought about it, the more I realised I had made my mind up as the Norwich gates closed behind me. As soon as I had filed my report and tried to clear Cade's name, I was going back. Now that I also had a job to go to, I had to plan ahead.

'I want a pay rise.'

'That comes with your new job title.'

The amount he quoted made me cough.

'Acceptable?'

'It will do. I also want Cade's full records, unredacted.'

Persephone stared at me and curled her lip.

'That won't be necessary. If you see him simply inform us and we'll take it from there.'

I shrugged and smiled at her and the others.

'It's the detective in me. I don't like unresolved cases and I don't like not having all the facts at my disposal.'

'We are paying you to catch smugglers,' she snapped, 'not chase ghosts.' Her comment about ghosts made me pause. Did she know about my map running skills? I didn't think so but I wasn't going to push my luck. I'd have to find another way to access his records.

'Very well, then. I have one final request.'

'And that is?' asked the CC desperate to defuse the tension in the room.

'Harry comes with me!'

Author's Note

This has been such a blast both writing this book and launching it. Writing a book is never a solo effort, and I am delighted to have worked with my agent John Berlyne and my editors Simon Spanton-walker and Julian Barr, and proofreader CS, who have all helped shape this into the epic adventure that it has turned out to be. My alpha readers, those who have been with me all through the Quantum Curators, have also helped me with their feedback and general cheerleading. God knows, on the darkest days, these readers are like effervescent rays of sunlight. This book was originally launched via Kickstarter and I would like to thank everyone of my backers who helped bring this to life.

Join my newsletter and get **The Fatal Night** for free. This is an origin story set on the night of the cataclysm.

https://bookhip.com/QMSVRAV

Book two will be launched the same way, via Kickstarter first with all the extras, but if you prefer Amazon and are happy to wait, here is the pre-order link for Flint in the Bones Book Two. I know, I know, I'm working on a better title!

Interview with Eva St. John

You grew up in Norwich, just like your protagonist. How did your own experiences in the city influence the creation of Detective Barnaby and her story?

I love Norwich; it was a great city to grow up in although at the time I didn't realise how special it was. Norwich is a small city, easily explored by a youngster with an enquiring mind and a taste for adventure. I explored all the alleys and yards, lost gardens, hidden passageways, many that I probably wasn't supposed to. I also grew up taking all the history for granted, and it was only when I left that I began to appreciate just how rare it was to live in a Tudor house on a Tudor street. Happily, unlike poor Bish, I managed to experience a Norwich without the plague and all its other obstacles that Bish encountered.

When did you first realise you wanted to be a writer, and how did that journey lead to Flint in the Bones?

I've always loved telling stories and dreaming of adventures. One day I decided to write them down. My first novel is also set in Norfolk, and it feels good for my fourteenth book to return home. And in this story the city a character in its own right. I hope that people who know Norwich read this and think yes; I got that right, even with all the chaos and magic, I hope the spirit of Norwich shines through. I also hope that those that don't know the city get to the end of the book and want to come and explore.

The idea for this novel sparked from imagining all of Norwich's timelines and architecture blended together. Could you tell us more about how that initial concept evolved into the finished story?

The idea of the setting came to me one bathtime, as the best stories often do. I was so excited by the idea of maps merging and timelines converging. But that was only a setting, a sort of Chernobyl, a very dangerous city, altered by magic. I needed a story to go with the setting and I thought that an escaped convict running to Norwich to evade capture would work. From there, it was obvious that someone would need to go and hunt him down. Enter Bish.

Did you always plan for magic to play a significant role, or did that element emerge later in the writing process?

The magic was integral. How else was I going to mush the maps together? I did enjoy turning the magicians into practitioners akin to nuclear physicists. We all sort of know what they do, but we really don't understand it. At least I certainly don't!

Detective Barnaby has mixed feelings about her hometown. Why did you choose to create a

character who is reluctant to save the city she left behind?

I don't think her feelings are mixed. She hates Norwich. But that adds a great dynamic tension to the plot, doesn't it? It gives the character room to grow, but also it gave me the opportunity to show just how devastating it was to be a child, growing up in the site of an ongoing cataclysm.

Without giving away spoilers, can you tell us what readers might expect from Barnaby's next adventure?

Well, we still need to find out who Cade is. It's also clear that the practitioners don't trust Bish but have to rely on her. And finally, Hitchman and Willoughby have some smugglers to catch. But that's all I can say, except for the fact that Harry will once again be by Bish's side.